Quintin
Jardine

AUTOGRAPHS
IN THE RAIN

headline

First published in 2001 by
HEADLINE PUBLISHING GROUP

First published in paperback in 2002 by
HEADLINE PUBLISHING GROUP

First published in this paperback edition in 2011 by
HEADLINE PUBLISHING GROUP

2

Cataloguing in Publication Data is available from the British Library

ISBN 978 07553 5868 7 (B format)
ISBN 978 07472 6387 6 (A format)

Typeset in Electra by Avon DataSet Ltd, Bidford-on-Avon, Warwickshire

Printed in Great Britain by Clays Ltd, St Ives plc

Headline's policy is to use papers that are natural, renewable and
recyclable products and made from wood grown in sustainable forests.
The logging and manufacturing processes are expected to conform
to the environmental regulations of the country of origin.

HEADLINE PUBLISHING GROUP
An Hachette UK Company
338 Euston Road
London NW1 3BH

www.headline.co.uk
www.hachette.co.uk

This is for Dr George Armour Bell, OBE,
uncle, medical adviser, and
all-round good guy

Acknowledgements

My friend and fellow mysterian, Richard 'Kinky'
Friedman, a star in two galaxies, who suggested the
title, unwittingly, in a Mongolian hut in Edinburgh.

Patsy, at Moonmare, wherever in the world, or on the
Internet, that may be.

Sylvia Cunningham, MBE.

William Crowe, a fellow escapee from an institution in
Elmbank Street, Glasgow.

A fine man, nameless on this page at least, who tried to
teach me chemistry in that very institution, but failed
through no fault of his own.

One

Christmas comes early in London. So does closing time.

The couple stood on the edge of the pavement and looked along Oxford Street; it was just over an hour before midnight, the lights were shining, their tableaux stretching all the way along towards Marble Arch. Buses and taxis flowed along Regent Street towards the Circus, business picking up again as the pubs began to empty.

'Jeez,' the tall man murmured. 'It's a shallow and inhospitable place, this. Damn near two months to Christmas and the fairy lights are on show already. Yet try and get a drink after eleven and you've no chance. To paraphrase an old Frankie song, London by night is a God awful sight . . . even on a Friday.'

'Come on now,' his companion laughed. In her high heels she stood only three or four inches shorter than his six feet two. She was golden-haired, stunningly beautiful in classic contrast to his rugged, life-formed features, and her pale blue eyes seemed to reflect the sparkle of the pageant light. Her voice was full and mellow, that of a contralto in her prime, refined and with the faintest trace, if one listened closely enough, of a Scottish accent. 'Glasgow was just the same when we were youngsters,' she said, 'but without the bright lights.'

1

'I never cared, when you were around.'

'No,' she countered quickly, a chuckle in her throat, 'nor when the other one was, either. You made your choice; and from the way you were talking about your daughter tonight, you've never regretted it.'

Suddenly, for the first time that evening, he was sombre. He hunched his broad shoulders inside his Barbour jacket, his sigh expelling a great cloud of breath into the frosty night. 'Regret is your enemy,' he said. 'If you give in to it, it can destroy you. It's a waste of time anyway; you can't change the past.'

'But would you, if you could?' she asked him.

'Why? Would you? The way you say that makes it sound as if I dumped you, yet I've always understood that our breaking up was a joint decision.'

She reached up and adjusted his tie, looking at the knot, rather than into his eyes. 'Then, sir, that just shows you how good I am at my job. Oh, I didn't make a fuss when it happened. I was a big girl; I put on my mature face and agreed with all the common sense you talked.' She put a fingertip between her breasts. 'But in here, my little heart was breaking.'

'I'm sorry. I really am,' he replied sincerely, 'but I still think it was for the best.'

'So do I, now; no doubt about it. But back while it was happening . . .' She smiled up at him, with a flash of mischief in her eye. 'Did you love me, then?'

He nodded, his steely hair glinting under the street lights. 'Yup.'

She opened her mouth to respond but broke off as a

pedestrian paused, and turned to stare at her. The man seemed to hesitate, then carried on his way. She looked back at him, the interruption over. 'But not as much as you loved her?' It was a statement as much as a question.

'It wasn't just that. I loved her, sure . . . although to be absolutely truthful, I liked you more. Ahhh . . .' He paused for a few seconds, gazing up at the night. 'Look, Lou, I don't care about religion or any of that stuff, just about what's right and what's wrong. My first personal commandment is loyalty. I've broken it twice in my life, and found that I hated myself for it, on both occasions.

'The way I came to see it back then was that I made a promise when I got engaged. If I had broken it off, I couldn't have hacked the guilt, and sooner or later, I'd have blamed it on you.'

'And I'd have hated that, for sure,' she conceded. She chuckled again, deep and warm, at his frown. 'Don't worry, I haven't spent the last twenty-five years pining for my lost love. I've found a few since then: two marriages, three serious affairs . . . not bad for a wee girl from Bearsden. I've never felt a pang of guilt, either. We're totally different personalities, you see: yours is set in concrete and mine's tossing about on life's restless ocean.

'I'd have left you by the time I was twenty-one. For sure.'

She paused as a red bus roared by, close to the kerb. 'When was your other fall from grace?' she asked him.

'A couple of years back,' he answered. 'My second wife and I had a major fall-out; she went back to the States, and I got involved with someone else. We got over it, though. We found out that we mattered too much to each other to let go.'

She smiled again. 'So there's no point in my asking you back to my place for a night-cap?'

He raised an eyebrow at her question, and glanced away, out into the street. 'That would depe . . .'

In mid-sentence, he stopped, threw his left arm round her waist and flung himself sideways, pulling her with him as he dived behind an abandoned newspaper stand. They heard the blast behind them before they hit the ground, and the scream of tyres as a dark coloured saloon accelerated away down Regent Street.

He was on his feet again in a second. 'Wait here,' he told the woman, then ran off down the street after the car, trying to catch a clear view of its number-plate, only to see it disappear round the curve in the broad street, heading for Piccadilly Circus. She too was standing once again as he returned to their safe haven. No one had come to her aid; indeed, none of the few people who had been passing at the time were anywhere to be seen.

She stared at him, bewildered, but apparently not in the least frightened. 'You swept me off my feet once before,' she exclaimed, 'but never like that. What was that about?'

He glared back down Regent Street. 'When someone shoots at me,' he said, tersely, 'I tend to get out of the way!'

Her hand flew to her mouth, and her eyes seemed to flash as they widened. 'Someone shot at you?'

'It's happened before,' he told her dryly. 'Didn't you see the gun?'

'I heard a bang, but that was all. What was it?'

'The guy in that car had a shotgun. I just happened to be

looking that way as he stuck it out the window and took a bead on me.'

'But who would want to shoot you?'

His mouth twisted in a grimace as he unfastened a pocket of his jacket and took out a hand-phone. 'More people than you could shake a stick at, my dear,' he murmured as he punched in the police emergency number.

Two

'Do you ever get enraged about anything, Sammy?'

'What?'

'Enraged, I said. As in, really steamed up with anger.'

He looked at her as she stood there, all lips and legs. 'Enraged? No, not so's you'd notice, anyway. Now if you'd said engorged . . .'

'But I didn't . . .' Ruth frowned at him severely.

He grinned back. 'Why d'you ask, anyway? Am I beginning to bore you, Ms McConnell?'

She shook her head, making her long, glossy hair ripple like a shampoo commercial. 'Not yet, Sergeant, not yet. All the same, you are getting predictable. You're the easiest going man I've ever been out with.'

'A typical copper, in other words.'

'Absolutely a-typical as far as I've seen. Where I work it's like a madhouse at times; I've never seen so many stressed-out people.'

He looked at her with a touch of scepticism in his eyes. 'Such as? I know the Big Man can go a bit stratospheric from time to time, but the Chief's an even-tempered sort, and DI McIlhenney's okay too, isn't he?'

'Up to a point.' She hesitated. 'I shouldn't tell tales out

of school, but . . .' She frowned. 'No, better not.'

'Aw, come on, Ruthie,' he exclaimed. 'You can't do that to me. Honest to Christ, I don't know. You seem to be making a career out of leading me on then slamming the bloody door in my face.'

'What do you mean by that?' She raised an eyebrow, provoking him even further.

'You know bloody well what I mean.'

'No. Spell it out?'

'You know.'

'No. Tell me.'

'Okay, we've been going out for . . . how long? . . . six months now, yet we've never . . .'

'So?' she asked, archly.

'So most people, most couples . . .'

'Shag on their first date?'

'No, I wouldn't go that far . . .'

'Well neither would I.'

He drew the car to a halt in a lay-by and switched off the engine. 'Fine,' he murmured, turning to her, 'but after this long, I'd have thought that our relationship might have . . . moved up a gear, shall we say.'

'You can say it if you like, Detective Sergeant Pye. But can you tell me why it should? Do you think you're God's gift or something?'

'No,' he protested, 'but it's not as if you . . .' He stopped himself short, and bit his lip. Fortunately, she laughed.

'. . . as if I haven't been round the block a few times? Was that it?'

'No! I wouldn't be that crude, Ruthie. But you've had

7

other relationships, okay: that's all I was going to say.'

'I didn't jump into bed with any of them either, no one long-term, at least. Sammy, the first time I screwed someone on a first date I was nineteen. Two days later I realised that I didn't really fancy him that much, but it took me six months and a lot of hassle to get shot of him. Ever since then, I've been careful to distinguish between short- and long-term things.

'There was a time when I had the hots for Andy Martin; given the chance I'd have shagged his brains out, but that's all he'd have wanted anyway. If I'd slept with you right at the start, then most probably it would have been all over by now. The fact that I'm still making up my mind; well, that's got to be good hasn't it? Unless, of course you're only after a quick legover yourself?'

'Which I'm not, as you well know.'

'In that case, trust me for a bit longer; being friends is more important than the other, believe me.'

'I know that,' he conceded. 'Karen and I were only ever pals, for all that half the force seemed to think.'

She laughed. 'Which is maybe just as well, given that you work for DCS Martin and that she's Mrs Martin now.'

He capitulated. 'Okay, I apologise,' he said. 'You are not a tease, and you have our best interests at heart . . . but you still led me on with that remark back there about stress in the Command corridor. Come on; I'm no security risk. Has Big Bob got another crisis on?'

'No,' she answered quietly. 'In both the operational and domestic senses, DCC Skinner is going along relatively quietly at the moment, thanks. But remember. I don't just work for him.'

Sammy Pye's eyebrows rose, as he grasped her meaning. 'Ah, Mr Theodore Chase, our new ACC Ops. Is he stirring things up, then?'

She looked at him. 'Not a word outside this car, mind you, but is he ever. "Come back ACC Elder," that's the word around my office.'

'Why did Jim Elder go in the first place? It was a real shock when he chucked it.'

'I have no idea. He just walked into my room one Monday morning a few months back and told me that he was leaving at the end of that week. No reason, no nothing.'

'Didn't Bob Skinner let anything slip?'

'Not a whisper. And if he wants me to know something he always tells me, so I know better than to ask.'

She sighed. 'Whatever happened, now we've got the new guy! God, he's Supercop, if ever there was such a creature. You know the first thing he did?' Fired up, she answered her own question. 'He appointed Jack Good as his exec., without consulting anyone.'

Pye gasped in surprise. 'Eh? He just did it? He pulled him out of his other job just like that?'

'That's right. Jim Elder never had an exec., but that didn't bother Ted Chase. He'd been through the door for no more than a fortnight before he had one. The worst thing of all was that he did it while the Chief was on holiday. Mr Skinner came in one morning and found Jack Good in Neil McIlhenney's office. When he asked him what he was doing there and Good told him, he went straight to the ACC's room. I was there at the time; Mr Skinner asked him what it was all about and Mr Chase as good as told him it was none of his business.

'For a moment the DCC looked as if he was about to explode, but he just turned and walked out. Next day he had Good moved out of Neil's office into a room of his own . . . Neil can't stand Jack Good . . . but it was on the floor below, and Mr Chase complained to the Chief when he came back. So a CID man was moved out to make room for him.'

Pye frowned. 'Remind me. Where did Chase come from?'

'He was an Assistant Chief in Cumbria. The job was advertised throughout Britain and he applied. Between you and me, I was surprised that Mr Martin didn't go for it.'

'I wasn't, but never mind. Jesus, does this guy have any idea who he's taking on, falling out with Bob Skinner?'

Ruth shrugged. 'If he does, he doesn't care. You're not going to believe what the latest is. Chase has written a paper for the police board; no one asked him to do it, he just did. In it, he argues that the executive structure of the force is wrong, and that given the nature of the Chief Constable's duties, his designated deputy from among the officers within the command ranks should be someone with extensive experience across the board.'

'Meaning him?'

'You guessed it. He also pointed out that he's been twice as long in the Chief Officer rank as Mr Skinner has.'

'He's after Big Bob's job?'

'Correct. But I think that ultimately, he's after the Chief's.'

'The man's mad, then. Mind you, who's going to take any notice of him?'

'The Joint Police Board might, for a start. The DCC has his enemies on that body; more than that, he thinks that Mr Chase has a direct route to them. He's found out that he has a cousin back in Cumbria who's a Labour MP at Westminster.'

'What's the Chief saying about it?'

Ruth pursed her lips and glanced at him. 'Nothing,' she said. 'He's playing it by the book; when Mr Chase wrote his paper, he sent it to him formally, with a covering memo asking him to put it to the Board. The Chief replied on paper, asking whether he was sure he wanted to do that. Mr Chase replied and said that he was.

'A couple of days later, the three of them . . . the Chief, Mr Skinner and Mr Chase . . . discussed it in private. Afterwards the Boss told me that the Chief thanked Chase and said that he would consider at some length whether it should go to the Board. It's on the shelf for the moment, as far as I can gather.'

'Has the Big Man said anything to you?'

'Only that if Chase thinks he's taking orders from him he's crazy.' She grinned. 'That wasn't quite what he said; I've left out the adjectives.'

Sammy whistled and restarted the car. 'I see what you meant about stress levels in your corridor. ACC Chase is either very brave, or very stupid.'

'Neither,' Ruth replied at once. 'He's simply ambitious. Possibly the most ambitious man I've ever met; he wants to be a Chief in a major force and to collect the automatic knighthood that goes with it. It's written all over him. As for his wife . . .'

She stopped in mid-sentence, slamming a metaphorical door on the subject. 'Come on, let's get under way again. I want to get to Uncle John's before dark.'

She smiled at him again, then reached out and ruffled his sandy hair. 'This is moving our relationship forward, you know. Quite significantly at that. If I take someone to meet my favourite uncle it's a sort of sign . . . if only you could read it.'

Three

'**B**ugger!' Neil swore quietly as the telephone rang; Lauren, his daughter, looked at him severely.

'Dad!'

'Come on, kid,' he appealed, 'right in the middle of the football results.'

'That's no excuse,' the eleven-year-old retorted. 'Do you want Spence to use language like that? Or me, even?'

'What are you talking about? You do already.' Still in his armchair, he leaned across and picked up the phone. 'Hello,' he answered.

'DI McIlhenney?' a Cockney voice enquired.

'That's me.'

'Hello mate. This is DC Crowther, from the Met. West End Central Division, Savile Row. I was tryin' to phone your boss, but his mobile number's unavailable. He left yours as back-up.'

'Is that right, Constable?' the Scots detective replied, his hackles risen instantly. 'Then tell me something. If he'd answered his hand-phone, would you have called him "mate" as well?' He paused. 'Not that I'm rank-conscious, mind.'

He heard a distinct gulp. 'Sorry, Inspector; it's just that I'm not used to dealing with Scotsmen.'

'Don't compound it, Constable. Now, what's this about? I haven't seen DCC Skinner since he left for London on Wednesday.'

McIlhenney thought he heard a faint chuckle at the other end of the line. 'Yeah, he's been busy down 'ere.

'Your guvnor called in a drive-by shooting last night from Oxford Circus; round about eleven. He said that a lone guy took a pop at him with a shotgun from a dark coloured Ford Mondeo. I'm just calling to tell him that we haven't had a sniff of a result so far. Not a bleeding thing.'

DC Crowther coughed. 'The thing is, sir, copper to copper, my guvnor's pissed off at your guvnor. Soon as his call came in last night we put a right shitload of effort into it; we alerted all our patrol cars. They pulled over everything within a three mile radius that even looked like a Mondeo. While they were doing that we had an armed robbery in a burger place in Oxford Street, a rape behind a pub in Great Titchfield Street, and a stabbing in Soho. As a result of your man's call we were late responding to every one of 'em, so we didn't feel a single collar.

'Tough, you'll say, but then we took a look at the scene of Mr Skinner's so-called drive-by, and guess what? It was as clean as a whistle. Someone takes a shot at you with a twelve-bore, even if 'e misses, you'd expect to find traces of it all around.'

Crowther sighed. 'Nothing. No damage to any shop windows, or to the news-stand your guvnor said he dived behind, and no lead shot lying around either, none at all. There were no witnesses either, not a bleedin' one.'

The Cockney seemed to hesitate for a second. 'Tell me

something, Inspector. I've heard about your man . . . who 'asn't? Is he the nervous type?'

'Not in the very slightest,' McIlhenney answered.

'Well, my divisional commander reckons that he is. He was in here this afternoon, effin' and blindin' about wasting police time. He reckons your man's shell-shocked, or paranoid, or worse. He's threatening to send a formal report to your chief and recommend that your man be made to have psych tests.'

'Is that right?' the inspector barked. 'Just you tell him, from me if you like, that he should wind his bloody neck in. If you don't fancy passing that on, have your DI do it, but get your guy calmed down somehow or . . . Commander or not . . . God help him. If Big Bob said there was a shot fired, then there was a shot fired, end of story. If he'd been carrying himself you'd have had fucking evidence all right, with a bullet in it!'

He waved an apology at Lauren, as she frowned at him.

'You get that report squashed, Constable. You do not know with whom you are dealing, and I mean that.'

'I'll do my best, sir,' said Crowther.

McIlhenney was unconvinced. 'Do that. By the way, what team do you support?'

'Eh? Spurs, as it 'appens.'

'That's good . . . they got stuffed four-nil.'

Four

'How long has your uncle lived here?' Sammy asked, as he drew up alongside the neat bungalow, the last house in a leafy cul-de-sac.

'He and Aunt Cecily came to Cumbernauld from Glasgow when they started to build the new town in the late fifties. They lived in a flat in an area called Kildrum at first, then moved here, closer to the town centre. They bought it from the Development Corporation about fifteen years ago, just after it was refurbished. They got it for a song too, as sitting tenants.'

'Your aunt's no longer around, I take it?'

'No,' said Ruth. 'She died of a heart attack in 1986, a year after Uncle John retired. He's been alone since then.'

'He'll be a fair age then?'

'He's just turned eighty. But he's very fit; he's been a member of Dullatur Golf Club just about all his life. He plays just about every day, hail, rain or shine. It's walking distance from the house.'

'What did he do for a living?'

'Something on the railways: in the office at the top of Buchanan Street, in Glasgow. He retired on a good pension, so he's quite well off, especially now that Auntie isn't here to help him spend his money.'

Sammy grinned. 'Are you looking out for your inheritance, then?'

She bridled at his joke. 'No, I am not! I may be the only blood relation he's got left, but he could be leaving his money to the cat and dog home for all I know . . . or care. We're here today because I'm guilty, that's all. I haven't seen him since his last birthday, in June, and that's not good enough. He's an old man, he hardly drives any more, and apart from his golfing pals he's all alone.'

'Come on, love. He must have neighbours who look in on him, or a home help, or someone.'

'No, not him. He's a very private man. Always has been.'

He opened the car door. 'Let's bring some company into his life then.'

She smiled as she stepped out, and led him up the garden path. Glancing around, Sammy noticed that the rose bushes in front of the house had gone to briar and that the beds in which they were planted were overdue for weeding. 'Old Uncle John's no gardener, from the look of it,' he muttered under his breath.

Although the short winter evening was almost over, no lights showed at the front door of the house, as Ruth pressed the doorbell. They waited, for almost a minute; eventually, Sammy patted her on the shoulder. 'You did call to tell him we were coming, didn't you?' he asked.

She looked up at him awkwardly. 'Well, no, I didn't. I wanted to give him a surprise.'

'Great! In that case, the old boy's probably still at the golf club.'

'No. He always listens to a football match on the radio on a Saturday afternoon.'

'Ring the bell again, in that case. He's probably got the sound turned up.'

'Sammy, he's not in.' She stepped across to the uncurtained living-room window and peered in. 'I can see his hi-fi set and it isn't switched on.'

'Maybe he's got another radio in the kitchen. Let's take a look round the back.'

As she looked at him, the first pang of fear shot through her. 'Okay,' she murmured, following him as he set off down the path which ran around the house. The small back garden lay to the east; the dusk, and the tall conifers which enclosed it on three sides, made it even gloomier than the front. There was no light in any of the three windows to the rear, the kitchen, the second bedroom or the frosted pane of the bathroom.

'Does your uncle see all right?' Pye asked. 'I mean would he normally have the light on at this time of day?'

'Uncle John's always reading something or other. He wears glasses now, but his sight's always been fine. Sammy, let's go up to the golf club; the old so-and-so's probably there, right enough.'

He held up a hand. 'In a minute. First of all . . .' He reached out and turned the handle of the back door; it swung open, into the kitchen.

'God,' Ruth snapped. 'He's gone out and left the place unlocked!' She stepped past him into the kitchen, and gasped. Looking over her shoulder, Sammy could see even in the dim light that the place was in chaos; worse, it stank of staleness. Dirty plates filled the sink and were strewn on the work-surface beside the cooker. A badly soiled tea-towel lay in the middle of the floor. A milk carton sat on the small table, surrounded by discarded food wrappers.

'What the hell's the old bugger living like?' she murmured. 'He's always struck me as such a neat man, yet this is pure squalor. If this is what happens when I don't warn him of a visit, I'll be here every Saturday from now on.' She screwed up her face. 'Jesus, the place stinks!

'Uncle John!' she called out, listening for a few seconds before turning towards the back door. 'Come on. Let's go up there and find him.'

The young detective handed her the car keys. 'On you go. I'll make this place secure; the front door has a Yale so I'll come out that way.' She bought the lie and did as he told her, although to be sure he turned the back door key in its lock as soon as she had left.

The smell became more obvious as soon as he stepped out of the kitchen; it was thick, and cloying. He had done this job before, but nonetheless he was a shade fearful as he moved up the hall and opened the front bedroom door. Crumpled clothes were strewn all around, and the bed itself was unmade, its sheets so soiled and tangled that they might have won a place in a modern art exhibition. But the room was empty.

He had seen on the way past, through its open door, that the second bedroom had been untouched for weeks, either by duster or vacuum cleaner; so that left only the bathroom. Hesitantly, he opened the door. As he did so, the smell, strong before, seemed to wash out and over him like an ocean wave, almost knocking him backwards, physically. He knew, before he looked inside, what he would find.

Uncle John McConnell lay full length, submerged completely in his big enamelled bath. He had played his last round of golf, and listened to his last radio football commentary.

Even before stepping into the bathroom Pye had guessed that he had been dead for days, and he had feared that he would find him in a state of hideous decomposition. Instead, and to his surprise, the old man's body was more or less intact, if a strange waxy colour, and if one ignored the strips of what looked like skin, floating on the surface. He looked almost like a statue, carved out of soap.

The young sergeant reached across the small bathroom and opened the ventilation panel set in the window, then stepped back out into the hall and closed the door behind him.

There was a phone in the hall. He picked it up, but to his surprise, the line was dead. Instead, he took out his hand-phone and dialled the main switchboard of his Edinburgh headquarters.

'Give me the Ops Room please, Duty Officer,' he asked the telephonist.

The line rang only twice before it was answered. 'Operations. ACC Chase speaking,' said a deep, North Country voice. 'How can I help?'

'Hello sir,' said the young detective, surprised. 'This is DS Pye, from Mr Martin's office. I didn't expect to find you in on a Saturday.'

'Spot check, Sergeant, spot check; something that should

20

happen more often here. What can I do for CID this fine day?'

Sammy hated being patronised, even by an ACC, but he ignored it. 'I've got a problem, sir,' he replied. 'I'm at Ruth's uncle's place, in Cumbernauld.'

'Ruth?'

'Your secretary, sir. Ruth McConnell. She took me to visit her Uncle John, only when we got here, the old chap was dead. In his bath.'

'Where's Cumbernauld?' Chase asked.

'Between Stirling and Glasgow, sir. It's in the Strathclyde area, but I don't have their Ops number to hand.'

'Okay, Pye, I'll turn them out for you. What do you need? CID?'

'To be on the safe side, yes, although it doesn't look suspicious at all. Like I said, the old chap seems to have taken some sort of seizure and died, in the water. He was alone in the house, though, so under Scots law we have to have police here, as well as the doctor.'

'I'm familiar with the law, son,' said Chase, heavily. 'What's the address?'

'Fifteen Glenlaverock Grove.' For a second Pye thought about spelling it out for the ACC, then thought again.

'Roger. You wait there for them. Is McConnell the next-of-kin?'

'Yes, sir, she is. She doesn't know about this yet, though, sir. She's out in the car.'

'Well, you better bloody tell her then, hadn't you, son, before the local emergency services descend mob-handed!'

Five

Bob Skinner laughed. 'The one place I can't be contacted, Neil, as you well know, is on Gullane Hill with my clubs over my shoulder. If I took my mobile out on the golf course with me, I'd soon run out of playing partners.

'I'm sorry they interrupted your Saturday though. I didn't really expect that.'

'No problem, Boss. My daughter was just about to bully me into doing the ironing.'

'Has she not taken that over yet?'

'No, she says she's too small to reach the ironing board properly. She also says that she doesn't expect to be tall enough till she's about eighteen. She's more like her mother every day, I tell you.'

'You don't have to, mate. I've seen her in action.' He smiled briefly at the thought. 'Anyway, what did this boy from the Met have to tell me?'

McIlhenney drew a breath. 'Nothing you're going to like.' He outlined the content of Crowther's call, omitting nothing. When he finished there was silence from the other end of the line.

Skinner broke it at last. 'The bastard must have fired a

blank,' he said, firmly. 'There was a gun, Neil, and it was fired. Believe me?'

'I never doubted you for one second, Boss,' his executive assistant replied. 'It's just a pity there weren't any witnesses.'

He heard the Deputy Chief Constable sigh. 'Aye, well, that's not exactly the case. The fact is, there was someone with me when it happened.'

'Why didn't you say so, then?' McIlhenney blurted out.

'Discretion, pal. Discretion. Does the name Louise Bankier mean anything to you?'

'Louise Bankier? The actress? The movie star?'

'The very same. Lou was there; she and I had just had dinner in a restaurant in Soho. We were looking for a taxi when the car drove by and the guy took his pop at me. For all sorts of reasons, I didn't want her about when the Met boys arrived, so I stuck her in a taxi and sent her home as soon as I'd called the thing in.'

'Boss, what the hell . . .'

Skinner laughed again, softly, at his friend's incredulity, '. . . was I doing up the West End with Louise Bankier? She and I go back a long way . . . a very long way.

'She was just starting at Glasgow University when I was in my final year; she was seventeen and I was twenty-one. We met at the Fresher's Fair when I was signing up new members for the squash club. She joined, and fortunately for the world, she also joined the drama club on the same day.

'She could play squash eff all, but when it came to the acting game . . . She wound up wangling a transfer to the Athenaeum – that was what they called the drama school in Glasgow – after her first year, and she's never looked back from there.

'I hadn't seen her in twenty-five years. I followed her career, of course, and went to all her movies, but I lost touch with her completely. Then last Thursday, I got a message at my hotel. There was a piece in the *Evening Standard* about last week's world terrorism conference. She saw it and phoned the organisers; they told her where I was stopping.

'I rang her back. She told me that she had called on impulse, for old times' sake; I said I was pleased to hear from her and we arranged to have dinner, last night. End of story.

'She hasn't changed a bit, you know.' He paused. 'No, that's crap. If anything she's even better looking than she was as a kid, and she's developed as a person in ways I could never have imagined. But I suppose we all have, have we not. Anyway, when all that nonsense happened last night, I imagined what the papers would do if they got hold of it. Lou does not need that sort of publicity and neither do I, so I got her out of the way.'

He could almost hear McIlhenney frown. 'Boss, that's . . .'

'Improper, at the very least. Obstructing the course of justice at the very worst. I know that, but I'll live with it. You just get back to that boy Crowther and tell him from me to pass the word up his line that if his commander doesn't want his gonads fricasseed, he'll pull that bullshit report of his.'

'I've told him that already. Mind you, he wasn't certain that it could be done.'

Skinner sighed again. 'I'll deal with that if it happens.

'The thing is, Neil,' he went on, 'Louise is not the only one I need to protect from too much press interest.'

'Apart from the gunshot . . . sure as hell she doesn't need to know about that . . . there's nothing that Sarah doesn't know, you understand. She was aware that I was meeting Lou all right; I told her as soon as it was arranged. But she wouldn't be best pleased either if the wrong sort of stuff appeared in the papers.

'The truth is that if any smart hacks did some digging, even though it'd mean going back a quarter of a century, there would still be plenty of people around to tell them that Louise Bankier and I were more than just squash partners.'

Six

Theodore Chase gazed down the driveway of the police headquarters building. Normally, every parking bay would have been occupied, and the street outside, even the school playground beyond, would have been thronged with vehicles, but on a Sunday afternoon most of the cars he could see belonged to shoppers at the nearby supermarket.

He stood in Ruth McConnell's tiny office, flicking through her in-trays, of which she had two; his own, which was empty, awaiting the Monday morning mail delivery, and Bob Skinner's, which was piled high with papers waiting for the attention of the DCC on his return from the London conference.

Ted Chase enjoyed lurking around empty offices, as he put it to himself. There was something about them; they seemed to him to be possessed by the auras of the people who occupied them through the week, each with its own unique signature. Take Ruth McConnell's small room as an example. She used the same fragrance as his wife ... *Rive Gauche*, whatever that meant; not that his nose would have told him that, for his sense of smell had been deadened by growing up close to a brewery. Since coming to Edinburgh he had discovered that he could even drive through Seafield without

26

the faintest wrinkle of his nose. He picked up the familiar blue *eau de toilette* tube, glanced at it, then put it back on the desk, carefully, on its side, in its original position.

He closed his eyes and he could feel her presence, could see her in his mind as clearly as if she was really sat there, long legs under her chair, close fitting skirt moulded to her thighs, riding just above the knee, her white blouse tucked into the waistband, covering the faintest roll of flesh. He let his mind roam further until he could actually feel the residual warmth of her body in the room, and sense the strength of her personality, filling its every corner.

In spite of himself he began to imagine her naked, hair tousled, glowing after sex; and then there was someone else in his vision. Sammy Pye? No, not the young sergeant, someone bigger, older, stronger, grimmer, frightening as his head seemed to turn towards the intruder . . . Bob Skinner.

Ted Chase opened his eyes wide, and was a shade embarrassed to find that he was breathing slightly heavily. He thought of Skinner and Ruth; they had worked together for a few years now. She was a woman and a half; he had a past that had made the tabloids. He couldn't believe that she would settle for a lad like Pye. There had to be something there, for sure.

He was startled when the phone rang on Ruth's desk. For a second he thought about letting it go unanswered, but that was against his nature. Somehow, it would have made him feel like a sneak. He picked it up, and was taken aback to hear Bob Skinner's strong, steady voice. 'Afternoon Ted,' he began. His tone was neutral, neither friendly nor hostile. 'Your wife told me I'd probably find you in the office.' Chase waited for the DCC to ask what the hell he was doing there, as, probably, he would have done himself in reversed circumstances. When he did not, he felt almost a sense of let-down.

'I've had a call from Ruthie,' he continued, instead. 'Asking if it would be all right for her to have a couple of days off. Her uncle's died, and she has to make all the funeral arrangements and stuff.'

'Yes,' said Chase, abruptly. 'I knew about that. I was in the Ops Room yesterday afternoon when Martin's man Pye called in after finding the body.'

He heard a soft chuckle at the other end. 'How the fuck did we manage without you, Ted? I really don't know.'

The ACC felt himself flush. 'I'm still getting the feel of the place, Bob, that's all.'

'You could have fooled me, mate, but let's not get into that. I told her that it was okay, and that I'd square it with you.'

'Yes, of course. In the circumstances, it's okay with me.'

'That's good. As it happens, the Chief's chairing an ACPOS committee meeting in Glasgow tomorrow, so Gerry Crossley'll have some time on his hands. We won't be neglected.'

'Ah, yes.' Chase did not approve of male secretaries, and could never keep the distaste out of his tone whenever the efficient young Crossley's name came up in conversation.

'He's a good lad, Ted,' Skinner said quietly. 'As you might find out for yourself, one day. See you tomorrow.' There was a click; the line went dead, then buzzed as the Cumbrian stared at the receiver, taken off-guard by his colleague's throw-away remark.

It wasn't that he disliked Bob Skinner, Chase told himself, as he replaced the receiver; he was an affable enough bloke. It wasn't that he was jealous of him; he took enough pride in his own career achievements not to feel jealous of anyone. It wasn't that he doubted his ability; he was one of the most famous policemen in the country, and the Queen's Police Medal wasn't awarded lightly.

No, he told himself, his concern was based on his distinguished colleague's attitude to The Book. There were accepted ways of policing, and these had been developed practically over many years. The relationship between police and public, in the eyes of Theodore Chase, was one in which the uniformed body had to stand aloof to command the respect which he saw as essential to efficient operation. Nevertheless, by no means did he see himself as being stuck in the past. He approved wholeheartedly of the new style of uniform, which was more comfortable, and had been designed to meet modern needs. He recognised the value of the Panda car, although he stuck to the view that walking the beat still had its place, especially in the inner city areas.

His problem with Bob Skinner was simply that he seemed to see it all differently. For example, the man had a little-disguised dislike of wearing the uniform . . . so little-disguised that it was a standing joke throughout headquarters. Chase saw the dark blue tunic as the basic symbol of authority. For example, for his Saturday drop-in to the Ops Room, he had worn it. A quiet Sunday in the office; well, that was something else.

Skinner had an overtly sloppy attitude to reporting channels also. It was one thing for ACC Operations to pay unannounced visits to his own Ops Room to keep everyone on their toes, but quite another for the DCC to involve himself in active criminal investigations. There was even a story about him taking his baby son on a stake-out of premises in the course of a hunt for a murder suspect.

Then there was his lax attitude to rank. He accepted that it was for the Chief Constable to determine whether he and his two assistants should be on first-name terms, behind closed doors, as they were. However, Skinner's easy familiarity with the men under his command posed in his view a clear and present danger to good discipline. He and DI McIlhenney played football in the same five-a-side group every Thursday . . . and sometimes, Chase understood, his daughter baby-sat the McIlhenney children to allow them to do it. He and DCS Martin had a fraternal rapport . . . so much so that Skinner had been best man at the Head of CID's wedding. He allowed McGuire, the Special Branch man, virtually open access to his office.

There were only two lines in Chase's controversial paper on the Force's command structure to which the DCC had taken outright exception; one had been a reference to 'the cult of the personality', as he had put it . . . and that was at the heart of his problem with Skinner. He would not . . . did not dare . . . suggest that the big Scot had built his own legend deliberately. No, he accepted that he was trapped within it. Yet that was the greatest obstacle to his efficiency as a chief police officer.

The Book of Proper Policing, Ted Chase's imaginary Bible, had been written by many people over many years. It had come under attack in a variety of ways, from direct assault by terrorism to insidious undermining tactics by those people to whom Chase referred most commonly as 'liberals', yet as he saw it, the solid dependable man and . . . yes, now, he had to concede . . . woman in uniform still stood, in spite of it all, as the cornerstone of society.

Image and perception were all-important; no personality could be allowed to overshadow either, yet that was what Skinner seemed to do. He was rarely seen in public in uniform. He was not the Chief Constable. And yet whenever anyone in Edinburgh . . . anyone in Scotland, probably, many people in England, perhaps . . . thought of a policeman, they were likely to think of him.

In his heart of hearts, Ted Chase disapproved of devolution. He was British first, Cumbrian second, and like many of his compatriots, English third; he had a niggling fear of anything which threatened the composition of the flag he saluted, and a downright dislike of anything which claimed to be an alternative to the National Anthem, which he took pride in bellowing lustily on public occasions.

However, he had accepted the political situation, and the prospect of working in a devolved Scotland, when he had decided to apply for the Edinburgh job. He had reasoned that it gave him his best chance of rising to command his own force. Now that he was in place, he had come to realise how different Scotland was, and how great was its potential for change. Virtually all of its institutions were under the control of a new breed of politician, able to tackle their manifesto objectives with none of the constraints of parliamentary time which had bedevilled the old Scottish Office at Westminster.

31

In particular, he had come to realise how easy it would be for his own views on policing, which had held sway under the old regime, to be swept away by the new administration, which he saw as a soft-centred coalition, committed to reform for its own sake. Nothing was beyond them.

And who better to serve as a model for a new Scottish breed of policeman than the home-bred hero, DCC Robert Morgan Skinner?

Chase was nobody's fool; he saw the danger more clearly than the man himself . . . and there, he saw also, might lie the saving grace. Skinner's intense dislike of politicians was a matter of record, certainly within the police force, and to an extent in the wider world, thanks to the circumstances which had led to his giving up his former responsibility as security adviser to the Secretary of State.

Yet what political power he could command through his reputation and his public profile, if only he realised it . . . 'Thank God,' the ACC thought, 'that he doesn't.'

He was so immersed in contemplation that he gave a small, involuntary jump when the phone rang for a second time. He picked it up, expecting Skinner once again, only to hear the voice of the security man on weekend duty at the main entrance.

'There's a UPS guy, here, sir, wi' a delivery for the Chief Constable. Since you're here, dae you want to sign for it?'

The ACC frowned. 'I suppose so. I'll be down in a moment.'

He left his secretary's office and walked briskly along the Command corridor, then down a flight of stairs which led more or less directly to the front door. The brown-suited messenger stood waiting, with a big brown envelope and the inevitable clipboard.

'Print your name there, sir, then sign ablow it,' he said.

Chase made a mental note of yet another Scots word, and did as the man asked, thanking him as he took the package. He glanced at it as he walked back upstairs, his curiosity aroused. The address was clear and simple: 'Chief Constable Sir James Proud, QPM, Police Headquarters, Fettes Avenue, Edinburgh', and it bore two red stamped injunctions, one 'Urgent', the other, 'Confidential'.

'But not, "personal",' he murmured to himself as he stood at Gerry Crossley's desk, holding the envelope poised over the in-tray. 'And Bob did say that the Chief isn't in tomorrow.'

He picked up a letter-opener, slit the envelope open and slid out its contents, three A4 pages, stapled together with a covering letter, on Metropolitan Police notepaper.

He was frowning as he began to read. By the time he was finished, he was wide-eyed and his mouth was hanging open in astonishment.

Seven

'Was that the first time you'd ever seen anything like that, Sam?' Detective Chief Superintendent Andy Martin asked his aide.

'Not the first time I've ever seen a body, sir,' the recently promoted sergeant replied. 'You know what it's like when you're in uniform. One way or another, you have to look at quite a few.'

He shuddered, looking older, suddenly, than his twenty-seven years. 'But it's the first time I've ever seen one like that; in that condition I mean. Lying there in the bath, the poor old bugger looked like …' His face twisted as he struggled to find words. 'Like a statue, like a tailor's dummy, like something that never had been human.

'It wasn't gross, Boss, not like something I saw once, when an old lady had died in front of an electric fire and lain there for about a week. There weren't any maggots in the eye sockets, nothing like that. But in its own way, it was pretty horrible, for all that.'

'Did Ruth see him?'

'No way. When I told her, I had to hold her back from going into the bathroom, but I did. She gave me bloody hell at the time, but calmed down pretty quickly.'

'No nightmares?'

'I wouldn't know, sir,' said Pye, abruptly.

'I didn't mean her, you clown!' the Head of CID chuckled.

The young sergeant flushed, embarrassed by his revealing slip. 'No, sir, not me.'

'You will have, Sammy, you will,' Martin murmured, his smile gone. He had known his own nocturnal horrors; happily, marriage seemed to be holding them at bay.

'I'll be ready for them, then.'

'No, you won't. No one ever is.'

Pye looked across at his boss; then changed the subject. 'How's Karen doing? Still being sick?'

'No, thank Christ,' he replied, sincerely. 'She seems to have stopped barfing up her breakfast. She's blooming, mate, blooming; she's not showing yet, but it won't be long.'

He picked up a pile of papers from his desk, and walked across to the meeting table. 'This is today's agenda, then?'

'Yes, sir.'

'Okay, then; on you go and see if the troops are here. If they are, wheel them in.'

The Head of CID's Monday briefing with his six divisional commanders was a practice established by Bob Skinner and carried on by his successors, Roy Old and Andy Martin. Its main purpose was to keep the Chief Superintendent abreast of all active investigations, but it was useful also in that it could reveal patterns of crime across the force area, and not least in the platform which it provided for fresh thinking on stalled cases.

This one was special, though.

As the six senior detectives took their places at the table, there was one among them who stood out from the rest. She was the only woman among the six, trimly built, attractive, in her thirties, with flaming red hair which shone under the neon strip lighting. But more than that, there was a presence about her, a bearing which could not help but say to the rest, *'Don't take me lightly. I've made it this far, and I may have further to go.'*

Martin stood as the rest composed themselves, and as Sammy Pye took his seat on his right, notepad at the ready to take down the bullet points of the meeting.

He looked along the table, and smiled. 'I'd like to begin this morning's meeting, gentlemen, by welcoming a newcomer in our midst. Okay, I know she's been here before on occasion as Brian Mackie's deputy, but this is her first meeting as commander of Central Division CID, only the second woman to hold such a post in the history of our force.

'Congratulations, Mags. You've earned your place here by being an outstanding detective as well as a good leader. I'm looking forward to your contribution over the months to come.'

Detective Superintendent Maggie Rose looked up at the Head of CID and smiled faintly, wondering whether any of the others had read anything into his time-frame. 'Thank you, sir. I'm honoured to be here. I know I have a lot to learn, but I'm surrounded by good teachers.'

Her promotion had come about following the retirement of Superintendent John McGrigor from the command of the

Borders division. Martin and Bob Skinner, feeling that a veteran would fill the vacancy best, had decided to move Dan Pringle south, and to promote Rose into his post in Central Edinburgh.

Martin laughed out loud. 'You're off to a good start. Flattery will get you everywhere with these guys.'

She looked back at him, and noted yet again the change in him. The strung-out, bitter man of a few months earlier had gone; returned was the laid-back, unflappable, pleasant colleague she had come to know and respect over the years.

'Okay,' said the Head of CID, taking his seat, 'to business.' He glanced along at Dan Pringle. 'I see from your first report from the Borders that you've been making an impact. I know that big McGrigor had trouble with the odd sheep-stealer, but what the hell's this? Trout rustling?'

The big superintendent hunched his shoulders and tugged at the heavy moustache which seemed to give him a permanently mournful look. 'Pour scorn on me if you like, Andy,' he muttered, 'but it's been a crime waiting to happen.'

'Aye, waiting for you, by the looks of it. Have you taken some of your old customers down there with you? Is that it?'

'Maybe. From what John told me in our hand-over, they've a pretty poor and unimaginative bunch of hooligans down there. They've got a long history of practically signing their names to every crime that's committed. Not this one, though; this was very professional, very efficient.

'It happened at a big trout farm, just off the St Boswell's to Kelso Road. The manager lives on site, but he was away on

Friday and Saturday nights. When he went in yesterday morning just to check that the automatic feeders and water pumps were all right, he found that all the bloody tanks had been emptied.'

'How, for God's sake?' chuckled Superintendent Brian Mackie. 'How do you nick a shoal of bloody fish?'

'Good question, son,' Pringle grunted. 'The very question I asked Gates, the manager. And the answer, it seems, is that you drive a bloody big vehicle in there, stick a wide-mouthed pipe in each of the tanks and pump out water, fish and all.'

'Jesus,' Mackie whispered.

His colleague raised an eyebrow in his general direction. 'These boys lifted far more fish than the Lord had to work with. This farm, Mellerkirk, it's called, is one of the biggest in the region. They supply two big supermarket chains on a daily basis, plus they run their own smoking business.

'All joking aside, the theft's a disaster for them. They're restocking from their hatchery as fast as they can, but it'll be a week or so before they can restart production.'

'What quantity of fish are we talking about?' asked Rose.

'Mr Gates couldn't say for sure, but he guessed around three tons.'

'Three tons!' Martin exclaimed. 'What the hell's anyone going to do with three tons of hot fish?'

'Freeze it,' Pringle replied. 'You'd have to. Anyone trying to shift that amount in one lot would draw attention to themselves pretty quick.'

'Sounds like a well-planned operation, then. Apart from

having the equipment to hoover up the stock, they'd surely have to have someone ready to receive and handle it.'

'Aye, that's right, sir. They'd have to do it right away too. Gates said that the fish would start dying pretty quick in those conditions. He reckoned that they'd have been driven straight to a processor for treatment. But where? That's anyone's guess.'

'What are you doing about finding out?' asked the Head of CID.

'We've put together a list of fish processors all over Scotland, and we're circulating it to all relevant forces this morning. As soon as that's done I'll want people going round all of the places on our patch. I'll need assistance from other divisions. That means you, Brian, you, Greg, and you, Willie.' He looked across the table at Detective Superintendent Gregory Jay and William Michaels, who commanded the Leith and West Lothian CID areas respectively.

'What are our chances, Dan?'

'Slim and none, boss. It's no' as if these bloody fish carry the owner's brand or anything. One deid trout looks just like another. I don't suppose for a minute that they'll show up in the major supermarket chains; they all vet their suppliers pretty thoroughly. We'll just have to keep an eye on the smaller outlets and hope.

'But if these boys are as smart as they look they'll keep the stuff in a freezer for a while . . . till the heat's off, you might say . . . then shift it in small quantities.'

'One thing we can do,' Martin suggested, 'and that's let the Central Intelligence Unit know, so that every fish farm in Scotland can be put on the alert.'

Pringle nodded. 'I did that yesterday.'

'Good man,' said the Head of CID. He ran his fingers through his curly blond hair, and chuckled softly. 'What a start to the week! Three tons of hot frozen fish! Welcome to the madhouse, Maggie.'

Eight

Bob Skinner had an aversion to St Andrew's House, the monolithic grey stone office building which housed many of the civil servants involved in the business of governing Scotland. Nevertheless, there were times when he had no choice but to swallow his dislike and visit the place.

With Sir James Proud engaged in a meeting with his fellow Chief Constables in Glasgow, it fell to him to represent the force on an *ad hoc* committee set up by the Scottish Executive to plan a new crime prevention publicity campaign. The big detective had serious doubts over the cost-effectiveness of government-funded media propaganda. He believed firmly that the whole exercise smacked of tokenism, a knee-jerk action by politicians who suspected, probably in error, that the public expected it of them.

In his experience, the messages washed over the heads of most of the honest citizens at whom they were aimed, while criminals were either too stupid to take notice of the warnings, or too intelligent to watch the television programmes on which they were normally screened.

However, the First Minister and his lackey, the Justice Minister, had decreed that it should be done and had

41

appointed Sir James Proud to chair the working group which would make it happen.

The meeting, when finally it began after a preamble of coffee and chat, was happily brief. The Scottish Executive Information Department's Head of Publicity, acting as secretary to the committee, introduced a hapless advertising agency team, who presented proposals which impressed none of the five policemen gathered around the table, and were sent away to think again.

Skinner smiled as he stepped through the great doorway of the building, which stood on the site of the old city jail, glad to be rid of an unwelcome chore. He was still nodding, grinning unconsciously, as he looked into Gerry Crossley's office and offered the young man a brisk, 'Good morning'.

'Good morning, sir,' the Chief Constable's secretary replied, but with a frown. 'ACC Chase asked if you would look in on him when you got in.'

'Aye, sure,' the DCC replied. 'Mail first though, Gerry, eh? Is it all in my office, or has Neil got it?'

'Mr Chase told me to leave it where it was, sir. He wants to see you right away.'

'*Tell him to go and fuck himself.*' Skinner stilled the retort on the launch pad. Instead, eyes narrowing slightly, he said simply, 'Tell him I'll be in my room: then get me my mail.'

'Very good, sir.' Crossley was reaching for his telephone even as the big detective left the office.

He had only just hung up his jacket and settled into his chair, when there was a knock at the door. Before he could reply, it opened, and Ted Chase strode into the room, brush-

42

ing aside the Chief Constable's secretary, almost knocking to the floor Skinner's pile of mail, which he was carrying.

Not bothering to suppress his sigh, the DCC stood up and pointed to the low leather sofas in one corner of the big panelled room. 'Ted,' he snapped, testily. 'Sit your arse down there.

'Gerry, thanks son. Just put that lot on my desk, then leave us.'

Chase was still standing as Crossley left the room. Skinner looked at him, frowning as he poured two mugs of coffee.

'Manners matter, you know,' he said. 'Gerry's a civilian employee; you wouldn't barge past a uniformed officer like that, and you sure as hell don't do it to him.'

Chase seemed to relax his ramrod stance just a fraction. 'Sorry,' he conceded. 'It's just that . . . Well, I was expecting you earlier.'

Skinner felt his temper rise in earnest; he made a conscious effort to control it and almost succeeded. 'Listen,' he hissed icily. 'As far as I know, I don't report to you . . . not yet, at any rate. You want to know where I am, ask McIlhenney; he always knows. You want to see me, just ask. Don't summon me, and don't lurk behind my fucking door. Okay?'

'I won't be intimidated, Bob,' the ACC countered.

The big detective shook his steel-grey head. 'I'm not trying to intimidate you. I wouldn't; you're a brother officer. I am simply telling you a couple of things that will make it easier for us to get on. Tact and diplomacy can be bloody difficult for career coppers like us . . . Jimmy has them both in abundance; that's what makes him so good . . . but we need to show them some time.'

He smiled, forcing himself to be conciliatory. 'Anyway, what's the problem, man? I hadn't put you down as a panic merchant.' He handed him one of the mugs. 'Look, sit down and tell me about it.'

Chase shifted a document to his left hand as he took the coffee.

'What's that?' asked Skinner.

'It's what I have to talk to you about. Believe me, Bob, when you see it, you'll see that I was being tactful.' He handed the paper over as he settled himself into one of the low sofas. 'It arrived by special messenger yesterday afternoon. It was addressed to the Chief and it was stamped as urgent. In his absence, and in yours, I deemed it proper to open it. Read it.'

The DCC took the document. *'Private and confidential,'* he read. *'To Chief Constable Sir James Proud from Assistant Commissioner Hector Plumpton.*

'Sir, I regret to have to make a formal report to you regarding an incident which took place in Regent Street just after 11 p.m. last Friday . . .'

'Bugger it!' he shouted, throwing the paper on to the coffee table. 'I know what this is. I had wind of it at the weekend, and I asked Neil to try to put a stop to it. Obviously, someone in London didn't get the message.'

'Be that as it may . . .'

'Yes?!'

'It's a complaint, Bob. A complaint against a senior officer.'

'*Your* senior officer.'

'Be that as it may too . . . I'll even forget your admission that you tried to have it suppressed.'

44

Skinner had given up the fight against his temper. 'Suppressed! If I had known the man would be that stupid . . .'

'Well, he has been! Now, what are we going to do about it?'

'We are going to do eff all. You are going to give that piece of shit to Proud Jimmy, to whom it was addressed in the first place.'

'But he won't be back till tomorrow.'

'Aye? So?'

Chase pushed himself to his feet and walked across to the window. 'Do I have to spell it out? That report questions your fitness for duty; it recommends that you be given a psychiatric assessment. In those circumstances, is it right that you continue in acting command of this force, even for a single day? What would you do if you were in my place?'

'I'd sit you down and ask you what happened. Then I'd accept your word.'

'Then you'd be in default of your duty. Listen, help me keep this thing in-house; let me call someone in, right now, to have a talk with you. O'Malley, for example; he's our top consultant, isn't he? That'll be the end of it.'

Skinner looked him in the eye, unblinking. 'You try that and it'll be the end of you, pal. No one, not even Kevin, is rummaging around in my head; not ever. I'll tell you something, Ted. For all your gauche attempts to take over my job, I respect you as a sincere man. That's why you haven't made an enemy of me. Believe me . . . and this is not intimidation . . . you don't want to.'

'Then help me deal with this.'

'Okay.'

The DCC stood, took two steps across to his desk, and picked up the phone. 'Gerry,' he said, 'I want to speak to the Commissioner of the Metropolitan Police.' He put the instrument down, then sat in silence in his swivel chair, waiting. It was over a minute before it rang again.

Skinner picked it up, his expression stony. 'Paddy? Bob here,' he began.

'Good to speak to you too. Yes, I thought last week was a great success; well done to your people for setting it up.

'Listen, I've got a problem up here that you can sort for me with one phone call. Last Friday night, I reported an incident in Regent Street.' He paused.

'You heard about it? Then did you know that one of your AC's, a guy called Plumpton, has written to Jimmy making a formal complaint against me, on the grounds of wasting police time?

'Yup, that's right. I've got it on my desk right now.' Watching, Chase saw him give a tight unconscious smile. 'No? Well, you'd better fucking believe it. I'll fax it to you if you like.

'It says that there was no evidence to back up my report, and goes on to suggest that I'm a fucking nut case. Well maybe I am, but someone discharged a shotgun in my direction, for sure. If I'd caught him, I'd have asked him if he had fired a blank, but probably not until after I'd killed him.

'What would I like you to do? I'd like you to send me Assistant Commissioner Plumpton's head on a plate. Failing that, I'd like an immediate letter to Jimmy withdrawing that report and a personal letter from the man apologising for doubting the word of a fellow officer. If his signature's in blood, I'll accept it with good grace.'

He paused, then smiled, broadly this time. 'Aye, okay, I'll do without the blood. But thanks for the rest. I appreciate it. So will Louise. Aye, she was there; you understand why I got her off the scene right away? Sure, for the best.

'And mine to Eleanor. So long.'

Skinner's smile disappeared as he replaced the receiver and looked across at Chase. 'There you are, Ted. I'm off the hook, and so are you. I'll keep that nonsense and give it to Jimmy himself. Have you spoken to anyone else about it?'

'No,' the ACC replied. 'Not even Crossley.'

'Fine. That's how it'll stay, then.'

'The reference to someone called Louise. What was that about?'

'My business, if it's all the same to you. The Commissioner knew about it, because his car dropped me off in Shaftesbury Avenue after the closing session of the conference.'

'Okay, if you say so. But Bob, what about the incident itself? Aren't you concerned that someone shot at you . . . even if it was a blank?'

'Sure I'm concerned. But there's nothing I can do about it, not unless and until the guy comes back for another go. It could have been anything, Ted. The conference was publicised; the chances are that some clown with a grudge against authority read about it in the *Evening Standard* and decided to stage a stunt, make a point, whatever.'

'Can you remember anything about him?'

The DCC snorted. 'Well seen no one's ever shot at you, mate. When it happens, all you can see is the fucking gun.'

'No, no one ever has, I'm glad to say. But then I'm not your sort of policeman.'

'No, you're not, are you? You'll never be like me, nor I like you; which is just as well for the sake of good order. We need traditionalists in the force, guys like you and Jimmy, who're at home in a uniform, as well as door-kickers-in like me and McIlhenney.'

'And Martin, I suppose,' Chase interjected.

'No, no. Andy's inherently a manager. He's better than I was as Head of CID. He lets the divisional heads do their job; I was always out there leading the charge. I still am on occasion; I can't help it.'

Skinner wandered back to the sofas and sat down, picking up his lukewarm coffee. 'You still after my job, then?' he asked casually.

'Bob,' the ACC protested, 'it's not that. I believe in that paper I wrote. It's honest, at least give me that.'

'Sure. And you have ambitions; give me that.'

'I can't deny it. What's wrong with that?'

'Not a bloody thing. I have some of those too; I just keep them close. No, that's not what worries me about you. To be frank, I think you're a zealot. Zeal and ambition can be a terrifying combination, especially in senior policemen . . . oh, aye, and generals.' He took a sip from his mug. 'Ever heard of Matthew Hopkins?'

'No. Policeman?'

'No.'

'General then?'

'Sort of. Three hundred and fifty years ago he styled himself the Witch-Finder General. He ran a personal crusade in England against witchcraft; he went from village to village uncovering so-called necromancers. Torture was forbidden even then, so he tended to use so-called bloodless methods, sleep deprivation, mainly . . . you could say he was ahead of his time . . . to extract confessions from his victims. Up to four hundred innocent people were hanged because of him, in only a few years.

'Actually, Hopkins did it for money, but it was his zeal that let him get away with it. He commanded authority.'

'But . . .' Chase spluttered, comically. In spite of himself, Skinner laughed.

'It's okay, I'm not saying you're another Hopkins. But you seem to me to have the zealot's belief in The Way Things Should Be. I don't see any bending in you, no compromise.'

'I don't compromise my beliefs.'

'No, but are you tolerant of those of others? I don't think so.'

'Does that matter, if you're right?'

Skinner threw back his head. ' "*Extremism in the defence of Liberty is no vice!*" ' he quoted. 'Barry Goldwater said that in 1964; happily the electorate didn't agree with him, and he didn't become President of the United States. It's not so well remembered that he also said, in the same speech, that moderation in the pursuit of justice is no virtue. As a philosophy, that's even more dangerous to civil liberties.

'Know what his campaign slogan was? *In your heart you know he's right.*

'You see, I believe that at heart you're a Goldwater Republican, Ted, and I won't have one of them running this force, either as Chief, or Deputy, not never, not nohow.'

'Can you prevent it?'

'I think so. I have my own constituency, and it's pretty powerful. As perhaps you've just seen.'

The DCC stood once more. 'Now, with all that clear, maybe you and I can just accept that we have fundamental differences in our beliefs, and use the contrast between us if we can to help us work together in the best interests of this force and the people it serves.'

Nine

Sammy Pye watched the door close on the last of the divisional commanders, then switched on his computer, to begin typing up his meeting notes. The session had gone on for longer than usual, thanks mainly to the extended brain-storming over the missing fish.

He had just booted up Microsoft Word and opened a customised template when the phone rang. 'DS Pye,' he announced, still feeling a prickle of pride at his new rank.

'Sam, thank goodness you're there.'

One of the things he loved about Ruth was her assuredness. Naturally, she had been upset when he had gone out to the car in Cumbernauld to break the bad news about her uncle. There had been tears when he had told her; there had been anger when he had prevented her from going into the bathroom; there had been self-recrimination when he had told her that the old man appeared to have been dead for some time. But it all had passed over, and the self-possessed woman had reasserted herself quickly, staying calm as the duty doctor and the police had arrived, even as the paramedics took the body off to the mortuary.

Now, he picked up the tension in her tone at once.

'What's up, love?' he asked.

'It's the police. They're being difficult; they won't let me make arrangements for Uncle John's funeral.'

'Eh? Why the hell not?'

'That's just it. They won't tell me. I don't like it, Sam. They won't tell me anything. There's even worse than that, too. I went to Cumbernauld this morning, to Uncle John's house, to start looking through his papers. There were police there, and they wouldn't let me in.

'Honestly, the way they're acting, it's as if they suspected me of something.'

Pye frowned so hard that he felt the muscles bunch in his forehead. 'Where are you right now?'

'I'm in what passes for a Town Centre in Cumbernauld. I'm going to go up to Dullatur Golf Club to see if I can find any of Uncle John's cronies there. Maybe they can tell me something about him . . . when was the last time they saw him, whether he'd been complaining of feeling unwell; that sort of stuff.'

'No!' the young detective said sharply. 'Don't do that, please.'

'Why not?'

'Because it wouldn't be helpful. Listen, Ruthie, like I told you on Saturday, when someone dies alone under any circumstances, technically the police have to be called, and they have to make a report to the Fiscal. Quite often that's overlooked; if the local GP is sympathetic and wants to spare a bereaved wife or husband from any more distress, he'll just certify death as if he's been there. We know that, and we don't bother about it.

'But when someone's died and lain undiscovered for a few

52

days, that's a different matter. The police will be called and they will make a report. What they're doing now is probably just routine.'

'Then why won't they let me into the house?'

Pye chewed his lip. 'That I don't understand, I admit. Possibly the local inspector's just an officious bastard. No, probably, he is; chances are that's the only reason. But if you go up to the golf club, you'll be doing something that the police may have done already, or worse, may still have to do.

'Give it up for today. Just go home.'

He heard her sigh. 'Okay,' she conceded. 'I will. Come and see me after work?'

'Sure.' He paused, and chuckled. 'Can I bring my toothbrush?'

There was a silence on the line. 'Okay,' said Ruth, eventually. 'But only if you bring your shaving kit as well. I'm funny about morning stubble.'

'Mmm,' he said, replacing the phone quickly; it took a conscious effort to force his mind back to the job, and to the minutes of the morning's meeting.

Nevertheless, he succeeded; he deciphered his notes quickly and had almost finished transcribing them, when the phone rang once again. 'DS Pye.' That flash of pride again.

'Sammy? This is Superintendent Rose. Are you alone?'

'*Christ,*' he thought. '*My lucky day.*'

'I mean are you free to speak?'

'Yes, ma'am. Why?'

'Because something very odd has happened, and I thought I'd talk to you about it before I did anything. My duty CID team here in Torphichen Place has just had a call from the

CID in N Division of Strathclyde Police, Cumbernauld Office. Fortunately Ray Wilding took the call himself; someone else might not have twigged to the name.

'Sam, the Strathclyde boys have asked that we pick up Ruth McConnell and deliver her to them for questioning about a suspicious death. Do you know what this is about?'

'Jesus!' Pye exploded. 'Some bastard's going really over the top now. The so-called suspicious death is Ruthie's uncle; we found him on Saturday when we went to visit him. Mr Chase knows about it; he was in the Ops Room on Saturday and he called out the local police for me.

'The old gaffer took a heart attack, or something similar, in his bath. That's all there was to it. The Strathclyde lot are being really heavy-handed, Ma'am. They wouldn't let Ruthie into the house when she went through this morning.'

'She's not at work?'

'No. The boss gave her the day off to make funeral arrangements and start tidying up the old boy's affairs. Leave it to me, ma'am, I'll speak to Mr Martin or Mr Skinner. One of them'll squash Strathclyde.'

'No, Sergeant, they won't. This is my divisional responsibility, and I'm not beginning my tenure of office by showing favouritism, or by getting a name in a neighbouring force as some weak woman who passes tough decisions up the ladder. If the Cumbernauld CID want to interview Ruth, that's their right in the circumstances, whether they're being officious or not.

'Where is she right now? Do you know?'

'I hope she's driving back through to Edinburgh.'

'Does she have a mobile?'

'Yes.'

'Okay, here's what I'll do. I will call N Division back and tell them that I don't have the resources to spare officers to act as delivery boys. I'll tell them that they can interview Ruth at this office at five o'clock. You call her and tell her to report here in time. Make sure that she does, mind.'

Pye felt anger rumbling up in him, but he suppressed it. He knew enough not to shout at Maggie Rose. 'Very good, ma'am. Can I sit in on the interview?'

'I shouldn't think so for one minute. But you can be here. From what you say, they should really be interviewing you as well.'

Ten

'You did the right thing, Maggie; don't worry about it. I appreciate your phoning to tell me about it, but the decision was yours all the way, and your assessment of the situation is spot on. You can rest assured that I won't go snarling at anyone through in Lanarkshire, either; I promise you, I'll keep my hands off this one, completely.

'All the same,' Bob Skinner continued, 'when the Strathclyde officers get to your place, I want them to be bloody clear as to who it is they've come to interview. I can't fault anybody for just doing their job, even if they are insensitive enough to ask for a bereaved relative to be brought to them for interview, but if I find out afterwards that they've been discourteous or aggressive to Ruth in any way, then I will have their tripes for supper, and no mistake.'

The superintendent smiled gently. 'I'll explain the background just as you say, sir, don't worry.'

'You do that. Who knows, they might even invite you to sit in on their interview. Don't let Pye anywhere near it, though. In fact, once he's dropped Ruthie off, send him packing. Tell him you'll give her a lift home once they're finished with her; you don't want him pacing the corridor outside the interview room.'

'You're right: I don't. I remember how Mario was when I got hurt, and I remember thinking that it was just as well Brian Mackie had the bloke who did it locked up in a cell. By the same token, the idea of having a serving officer in the building while his girlfriend's being interviewed . . . even if it is a formality . . . does not appeal to me: too many potential complications.'

She paused. 'I suppose it is a formality,' she said tentatively.

'Of course it is,' the DCC responded at once, then he too hesitated. 'They're being heavy-handed about it, right enough, but I'm sure that's all it is.'

'Still, it's unusual . . .'

'For someone to be brought in for interview in a run-of-the-mill sudden death investigation? Yes, it is. You know, Mags, with every minute that passes this is becoming more difficult for me. As Ruth's boss, and more than that, as her friend, I want to pick up the phone, call the officer in charge of this investigation, and ask him what the bloody hell he's playing at. Yet as the DCC I can't be seen to be leaning on another force, especially not at this time.'

She caught his veiled meaning.

'If Jock Govan was still in the Chief's chair in Glasgow,' he continued, 'it would be okay. I could just have called him; or even Willie Haggerty, if he hadn't been moved back into uniform as a divisional gaffer. But I don't know the new guy yet, so I have to be careful not to provoke any diplomatic incidents. I've already had to defuse one bomb today; I don't fancy handling another.'

'Why don't you ask Mr Chase to make enquiries?'

'Are you being mischievous, Detective Superintendent Rose?' Skinner snorted. 'I don't believe in introducing foxes to chicken coops, and that's all I'm saying. No, we'll just have to be patient, if we want to find out whether there's anything sinister behind this request. It does help having them on our turf, though.'

'In what way?'

'Well, not interfering in advance of the interview is one thing. But afterwards . . .'

'Don't worry, sir. These people won't leave this office without me knowing what all this is about.'

'Good for you. Keep me in touch.'

The DCC hung up the phone and returned to the pile of papers through which he had been wading when Rose had called. There was nothing there of any drama or import; over the previous few months the force had gone through a period of calm almost unprecedented in recent years. It had been so quiet that Skinner had even taken to reviewing old and unsolved investigations, reading the notes to see if anything caught his eye in a way that might offer a new line of inquiry.

The latest of these, the file on the unsolved murder of two teenage girls, still lay on his desk. He glanced at it, and was reaching for it, when the phone rang again.

'Yes, Neil,' he said, knowing that it would be McIlhenney on the other end of the line.

'Call for you, Boss.'

'On your number?' Almost invariably, calls for Skinner came through Ruth McConnell's extension.

'Yes. Remember the lady you mentioned to me on Saturday? It's her. Do you want to talk to her?'

'Course I do. Put her through.'

He leaned back in his chair, hearing the click on the line. 'Hi Lou,' he began. 'What a surprise. Right on cue too; my day was beginning to drag. What can I do for you?'

'Nothing, really. I just wanted to talk to you; to make sure you were all right after Friday night, I suppose. I guessed that you wouldn't have given me this number if you didn't want me to call, so . . .'

'Yeah, sure. But never mind how I am. Did you get back home okay? And are you all right? It's me should have phoned you, really, after chucking you as broad as you're long down Regent Street.'

Her deep throaty laugh sent a warm familiar feeling down his spine. 'You're forgiven: just like old times in a way. I'm fine, honestly. You owe me a pair of tights and a cleaner's bill for one Dior jacket, but apart from that . . . . Tell me,' she asked, with sudden concern, 'did the police catch the man?'

'Hah! The police didn't even believe that there was a man. There were no signs of a gunshot at the scene. The borough commander got very Humpty Dumpty about it.'

'But that's ridiculous! There was a shot. I heard it. I saw the car drive away, and I saw you chase it. I'll bloody well call and tell them.'

'No, Lou. You won't. That would not be a good idea; not at all. Don't you worry about old Humpty. He's fallen off his wall since then; all the king's horses and all the king's men are looking for the bits, even now.

'As for the incident itself, I'm not worried about it. London can be a wild place at night; any city can. Chances are it was a random thing, some cowboy who gets a buzz out of scaring the posh people up the West End. It happens.'

'Why don't I believe you believe that?'

'Because of who I am, that's all; it's as likely an explanation as any.'

'But not the only one.'

'No, but really, Lou. Don't concern yourself.'

'Because big tough Bob can take care of himself? Sure you can; you always could, even at university. But I've read about you. I didn't tell you on Friday, but I've followed your career ever since you began to get your name in the papers. Remember Lucy, my sister? She was only a toddler when you and I were going out together, but she's kept me in touch with your adventures over the years. I know about some of the scrapes you've been in, like that time when you were stabbed and almost killed. You probably didn't even know this, but while you were in hospital, your wife had a delivery of a bouquet of red roses. There was no card, but they were from me.

'You're not a cat, Bob. You don't have nine lives. Too damn right I'll concern myself, even though I'll concede that Friday night probably had nothing to do with your past.'

He scratched his chin. 'God, do that speech in an upstate New York accent and you'd sound just like Sarah.'

'She's welcome. I'll tell you something, my love. It's great to have a past with a man like you, but I don't envy Sarah the present.'

'That's comforting to know. In that case you won't want to have dinner with me again, when I'm in London after the New Year.'

'I didn't say that. Actually, you'll have an opportunity before then; unless you don't want to be seen with me in Scotland, that is. I've been offered the lead in a new movie, and it's going to be shot in Scotland. I get to play a lady lawyer involved in some sort of shenanigans; I've only just been sent the script.

'I'm coming up to Edinburgh on Friday; I'm meeting the director and the executive producer in the Balmoral, then being driven round the locations.'

'Okay,' he responded. 'If you're free in the evening, let's have dinner. But why don't we do it at my place? You can meet Sarah, and give her your sympathies. You can tell her about the roses too if you like. If you take the part, you'd better meet my daughter as well. She's a lady lawyer; she'll help you research it.'

He heard her draw in her breath. 'Are you sure about that? Introducing me to Sarah, that is.'

'Sure I'm sure. Are you up for it?'

'Yes,' she said, firmly, a decision made. 'Thank you; I'd like that.'

'Okay, it's a date. I'll collect you from the Balmoral around six.'

Eleven

'Is this normal practice with you CID people?'

Ruth McConnell was bristling with anger as she stood on the pavement staring at the entrance to the Torphichen Place police office. As she turned her fury on Sammy Pye he had a mental picture of his toothbrush, standing alone in its glass beside his bathroom mirror.

'No, it isn't,' he assured her. 'But different forces do things in different ways. These people are sticklers, and there's nothing I can do about that.'

She was only slightly mollified. 'Okay, I won't blame you. All the same, this is ridiculous. Telling me to report to them, indeed! Why couldn't they have come to see me at home? That's what you'd do in the same circumstances, isn't it?'

Pye was inwardly thankful that he had not told her of the original request from the Strathclyde officers, that she be brought to their office. 'Sure it is, love,' he answered, 'but like I said, I can't speak for these punters.'

She shook her long shimmering hair and straightened her back. 'Oh well,' she snapped. 'We're here now, so let's get it over with. Then may be I can get on with burying my poor uncle.'

'Where do we go?'

'I've to take you to Maggie Rose's office.' He held the door to the building open for her.

'Will you come with me when I see them?'

'I don't think they'll allow that.'

She stopped in her tracks. 'What? In that case I'm not going to speak to them. Take me home, right now.'

'Ruthie,' he pleaded. 'Don't be difficult. If I was them I wouldn't want a man from another force sitting in either. But I've told you, it's just a routine interview. So come on.'

She shot him a look. 'Okay. But you be here when they're finished with me.'

'I will be, don't worry. We've got a date, remember?'

'What? Oh yes. We'll see how I feel after this. Who knows, I might be right off policemen by then.'

He knew that she was serious, as he led her up the stairway which led to the CID suite, rapping on the divisional commander's door and stepping inside on her call. 'Ma'am. Ruth's here.'

Maggie Rose looked at him, unsmiling, and at his companion as she stepped into the room. 'That's good; right on time.' The red-haired detective superintendent nodded in the direction of two visitors who stood beside her desk, a man and a woman. 'These are our colleagues from Strathclyde; Detective Inspector Mackenzie and DS Dell. People, this is DS Pye, and this is the lady you want to see.'

She looked at them, her expression suddenly sharp. 'This summons had better be justified, otherwise you might find yourself having to explain to Ms McConnell's boss.'

As the tall, dark Mackenzie smiled, his face took on an expression of pure menace. Pye took an instant dislike to him, and wondered if, after all, he should force his way into the interview. 'And who's that?' the man asked.

'DCC Skinner,' Rose replied. 'You'll have heard of him.'

'Aye, vaguely,' Mackenzie chuckled. 'Have you an interview room for us?'

'Use this office.'

'We need a tape, ma'am. This is an official interview.'

Pye knew Rose well enough to read the sign as her eyes narrowed. 'Very well,' she said icily. 'Ruth. Would you like me to sit in with you?'

'I don't know if we can have that, ma'am.'

'Inspector,' she snapped, 'in my station you'll have what I tell you. Ruth?'

The woman shook her head. 'Thanks, Maggie, but it's all right. I just want out of here with a minimum of fuss.'

'Okay. Mackenzie, there's a vacant interview room at the end of the corridor. Use that, and bring Ms McConnell back here when you're finished.'

The big detective chuckled again. 'Aye, we'll have to see about that too, ma'am.' Pye took half a pace towards him, until a glance from Rose stopped him in his tracks. Instead, he stood aside and allowed the Strathclyde officers to escort Ruth out of the office.

'There's something about that bastard,' Maggie Rose murmured as the door closed on the trio, 'that reminds me of Flash Donaldson . . . and we know all too well about him.'

The interview room was three doors along the corridor. Detective Sergeant Dell held the door open for the other woman and ushered her inside. The only furniture was a table, upon which there sat a black tape recorder, and four chairs, two each on opposite sides.

'Sit down,' said Mackenzie curtly. He took a tape cassette from his pocket, slipped it into one of the twin slots of the recorder, and switched it on. The interviewee sat down with her back to the door, laid her handbag on the table, then delved into it. Finally, satisfied, she produced a tissue and settled back into her chair.

The inspector stared across at her coldly. 'This interview is being held at Torphichen Place police office, Edinburgh, at five ten p.m. on November 27, 2000. I am Detective Inspector David Mackenzie, N Division, Strathclyde Police. Also present are Detective Sergeant Gwendoline Dell and Miss Ruth McConnell.'

Then he astonished Ruth by reading her a formal caution.

'What the devil?' she exploded.

'Quiet please, Miss McConnell,' barked Mackenzie. 'You'll answer questions only, not ask them.'

'The hell with that. Have I been arrested here?'

'And why should you be?'

She blazed back at him. 'Don't fence with me. For that bloody tape, what's my status here?'

Mackenzie nodded a concession. 'For the record, you are here voluntarily to assist our investigation into the suspicious death of your uncle, John McConnell, of number fifteen Glenlaverock Grove, Cumbernauld.'

'Suspicious? What do you mean?'

The detective reached across and hit the stop button on

the recorder. 'There you go with the questions again. Listen, McConnell, I don't care whose fucking secretary you are. As far as I'm concerned you're just another fucking suspect.

'You know what my nickname is? They call me Bandit; not just the other coppers, but our local villains too . . . and believe me, through in the west we have some real villains, not like the poofs . . .' He laughed, suddenly, harshly, '. . . oh aye, and fucking fish rustlers you lot have through here. It's a mark of respect, so they tell me; they call me that because I'm a bad bastard and because I'll nick anyone.

'They say about some coppers that they'd lift their own brothers. I did, once. So be advised; behave yourself and don't try to pull rank or influence on me.'

He switched on the recorder once again. 'Now, if you're ready, Miss McConnell.'

She looked at him, then turned her head and spoke directly to the microphone. 'I am, if you've quite finished spraying the room with testosterone.'

The inspector glowered back at her. 'When was the last time you saw your uncle?' he asked, abruptly.

'Last June. I took him a birthday present and took him out for lunch.'

'What? You haven't seen him since?'

'No, I have not.'

'You didn't see him on or around Saturday the eighteenth of November?'

'No. I went to see him last Saturday, as you know quite well. You're getting your dates mixed up.'

'No, I'm not, lady. I meant the Saturday before.'

She shook her head. 'I did not see my uncle on that date,' she said, loudly and firmly.

'We have information that you did.'

'Then your informant is either mistaken, or a liar.'

The detective's face twisted into an ugly grin. 'And when your uncle told a neighbour that afternoon that he was expecting a visit from his niece, would he have been a liar too?'

'Either he or the neighbour would certainly have been mistaken.'

Mackenzie glanced sideways at Sergeant Dell. 'It's amazing the number of times people say that to us, Gwennie, isn't it?'

'It is, sir.' Ruth looked at her for a sign that she might be the soft cop in the old routine, but found none.

'They're usually the ones that are lying, though. Isn't that right?'

'It is indeed, sir.'

'Well this time she isn't, Inspector.'

'So when was the last time you spoke to your uncle?'

'A few weeks ago.'

'How did he sound?'

'Old, Inspector, he sounded old. He was eighty.'

'And what did you say to him?'

'I promised him a visit soon, but I wasn't specific about it. I couldn't tell him any date for sure.'

'What kind of car do you drive?' Mackenzie asked abruptly.

'A Corolla hatchback.'

'What colour is it?'

'Blue.'

'So if a blue hatchback was seen outside your uncle's house on the day he died, the day he told his neighbour that he was expecting a visit from you, that wouldn't have been yours, then?'

'No, it would not.'

'What do you earn, Miss McConnell?'

'Mind your own business.'

'It is my business, hen. Have you not worked that out yet? No point in being coy anyway; I could find out by picking up a telephone.'

'Okay; my salary is around twenty-two thousand.'

'Not bad, eh?'

'Reasonable. I work for two of the most senior police officers in Scotland, on a confidential basis. I have their trust,' she added, pointedly.

Mackenzie laughed again, this time with undisguised mockery. He reached across and switched off the tape once more. 'And your man Skinner's never made a mistake about a woman has he? I seem to remember he was all over the tabloids not so long ago. Something to do with him shagging a woman detective sergeant on his staff.

'Does he give you one as well, now and again?'

'This is outrageous,' Ruth spluttered. 'Listen, Bandit, or whatever your damned name is, unless you stop peddling innuendo and get specific about the purpose of this conversation, I'm walking out of that door, and I am going to see Mr Skinner . . . and if that doesn't worry you, then you are an even bigger fool than you are a playground bully.'

The Strathclyde inspector reached across and pressed the record button of the tape once again. 'All right, let's just jump to the "Detective Sums Up" bit. Your old Uncle John tells a neighbour on Saturday the eighteenth of November, in a state of some excitement, that he's expecting a visit from his niece . . . namely you, because I've confirmed that you're the only niece he had.

'Later that afternoon, just as it was getting dark, a blue hatchback vehicle, just like yours, pulls up outside his door. A tall, dark-haired woman, whose description you fit perfectly, is seen to get out and walk straight into the house.

'And right at that time, someone sticks the old man in a scalding bath and drowns the poor old sod.'

She stared at him across the desk, speechless, truly shaken for the first time.

'And there's more. Your uncle hadn't shown up at his golf club for a while, so one of his cronies went to see him. He found him concerned and confused, as if the ageing process had caught up with him, finally.

'But he noticed that things were missing from the house. There was a silver trophy he won at golf years back; there was a very fine grandfather clock; both missing. When your uncle's pal asked what had happened to them, all he said was that his niece had money troubles.

'Then he told his old friend to bugger off and mind his own business.'

Mackenzie paused. 'So you see, Miss McConnell. I'm engaged in a search for a cold, cruel murderer, and all the evidence I have points straight at you, his only niece, the sole beneficiary in his will.

'Yet when I ask a neighbouring force to do me a favour by picking you up and bringing you through for interview, I get a call from some jumped-up woman refusing and telling me to report to her. I don't mind telling you that pisses me off, and it doesn't make me inclined to go any easier on you than on any other suspect.

'So . . . If you weren't drowning your uncle on November the eighteenth, what the hell were you doing, Miss McConnell?'

'I was with my boyfriend.'

'Who is?'

'Detective Sergeant Pye; he's on the staff of Detective Chief Superintendent Martin, the Head of CID.'

'There you go dropping those names again. Is he the lad who brought you here? The same guy who found your uncle's body?'

She nodded. 'Yes, that was Sammy.'

'Do you live with him?'

'As of today, yes, I think I do. But not then.'

For the first time she sensed Mackenzie becoming more cautious. 'Did you spend all day with him?'

Ruth took a deep breath, and decided to tell the truth. 'No. I went round to his place in the morning; we had a sandwich lunch, watched television for a bit, and then I went shopping in Jenner's and John Lewis. I left Sammy's at about two thirty, and I got back just after six. Later we went out for a meal and a drink.'

'I see. And can you prove you were in Jenner's or in John Lewis? Do you have any credit card slips, for example, with your signature and the date and time?'

'No,' she admitted. 'I didn't buy anything. I didn't see anything I fancied.'

At once all the hardness was back in the dark-haired detective, as he turned to his sergeant once more. 'I see. Piss poor cover story, Gwennie, isn't it?

'Miss McConnell, even by your own account you had plenty of time to drive through to Cumbernauld that afternoon, do the old man, then drive back to the love nest in time for a nice evening out.

'It was a really smart touch too, going back the following Saturday and arranging for the boy Sammy to find the body.

'Miss, I want to see your car, I want to see any record you have of petrol purchases, and I want to see all your bank accounts. I expect that when I've done all that I will have more than enough evidence to justify a charge of murder. In fact, I could arrest you right now, and take you back to Cumbernauld, but that would just be too much fucking hassle. Since your man's a DS, I'll trust him to be professional enough to ensure that you don't do anything silly, and that next time, when I send for you, you're delivered, gift-wrapped.

'This interview is terminated at five thirty-seven p.m.' He switched off his tape. 'You can go. I'll tell Rose what's happening. Be available to us at any time tomorrow.'

Ruth picked up her bag, looked down her nose at the two detectives, then stood up from the table and left the room.

She was shaking as she walked up to Pye, who was waiting for her outside the building, in accordance with Skinner's order. He saw her agitation at once. 'What's up, love?' he demanded.

'Not here! I can't tell you here. I have to get out of this place, right now. Sammy, love; please take me to Mr Skinner, wherever he is. I need to see him, right now!'

Twelve

Dan Pringle looked around as he stepped out of his car. It was eight thirty-five on a late November morning, and the sun had only just struggled above the eastern horizon. Yet as he breathed in the clean, crisp, morning air, the burly detective superintendent felt a sudden, strange burst of pleasure and relief.

To his great surprise, he was discovering that, with each passing day, he liked the Borders more and more. When Bob Skinner and Andy Martin had invited him to move south, following John McGrigor's decision to hand in his warrant card, he had felt that it was no more than a step towards his own being put out to grass.

Sure, they had said all the right words; they had explained that the Borders division was a mature area which required maturity and experience of its senior police officers, even . . . especially, perhaps . . . those in the detective branch. Yet he had felt a niggling suspicion that he was simply being put out of the way, a belated punishment for his scarcely disguised annoyance when the young Head of CID had been appointed over his head.

Now, only a few days into the new job, he realised that they had been right. He took a sniff of the agricultural air and smiled. 'No bullshit,' he whispered. Never before had his career taken him on to a farm of any description. Never before had he consciously mixed with countrymen; a different sort entirely, stolid, straightforward, undissembling men who looked you straight in the eye, unimpressed by titles or authority.

He knew that no bright young lad, or fast-tracking young woman from the city could hope to step into a place like this, particularly not to follow a massive son of the soil like McGrigor, who had carried an awe-inspiring reputation from the rugby field into the senior ranks of CID.

More than that, he knew that Skinner and Martin had done him a favour. He thought back a year, to a time when he and Stevie Steele had visited an office on the attic floor of a city centre building. The breathlessness which had almost overwhelmed him at the end of the climb had been like a first intimation of mortality, a quiet message, gasped, not whispered, that he was a prime member of an 'at risk' category.

He had tried since then to improve his physical condition; however, being in his fifties, and as prone to a drink as the next polisman . . . sometimes, he had to admit, being prone as a result of it . . . he had found it difficult.

Now, translated with little warning from a city to a country copper, he felt instantly the better for it. As he trudged up the curving track towards the distant building, looking at the rolling hills all around him, he did not regret for a second his decision to come in his own road car rather than a force Land Rover. He realised with astonishment that this morning walk was the most pleasurable thing he had done at work . . . apart,

74

maybe, from belting that Russian . . . for more years than he could remember. He breathed deep and drank in the physical and psychological good that it was doing him.

As he neared the two squat stone cottages, he saw two cars parked in front, both off-roaders. He recognised one, a blue Suzuki jeep, from his earlier visit, but the other, a massive Toyota Land Cruiser, was new to him. Its vivid green metallic finish seemed to shine through the mud which caked its sides.

As he looked at it a voice called out. 'Hey there. What dae ye want?' A deep, rough-hewn voice, that of a man given to asking only simple questions.

Pringle fixed him with a policeman's glare. The man looked to be in his late fifties, strong, with a labourer's build. He held a black sack in his left hand and in the other, a dead trout.

'I want the manager,' the detective barked, his answer as aggressive as the question.

The worker backed down. 'Over there, sir,' he said, at once as threatening as his trout. 'Thae cottages.'

Pringle was about to knock on the door of the first of the twin houses, when it opened, leaving him with his knuckles poised in mid-air, descending towards nothing. 'Good morning, Superintendent,' said Bill Gates, the young manager of the Mellerkirk Trout Farm. 'Sorry about old Harry's welcome. He's a bit narked; he thinks he's going to be laid off because of this.'

Gates was fair-haired, slightly built inside his waxed cotton jacket . . . a Marks and Spencer job, Pringle noticed, rather than the more famous brand . . . and wore a harassed

75

expression. 'Come on into the office. We've been watching you coming up the track,' he added. 'That was a long walk you left yourself.'

'A nice morning for it, though, Mr Gates.' The police officer stepped inside and looked around. The first of the buildings, which had once housed labourers of the land, served as the office of the fish farm in the new era. The other was still a dwelling, occupied by the farm manager, a single man.

On the other side of the room, a door opened and a third man stepped through; tall, straight-backed, silver-haired, with a long, patrician nose and small sharp blue eyes. 'Detective Inspector Pringle,' Gates announced, 'this is Sir Adrian Watson, Baronet, the owner of the farm, and of the Mellerkirk Estate.'

The newcomer offered no handshake; nothing but a curt nod. 'Good day, Superintendent,' he barked. 'You're the new fellow, are you; McGrigor's successor.' He looked Pringle up and down, as if he was inspecting livestock. 'Less of a stereotype than him, I must say.'

'Wish I could say the same for you,' the detective thought as he gazed back at the landowner.

'Big John's a good man to follow, sir. He ran a tight ship down here.'

'In that case, you're not living up to it very well, are you, man?'

It seemed to Dan Pringle as if all the good of his morning walk had been undone in an instant, as he felt his blood pressure soar. 'Would you like to expand on that, Sir Adrian?' he asked coldly.

'I may expand on it to Sir James Proud, the next time I see him in the New Club.'

'You do that very thing, sir. But right here, right now, I'd like you to explain to me what you meant by that remark.'

The baronet looked at the policeman, taken aback slightly by his bristling aggression. '*No, you bastard*,' Pringle thought. '*I haven't gone completely native, not yet, anyway.*'

'Where are my damn fish then?' the estate owner snapped, trying to bluster his way out of what had become suddenly an uncomfortable corner. 'You don't look as if you've come to tell me you've caught these damn thieves.'

'No, I haven't.'

'Well, what are you doing here? Go away and get on with it, man.'

'Listen, Sir Adrian,' said the detective, 'it's time you came to terms with the facts.

'Fact one: I've got officers all over Scotland and beyond involved in the search for your stock. We're checking every possible processing centre we can find. We're checking every supermarket chain in the country to see if they've been offered any surprise consignments of trout. We're interviewing every resident in this area to see if anyone saw a large vehicle enter or leave your farm on the night of the theft.

'You know what? They're all wasting their fucking time.

'Fact two: we've got little or no chance of recovering your fish. By now they're probably killed and frozen down, and in a store that we've got no chance of finding. In a few months' time they'll start showing up in the sort of street-corner mini-market where you have to check the sell-by date on every can of beer, the sort of place where the owner won't ask questions if he's offered some bargain stock.

'Either that or they'll be disposed of in bulk through a cash-and-carry somewhere down south, or possibly in France or Spain.

'But suppose we do catch some joker trying to flog some frozen trout? He's going to spin us a story about having netted them. What are we going to do then? Stick the fucking things in a line-up and ask you and Mr Gates to identify them?'

He glared at Watson. 'Fact three: you are not only the victim here, sir. You are also a contributory factor to the crime.

'You're running a business here with a multi-million-pound turnover. You've got a massive investment in stock, in rearing tanks, in sterile conditions for harvesting, handling, killing and distribution. Yet you grudged the relatively small investment it would have taken to protect you against the possibility of a theft like this.

'Fact four: John McGrigor visited you personally a couple of years ago, and another time before that, and he advised you to install perimeter alarms linked to the nearest fully manned police office, plus a video system with cameras on inaccessible steel poles linked to a recorder off-site.

'The cost of all that would have been a relatively small addition to your total capital investment here. You could have written it off against tax in the usual way, and reduced your insurance premiums significantly.

'Did you do that? Did you fuck! You told him that the fact that the manager lived on site was security enough. You were dead bloody wrong, of course, and that's why the three of us are standing here today.'

Pringle turned towards the door. 'That's what I came here to tell you this morning. Those fish have bolted now, of course, but it's not too late to bar the gate against a repeat performance.'

He grasped the round brass handle, then paused and took a deep breath. 'Oh aye, there's one more thing.

'Fact five: if you ever try to threaten me again, or try to dismiss me in that way, then do not from that time on drink as much as a thimbleful of whisky and get into your car, or park on a yellow line, or give a sweetie to a kid in the street, or do anything else you could be had up for, or, believe me, you will be.

'If you want to tell all that to Sir James Proud, in the New Club, in his office, or anywhere fucking else, be my guest. But tip me off when you're going to do it, because I'd like to be there.'

The heavy door crashed shut behind the detective. As he began the long walk back to his car, down the rough track, feeling the recuperative power of the morning country air, there was a broad smile on his face.

Thirteen

Ruth McConnell made a soft sound as Pye pulled his car into his space in the park behind police headquarters, directly alongside a sleek red MGF sports car.

'What's up?' Sammy asked.

'I was just thinking about your boss's pride and joy, parked next to us. That'll be going down the road soon. Karen won't be able to get into it in a couple of months, and once she has the baby ...'

'Don't you believe it. Andy Martin and that motor are joined at the hip. But it's not a problem; they've got another car, a new Ford Focus. They got it after they sold Karen's flat.

'Anyhow, just for a minute there I thought you were pissed off at me, or something.'

She reached out and touched his cheek. 'And why would I? Sammy, you were really great last night, really understanding. I was just so stressed out that if we had, it would have been awful, disastrous even. Having you there beside me . . . I really needed you; but I have never been less in the mood.'

He glanced at her mournfully. 'I've never been more in the mood.'

She laughed again brightly. 'I could see that. Very impressive, even under cover.'

She laid her hand on his thigh. 'Once the boss gets back, I'm sure all the strain will be off, but until it is, until I know for sure, I'm still in this nightmare.

'Once it is over . . . Would you like to move in with me? Or would you like me to move in with you? Or do you prefer it the way it is?'

He sighed, and smiled. 'You know what I want. Your place is bigger than mine; your bathroom's nicer, your kitchen's better equipped. I'll move in with you; after a while we can look for something together.

'I won't be in this job forever. Who knows, Mr Martin might post me down to the Borders, beside Dan Pringle.'

'No danger; Jack McGurk's there already, remember. You're going back east, eventually, to Brian Mackie's division. Stevie Steele's going to team up with Maggie Rose again, once a certain DS in her team retires.'

'How do you know all that?'

'I just do. Now please forget I said it. We'll have to be careful with the pillow-talk, you and I.'

'I'm just looking forward to starting it.'

'Me too,' said Ruth. 'But now we'd better get inside. My big boss might be away for the morning, but the other one's probably been in for an hour already.'

Fourteen

Detective Inspector David Mackenzie stepped into his office, closed the door behind him, then stared in astonishment at the man sitting behind his desk. His mouth hung open as the visitor pushed himself out of his chair and walked round toward him.

The blow was faster than anything he had ever seen; the tips of three stiff straight fingers stabbed into the pit of his stomach at the top of the inverted V-shape below his rib-cage. A bolt of pain, worse than anything he had ever known, flooded through him and stayed. His legs gave, and his bladder almost followed, but despite the agony he managed to keep it under control.

As he started to fall, the man caught him by the lapels of his overcoat, held him up, then dropped him on to a straight-backed seat. Mackenzie wanted to shout for help, but he felt as if he had no breath left in his lungs, only fire. Also, he guessed that there was a fair chance that if he tried, no sound would be allowed to escape his lips.

'Who?' he croaked eventually.

'You know who I am,' said the intruder icily. 'You know all about me, Bandit, or so it seems.'

He reached into his pocket, produced a small, palm-sized

tape recorder and pressed a button. The inspector froze as he heard his own voice, tinny but unmistakable.

'*And your man Skinner's never made a mistake about a woman has he? I seem to remember he was all over the tabloids not so long ago. Something to do with him shagging a woman detective sergeant on his staff.*

'*Does he give you one as well, now and again?*'

'The answer is "no", Mackenzie, although the man who does is a lucky son-of-a-bitch.

'Mister, you've just committed two of the biggest mistakes any detective officer can make. The first is stupidity, and the second is underestimating a suspect. I've been guilty of both myself in my time, but never as crassly as that. Ruth works for me; she's a very intelligent lady, and she's picked up a few touches from me in her time.

'For the purposes of your investigation, I'll tell you this, you arrogant young bastard. Last night, after your failed attempt at intimidation, Ruth came straight to see me. She played me that tape, which sealed your fate on the spot. Then I asked her to think very carefully about all the time she spent away from Sammy that Saturday afternoon.

'Happily she remembered something. She remembered seeing my daughter in Jenner's, just before five o'clock. She didn't speak to her, but she saw her on the other side of the second-floor balcony, in the glassware department.

'I called Alex, and she confirmed that she was there. And she does have a date and time stamped credit card slip to prove it; for half-a-dozen whisky tumblers, as it happens. My Christmas present; she's pissed off because now she'll have to get me something else.

'So you can forget about Ruthie as a suspect. That was always far too fucking easy, anyway. I'll grant you that all the circumstances pointed straight at her, but even at that, you must have been out of your fucking mind to think that a DCC's secretary would off anyone and let herself be seen doing it.

'So look somewhere else, Bandit. Your investigation's back to square one again. Understood?'

Mackenzie nodded, still incapable of coherent speech, still racked with pain.

'You know, son,' Bob Skinner continued, 'there're two ways a copper like you can go. He can go to the top or he can go to hell in a handcart. Make me your enemy and you are on route two: you can be dead certain of that.'

He held up the recorder for the Strathclyde detective to see. 'I could use this tape to have you sent to Oban in a uniform by tomorrow morning at the latest. I've got the power to halt your career in its tracks.

'But I'm not going to, because I asked my pal Willie Haggerty about you. You remember him? Yes, I thought you would.

'He told me that you're undoubtedly the cockiest, most conceited bastard he's ever met, and that you have been in need of a really good doing for some time. But he said also that you've made DI in spite of your weaknesses, and that with them knocked out of you, you could become a great detective officer.

'Now you've got the chance to prove him right. Get out there and find out who killed old John McConnell. And keep me informed of progress every step of the way. Don't worry about jurisdiction; I'll square that with your gaffers. They owe me a couple of favours, and I've got a personal interest in this one.'

He looked down through what David 'Bandit' Mackenzie realised were the coldest blue eyes he had ever seen. 'I'm backing Willie Haggerty's judgement of you, son. You prove us wrong and I might just come back here and teach you everything I know about intimidation.'

Fifteen

As the door of his office swung open, Ted Chase sighed his irritation. 'Inspector Good,' he began, 'I thought I told you to call before . . .' Then he looked up and saw a figure, clad in a uniform which was heavy with silver braid.

He stood up straight behind his desk, almost by reflex. 'I'm sorry, Chief, I didn't realise.'

'Not at all, not at all,' said Sir James Proud. 'I should apologise. I ought to have knocked.' He waved some correspondence which he was holding. 'I just thought Bob might have been in here, that was all. There's something I wanted to ask him about.'

'It wouldn't be the London incident, would it?' Chase ventured.

'As a matter of fact it would. How the hell did you know about that?' The normally affable Chief Constable frowned slightly.

'I happened to be in the office on Sunday when the document arrived. Since it was marked urgent I took it upon myself to open it, in your absence. I took it upon myself also to show it to the DCC, and to discuss it with him.'

'Did you not think you were taking rather a lot on yourself, Ted?' asked Sir James. 'You've only been here ten minutes, and five of them must have been taken up writing that paper of yours on the command structure of the force.'

'I exercised my judgement, sir. That's all I can say.'

'Even though for all you knew this could have been a report from the Security Services exposing you as an Iraqi spy?'

'All the more reason for me to open it, sir.'

Proud Jimmy laughed. 'Aye, maybe so. Anyway, Ted, you've explained everything. I get this daft report about Bob, which you've already showed to him. In the same in-tray, I find this grovelling apology from the bloke who wrote it. You don't have to tell me what happened when Bob read the bloody nonsense. Even Assistant Commissioners aren't beyond his reach.'

'Yes,' Chase concurred. 'He does seem to have his own power-base, doesn't he.'

The silver-haired Chief Constable looked at his Assistant for a few seconds. 'Maybe you didn't mean that remark to have a barb in it, Ted. If you did, please desist. I have your paper under consideration, and I am taking it seriously. I'm seized of your underlying point that criminal investigation is only one of the responsibilities of a modern police force and should not be allowed to dominate it. So, incidentally, is Bob Skinner. He and I have discussed that very concept on many occasions.

'However, I and I alone will decide what happens to your document, and I'll do it in my own good time. So just leave it at that, eh?'

'Very good, sir, but I really didn't mean anything by my last remark.'

'Good. Then forgive me for reading anything into it.' Sir James paused. 'Want a coffee?'

Chase took the invitation as an order; he nodded and followed the Chief back to his own office.

'Do you happen to know where Bob is anyway, Ted?' Proud Jimmy glanced across the table as Gerry Crossley set a coffee pot and crockery on his low table.

'Not really, sir. I asked Miss McConnell, but she said simply that he had an appointment out of the office.'

'Mmm. I asked her too. She said all she knew was that he had to see someone through in Strathclyde. That's funny. I'm not saying it's unique, but it's unusual for Ruth not to know exactly what he's doing.

'Unless she does, and for some reason she's not telling.'

He smiled, almost to himself. 'If she does . . . Well, sometimes it's best not to know what that bugger's up to.'

Sixteen

'If God had meant people to play golf in this valley, he wouldn't have put the prevailing wind in this direction. It can be as cold as charity here, in the middle of summer.'

'Have you played Dullatur, sir?' Mackenzie asked.

'No, but I have played the course across the road, Westerwood. Middle of June it was, and fucking freezing. This one won't be any different. The west of Scotland new towns, East Kilbride and Cumbernauld, were established on land within easy reach of Glasgow but where no major community had grown up before. The planner should have realised that that was no accident. EK's always snowed up in the winter, and Cumbernauld's swept by this bloody Arctic wind.'

'You sound as if you're from the west, sir.'

'Motherwell. I dug an escape tunnel twenty-five years ago.'

'Would you ever come back?'

Bob Skinner shook his head. 'Not to live,' he said, vehemently. 'I like Gullane, and my family are happy there. But crime tends to move around; I'll go wherever it takes me. I'm a specialist policeman, Bandit, just like you. My Chief Constable and I have long philosophical discussions about that. His strengths complement mine; he couldn't run today's force without me, or another specialist like me, and I couldn't run one without someone like him.'

'Aye but how does that help the punters, sir?' the younger man interposed, showing a renewed trace of his customary brashness. 'Red tape's always fucking up our job.'

Skinner looked sideways at him. 'See? There is a brain hiding behind that designer raincoat of yours. That's a bloody good question. Should we have separate bodies, one responsible for public protection and the maintenance of order, and the other charged with criminal investigation?

'If I was a politician, which thank God I am not, because I distrust the bastards totally, I would answer "yes", and do something about it. However, they do tell me that I can move and shake things, so you never know.'

Mackenzie picked up a bacon roll from the table before them. 'I'll watch developments, sir.' He took a bite. 'Why did you want me to bring you here?' he asked.

'Several reasons. I missed my breakfast to come through and sort you out, so you owe me one. Old John McConnell was a member here, so I wanted to get a feel for the place. As it turns out you're a member too, so that was handy. On top of all that I wanted to get you out of that office, to see if I could kick-start your thinking on this investigation.

'After all, I've just blown your easy assumption right out the window. So maybe I owe you one.'

He looked around the members' lounge. 'Impressive place this is, David, for an ordinary urban golf club . . . if you don't mind me saying so.'

Mackenzie nodded agreement. 'Too right.' He pointed

to his right, out across the first tee where two golfers stood in weather-suits, ready to set off into the wind and rain. 'The original clubhouse was away down there. The New Town Development Corporation, before it was wound up, did a complicated land deal with us which involved them building this place for us, plus laying out some new holes as well.'

'Good deal.'

'Aye, sir. Everybody won, I'd say.'

As he spoke a door behind him opened. An elderly man in casual clothing walked into the room, holding a cup of coffee. 'Morning,' he said, nodding towards the players outside. 'Rather them than us the day, eh gents?'

'Too right,' Skinner agreed. 'You wouldn't get me out on a morning like this.'

'Ye don't look as if ye're here to play anyway, though,' the old man observed.

'No, we're not, although my colleague here's a member. Actually we're police officers; we were just talking about poor old John McConnell.'

The veteran grimaced. 'Aye, damn shame that. Poor old John; he'll be missed. Him such a fit man, too, tae go downhill so fast.'

'How d'you mean?' Mackenzie asked.

'Well he jist did. He used tae play every day. Ye'd have found him out the day, even. Then about four months ago, he started missing days, until he wisnae here at all. Ah heard fae somebody that went tae see him that he was jist sitting there in his hoose, fair wandered.

'That Alzheimer's, eh. It's jist as well he's awa' quick.'

'Yes, I suppose it is,' Skinner murmured, waving a brief farewell to the senior member as he wandered across to a table on the far side of the big lounge.

'Interesting,' he said, his voice still low. 'I envy you this one, Bandit. It's a real challenge.'

'Too right. But where do I start?'

'Come on, man; you start at the beginning. Who knows so far, apart from us, that this is a murder investigation? No bugger does. Well, it's time they did. Call in the press; tell them that you're starting a full-scale investigation.

'Re-canvass the neighbours while their memories are still reasonably fresh. The dark-haired woman; you know who she isn't, so get a better description of her to help you find out who she is. Try to establish what make and model of car she was driving.

'Then there are the missing possessions: grandfather clock; big silver trophy. They'll be somewhere: find them. After you've apologised profusely to Ruth,' he leaned on the adverb, 'ask her to go through the house to see what else might be missing. If that doesn't help look at the whole scene in a mirror.

'Look into his bank accounts to see what was happening there.'

Mackenzie frowned. 'I know that already, sir.'

'Fine, in that case, go back to everyone who spoke to old John before his death. Turn up people you haven't even looked for yet. Did he have any interests other than golf? Find out what was happening to him.

'I will bet you one thing, Detective Inspector Mackenzie. Even suppose that was a district nurse who went into his house that Saturday, that old boy didn't have Alzheimer's. He's been a victim of something all right, but it was man- or woman-made.'

Seventeen

'Sir Adrian Watson. Sure, I'll remember that name, Dan, and yes, I'll pass it on to the Chief, and the DCC too, just in case.'

'Thanks, Andy. Not that anything happened that I couldn't justify to myself, but threatening to nail him to the fucking wall might look bad if he wrote to the *Scotsman*, or got his tame Lib Dem MSP to raise a question in the Scottish Parliament.'

'I'd be surprised if he did. But what about this chap Gates? How would he swing if Watson did get stroppy?'

'Gates told me the first time I met him that he recommended that Watson should follow John McGrigor's advice and install an automatic security system, but he was advised, bluntly, to wind his neck in. I could tell that inside the boy was cheering when I gave Sir Adrian the benefit of my own advice.

'Nonetheless, he's an employee. And he did hear me threaten Watson.'

'Presumably he also heard Watson threaten you.'

'Aye, but he might forget, though. Look, I'm no' that worried about it, Andy. I'm just telling you in case there was any comeback that might cause embarrassment.'

'I appreciate that, Dan. Leave it with me; I'll deal with it. Cheers.'

Andy Martin ended the call, then buzzed his junior assistant, Detective Constable Rhind. 'Lorna,' he said. 'I want you to trace a number for Sir Adrian Watson. He's a landowner down in the Borders. Get him on the line for me, please.'

He turned to Detective Sergeant Pye, who was seated across the desk, waiting. 'Sorry about all that, Sam. You probably gathered; Dan Pringle's had his first run-in with the local Establishment down on his patch.'

Pye grunted. 'And he's been there for a week, already; I'm surprised it took him so long, sir.'

The Head of CID laughed. 'Me too. But it proves us right in sending him down there. Nothing against big John, but the division needed shaking up a bit, needed his successor to be a different sort. We could have sent Brian Mackie down there, and the place would have fitted him like a glove, but the DCC and I reckoned that Dan's occasional lack of diplomacy made him best suited for it.'

'Oh, I get it, sir. He does the plain speaking, with you in the background to smooth over any incidents.'

The phone rang. 'Yes. As you're about to hear.'

He picked it up. 'Sir Adrian? Good; Detective Chief Superintendent Andy Martin, Head of CID. I thought I'd give you a call . . .'

Pye, across the desk, saw his boss pause and nod.

'Yes, Superintendent Pringle's told me about your discussion. Yes, sure . . .

'Dan's a plain-spoken man, sir, and he's spent most of his

career in the city. But there's no better, or more committed, detective officer on this force . . .

'I'm glad you appreciate that, sir. I'm sure you'll appreciate also that he didn't intend to threaten you, any more, I doubt not, than you meant to give the impression that you were threatening him, or were dismissive of his efforts and those of his officers . . .

'No, of course not. We have a simple operating principle in dealing with the public: equality for all under the law. Every law-abiding citizen can expect the same treatment from us, sir, and no individual is subjected to inappropriate scrutiny, unless he or she is suspected of committing a crime or offence, or unless we have reason to believe they may be about to commit one . . .

'Why should I believe otherwise, sir? I played rugby in the Borders many times in my career. I've been in many a club bar after many a match . . . I may even have seen you once or twice. And I can't recall ever seeing anyone have an excessive amount to drink and get into a car . . .'

Pye searched Martin's face for any sign of sarcasm but found only bland innocence.

'Sure, Sir Adrian: a slight excess of zeal. Yes, of course I'll convey your apologies to Dan also. I'm glad you see it that way, and I'm pleased that you're so supportive of the work we're doing to trace these thieves . . .'

'And good afternoon to you too, sir.'

He replaced the receiver. 'There you are, Sam,' he said. 'Smoothed over. And I never told a single porky either.'

'What! What about never seeing anyone in a rugby club get into a car over the limit?'

Martin grinned. 'I never looked. Anyway, although I didn't play for all that long after I joined the force, word gets round if there's a copper in the bar.

'I do remember Watson, by the way; he was pointed out to me at a club once. Real arsehole, and he was pissed as a rat.'

He swung round in his chair to face Pye. 'So, Sergeant. Why's your face been tripping you all morning? . . . as if I had to ask.'

'You know?'

'Of course I bloody know. Superintendent Rose called me as soon as Mackenzie and Dell had left last night; she told me what had happened. Then about an hour-and-a-half later, after you and Ruth had been to see the Big Man, he phoned me, absolutely fucking incandescent with anger.

'What was on that tape Ruth played him? He wouldn't tell me.'

The young detective winced. 'Then don't ask me to tell you either, sir.'

'That bad, eh. It could be "Goodbye Mr Mackenzie", then. Because the said DI had a surprise early morning visit from DCC Skinner, cleared in advance with Max Albright, the Strathclyde Head of CID . . . I phoned him this morning, just in case another diplomatic mission was necessary.

'Max said that Big Bob called him at home last night . . . I knew he was going to . . . and asked formal permission to jump on Mackenzie's toes from a great height. He told me he said to go ahead, please, because the bloke's been in need of it for a while, only he couldn't find an excuse.'

Martin leaned back in his chair and grinned at Pye. 'Then, just before Dan's conscience call from the Borders, the DCC phoned me from his car, on his way back through here. Ruth's off the hook, Sam, with a grovel from the Bandit as well. He said we should listen to the news any time after midday.'

He checked his watch. 'It's close on twelve thirty now.' He reached back to a small table to switch on a small Sony radio. Before he could do so, his office door opened unexpectedly and a tall, beautiful woman, in full bloom, stepped into the room. 'Hello Karen,' Pye exclaimed, jumping to his feet and pulling a chair from the wall up to the desk.

'For God's sake, Sammy,' Karen Martin laughed, 'I'm not that pregnant!' She turned towards her husband. 'Hope you don't mind me being early for lunch, but shopping for a lump dress took less time than I thought.'

Andy grinned back. 'Miracle of miracles. No, that's fine; but hold on for a minute, okay. There's something we want to hear.' He pushed the radio's 'on' button.

They had to wait for only a minute before the bulletin began. The second item was a report of a midday press conference held in Glasgow by Strathclyde Police, to announce that a full-scale murder investigation was under way into the death of Mr John McConnell, of Cumbernauld.

It included a short soundbite from Detective Inspector David Mackenzie, appealing to the public for information about Mr McConnell's last days, and in particular for any sightings of a tall, dark-haired woman, and a blue car, seen outside his house on the afternoon when he was believed to have died.

'Well, there you are,' murmured Martin, switching off the Sony as his ex-detective wife looked at him, with her former professional curiosity aroused. 'The wrath of God hath fallen upon the woeful Bandit, who repenteth, plenty.'

Eighteen

'Where do we start, though sir?' asked Gwendoline Dell. 'Now that your first principle of detection's been stood on its head, "Never look further than the obvious without good reason", how do we actually progress this investigation?'

'Don't chance your arm, Gwennie,' Mackenzie growled. 'We're going to do the things that the uniformed numpties who handled the thing until the post-mortem report came in never bothered to do.

'For a start, no one's even talked to Mr McConnell's GP. We don't know anything about the old man's medical history. All we have is assumption and hearsay. For all we know the mystery woman in the blue car could have been a doctor. The old boy might have been under treatment for something that didn't show up in the PM.

'We should go back to the people we've interviewed so far, see if we can get them to be more specific about the things they told us. For example . . . not that we're going to get it . . . a registration number for that motor would be more than useful.

'You get your wheels turning on that, instead of sitting there laughing to yourself about me getting turned over.'

'As if I would, sir,' the blonde sergeant chided, with the very faintest of smiles.

'Gaun, bugger off,' Mackenzie laughed. 'There's something else I've got to do and you're not sitting in on that. Seeing a grown man crawl can be an awful experience.'

He waited until the door closed behind Dell and he heard her footsteps recede down the corridor, before picking up the phone on his desk and dialling a number which Bob Skinner had left him.

Bob Skinner. Mackenzie felt a cold pang at the memory, still fresh, of his introduction to the man. He knew within himself that it would stay fresh, always. What a mixture; cold and terrifying one minute, then, message transmitted, received and understood, affable, positive and helpful the next. He had heard stories about the Edinburgh DCC; his old boss, Willie Haggerty, spoke of him often. But nothing had prepared him for the reality, or warned him of the extent of the folly of crossing him.

He made the call and heard two rings at the other end of the line before the woman answered. 'Ms McConnell,' he began, doing his best not to sound ingratiating, 'this is an apologetic David Mackenzie, from Cumbernauld.'

'I've been told that it's up to me whether I accept your apology or not, Inspector,' she said coldly, '. . . but it's been suggested that I should, and so I will. What can I do for you?'

'You could come through here, if you'd be good enough, and meet me at your uncle's house. I promise we'll let you in this time. Please, if it would make you feel easier, bring someone with you; DS Pye, maybe.'

'Sammy's my boyfriend, Mr Mackenzie, not my minder. Anyway, I don't imagine I'll need company, do you? I'm sure you'll be as considerate today as you were inconsiderate yesterday, bearing in mind that the last time I was in that house, my uncle was lying dead in the bath.

'I'll need to clear it with both my bosses, but assuming that it's all right, I'll meet you there at four o'clock.'

Nineteen

'The Ruth business is all sorted out then, boss?' Detective Inspector Neil McIlhenney asked, rhetorically. 'What sort of a super-hero does that guy Mackenzie think he is, waltzing on to our patch and giving one of us . . . . as Ruthie is . . . the third degree?'

'Ach,' said Skinner, 'we can all get a bit carried away with ourselves from time to time. The boy Bandit got carried too far away, that's all. He's a good copper, when you strip the bullshit away.'

'You sound as if you wish he was working for you.'

'He is working for me. I'm taking a personal interest in this investigation; apart from bloody terrifying Ruth last night, they owe it to her to find out what happened to her uncle. Fucking weird, Neil, I tell you. A fit old man till last summer, still with two good hips and playing single-figure golf going into his eighties, shooting well under his age practically every time he set foot on the course, then a few months later he just drowned in his bath.

'Mackenzie's promised to copy me all the reports coming out of his investigation. Meantime, there's something I'd like you to do for me. Get on to the pathologist in Glasgow who did the PM on the old boy, and ask him to fax or e-mail me his complete report, photos and all. I think I'll show it to Sarah, to see if anything occurs to her. I suppose you'd better tell him that, too; I don't want to ruffle any professional plumage.'

McIlhenney nodded. 'Will do, boss. I've got something for you, though.

'I've just had a call from that lad from the Met, the one who called me at the weekend. He told me that one of their uniformed women was on foot patrol in Regent Street early this morning when she spotted something in the gutter about two hundred yards away from the spot where you had your bother.

'It was bent out of shape, and looked as if it had been run over by a car, but it turned out to be a spent shotgun cartridge.'

'Is that right?' The DCC's eyes shone in triumph. 'I'd like to shove it up Assistant Commissioner Dumpty's arse,' he muttered, 'just to teach him not to doubt the word of a brother officer.'

He paused, still smiling. 'Oh aye. Thinking about Regent Street and all reminds me. Lou Bankier's coming up to Scotland on Friday, and I've invited her to dinner at Gullane. I was going to ask Alex to join us, and to take her back to the Balmoral afterwards, but it turns out she's going to Paris on business.'

He caught the twitch of McIlhenney's eyebrows. 'I know. Bloody lawyers move in a different world these days.

'Anyway, if you can find a child-sitter, Sarah and I wondered if you'd like to join us. You can do the taxi run, of course, which won't be a problem since you insist on being teetotal these days.'

The big inspector looked at him oddly. 'It's nice of the two of you to ask, Boss, but . . . I don't know. The truth is, I haven't sat down to dinner with any adult other than you and Sarah since Olive died. I don't know what kind of company I'd be.'

'I do, or I wouldn't have asked you. I'll tell you from the perspective of one who's made such a mistake; you can't be a social hermit all your life, man. Furthermore, you know damn well that your wife would have been the very first to agree with me. Anyway, for God's sake, I'm offering you a date with a movie star!'

McIlhenney grinned. 'Now that would give Olive a laugh!' He glanced upwards for a second. 'Aye, all right, Boss. She says it's okay. Thanks.'

'That's good. Now go and get me that PM report, and let's see what I can stir up.'

Twenty

There was only one car parked in the street, when Ruth turned into Glenlaverock Grove; it was a bright red Ford Ka with colour-matched plastic bumpers, and it stood directly outside number fifteen. She pulled up her blue Corolla close behind it.

As she did so, Bandit Mackenzie climbed out of the driver's seat, almost catching his long overcoat in the door as he closed it behind him. 'The coat suits you, Inspector,' she said, a shade archly. 'It goes with your image. The car doesn't, though; of course, if you were wearing a pointy blue hat with a bell on the end . . .'

'It's not mine, honest,' he assured her, hurriedly. 'Mine's in for a service; this is the wife's.'

'My God, you have a wife?'

'Aye, and three kids.'

'Indeed? And what do you do if one of them comes home with a bad school report? Shine hot lights in his eyes and give him the third degree?'

Mackenzie smiled at her. The hostility of the day before had vanished; if she had never met him before she might have taken a liking to him at first sight. 'My kids don't get bad reports,' he said. 'Other than my four-year-old, when he tried to correct a playgroup teacher's spelling.'

'I wonder where he got that trait from?'

'Ah, but he was right.'

'He must take after his mother, then.'

The inspector sighed. 'I'll tell you what, Ms McConnell; I know this is a smokeless zone, but if you can come up with some ashes, I think I could lay my hands on the sackcloth. I am really sorry about yesterday; all our information did point to you, and I got pissed off at having to traipse through to Edinburgh. But still I went over the top; I must have scared the hell out of you.'

'A big mistake on my part, I tell you.'

Finally she smiled back at him, with a degree of satisfaction. 'You don't have to.'

She paused. 'Very well, Inspector. Apology accepted; let's start off fresh. Let's go inside; it's chilly out here.'

Mackenzie nodded, then reached into his overcoat pocket and produced a labelled key ring. 'Here,' he said, handing them to her. 'You can have these back; our forensic team are all finished here. I'll keep the second set for a while, if you don't mind; just in case Gwennie and I need to go back to check up on something.'

'Such as?'

'I have no idea at this moment, but you can never tell. It would be useful, that's all.'

'Okay, if you have to.'

She looked at the keys and found the two which opened the front door, as the detective ripped away the plastic crime-scene tape.

The house was cold as they stepped inside; Ruth looked at a wall thermometer in the hall, with a circular switch alongside. 'This controls the central heating,' she said. 'It's set at five centigrade. One of your people must have turned it back.'

'No,' replied Mackenzie. 'It was like that when we were called out.'

She frowned. 'Yes,' she murmured. 'I remember now; it was cold when Sammy and I came in at first. I'd forgotten. That was unusual; I always remember Uncle John's house as being uncomfortably hot.'

The inspector stepped up to the control wheel and peered at it. 'There you are, right away; that's something we'll need to come back for. This doesn't look as if our technicians have dusted it; we must, though, just in case our dark-haired lady found it uncomfortably hot as well.'

He turned back to Ruth. 'Where do you want to begin?'

'What about the garage?'

'What about it?'

'He didn't drive much, Mr Mackenzie, but he still had a car, a big old Rover coupé, with real leather seats. He's had it all my life, so it must be over thirty years old. It was his pride and joy; he used to spend hours cleaning and polishing it.'

'I've been in the garage, Ms McConnell,' said the detective quietly. 'There's no car there; a back wall racked with carefully arranged tools, but no car.'

For a few moments, Ruth had to fight to hold back tears. 'Oh no,' she whispered. 'The grandfather clock, the trophy; okay, they're gone. But something very bad must have been happening for Uncle John to sell his car.'

'Maybe he didn't sell it. Maybe someone just took it.'

'But who? Why?'

'I don't know. But presumably the same people who've been emptying his deposit account in the Hibernian Building Society in Coatbridge over the last few months.'

'What?'

Mackenzie nodded. 'I'm afraid so. How much did you know about your uncle's finances?'

'Only that he was comfortably off; nothing much else.'

'Mmm. He had two bank accounts; a current account with the Bank of Scotland that his pension was paid into, and the other one, with the Hibernian. Last summer, that had over seventy grand in it. Just under three weeks ago the last of the money was drawn out. Each of the withdrawals was made by a third party, on the basis of a form signed by the old man, nominating Ms Ruth McConnell as his representative.

'The tellers who handled the transactions all described a tall, attractive woman, with long dark hair.'

'Didn't they ask for evidence of identity?'

'They did. She showed them a credit card with your name on it.'

He looked at her. 'So you see, Ruth, on the basis of all that, plus what the old man said to his friend about you having money troubles, maybe you can understand a bit better why I was so bloody sure of myself yesterday.'

She bit her lip, unconsciously. 'Yes,' she conceded. 'I'll give you that.'

'Can you remember the car's registration number?'

'Yes. CDV 32.' She laughed quietly, taking the policeman by surprise. 'I remember Uncle John telling me, about ten years ago, that a man called Charles de Vere offered him five thousand pounds for it ... for the plate alone, that is, without the car.'

'That looks like another asset stripped out, then. Mind you, maybe this woman will surprise me by being really stupid and offering the number for sale in *Exchange and Mart*.'

'Do you expect her to?'

'Not for one second. Come on,' he said briskly. 'Let's see what else, if anything, she's got away with.'

Ruth nodded, and followed him into the living room. 'What about his watch?' she asked.

'There was one watch among his effects; a cheap battery thing.'

'There wasn't a Rolex?'

'No, absolutely not. I'd have remembered.'

'There should have been. My aunt gave it to him on their fortieth wedding anniversary. She retired about a month before that; she was the matron of a hospital in Stirling. She bought it out of her lump sum.'

She pointed to a wall cupboard, near the fireplace; it was split into two halves, and the upper section had a glass door. 'There was a silver tea service in there; my aunt's. What about her jewellery? My mother and I were left a couple of pieces, but Uncle John kept her diamond engagement ring and a sapphire and diamond ring that had been my aunt's mother's. That in particular was worth a lot of money.'

'They've gone too, then. What can you tell me about the grandfather clock?' he asked.

'Not a lot. I'm no expert. I can tell you that it was a big

one, though, with a shiny brass face that Uncle John always kept polished. It always kept good time as well; he knew a watchmaker who serviced it for him.'

She dropped to one knee and swung open the doors of a big sideboard. 'Bastards,' she hissed in anger. 'There's nothing in here either. There should have been an eight-piece Wedgwood dinner service, and a canteen of Sheffield steel cutlery.

'Inspector,' she said, as she stood up once more. 'There doesn't seem to be anything of value left in this house. It's been picked clean. I don't know who this woman was, but she's a vulture.'

'No, Ruth,' said Mackenzie slowly. 'She's worse than that. Vultures are carrion birds. This creature does her own killing.'

Twenty-one

Detective Sergeant Gwendoline Dell had sore feet; she had spent the afternoon on fruitless visits.

One had been to John McConnell's doctor, who had declared that on his last visit, for a pre-birthday check-up, the old man had been the fittest eighty-year-old he had ever seen. 'Strong as a horse, he was. All that golf over all those years gave him forearms like a blacksmith.'

Another call had been to his club cronies gathered in the bar, sheltering from the awful day. One of them had directed her to a railwayman's club in the nearby village of Croy, but the steward there had never heard of the old man.

Finally she had canvassed every house in the streets around his home, trudging from door to door, ringing bell after bell, most of them without reply. Those people who were in were either wrapped up in afternoon television or struggling with pre-school children.

They were all concerned citizens; every one of them frowned sympathetically as they denied even knowing John McConnell, far less being familiar with his visitors and his habits.

She had kept the unlikeliest prospect for last: Miss Alice Lind, retired schoolteacher, of Number Twelve Glenlaverock

Grove . . . unlikely because it was she who had reported seeing the tall dark woman heading towards her neighbour's door on the last day of his life. More than that, she had given impetus to the wild goose chase by suggesting that it might have been his niece.

'Come away in, dear,' said Miss Lind, in an accent which suggested a genteel Glasgow upbringing. 'You poor soul,' she clucked, 'you look absolutely worn out. Let me make you a cup of tea.'

Normally Gwendoline would have declined, but the old lady was right. She was worn out, and dry as a bone. And there was another reason to accept: she guessed that the blue Corolla parked behind Lorraine Mackenzie's Noddy-car belonged to Ruth McConnell, and she had no wish to bump into her again.

She looked around the neat living room as her hostess rattled crockery in the kitchen. It was of another age; it felt just like visiting her granny.

Miss Lind's return broke into her thoughts. She took the proffered cup of tea gratefully, and even accepted a Tunnock's caramel wafer.

'I heard the news at lunchtime,' the former teacher said. 'Poor Mr McConnell; how very awful. No wonder your people spent so long at the house.'

She paused then added, casually, 'Was his niece of any help to you?'

'She's helping us right now,' DS Dell volunteered. 'But I'm sorry to tell you that wasn't her you saw ten days ago.'

The old lady looked genuinely surprised. 'Oh, was it not? I don't know the girl, of course, but I've seen her on the odd occasion she's been to see her uncle, and from the back, it did look very like her.'

'Ah. So you only saw her from the back.'

'Well yes. I suppose I did. It was the hair, though. The girl Ruth's is long and well-groomed, like those lassies in the shampoo ads, and this other one's was just the same. I was absolutely sure too. I hope I haven't caused Ruth any upset.'

'None at all,' Gwendoline lied. 'No, I was just wondering, Miss Lind, if you could remember any more about this woman. Her car, for example; can you recall what make it was?'

'My dear, I can't tell one car from another. I grew up in a time when there were shooting brakes and running boards and things like that. Today, they're all the same: not like that lovely Rover of Mr McConnell's. Now that is what I call a car. The woman's? I'd enough trouble remembering that it was green.'

'Green? But you said before that it was blue.'

'Did I? Well maybe that's what I thought at the time. When you get to my age, my dear, the memory goes funny.'

The detective moaned inwardly. 'Do you have any idea how long the car was there?' she asked.

'Not really, dear,' the old teacher replied. 'I don't think it was there when I closed my curtains at six o'clock, but it was dark by then, so I can't really be sure.'

'What about the woman herself? Think back please, Miss Lind. Can you remember what she was wearing?'

'A long coat and boots. That I can remember; they made her legs even longer.'

'Anything else? Anything at all?'

114

The old lady pursed her lips and put a hand to her head, as if she was rummaging about in it. 'Well, there was her bag, I suppose.'

'Her handbag?'

'No dear, not a handbag, more of a shoulderbag. Only it was bigger than that. A big square thing, almost the size of a suitcase. Yes, I remember thinking that, from the size of the thing, Ruth must have come for the weekend.'

Twenty-two

'Should I be doing this?' Dr Sarah Grace Skinner asked, as she took the folder from her husband. 'By that I mean have you cleared it with . . .' She opened the folder and peered at the top sheet, '. . . Dr McCallum?'

'Of course I have,' her husband replied. 'Neil spoke to her. She told him that she was more than happy to have someone else look over the papers. The impression he got was that she feels a bit exposed, now that all the background circumstances have come out.'

'I don't blame her. Okay, drowning in the bath is not an everyday cause of death among adults, but this man was eighty years old. In this case, the pathologist's natural instinct would not be to ring alarm bells.'

'Maybe not,' said Bob, thoughtfully. 'But maybe it should have been.'

She grinned at him as she laid the folder on the kitchen work surface. 'I will read this later, once the kids are in bed.' She handed him a china bowl with Beatrix Potter rabbits around the edge. 'Meantime, take this and feed your younger daughter.'

He took the dish and pulled up a chair, beside the high seat in which Seonaid, the newest member of Clan Skinner, bounced up and down in anticipation. She was a sparkling, sturdy baby, and a fast developer like her brother James Andrew had been in his infant days, before he grew into a rough and ready three-year-old.

'Okay, Junior Miss,' her father murmured, spooning up some of the blended food. 'What the hell's this gunge I've been asked to give you?'

'Beef and vegetable,' Sarah called across; her accent was still upstate New York for all her years in Scotland. 'And before you knock it, it ain't out of no jar. I made that myself. It's not unlike what the rest of us are going to have once you've put Tootsie to bed. I've just mashed it down with the hand blender, that's all.'

Whatever it was, the baby demolished it with impressive concentration as her mother headed upstairs to round up Jazz, and their adopted son, Mark, who were along the corridor in their playroom, engrossed in Deep Space Nine.

Bob Skinner was an enthusiastic parent; he had been left to bring up Alex alone for most of her young life. He reckoned that he had done a pretty fair job, but it gave him a secret inner delight that he had been given a second opportunity to share the experience with someone else.

He made a point, whenever the job permitted, of being home early enough in the evening to be able to feed Seonaid, bath her and put her to bed, then to spend time with the boys before their curfew.

That evening was typical of the domestic regime which he and Sarah had established; they were both pleasurably tired by 9 p.m., when Mark and Jazz went upstairs for the night.

'Okay,' said Sarah at last, as she slumped down on to the

sofa in their living room. 'Let's see that report.'

Obediently, Bob walked back through to the kitchen and brought the folder to her. Making herself comfortable in her seat she opened it, counted the pages briefly, then turned to the colour photographs which were appended to them. 'Did you get these by e-mail too?' she asked.

'Yes. They were sent through as files. I had our IT people print them out as clean as they could.'

'Very impressive. If only they could e-mail autopsy subjects to me, I'd never have to leave Gullane.'

Bob scratched his stubbly chin. 'If we had the garage converted to a mortuary, I could arrange to have them brought to you. I doubt if the boys would fancy Mum nipping out twice a day to carve up a cadaver.'

'You kidding? They'd love it. We'd be the talk of the village, though.'

'I've got news for you, kid. We're that already.'

She smiled, then turned her full attention to the photographs. 'This was taken in situ?' she asked, looking at the first.

'There's an index at the back, but yes, it was. It was shot as soon as they'd drained the water from the bath.'

'I wish they had taken one before they did that.'

'Why?'

'See those patches discolouring the white enamel?' She pointed to marks on the photograph. 'They could be strips of skin.'

'What would that tell you?'

'Nothing for sure, but . . .' She hesitated, frowning. 'Suppose the old man was suffering from rapidly developing dementia. If, in his confused state he ran himself a bath straight from the hot tap, then climbed in, in his senile condition the scalding effect could have induced shock causing him to faint and slip below the surface, absorbing a lungful of water which would have killed him immediately.

'The body would have blistered, causing those strips of skin to detach themselves post mortem. If I were you . . .'

He held up a hand. 'Not me. Detective Inspector Bandit Mackenzie, Strathclyde CID.'

'Bandit?!'

'Aye. The lad believes in his own legend just a bit too much. He's proud of his nickname.'

'Well in that case, if I was Bandit I'd go back to the house and see if there's anything still clinging to the inside of that bath.'

'What might that tell him?'

'That this isn't a homicide at all. On the basis of this photograph alone, the Strathclyde police have been precipitate here. Their investigation is based purely on this woman who looks like Ruth being seen going into the house on the day Mr McConnell probably died.'

'Probably?' interjected Bob.

'Yes, probably. I'm sure the estimate of time of death was scientifically based, but there's always a margin for error. Stop right here; find the mystery woman, charge her, and I'll give evidence for the defence.'

'She walks in ten minutes. The Crown Office wouldn't let it anywhere near court.'

'I see. Yet . . . my gut feeling is that Mackenzie's right. Read on, and let's see if we can help him prove it.' He pointed to the photograph. 'Why's the body in that condition?'

'That's called saponification. It can be caused by burying a body in very damp conditions . . . or in this case, immersing it in water. Essentially it means that the corpse is turned, or largely turned, into something akin to soap. That might have helped Dr McCallum establish time of death, but it could have given her other problems; for example the process might have destroyed major organs.

'Let's find out.' Sarah turned back to the narrative of the e-mailed report, and began to read.

As she did so, Bob went into the kitchen, took two bottles of Sol from the fridge, uncapped them, and carried them back to the lounge.

'Thanks,' said his wife, without looking up, as she took one from him.

She finished the beer before she finished her study. She thanked him again as he gave her another, and as she laid down the report.

'Weird,' she pronounced. 'There's no evidence of cerebral degeneration at all. Dr McCallum notes that the brain is the healthiest she'd ever seen in an eighty-year-old man. This doesn't preclude mental illness, of course, or severe depression. Yet . . .

'Think of one of the senior section of our own golf club; you know the people I mean, there are plenty of them in their late seventies or into their eighties, playing every day and looking ten, sometimes fifteen years younger than they really are. Imagine if one of them suddenly withdrew from the world for no obvious reason, and degenerated physically over a period of weeks to the point of pouring himself a scalding bath by mistake and dying in it.

'You can't, can you?'

'Only with difficulty,' Bob admitted.

'Well, from what you've told me and from what I've read, that seems to be what happened here. Dr McCallum reports some degeneration of vital organs, but she was able to record that they were all in excellent condition. Analysis of the liver showed that Mr McConnell had never been an excessive drinker, his kidneys were almost donor class, the alimentary system was clear.

'The muscles, particularly those of the arms and legs, appeared to be wasted, but there was sufficient bulk to indicate that this process had begun recently.

'There was clear evidence of cardiac seizure, but this is consistent with my supposition that the old man might have been immersed in a scalding bath. It might have rendered him unconscious, but it didn't kill him. He drowned all right.'

'So are you saying that Mackenzie should scale down his investigation, even though the whole thing screams "Suspicious death" at both of us?'

She smiled at him. One of those specials which, as he knew so well, always preceded a metaphorical rabbit appearing from an imaginary top hat.

'I would, save for one thing. Analysis showed bloodstream traces of temazepam – significant traces, I'd say, given the man's age and rapidly deteriorating physical condition. You told me earlier that Mr McConnell hadn't been under any form of medical supervision or treatment.'

'That's Mackenzie's information.'

'Okay. He'd better check with his GP and with the local pharmacies, to find out who prescribed or dispensed such a strong sedative, and why. And here's something the clever lad's missed. He should also ask Dr McCallum to repeat her analysis of the stomach contents, because she reports no temazepam residue there.

'However, she has a reputation for being very efficient, so I'm sure a second check will come up with the same result.'

'Meaning?'

'Meaning that the drug was injected. You can forget examining the body for puncture marks; they'll be long gone. But there can be no other conclusion. I take it that no hypodermic syringe was found in the house.'

He took her meaning at once, and gave a soft whistle. 'There's no mention of that in the papers I've read. It wouldn't have been left out either; it would have hit Mackenzie right between the eyes.'

'In that case, even though it'll still be damn near impossible to prove homicide at the end of the day, the inspector's investigation is still up and running.

'However, what he should be looking at first and foremost is the possibility that this old man was a temazepam junkie, and that someone . . . maybe Ruth's lookalike . . . was feeding his habit.'

Skinner's scowl was thunderous. 'And stripping his assets in the process. In which case it's a good bet that when they'd bled him dry of cash, they simply killed the poor old sod.'

Twenty-three

'Honest to God,' Sammy Pye murmured. 'Women are unpredictable creatures; and you more so than any other I've ever met. Yesterday this Mackenzie had horns and a tail. Today he's not such a bad bloke.'

She laughed softly; it sounded in his ear like the tinkling of a small bell. 'That's the power of Bob Skinner. I don't know what the boss said to him, but it had a dramatic effect. He couldn't have been more considerate, really.'

'What about that torn-faced witch of a sergeant of his? Was she there?'

'No. He said she was out pounding pavements. You're being too hard on her; she might have looked severe, but she was taking her lead from Mackenzie. All she did in the interview room, more or less, was nod her head when he expected it.'

'So what did you find in your uncle's house?'

'Nothing. Somehow or other, he's managed to dispose of all of his assets, save the house itself. On what, God alone knows.'

'Is Mackenzie still convinced that he was murdered?'

'Yes. And so is Mr Skinner. He's taking a personal interest in the investigation; on my behalf, I suppose.'

'That's nice of him.'

'Ah, but I think it's professional too. He's fascinated by it, I think. His nose has started twitching. When he starts to follow it, anything can happen.'

'Wait till he gets a whiff of Dan Pringle's first big case down in the Borders. That should stir his imagination.'

'Why? What does that involve?'

'A couple of ton of farmed trout; missing, presumed dead.'

She beamed as she made a connection. 'So that's what Mackenzie meant yesterday. At the start of the interview he made some crack about fish rustling. At the time I thought he was loopy.'

'No, he'd know about it all right. Dan's got an All Points Bulletin out on those trout.'

She laid a hand on his chest, smiling sadly as she leaned across and kissed him. 'The lives we lead, Sammy, eh.'

He combed his fingers through her long hair, running their tips lightly down her naked back, drawing a gasp from her.

'Well, Sergeant,' she whispered. 'You've got me into bed again. What do we do now?'

'Let me show you.' He breathed the words in her ear as he eased her on to her back. They kissed, long and slow. She felt for him, down beneath the duvet, but he moved downwards out of her reach, licking her nipples lightly, left, right, left again.

'Hello ladies,' he murmured, then slid further down her body. She cried out, a soft scream, as she felt his tongue again.

'God, Sammy,' she moaned. 'If I ever tell you to stop that, ignore me; please.'

She thrust her pelvis upwards, opening herself to his touch, writhing with it, until he slid back upwards and she could grasp him, big and rock-hard, and guide him towards her, towards where she wanted him. She called out again, louder than before, as he entered her, bucking and heaving beneath him, surprising him with her strength, exultant as he matched her.

They were still breathing hard, lying there entwined, glowing with sweat and satisfaction, when the phone rang out, beside the bed. They looked at each other and laughed in unison.

'Let it ring,' he said.

'No, better answer it.'

He reached across her and picked up the instrument. 'Yes?' he began, still smiling, his tongue working to free a hair which had become trapped between his front teeth.

'Sure, sir,' he continued at last, forcing himself to speak evenly. 'She's right next to me.' Ruth's eyes widened as he passed her the telephone. 'It's Mr Skinner. He's got some news for you.'

Twenty-four

'Have we got any other crime on this patch apart from vanishing bloody trout?' Dan Pringle asked Detective Sergeant Jack McGurk.

'A farmer down Hawick way shot a dog that was worrying his sheep, sir,' his tall assistant replied. 'But other than that, that's it.'

'Shooting a dog's not a crime to a farmer.'

'I was talking about sheep-worrying, boss.'

The superintendent drew him a long look, and a half smile. 'You know, son, there's times I wish I'd left you in Edinburgh.'

'We've only been here for a week and a half, sir, but there's times when I wish you had too.'

'Listen,' said Pringle. 'When Big Bob and Andy Martin posted me down here, they said I could take my ten favourite records, one book, and a familiar object. The last one's you; end of story.' He laughed at the young sergeant's mock outrage. 'Ach, don't worry, Jack. There'll be plenty to do down here. Up in the city, it was as if crime came to you; busy all the time. It's different here, with different styles of crime and maybe of criminal, but the basics are the same.

'Our good colleagues laugh at the notion of fish rustling,

but it's theft of property nonetheless. It's just as serious as a wages snatch, or a jewel robbery, or a housebreaking.

'Anyway, if there's one thing I've learned in the two centuries in which I've been a detective officer, it's never to complain when things are quiet, because sooner or later, they won't be. Don't you forget that the thing which drove John McGrigor to early retirement was the murder of his best friend in an armed robbery, right in the middle of this patch.'

McGurk winced. 'I suppose you're right, boss,' he conceded. 'Anyway, the fish are keeping us busy, up to a point, even if the chances are they're long gone from our patch. All the out-stations have finished the rounds of fish farms in their areas . . . and there's more of them than you'd imagine. Some are just cottage industries, but there are a few as big as Mellerkirk.'

'What sort of fish do they farm?'

'Trout, boss, all of them. They're the only sort you can farm around here.'

'What about salmon?'

'No,' said the sergeant, with a shake of his head. 'Salmon are farmed in salt water, in the West Coast sea lochs mostly, and in the fjords in Norway. There are hatcheries on shore, but they're all close to the farm sites.'

'You seem to know a bit about this, Jack,' the super-intendent remarked.

'I've done a bit of research, sir. Bill Gates at Mellerkirk was a big help.'

'So is there money in this fish farming, then?'

'Oh yes boss, there's money in it all right. But it's high-risk too. If you're a salmon farmer, once you've put your smolts into the cages . . .' He caught Pringle's puzzlement. 'Smolts are young fish, raised in the hatcheries.

'Once you've put them to sea, you have to feed them, treat them, and medicate them for two years before you can harvest them. It's high-cost, long-term husbandry, and it calls for patience from everyone, not least the industry's bankers. During that two-year rearing period there's lots of things can go wrong. The stock can become infested with sea-lice, so they have to be constantly treated. They're subject to disease, so they have to be given antibiotics. They're prey to things like red algae bloom, that will kill all the fish on a farm site if it flows through it. On top of that, there are the grey seals, tens of thousands of the buggers, that can sometimes swim up to a pen and take a bite out of a fish right through the net.

'When salmon farming started, there were lots of small operations, but the costs and the risks resulted in it consolidating to the point where now there are a few big producers and that's it.'

He paused. 'Trout farming's different; a much more attractive proposition as a small business. Less risky all round. You can do it on land, in sheltered sites. Other than a few otters, and man, of course, there are no natural predators. You can harvest your stock much quicker, and sell it more easily. Some small farmers sell at the roadside more or less; the punters walk in, pick a fish and they just whip it out with a net and hit it on the head.

'The bigger boys, like Mellerkirk, are more sophisticated. They go for volume production and sell to specialist fish shops, supermarkets, or processors.'

'And how many of the bigger boys have we got on our patch?'

'Three,' replied the big sergeant. 'One in Berwickshire, one just outside Jedburgh, and one in Langholm.'

'What's their security like?'

'The Langholm one's good, but the other two are crap. Like Sir Adrian Watson, they had advice from Mr McGrigor, but they felt that, with a manager on site, they didn't need to spend that amount of money. The truth is, sir, in trout farming it's cheaper just to insure against stock loss.'

'I must have a word with the Insurers' Association,' said Pringle, 'or ask Big Bob if he'll do it. They need to change that situation.

'Meantime, you'd better talk to the managers. Don't scare them, but warn them to sleep with the light on this weekend. D'you know anything about them?'

'According to Gates, they're both young, single people like him; that seems to be the type you find in that job. One's a woman.'

'Jeez,' the superintendent muttered. 'Security! I don't suppose they ever go to the pub of an evening, or anything like that . . .

'You got the names and addresses of the owners of those two farms? John McGrigor's rugby club network approach doesn't seem to have worked with these people. Let's see if a touch of Pringle diplomacy does any better.'

Twenty-five

Never having met Sarah Skinner, Bandit Mackenzie found Dr Helga McCallum a break from the normal run of forensic pathologists. She was tiny, no more than five feet tall, ash blonde, and with facial features that made him think of a delicate china doll. She looked as if she was in her early twenties, although the policeman knew from the job she did that she was probably at least ten years older.

For a minute or so he felt himself falling in love, until he fought it off by imagining her at work, standing on tip-toe and up to her elbows in innards.

'I'm sorry to have brought you here, Inspector,' she said in a slow Glasgow drawl, looking round the mortuary. 'You've taught me a professional lesson. I thought it was bloody obvious that if there were no stomach traces of a drug, then it was introduced by other means; either up the bum, or by injection.

'Obviously, I have been guilty of not spelling everything out in my report. It hasn't been necessary with the officers I've worked with up to now.

'Henceforth,' there was a cutting edge to her voice, 'every "t" will be crossed, and every bloody "i" dotted.'

Mackenzie slipped immediately into mollifying mode.

'My fault, Doctor, not yours. The report was quite clear; I just misread it.

'I'm sorry to have to ask you to repeat your analysis of the stomach contents, but their absence has become a crucial factor in my chain of evidence. And since you might wind up in the witness box, it's in your interests as much as mine that we're dead certain on this.'

'Don't worry,' said Dr McCallum. 'I'm well aware of that . . . although I am used to the Court taking my word on the basis of one analysis.

'I've repeated the tests, and done some others, and I can promise you that the subject did not ingest temazepam within two days of his death. Any he may have swallowed before that would have been gone from the bloodstream by the time of death.'

She turned, stepped over to a long trolley, and with a single movement of her forearm, whipped away the sheet which covered it. 'You haven't met Mr McConnell, have you, Inspector?'

The sudden sight of the naked, chalk-white corpse, with its roughly stitched incision from neck to groin, made Mackenzie's stomach clench as if it had been gripped by a fist. He felt himself gagging and hoped that it did not show.

'Dr Grace was quite right in her observation. The saponification of the body has made it virtually impossible to detect any puncture marks. I've checked, nonetheless, if only to confirm there are none visible. However, examination of what's left of the veins of both forearms does reveal the likelihood that the subject was injected repeatedly in the period leading up to his death.

'This old man wasn't given a fatal shot of temazepam, but I'd say that he took it or was fed it, intravenously, on several occasions.

'Does that help?'

The detective looked at the diminutive pathologist. 'It confirms our suspicions about Mr McConnell's death, short of proving conclusively that he was murdered.

'But as for finding the person who stole just about everything the poor old man had, it takes us not one step further forward.'

Twenty-six

Louise Bankier was in her hotel suite when Skinner arrived at the Balmoral, at exactly six o'clock. He parked his BMW directly in front of the hotel, nodding to the familiar figure of the doorman on his way in, and announced himself at the reception.

She appeared from the lift in less than two minutes, walking over to him, at the desk. Her key deposited, she kissed him quickly on the cheek, then took his arm as they headed for the door. Heads turned as they stepped out into Princes Street and crossed the narrow pavement to the car; Bob was quite certain that no one was looking at him.

'Did you get your business done?' he asked, as he pulled out from the kerb and drove away, signalling a left turn on to Waverley Bridge.

'Yes I did, thanks.' He saw her nod, out of the corner of his eye, as he swung past the green light. 'I've taken the part; we start shooting in Edinburgh next month, while the Christmas lights are still there. I liked the script, my co-star will be Ralph Annand, a very fine Scottish actor, and I know Warren Judd, the producer, of old. He's an ex-, as a matter of fact.'

'Husband?'

'No. Informal.' Her voice dropped. 'We didn't part friends, and we haven't worked together since; it took a lot of soul-searching before I even began to consider doing his movie. My other hesitation was that I've never worked with the director before.'

'Is that a big factor?' Bob asked.

'It is for me. I'm sufficiently stellar now to be able to turn down parts if even one aspect of the project doesn't feel right. The relationship between cast and director is very important. It's his movie . . . at least in theory it is . . . and he can, if he chooses, try to impose his will on the actors.

'So nowadays, before I commit myself to anything, I make sure that the director and I are thinking along the same lines.'

'And this bloke's okay, is he?'

'Personally, he's a limp-wristed little jerk. Professionally, however, he's one of the real up and coming young men. More than that even; he's up and he's come, if I can put it that way.'

He chuckled at her earthiness. 'You may, Lou, but possibly not in front of the wife. Who is he anyway?'

She twisted round in her seat to face him. 'Have you ever heard of Elliott Silver?'

His eyebrows rose slightly. 'Ah yes, him.' Then he grinned. 'Wouldn't know him from Adam. Who he?'

'Very trendy, very good; he's a young Londoner, in his late twenties. He made a couple of things for television, then when he was twenty-five, he wrote and directed a gangster movie set in the East End. It won two BAFTAs and an Oscar for best screenplay. In the four years since then he's won two more BAFTAs, and had an Oscar nomination. Early this year he did his first Hollywood movie; they say it's a cert. for Academy Awards for best picture and best director.'

Bob whistled. 'Wow! And here was me thinking that a BAFTA was an Islamic curse.'

Louise laughed. 'Philistine!'

'Don't knock them,' he protested. 'I've got a soft spot for the Philistines. They had bad reviews, but even from them you can see that they were pretty good at getting the job done. They were artists in their own way too; look at what they did to King Saul. It wasn't dissimilar to some of the things that have won the Turner Prize in recent years.'

He swung the car past the Palace of Holyroodhouse, and, on the right, the floodlit site of the Scottish Parliament building. 'How many of those things have you won?' he asked.

'BAFTAs? Four; three film, one television.'

'And Oscars?'

'Three, plus two Golden Globes.'

In the darkness of Holyrood Park, she could see his soft smile in the dashboard light. 'Oh, I remember them well,' he whispered.

Her laugh was deep and raunchy. 'They're still doing all right. Moved a little south, but still all right.'

'I know,' he said. 'I saw that film of yours a couple of years back; the one where you got your kit off. That felt very weird, I'll tell you. It's as well the cinema was dark.'

'Have you seen many of my movies?'

'Several of them. I have them on video.'

'Good boy. You're helping to make me rich.'

'You like that, do you? Being rich?'

'It's okay. Why? Is that your ambition?'

He shrugged. 'A lot of people would say I am already; you'd probably just say that I'm comfortably off. I've had a few legacies in my life, and I've invested them well. Give me five years and I could retire in considerable comfort on my police pension and my investments.'

'And will you?'

'Not a chance. The day I feel burned out as a copper, then I'll go; but I'm a hell of a lot more than five years away from that. Lou, even back then, when we were kids, I had a vocation for police work, and in particular, for the investigative side. My father wanted me to be a lawyer; when I told him I was joining the police, he felt let down, as if the money he spent sending me to school in Glasgow, then to university, had all been wasted.

'But I said to him . . . I remember it, clear as daylight . . . "Dad, I am going to be a lawyer. I'm going into the justice business; the only difference between your ambition for me and my own is that I want to work at the sharp end."

'And you know what he replied? He looked at me and muttered, "I bred a fucking idealist!" But the last thing he ever said to me, the night before he died, was "Son, you were right." On the two occasions in my career when, for a fleeting moment, I've thought, "Why, Bob, why?", that's been my answer.'

He drew to a halt in the queue at the Willowbrae traffic lights, and glanced sideways at Lou, her profile framed in the lights of the Mercedes dealership. 'How about you? Why do you do it? It hasn't brought you happiness; I can tell that. So what is it? Fame? Money?'

She laughed, but it was a brittle sound. 'Of course it is . . . especially money.' The traffic began to move through the lights, and he eased forward with it.

'I am happy, Bob, really. Not like you are, with your wife and young family, but I'm happy with what I do. Even way back then, the very day I met you, when I joined your squash club because I wanted you, that same day I joined the drama society because I wanted that even more.

'When we split, it was because you followed your Presbyterian conscience. But if we'd stayed together then, I'd have left you eventually for my other lover . . . either that or I'd have destroyed your life.

'I spent a long time wondering what it was about, why I was addicted to the hot lights, the roar of the greasepaint, the smell of the crowd, as they say. For a while, I thought I was the most self-indulgent being alive.

'And then, one night, I was in Los Angeles, at an Academy Award ceremony. I wasn't nominated that year, so when it was over I started to leave, to meet some man, at some party somewhere. It had started to rain during the show, and it was hammering down outside like a bloody monsoon. It was chaotic, some very famous people were running for their limos under inadequate umbrellas, and twenty-thousand-dollar dresses were being ruined in five seconds flat.

'In the middle of it all, I saw a man; he was a singer, a minor figure in the movie industry, but a legend in his own field. He was standing there, his buckskin jacket soaked, his long hair plastered to his head, and he was signing autographs, not just one or two but dozens, maybe hundreds, for all the people who were pressed around him, wanting a piece of him.

'I don't know how long I watched him, standing there signing those soggy books, tee-shirts, programmes, anything, as best he could, as all those bloody movie stars ignored the crowds and ran as fast as their dignity and their heels would allow. But eventually someone spotted me, shouted to me above the noise "Louise", and waved a baseball cap at me.

'I walked out from under the marquee, into the rain, I took the marker pen he gave me, and I signed, watching the ink run even as I wrote. Then another, and another. The signatures were barely legible, and probably didn't survive the night, but I knew as that singer knew that it didn't matter.

'Those people out there in the storm were representatives of all those who make people like me. I hate the word "fans"; they are our patrons. They give us something of themselves . . . love if nothing else . . . and it's our solemn duty to give them something back. Even if it does cause us momentary discomfort.

'So that's why I do it, Bob. So that I can sign autographs in the rain.'

They drove on in silence for a while, leaving the city lights behind. They had just turned off the A1, when Louise reached out and touched his cheek. 'Speaking in general terms of course, do you ever wonder,' she asked quietly, 'what it would be like to be with someone again, an old lover, after a quarter of a century? Would it be as good as it was, would it be better, would it be a let-down?

'In your deepest thoughts, do you ever wonder that?'

'I can't speak in general terms, Lou,' he murmured. 'In terms of bygone lovers, Myra's dead, there was someone I never want to see again, and there are a couple of others I can barely remember; which leaves only you. I can only speak of you.

'Of course I wonder. Do you think I could ever forget what it was like? We were only youngsters, you and I, but we were tremendous together. Today, given maturity, experience, and everything else, sure, most people might be tempted to play those scenes over again.

'But not me. It's a delicious thought, but that's all it can be; for me at least. Because where I am now is where I want to stay for the rest of my life. I am happier than I have ever imagined; in ten minutes or so, you'll find out why.

'Just suppose you and I did indulge ourselves, even just for one night. We could contrive the circumstances without difficulty, and afterwards say "Thanks" and walk away. Sarah would never know or even suspect.

'But I'd know; I'd know I'd betrayed her, the kids, the whole thing. And because I had, even though I'd got clean away with it and things might appear to be as perfect as before . . .' He tapped his chest. '. . . in here, they would never be quite the same again.

'I speak from experience here; I only have what I have now because Sarah was tough enough to see us through our tough time. That alone means that I feel guilty even fantasising about you.

'There's something else,' he added. 'I love her like crazy, and I'd die before I'd betray her again.

'Don't get me wrong, Lou,' he said, glancing across at her,

'I cherish the memory of the time we had as youngsters. We were perfection together, even if it was too good to last. However, it can provide a great foundation for lifelong friendship if we both see it that way. Deal?'

He took his right hand from the wheel and held it out. She smiled, and shook it firmly. 'Deal,' she said. 'Not even for the part of the world which I don't yet have, would I spoil what you have now.

'For the truth be told, my old love, to be as happy as you, away from all the glitz and glam, is what I want for myself, far more than another fifty Oscars.'

They drove on towards Gullane, Bob's eyes on the road, Louise looking out of the window at the lights across the Forth.

As they reached the village, Bob shifted in his seat. 'Oh,' he exclaimed, 'I almost forgot. Alex can't make it tonight, so we have another dinner companion, my pal, and colleague, Neil. He'll be your taxi back to Edinburgh, too. He's probably there ahead of us.

'One word, of explanation rather than warning, about him. His wife died less than a year ago, so if he seems a bit withdrawn, that's why.' He chuckled. 'Don't go thinking he's star-struck or anything; big McIlhenney's the least impressionable guy I know.'

Twenty-seven

'What exactly is it that you do in Bob's team, Neil?' asked Louise, as McIlhenney's car accelerated out of Gullane, towards the amber glow which hung in the sky over Edinburgh. 'We talked about everything but that. I noticed one thing though; you never called him by his Christian name all night, not once.

'Sarah yes, but not him. All the other policemen we talked about – Dan Pringle, Andy Martin, Mario McGuire, Maggie Rose, all first names – but not him.'

'I can't, to his face,' the big dark-haired man answered quietly. 'I respect him too much. He's told me I should away from the office, but I've told him I just can't do it.' He gave a soft laugh. 'Not till he promotes me another three ranks, at any rate.

'It's a police thing; part of being in a disciplined service. An inspector might be on first-name terms with a chief inspector, when there are no PCs around, maybe even with a superintendent, if they've come through the ranks together. But when an officer moves into the Command corridor, when he becomes an ACC or a DCC, he goes on to another level.

'His rank carries with it an extra degree of respect; if he's

141

Bob Skinner it makes him a demi-god.'

Although he could not see it, she smiled at him. 'And to think he told me you were the least impressionable man he knows.'

'Maybe he's right; but he's the exception, although it would embarrass him to know it. I'm not alone. Bob's greatness is that although he's the most natural leader any of us who work with him have ever met, he's also a man of the people.

'That's what the word police means, you know, if you trace it back to its root. Linguistically, policemen and politicians are both the same thing . . . men of the people. Now isn't that bloody ironic; how a single root could have produced such different fruits.'

'The twain never meet?'

'Not quite. Chief Officers have to live with politicians, so they have to acquire some of their skills. Proud Jimmy . . . Sir James Proud . . . our Chief, has them under his thumb, and Mr Chase, our new ACC, is that sort of animal too. But a police officer with a politician's duplicity . . . now he'd be a dangerous man.'

'What about Bob?'

'He hates them. He'd drown the buggers at birth. The irony is that he used to work for them, as an adviser, but one Secretary of State let him down. He walked away from that job and he's never forgiven the man since.'

'Is that politician still in office?'

'No. You don't want to get on the boss's wrong side. That's the irony, you see; he hates politicians, yet he's hugely influential himself. He's come to realise that, too.'

'Maybe he should become a politician himself, then,' Louise suggested. 'New blood to change the breed. You're right; I travel internationally, and it's the same everywhere I go. Politicians have become so ideologically inbred that you can't tell them apart.'

Neil shuddered. 'Don't wish that on him, please. If Bob Skinner ever went into politics he'd be like Julius bloody Caesar. He'd frighten the weak and the venal among his enemies so much that eventually they'd pluck up the courage to kill him. Some of the old-guard lefties on the Police Board have tried already, metaphorically.'

She chuckled at his reaction. 'Okay, I withdraw that wish.'

They drove on in silence for a while. There was a new moon, but the night was clear and crisp. Out on the Firth of Forth, lights shone on several moored tankers and rigs.

'Hey,' exclaimed Louise suddenly, 'you didn't answer my question. What do you do in Bob's team?'

'I'm his exec.; his ADC, his personal assistant. Andy Martin, the Head of CID, calls me his Vicar on Earth.'

'So you'll know where all the bodies are buried, then.'

'Those that I don't know about, I don't want to know about.'

'Did he tell you about the trouble in London last Friday night?'

'I know about that.'

'Was there an aftermath? He mentioned something on the way out.'

Neil detected an underlying concern in her question. 'There was, but it lasted about two minutes. A high-ranker in the Met did something very stupid; he doubted my boss's judgement, and worse, his word. He won't do that again.

'Let me guess,' he went on, looking across at her. 'You're blaming yourself for letting him stick you in a taxi and get you out of there before the police turned up?'

'Sort of.'

'Well don't. He doesn't use his position very often, but when he does, it's for the right reasons. In this case, he made you disappear to protect you from the possibility of unwanted publicity . . . and to protect Sarah, as well.'

Louise nodded. 'I understand that now. She's a stunner, isn't she? And those children are lovely.'

'All children are lovely,' McIlhenney murmured, in the dark. 'Even those that ain't.'

'How many do you have?' she asked.

'Two. Lauren and Spencer. Lauren's eleven, going on twenty, Spencer is nine, going on ten. How about you? Do you have children?'

'No. I've never been in one place, or one marriage, long enough. The up-side is that . . . apart from one time, about twenty-five years ago . . . I've never stayed long enough to get really hurt, either.'

She sighed in the dark. 'God, I shouldn't have said that, should I; not to you.'

'It's okay. Honestly, no one can say anything that'll make it hurt any worse than it does already. It's better when people don't walk on eggshells around you. I'm just younger than the average widower or widow, that's all. You know what? I sat in the church during Olive's service, and I thought of all the couples gathered round me, and I realised that one out of every pair will sit in a front-row seat at a funeral one day.

'It's part of the deal. If it's a good marriage, the hurt is a cross worth bearing, even though you might be selfish enough to wish that she was the one left to bear it.

'So really, don't feel awkward or sorry for me, Louise. Envy me, if you like, but don't pity me.'

Spontaneously, she reached out and squeezed his arm. 'Sorry,' she said. 'I mean . . .' They laughed, in harmony.

'Jesus Christ,' she exclaimed, suddenly sounding more Glaswegian. 'What a bloody evening. I haven't had a deep conversation with a man in five years or more, and here I've had two in one night.'

'I'd better just shut up, then.'

For a moment she thought he was being serious. 'Oh no,' she said, quickly. 'Don't do that. I like talking to you. I like meeting someone who isn't impressed by who I am or what I do.'

'Who said I wasn't? You're a Scottish heroine, Louise, right up there with Connery . . . even if you are about forty years younger.'

'That's very gallant of you, sir, but actually I'm just under thirty years younger. How old are you?'

'Pushing forty . . . hard!'

'Don't worry about it; it's no big deal. In fact I find it better to think of myself as being in my early forties, than in my late thirties.'

'I'll bear that in mind. The truth is the only age ambition I have is to stick around long enough to see the kids through university. After that, I can keep my date any time.'

'Your date?'

'I had a dream a few weeks . . . after. It was about a grey bridge. Olive was on the other side, I was able to see her but I couldn't cross, not then.' He broke off. 'Sorry. This is getting heavy again.'

'Hey,' she said. 'Not having to say sorry cuts both ways you know. You don't need to worry about what you say to me either. I get fan mail, Neil. People tell me all sort of things; some of them would break your heart, but I still read them.'

He smiled across at her. 'You're quite a lady, Louise . . . for an actress.'

'And you're quite a bloke . . . for a copper. You must have some interrogation technique . . . just like Bob's, I suppose.'

'Not at all, in fact. I let people talk to me; he makes them.'

As he spoke, he drove through the traffic lights at the foot of Waterloo Place, and pulled up outside the Balmoral.

'Thanks Neil,' she said, 'for the lift and the deep conversation.'

'My pleasure, Louise.'

'Lou, please. Call me Lou; all my real friends do.'

He stepped out of the car and went round to open her door, but she had let herself out and stood waiting for him on the pavement. 'This is where I let myself down,' he said, big and sheepish. 'Can I have your autograph?'

'Just a punter at heart, eh?' she laughed, as he found a pen and fumbled in his pockets for a piece of paper. 'I'll send you a photograph, signed to Neil, Spencer and Lauren. Will I post it to the office?'

'God no. Some bugger would open it. Send it to my home

address.' He found a business card, scribbled on the back, and gave it to her.

'I'll tell you what,' she said. 'I'm off to London tomorrow, then I'm back here next Friday for another meeting about the movie, and I'm staying until we've done all our location shots. I'll deliver it myself, if you like.'

'Would you? That would be really nice of you; the kids would love it.'

He stood there watching her as she stepped into the hotel. 'See you then,' she called, with a final wave.

Twenty-eight

Bob rolled over on to his back, and sensed that Sarah, although he was lying still, was awake also.

'What's up?' he whispered.

'Nothing at all. I was just lying here thinking about this evening, and about Louise. She's a very nice lady; not at all precious considering all she is.'

'That's a Scots thing,' he told her. 'Jocks and Jockesses who make it big internationally in entertainment or sports have to be very careful when they come home. If they're even suspected of putting on airs and graces, they don't half catch it in the neck. We like our heroes to be ordinary; sometimes we even like them to be fallen.

'Lou could never turn into a prima donna though. She was always too nice a girl for that.'

'She's beautiful now, so she must have been a stunner as a girl.'

He whistled, softly. She could see his smile in the pale light of the bedside alarm clock. 'Oh she was. I remember the first time I saw her, in a crowded corridor at the Fresher's Fair. I was flogging squash club membership; I knew just from looking at her that she'd never played in her life . . . hardly anyone did then . . . but I pitched her just the same.'

'Was it tough to leave her?'

'You better believe it. I shouldn't have got involved in the first place; Myra and I had just got engaged, so I was spoken for, but she did my head in.'

'Just your head?'

'Aye, okay, that too.'

She frowned. 'Aren't you surprised she's never settled down herself?'

'Not really. Back then she was always looking for something, without knowing what it was. She still is, I think.'

'Maybe back then she was looking for you.'

She heard him chuckle. 'Nah. Her ambitions ran beyond me, even then, as she'd tell you herself.'

'Did you ever regret it?'

'Which? Getting involved, or chucking her? I should have regretted the first, but I never did. As for leaving her . . . to be honest it was touch and go which of them I split with, but I wouldn't have made Lou happy long-term. I know that now, although I didn't at the time. No, I stayed with Myra because she had a hold on me; I loved her. Plus, she had me fucking hypnotised, just like everyone else.

'But it's worked out. We had Alex. Then, down the road, you came along and the kids. The icing on the cake of my charmed life.'

She rolled towards him. 'Oh, you're working well tonight,' she murmured.

The inescapable telephone rang quietly by the bedside. 'Whothehellisthat!' Bob grumbled, but as always, he picked it up.

'Bob?' Andy Martin sounded tense. 'Sorry, but you'll want

to hear this. I've just had the manager of the Balmoral on the blower in a flap. There's been a fire in a guest's suite. It's Louise Bankier's; she's a friend of yours, isn't she?'

Skinner sat bolt upright. 'Is she all right?'

'Smoke inhalation,' Martin answered. 'She'll be all right but they've sent for an ambulance.'

'Okay. Tell them to take her to the Murrayfield Hospital, not the Royal. Then call there and make sure they're ready to receive and treat her. If it's non-emergency, she'll be more comfortable there, and she'll have more privacy. I'm on my way there now.'

He paused. 'Hey, Andy. How come the manager called you?'

'Because he's shitting himself. He says it wasn't an accident.'

Twenty-nine

'I've no idea how it happened, Andy,' exclaimed Guy Bronte, the general manager of the Balmoral Hotel. 'I only know that as soon as the senior fire officer looked at it he said that it couldn't have been ignited by accident.'

'Tell me what happened, exactly.'

'It was just after 2 a.m. The fire alarm went off, and our board pinpointed the location as number two-ten, Miss Bankier's suite. I was sleeping here tonight, rather than at home, so I was wakened with everyone else. When we got to the room, one of my under-managers opened the door with an emergency pass key.

'Our sprinkler system had dealt with the outbreak by that time, but there was still a lot of smoke around. Miss Bankier was still lying in bed, soaked by the spray and coughing very badly. We have a doctor as a guest tonight. He examined her and said that she was in no danger, but recommended hospitalisation as a precaution.

'The ambulance took her away ten minutes ago.'

'Did you evacuate the hotel?'

'Yes, but only very briefly. We were able to let everyone return to their rooms almost at once.'

'Are the firemen still here?' asked Martin.

'Yes. They're up in two-ten.'

'That was a daft question,' the detective murmured to himself as an afterthought, 'with a fucking big fire appliance parked outside.'

Bronte led the way up to the second floor, using the stairs rather than the lift, even though the firefighters had declared the emergency officially over. A bulky figure in a fire suit and white helmet stood outside the door; for all his armour the chief superintendent recognised him at once.

'Hello Matt,' he called out. 'You're a bit over-dressed for this one.'

'That's the way I like them, son,' said the veteran Divisional Officer Matthew Grogan. 'There's nothing nicer than turning up at a fire to find that it's out.

'No' that this one really was a fire, mind you.'

'What do you mean?'

'It was the smoke alarm in the room that went off. But there was nae flame.'

'So what was it?'

'A pair of smoke canisters, hidden in a laundry basket, with a timer on it that must have been set for two in the morning or thereabouts. Together they'd have generated a hell of an amount of smoke. It was non-toxic, the sort of stuff that we use in our training exercises, but you wouldn't know that if you were in the middle of the stuff. It's bloody realistic and if you inhale enough of it, you'll still have a right bad cough.

'The woman in this room must have had a hell of a fright. What was her name, anyway?' Grogan nodded in the direction of Bronte, who was heading towards the stairs. 'She had an oxygen mask on when the paramedics wheeled her out of the room they transferred her into. That fella got all coy when I asked him who she was. He said that he wisnae at liberty to say. Ah nearly told him that I was at liberty to close his fucking hotel, but what the hell.'

'So who is she?'

'She's a friend of Bob Skinner,' Martin told him. 'I asked Guy to keep the name quiet, because, to be frank, I didn't want any of your boys to be tempted to make a few quid by phoning a tip to one of the tabloids. Don't take it personally, though, Matt.'

'Don't worry, son,' the big fireman assured him. 'I live in the real world. You were right.'

'Where's the device?'

'In here. I had a good look at it, but I didn't touch it. The ignition blew the lid off the basket, so it got soaked like everything else.'

Martin looked into the suite. It was in fact a single large room, with a seating area and a double bed against the far wall. Every item in it – carpets, furniture, bedding – was drenched with water.

'The basket's in the bathroom,' said Grogan. 'There was a towel in it, over the canisters. Maybe the woman chucked it in herself, or maybe someone put it in there so she wouldn't see them if she looked in.'

'That's quite likely,' the detective concurred. 'We'll find out soon enough.' He reached into the pocket of his leather jacket for his mobile. 'Meantime, I'd better get a CID team along here.'

Thirty

'Twenty-five years on,' Bob Skinner grinned, 'and you still look just as good in bed.'

'I promise you I don't feel as good,' Louise replied, in a hoarse whisper. She lay in a blue-covered bed in a well-appointed private room. 'In fact,' she said, 'I feel as if I've had something large, rough and hard down my throat.'

'Just like old times then,' he muttered, wickedly.

She started to laugh, then broke into a coughing fit; quickly, he poured her a glass of water from a jug by the bedside and handed it to her.

'No more funnies, please,' she entreated him, when the paroxysm had passed. 'I really am bloody sore.'

'No more, I promise. You fed me that one, though, you have to admit. You always had an earthy sense of humour, Ms Bankier.'

He paused, and the smile left his face. 'The problem is that someone out there isn't seeing the joke any more.'

'What do you mean?' she whispered, frowning back at him.

He sat on the edge of her bed and took her hand in his. 'I mean, my dear, that what happened in your room tonight wasn't an accident.'

She gasped, and he felt her grip tighten. 'What . . . ?' Her question tailed off.

'Someone planted a smoke-bomb in the linen basket in your suite, timed to go off during the night.'

She stared at him, astonished. 'You mean someone tried to kill me?'

'I don't think so. The smoke itself was harmless; there was just a hell of a lot of it. Someone did want to give you a fright, though, at the very least.'

He looked at her, as if he was choosing his words very carefully. 'Which raises a clear and obvious proba-bility, one that should have occurred to me before, but didn't, maybe because I've fallen victim to my own legend. Conversely, maybe it didn't occur to you because you haven't.

'Last Friday night's incident might well have had nothing to do with me; it might not have been random. Given what's just happened, I'm bloody near certain that it was aimed at you.'

Her eyes widened; her mouth opened as if to speak, then her throat constricted and she started to cough. She sipped more water, until she was settled.

'Lou,' he asked her quietly. 'Have you ever suspected that you might have a stalker?'

She stared at him, then at the wall, then out of the window. Suddenly, outside, a lion roared. She started, eyes widening still further.

Bob smiled at her surprise. 'Don't be alarmed. Edinburgh Zoo's right next door.'

'What is this place?'

'It's a private hospital. I thought it would be better for you if you came here. Listen, we can talk about this in the morning; I'll have the staff give you a knock-out pill for tonight. But when you waken, I want you to think about what I've just asked you.

'You'll be okay to leave here in the morning. But do you have to go back to London?'

She shrugged her shoulders, wincing at the movement. 'My schedule for next week was learning the script for my new movie, that's all; that and packing for a longer stay up here. But other than that, no, I don't have to.'

'You have an assistant, don't you?'

'I have a secretary. She's based at my agent's office.'

'Would you trust her to pack for you, and to courier the cases up here?'

'Sure.'

'Good. In that case I want you to stay up here, under my protection. I don't want you in a hotel, though; you can move into our spare room for a while.'

'No.' She snapped the word out, with no little discomfort. 'If someone's after me, Bob, I don't want to be anywhere near Sarah or your children.'

'Okay,' he conceded. 'We'll find another solution long-term, but for a couple of days you'll be okay in Gullane. No one will know where you are, other than you and us. That'll give us time to find you a safe house.'

'Bob,' she protested. 'I'm not living like a prisoner. I can't.'

'No, but we can take precautions.'

She smiled and gave in. 'Back to the old days, again.'

'Better than dealing with it after it's happened. You get some sleep, now. Phone your secretary first thing in the morning; I'll be back to pick you up around ten.'

Thirty-one

Dan Pringle opened one eye, experimentally. Exposure to light did not send a shaft of pain shooting through his head, and so he opened the other. 'What time did we get in last night?' he asked, huskily.

'About two thirty.' He turned round, to see his wife standing beside their bed with a mug of tea in her hand. 'Dan,' she said, severely. 'You had better be aware that I am not driving you back from Edinburgh to Galashiels every Friday night in life. We have moved and that's that; get used to it.'

Like many police officers, Dan Pringle enjoyed a drink. He enjoyed also to get away from the job at least once a week, among a group of friends with whom he could discuss sport, sex, current affairs, and even politics, on occasion, but never work. The biggest sacrifice which he had made in revitalising his CID career was in wrenching himself away from his social circle, to move on to his new Borders territory.

'I know, love,' he sighed. 'Last night was a one-off, I promise. It was only our second Friday away; I had to have a fix.'

'Well if you want another,' countered Elma Pringle, 'you can get a patrol car to run you home afterwards.'

Dan pulled himself up in bed. 'Oh no; I can't do that. Jim

Elder was bad enough about CID using Pandas as taxis, but this new ACC Ops, Chase, he'd have my guts. There's a story about, that Willie Michaels got a car to take him back to Broxburn after a Masonic dinner in Edinburgh, and when Chase found out about it, he sent him a bill for the equivalent taxi fare.

'The Ops Room Superintendent was telling me that he has his lackey, Jack Good, spot-check the logged patrol movements every day, looking for that very thing.'

'Why should you call Inspector Good a lackey? I've never heard you speak like that about DI McIlhenney, and he does the same job for Mr Skinner. Or about Jack McGurk, for that matter.'

'Does he hell as like. Jack Good's a tea boy in uniform. Big Neil's a first-class detective doing a valuable CID liaison job, and he's a hard man, to boot. Good's next job will be to draw his pension; Neil's will be on up the ladder, either to Special Branch or deputy divisional commander. I'd have him down here, I'll tell you.

'As for Jack McGurk, he's a good lad too. I trust Jack; I like him close to me.'

'That's good,' Elma remarked. 'Because he's downstairs.'

'He's what?! For Christ's sake, why didn't you tell me?'

'I just did. Anyway, didn't you hear the doorbell?'

'I heard fuck all,' Dan moaned, climbing out of bed and stumbling into the en-suite shower room. 'Give him a coffee and tell him I'll be down in ten minutes. What time is it?'

'Ten to ten.'

'Jesus! I'll bet I'm the only copper has his Saturday morning disrupted.'

'Better than you disrupting mine with your bloody snoring. I'll tell him, but you hurry up.'

Jack McGurk had just finished the *Scotsman* Saturday sports section when his boss appeared in his living room, unshaven, but showered and dressed in jeans and a crew-necked sweater.

'What the hell brings you here?' The superintendent growled his greeting.

'Fish,' the sergeant growled back.

Pringle seemed to stop in mid-stride. 'Never! You mean we've found it.'

'No, sir,' McGurk replied. 'I mean we've lost another few tons.'

There were times when the young detective regretted being six feet four; it meant that there was more of him to be glared at. 'Jesus Christ,' Pringle barked, 'how the fuck did we manage that?'

'I don't know yet, sir.'

'Where was it?'

'Howdengate Trout Farm; that's the one just outside Jedburgh. I've called DI Dorward's forensic team down; the owner and the manager should be waiting for us when we get there.'

'Aye, okay,' the superintendent muttered, resigned to the loss of his Saturday, but thankful that he had declined the last whisky on offer the night before. 'Let me run my shaver over my chin and we'll be on our way. You're driving, son.'

Thirty-two

'Are you sure he'll be here?' asked Andy Martin.

Skinner nodded. 'It's a clear morning, there was no reply when I called the house and his mobile's switched off. There's nowhere else he'll be.' He pointed across the playing fields. 'Look. There he is.'

Across three practice rugby fields in the training area behind Murrayfield Stadium, half a dozen mini-pitches had been laid out. Neil McIlhenney, bulky in a North Face fleece, stood on the touchline of the third. Walking towards him, Skinner and Martin saw him tense as a small figure in white shorts and a red bib took a pass from the player inside, and accelerated effortlessly towards the line leaving his immediate opponent floundering in his wake.

As he touched the ball down, McIlhenney punched the air with his right hand. By his side, a rangy, dark-haired girl jumped up and down, clapping. Then she caught sight of the two newcomers and tugged at her father's shoulder.

'Lovely turn of speed, Neil,' said Martin. 'He's got the gift as he runs, of making his marker think he's got a chance and getting him to commit himself far too early. You just can't teach that; if his basic speed grows with him, and he keeps that knack, I'd say he could be a bit special.'

McIlhenney nodded, not trying to disguise his pride. 'That's what the coaches here say, too.'

Martin glanced at the two adults on the field, who were rounding up their sides, now that the final whistle had gone. 'I know these guys; I played with them, and against them. They're top class.'

'So were you, pal,' Skinner murmured. 'You gave up the game far too soon.'

'I know,' his friend conceded. 'But there's no point in dwelling on it. On the other hand, I played ten years too soon; if I had carried on, and suppose I had done all the things they said I was capable of – caps, British Lions, all that stuff – where would I be now? Retired and sitting in the stands watching guys who couldn't have laced my boots making silly money for playing the game while I did it for love and travel expenses.'

'Now you, pal,' he said as Spencer McIlhenney ran towards them, 'with a fair wind, a run of luck, and given that you get to be the size of your old man, you've got a future.'

'Hello Mr Skinner,' the boy called out. 'Did you come to watch me?'

'Spence!' Lauren chided her brother. 'Don't be silly.'

'Ah but I did . . . and to talk to your dad.'

McIlhenney ruffled his son's hair. 'Go and get changed, and have your Bovril. I'll see you back at the car.' As the youngster ran off he handed the keys to Lauren. 'Go on ahead of us, honey, while I talk to Mr Skinner and Mr Martin.'

As she took them from him and turned to leave them, Bob watched her. Tall for her age, almost ready to burst into womanhood, she was a younger version of her mother, so much so that he wondered whether, on occasion, it broke Neil's heart just to look at her.

'I'm a lucky man, eh?' said the inspector. 'What a legacy. Now, what dug you two from the bosoms of your respective families? You didn't just come to see mine.'

'No,' the DCC admitted. 'It has to do with Lou. After you dropped her off last night, she had a mishap.' He outlined what had happened in Louise Bankier's suite, and was struck by the mix of horror and anxiety which crossed the face of his exec.

'Who the hell would do a thing like that to the woman?' he exclaimed.

'I'm betting that it's the same bastard who fired that shotgun in London last Friday night . . . not at me, but at Lou. Do either of you disagree with that assumption?'

'No,' said the Head of CID. 'Someone's stalking her, trying to scare the life out of her. A blank cartridge, then a smoke bomb; nasty stuff.'

'Yes, but who's to say that the next one won't be lethal? We have to assume that it will be, and we have to give her protection. Who she is, the fact that she's a friend of mine, that doesn't come into it. There's a clear threat to her safety and she has to be protected. At the same time, we have to keep it quiet. This sort of craziness can bring all sorts of bugs out of the woodwork; we don't want any copy-catting.

'However, there's a limit to what we can do. Lou has a movie commitment . . . fortunately it's here in Edinburgh, but she won't cancel it.'

'No,' McIlhenney murmured. 'She's not the sort of lady to be frightened into seclusion.'

'Exactly. So we have to help her get on with her life, as safely as we can.'

'We need a safe house then, Boss,' the inspector suggested.

'She won't have it. But I won't have her in a hotel. Nor will she agree to stay at my place; not with the kids there, she says . . . as if I couldn't fortify it, but there it is. So what I plan to do is have her rent a house for her stay here . . . a detached house, not a flat or a semi . . . install certain security devices that she doesn't need to know about, like geophones to detect movement in the garden, and an alarm system linked to the nearest nick, or somewhere suitable. Then I'm going to persuade her to bring her secretary up here, for company as much as anything else.

'On top of all that, I want to give her a minder; someone to watch over her, to make sure she gets to work safely, then home at night, to take her shopping if she wants to go, to keep an eye on her if she wants to go out for a meal.'

'Got anyone in mind?' McIlhenney asked, casually.

'Yes. You; but it's not an order.'

'It doesn't need to be; of course I'll do it.' He frowned. 'There is just one problem, though.'

'I know,' said Skinner, 'and I've anticipated it. If there is an emergency, you can't just run off and leave Lauren and Spence. So . . .

'That girl you have as a part-time help. D'you think she'd work for you on a live-in basis for the duration of this job? Don't worry about the added cost; I can take care of that.'

'I'll have to ask her, Boss, but I'm sure she will.' Neil paused. 'But what about Sammy Pye? He's single.'

164

'Maybe, but he's too young. Whoever does this job has to be someone with whom Lou can feel comfortable, and safe. She knows you, plus she likes you; I could tell that last night over dinner. Besides, Sammy's full of Ruth McConnell at the moment, and Ruthie has her own problems, with her uncle's death and its aftermath.'

He looked from one friend to the other. 'So that's it sorted then. Neil, you'll look after her. Andy, you'll catch the bastard who's after her.'

Thirty-three

The approach to Howdengate Trout Farm was the opposite of that to Mellerkirk. It ran along a tight, steep-sided valley, through which a river ran; Pringle was in no mood for a walk, so McGurk drove his Astra along the rough forest track, looking ahead carefully for boulders.

They drove through woods for over a mile until they came suddenly to an end, and the unmade road opened out into a flat field with hills rising on either side. In the middle distance, they saw a number of buildings close to the river, and next to several large rectangular tanks half-buried in the ground.

'Looks bigger than the other one,' the superintendent observed.

'It is, sir, if the size of the loss is anything to go by. When I spoke to the manager he estimated the stock nicked at four tons.'

'What's his name?'

'Arthur Symonds,' McGurk replied. 'He'll be waiting for us, with the owner. His name's Glenn Lander; like Sir Adrian Watson, he owns the estate on which the farm stands. Trout's an extension of his business.'

The sergeant drew to a halt beside half a dozen cars which

were parked beside the first building. As the detectives climbed out two men walked towards them. They were both in their twenties. One was very tall, taller even than McGurk by a few inches, but more heavily built, with fair hair; the other was stocky, with a ruddy complexion and very wide shoulders. In build, he reminded Pringle of Andy Martin; as he approached with hand outstretched, he imagined him, too, in the back row of the scrum. Looking at the other man, he guessed that he might pack down immediately in front.

'Mr Pringle? I'm Glenn Lander. And this is my manager, Arthur Symonds.'

'Morning.' The policeman shook the landowner's hand, and nodded sideways. 'This is DS McGurk.'

He was pleasantly surprised by the contrast between Lander and Sir Adrian Watson, but he saw no reason to show it. 'Well, gentlemen,' he barked. 'Have you two been living on another planet? I mean after what happened last weekend, how the hell could you manage to lose another farmful of fresh fucking fish?'

Arthur Symonds blushed bright red. 'It was my fault, I'm afraid.'

'I'd have done the same thing, Art,' said Lander, at once. 'Don't blame yourself, because I won't.'

'So what did happen? You guys were warned, weren't you, to keep the farm guarded overnight.'

'Aye, we were,' the giant agreed. 'And I was here; only I had a phone call just before midnight. From the police in Hawick, or so they said. They told me that my father had been hit by a car on his way home from the pub and that he was critical. They told me that they were taking him to the Borders General, but that it was touch and go whether or not he made it.

'I never thought, or doubted it for a second. I just jumped in the Land Rover and bombed out of here. When I got to the hospital they didn't know what the fuck I was talking about. Eventually I worked out what might have happened and called Glenn.'

'You never thought to call home before you went tearing off?'

'My dad lives alone, Mr Pringle. He's in the pub every Friday night, and every Friday night he's the worse for drink . . . no' just Fridays, either. I just took it at face value.'

'So how long would it have been before you realised you'd been set up?'

Symonds knotted his eyebrows. 'I never thought to check my watch, but given the time it took me to get up to Gala, then the time I spent farting about the place trying to find my old man, it would have been over an hour, anyway.'

The superintendent looked at the young estate owner. 'And you, Mr Lander? How did you react when Mr Symonds called you?'

'Apart from calling him a dim-witted fucking second-rower, you mean, then having to apologise to my girlfriend for my language? After what happened to Mellerkirk last weekend, I jumped straight out of bed and drove to the farm. I was here inside ten minutes.'

'Didn't you ever stop to wonder what you'd have done if you'd driven right into the middle of them?'

'No, but I'd a shotgun in my jeep.'

Pringle ran a hand over his eyes. 'I never heard that, son,' he murmured.

'So what did you find?' he continued.

'An empty farm, basically. There was nothing here but a lot of tyre tracks, a few fish left swimming in the tanks, and a few dead ones, on the ground and floating on the surface.'

'Did you pass any large vehicles heading in the opposite direction as you were driving here?'

'I didn't pass anything, Mr Pringle. I hit a deer on the road but that was all I saw.'

'How many people do you employ here, sir?'

'Two, in addition to Art. Then we have a vet who looks in regularly to check on the stock.'

'We'll want to speak to all of them.'

Glenn Lander reached into a pocket. 'I guessed as much,' he said, pulling out a single sheet of paper. 'There are their names and addresses.' He made to hand it to Pringle, but Jack McGurk took it from him.

'Do you have doubts about any of them?' asked the sergeant.

'No. I've known the two workers since I was a kid, and Mr Gibb, the vet, has looked after the estate since God was a boy.'

'We'll talk to them, nonetheless,' said Pringle. 'Who are your insurers? I assume you are covered.'

'Royal Sun Alliance.'

'Mmm. Mellerkirk's with CGU.'

Lander laughed. 'Just as well. One company might not have fancied two claims in a week.'

The bluff superintendent snorted. 'I think you'll find that the big commercial insurers all compare notes. You'd better budget for double the premium next year. Unless . . .' he barked, suddenly, 'you finally take police advice and install decent security.'

'It'd still have to be cost-effective, Mr Pringle.'

'We can arrange that, by advising the companies to adjust their premiums accordingly. They take police advice as well, you know, and I'll make damn sure they get it. I don't like being hauled out on a Saturday because you boys are too tight to pay for proper alarms and surveillance equipment.'

The landowner shrugged his wide shoulders. 'Do that if you must. Now can Art and I go? We've got a game up at Raeburn Place this afternoon; Edinburgh Accies Seconds.'

'Don't let us keep you, then,' the superintendent muttered. 'But don't let the opposition sell the Big Yin here any dummies. He's bought one already this weekend.'

Lander laughed, and the two turned to leave, Symonds wearing a wounded look on his lofty face.

The detectives watched them as they drove off, then walked across to one of the men who were left on the site. He was wearing a white tunic with black wellingtons, and he had red hair. 'Morning Arthur,' Pringle called out. 'Solved the crime yet?'

Detective Inspector Dorward, head of the forensics unit, turned and scowled at him as he stepped out of a taped-off area. 'You wish, sir,' he said, sourly. 'I got no fingerprints off any dead fish last week, and I don't suppose these'll be any different.'

'Can you tell us anything?'

'Oh, yes. I can always tell you something. Last week I told you that there were four people involved in the raid, going by the footprints that were left around. They were all wearing wellies; we established from the casts we took that three sets were cheap own-brand jobs, bought almost certainly from Milletts, but the fourth was a more expensive brand whose stockists include Dickson and Tiso, both of Edinburgh, and various other country-wear specialists.

'Judging by what I've seen so far, I'd say that the same people did this, and going by the tyre tracks, I'd say that they used the same two vehicles.'

'Two?'

'Oh yes, sir. That volume of fish, and water, takes some shifting.'

'Is there any chance of you being able to follow the vehicles to their destination by following the mud on their tracks?' asked Jack McGurk.

Dorward eyed the tall sergeant up and down, then looked at Pringle, as if over the top of imaginary spectacles.

'Who is this, Dan?' he murmured. 'Your faithful Redskin companion?'

He turned back to McGurk. 'If you look up,' he said, 'you will see dark clouds; you should see them okay, since you're a lot closer to them than I am. It's going to rain, any minute now, and the forecast is that it will spread to all parts by mid-afternoon. On top of that, the track through those woods leads to a minor road which leads very shortly thereafter to a trunk road, which in turn has had traffic pounding up and down it all night.

'I can take a sample of mud here, and if you find these vehicles I'll probably be able to prove for you that they were here. That's bloody clever as it is, lad; I draw the line at the impossible.'

The red-haired inspector turned, and went back to his white-coated team. Pringle grinned up at his aide. 'Nice one, Tonto,' he chuckled. 'Now here's what you will do. Everyone's come up kosher at Mellerkirk so far, but the possibility remains that it was an inside job. If this was an inside job as well, then with the same thieves involved there is a chance that it's a conspiracy.

'So I want you to have our people check into all the staff at the two farms, to see if there's any connection between any of them. But if it's anyone, I fancy the managers. Gates just happened to be off watch last weekend and Symonds says he had what turned out to be a hoax phone call.'

'But we can verify that he had a call, sir.'

'Can you verify that he wasn't expecting it? I tell you, Jack, the team that's doing it either has inside info, or it's done its homework bloody well, to know about Symonds' father being a piss artist. The lad Gates and big Lurch, there; I want them watched.'

'I'll get people on to it, sir.'

The superintendent scowled again, and tugged at his moustache. 'One thing does seem bloody clear, though, Sergeant. These people must have an outlet, somewhere. They stole three tons last weekend; now another four. There's no way they're going to stockpile seven tons of frozen trout.

'They've found a buyer for the first lot already; it's the only explanation. And if they can shift this lot quickly as well . . .'

'They'll be on the lookout for more.'

'Exactly, son. So it's up to us to be waiting for them if they do. And if there is someone on the inside, that could be bloody difficult.'

Thirty-four

'Can you really do all that for me?' Louise Bankier asked. The remnants of lunch lay scattered around her; Seonaid was gnawing happily on a rattle in her high chair, abandoned by her brothers who were watching cartoons in their playroom.

'Not just for you,' Bob Skinner assured her. 'I'd do it for anyone in your situation. Not that I've ever had anyone in your situation before . . . it's a bit unusual, in Scotland . . . but my colleagues down south have. As a matter of fact, protection from stalkers was on the agenda at my London conference. It's been decided to treat it as a form of terrorism; which is exactly what it is.'

'What about your secretary?' Sarah interposed. 'Can you bring her up here?'

Louise nodded. 'Yes. I'd have done that anyway, for the duration of the Edinburgh filming. Glenys always goes on the payroll when I'm working on a movie; name on the end titles and everything, after the dress designer but before the hairdresser.'

'She's single then?'

'She has a boyfriend, but I'll fly him up at weekends, so don't miss each other.'

nly after he's been thoroughly vetted,' said Bob.

'But I know him! He's been to my house.'

'Fine, but he doesn't get in again without being quietly checked out. Sorry to lapse into police-speak, but in nine crimes against the person out of ten, the victim knows the attacker.' He read her expression. 'Don't worry, Lou. I say vetted, but he won't feel a thing, I promise . . . unless he's our man, in which case he'll feel plenty.'

'The man in the car in London,' she said. 'I know you didn't see his face, but did you notice anything about him? Skin tone, for example.'

'Yes, he was white, I saw his hand.'

'It wasn't Clarence, then. He's black, and very dark-skinned.'

'Then that's a relief, but I'm still not making any exceptions to security procedures. Please, Lou, forget about that side of it; that's our business, and my people are good at it.'

He poured her more coffee. 'Are you happy with Neil as your minder?'

'Very happy. I like him, and he strikes me as formidable too. I'm sure I'll feel safe with him around. But can you spare him from your office?'

'I have a very good secretary, just like you. She can cope for a while. Anyway,' he added, 'it won't be for long. I intend to catch this bastard, double quick, and lock him up.'

'Let's hope you do.' She glanced out of the window, towards the sea; it looked grey and cold. The threatened rain had made its way up from the Borders, and was falling hard. 'I don't like this feeling of being constrained. I've never suffered from claustrophobia before, but that's what this feels like.

'I'm just like everyone else; I like mixing with people, and I know that not being able to will do my head in.'

'It needn't be as bad as that. With Neil around you can go out.'

She looked at him. 'I really should too, shouldn't I?' she suggested. 'You won't catch this man unless he shows himself again, will you?'

'Maybe we will.'

'But it's unlikely, isn't it? Yes, of course it is. But how will you draw him out if you've got me holed up in a house somewhere?'

'Honest to God, even if I was ruthless enough to use you as bait, I don't think I'd need to. This man followed you to Soho with me. He followed you to Edinburgh, and he found your room number in the Balmoral. He'll find out where you're living all right. Maybe, if we're lucky, just trying to will get him caught, but I doubt it. Sometimes people like this are dumber than you think, but it always pays to assume that they're intelligent.'

'He must be to have got into my hotel room.'

'Not really,' said Bob. 'What did you do with your key when you were out here last night? You don't need to tell me; you walked over to me at reception, left it there, and then we headed off in my car. You're our stalker, you distract the receptionist for ten seconds and you're in there.'

'But how do you put the key back, Uncle Bob?'

A small voice came from beside the fridge. Skinner looked over his shoulder in surprise and saw Mark, standing behind him, with a Seven-Up in each hand. 'You don't, son. It's a card key, you see. So all you do is go down to the foyer again, wait till the receptionist's back is turned, and chuck it on the floor, behind the desk.'

He grinned at his adopted son, reaching out a hand to ruffle his hair. 'Clever little so-and-so, though, aren't you? I'll make you either a master criminal or an ace detective when you grow up. Which'll it be?'

'Detective,' Mark replied at once. 'Better security and long-term prospects.'

The three adults laughed as he headed back to the playroom. 'You think he's kidding?' Bob joked. 'He'll have worked that out. Mark's always had a phenomenal memory; now he's developing the mental power to back it up.

'What he's actually going to be is a mathematician, and probably before he grows up at that.' He rapped the table top. 'But back to our discussion. See how Mark wandered in here without us noticing him?

'That's how easily the stalker could have got into your room.'

'God,' Louise murmured. 'What advantages do we have?'

'Privacy, for the moment. You're out of the spotlight for now, in that nobody knows where you are. Possibly one other edge also. If this man's from out of town, and let's assume he is, there's just a chance that he doesn't know who and what I am.'

That illusion lasted for five minutes longer, until the phone rang. 'I've found a house, boss,' Neil McIlhenney announced. 'I checked the "to let" section in the ESPC office after we all split up. There was a place listed in Craiglockhart Avenue, a detached bungalow; rang the viewing number and had a look. It's newly refurbished, new kitchen and stuff, very well furnished, with a nice big open garden that you couldn't hide a mouse in. To cap it all, it's just a couple of minutes' walk from my place.

'Couldn't be better. We can show it to Lou tomorrow afternoon, if you like. Keith Stanley's the letting solicitor; we know him, so he shouldn't be hard to deal with.'

Skinner smiled at his exec.'s pleasure over a job well done. 'Yeah, we'll do that. You make the arrangements and tell us where and when. We'll meet you there.'

'Fine,' said McIlhenney. 'There's one more thing.

'I just had a call from Alan Royston, the press officer. He was a bit leery about phoning you, but there's a piece in the News today, in their gossip column. It talks about Lou being seen leaving the Balmoral last night, and here I quote, "looking starstruck herself, on the arm of a very senior Edinburgh policeman."

'Royston's already had the News of the Screws, the Sunday Mail, the People and the Sunday Herald on the blower. He wants to know how he should play it.'

'Shit!' Skinner snapped, drawing startled looks from the two women. 'Tell him to play it straight, Neil; the plain truth, that we're old friends from way back and that I was taking Lou to dinner with family and friends. Tell him also to make it clear what will happen if anyone as much as suggests anything different.

'Thanks mate. See you tomorrow.'

'What was that?' Sarah asked.

'If our man was in any doubt about who I am, he knows now, courtesy of our well-meaning and very well-informed local evening newspaper.'

Thirty-five

'Are you sure I'm on overtime for this, Dave?' Gwendoline Dell looked at the detective inspector doubtfully.

'Don't worry about that, Gwennie,' he told her, in a tone of voice which made her worry even more. 'I'll square it with the DCI on Monday. Anyway, look at me; I'm missing out on the joys of an afternoon in the St Enoch Centre with the wife and weans.'

'No wonder they call you Bandit,' she muttered, looking out of the car at the bungalow, and at the rain, which was lashing down. 'Okay, I'm here; now will you tell me why?'

Mackenzie nodded. 'Ach Gwennie, it's just . . . well I've always fancied you, and here's an empty house . . .'

Her mouth fell open in astonishment; she glared at him with instant fury . . . until she saw the laughter in his eyes.

'If you didn't sign my fitness reports . . .' she exclaimed. 'Listen, cut the crap. What are we here for?'

'It's that bag that the old dear told you about. I've been wondering about it. Bigger than a handbag, she said; big enough to make her think that Ruth had come for the weekend. I've been wondering what was in it, and why, if it was that bulky, and she wasn't staying for the weekend, she bothered to bring it into the house . . . unless there was something in it she needed.' He smiled at her again.

'The obvious answer is that there was something in it she needed.'

'Drugs,' Dell suggested.

'She could have got a whole fucking pharmacy in there. Even if we're right and she was feeding the old man's habit, she could have carried the temazepam, and the works in her pocket. No, there was something else in that bag.'

All joking over, he looked at the sergeant. 'I've been trying to think like Skinner,' he told her.

'He impressed you that much?'

He nodded, emphatically. 'That much. Just talking to him changed my outlook on a lot of things. We were trained to look for the obvious first and foremost; so was he, but once he sees it he questions it. He told me that when he was in the field he'd turn up at a crime scene and ask himself a few simple questions. What type of crime was this? Was it opportunistic or was it premeditated? Was it driven by anger or financial gain? Was it a stupid crime, or was it well planned?

'I've been asking myself all those questions, and I find myself looking at something that was clearly premeditated, money-driven and very well planned. A very intelligent crime, so fucking intelligent that we're not even sure if it's been committed or not. Is this murder? Is it extortion? Is it both? Or did the old boy give this woman all his money just because he liked her? Did he just run his bath too hot, take a heart attack from the shock, and drown in it?

'We don't bloody know, do we? Now that Ruth McConnell's

been taken out of the frame and our faith in the obvious has been destroyed, we know hardly anything.'

'Agreed,' said DS Dell. 'So what would your new hero Skinner do in our shoes?'

'That's what I've been asking myself. And then I remembered something he said, when we were at the golf club. He said he'd look at the whole scene in a mirror.'

'What did he mean by that?'

'Well, so far we've been concentrating on what's missing from the house. Now we know, but it's taken us nowhere. But instead of that, what if there's something in the house that shouldn't be?'

'Such as?'

'Maybe we'll know when we find it. Maybe we won't, but let's just have a look round with that objective in mind, and maybe we'll find something that will give us a clue about what was in that big bag the woman was carrying.'

'Is that likely?' Dell asked, doubtful once more. 'We know that the old man was injected within a short time of his death. It'd be reasonable to assume that the woman did it, but she was very careful to remove the syringe from the house.'

'Exactly!' exclaimed Mackenzie. 'And as big Bob Skinner pointed out when we had our chat, that was a major mistake. Like he said, she should have chucked the thing in the bath. We'd just have assumed that the old chap had shot himself up. The woman could have been the Avon lady going to the wrong address.'

'How d'you know about the Avon lady?' she shot back at him.

'My mother told me.' He opened the car door and stepped out into the rain. 'Come on, let's get on with it.'

The sergeant followed him up the path, with the collar of her heavy coat turned up to protect her hair against the rain as much as possible, then waited as he fumbled with the keys. Finally, he swung the door open.

The house was cold, with an unpleasant musty reek clinging to it. Dell shivered. 'I don't like this place,' she said.

'Eh? D'you think it's haunted?'

'In a way. I believe that evil clings to places and takes a long time to go away, and I feel that something evil happened here.'

He gave her a look that was a mix of scorn and cynicism. 'That'll sound good in the witness box. Let's find some evidence; in my experience that works better with juries. I'll take the bathroom and bedrooms, you take the kitchen.'

'Okay. But what am I looking for?'

'Look at, not for. Look at everything, and ask what it's doing there. If there's no good answer . . .'

She did as he instructed and went into the kitchen. She looked around; it was neat and tidy, with neither utensils, cups nor saucers scattered around. She began by opening the high fitted cupboards on the wall facing the door. One contained only food, in tins and packets; the other was full of crockery and glassware.

She went from cupboard to cupboard, drawer to drawer, but saw nothing in any of them that would have been out of place in any kitchen. Finally she glanced along the work surfaces. 'Toaster, microwave, blender,' she said, absently, coming to a rack on the wall, and flicking through its contents. 'Bills, bookmark, empty cassette box, postcard . . .' She took it out and looked at it. '. . . from Ruth. "Love from Corfu." Nice thought on a day like this.'

She left the kitchen and walked across the hall, into the living room. It was just as neat; two chairs were placed on either side of the gas fire, so that both looked at the television set in the corner. Redundant fire irons stood in the hearth, a brass knight in armour with poker, tongs, shovel and brush as weapons. Alongside a rack held newspapers and magazines. She looked around as Ruth had done; virtually the only other items left were the old man's hi-fi equipment and his small collection of vinyl records and CDs, all of it gathered together in a purpose-made unit. The system looked impressive, if not new. It was made up of carefully chosen separates, like her own, all except the turntable from the Mission Cyrus range. She peered at it. 'Amplifier, power amp, CD player, tuner, Systemdek turntable.'

She paused, and her eyes narrowed slightly. She bent and looked at the recordings, lined on their shelves. Twelve-inch LPs and compact discs. Straightening up she went back through to the kitchen and took the cassette box, empty of tape or label, from the rack.

'Dave?' she called, stepping back into the hall. 'Have you come across a tape player through there?'

The inspector emerged from the front bedroom. 'No. Why?'

She held up the box. 'He didn't have a deck in his system either. I was just wondering what this was doing here. It was in the rack in the kitchen, but Ruth could have put it there. I think she must have tidied up, after you left her here the other day.'

He took it from her and looked at it. 'Maybe. We'll take it anyway. It doesn't look as if it's been dusted, so we can always see if we can lift a print off it, other than Ruth's, the old man's and ours.

'I don't know what it'll tell us though.' His wicked smile flashed back. 'Here, maybe she had a karaoke machine in that box. Maybe the old fella was hooked on that as well!'

Thirty-six

When a man is six feet four inches tall and is brought up in Edinburgh, there has always been a fair chance that at some time in his youth, someone will persuade him to pack down in the back row of a scrum. (Today, when a woman is six feet four inches tall, that fair chance becomes a certainty.)

In Jack McGurk's case, most of his classmates in his year at the Royal High School had been vertically disadvantaged, and so, in his penultimate year, he had been pitched into the second row of the scrum and the middle of the line-out.

He had done well in schools rugby, not because of any inborn technical skills, but because his natural aptitude for violence in close-quarter situations, particularly those on the blind side of the referee, had quickly earned him a reputation which had made most opponents back off.

Unfortunately he had carried this trait with him into senior rugby; his career had come to an end before his nineteenth birthday, two seconds after he had squeezed the testicles of a twenty-six-year-old policeman, and one-time Scotland B flanker, named Andrew Martin, in the middle of a ruck.

A trip to Casualty, a bad case of concussion, and four lost

teeth had been all that it had taken to make him realise that the game at that level was something entirely different, and that he wanted no part of it.

McGurk was fairly certain that ten years on there was little chance of the Head of CID, even if he remembered the incident . . . and it had been a fairly powerful squeeze . . . identifying him as the culprit. As it happened he was wrong, but Martin was not a man to bear a grudge, particularly since the referee, having seen the provocation, had been blind to the retaliation.

The detective sergeant's jaw ached as he wandered into Raeburn Place, the traditional home of Edinburgh Academicals Rugby Football Club, the very ground where his brief flirtation with the game had ended. The Second XV was the only side in action that afternoon, pitted against Jedforest Seconds; he had decided to go along to the match out of nothing more than curiosity, to see whether Lander and his manager chum were any good at the game.

The rain was hammering down as he wandered into the ground, under his golf umbrella, and found shelter in the small grandstand. The first half was almost over and, already, Jed were fourteen points down. He could see why at the first line-out, when Arthur Symonds, on his own hooker's throw, had the ball stripped from him easily by a smaller, but more committed opponent.

'Look at that big lad,' a disgruntled Jed supporter moaned, in the general direction of McGurk, as the nearest available listener. 'He looks like a fucking tree stood among all the rest of them, but all he is is the fucking fairy on top!'

Accies' scrum-half used the unexpected good possession

to feed his backs, but the inside centre was tackled in open field by a determined form whom the detective recognised as Glenn Lander. Unfortunately the flanker missed an easy opportunity to turn his man and regain possession. Accies' scrum-half used the resulting ruck to reset his attack, before spinning a long pass directly out to his left wing who crossed the line and ran behind the posts.

'Look at them,' roared the Jed diehard beside McGurk. 'Boys against men . . . and the boys are still stuffing us!'

Had it not been for the incessant heavy rain, which continued all through the match, the policeman would have left at the half-time break. Instead he stayed under his shelter and watched the debacle until the end. A further converted try soon after the restart put the result beyond any doubt, and the home side seemed content to contain their opponents from that point on.

Happily, the referee exercised merciful common sense; with almost twenty minutes left to no-side, he abandoned the meaningless match because of the deteriorating ground conditions. Thirty players, and around the same number of spectators applauded his decision in evident relief, and, as a man, headed directly for the pavilion and the sanctuary of the bar.

The tall detective, who had come to the match by bus, saw the sense of this approach. As he hustled across the pitch, avoiding, like the rest, the most churned-up areas, he saw a man in a waxed cotton coat and matching flat cap walk over to Glenn Lander and speak to him. The young estate owner, his face a mask of mud, turned as if to reply, then caught sight of McGurk.

At first, it was impossible to read his expression beneath the camouflage, until he grinned, said something to the other man and, as he turned towards the exit, headed in the direction of the policeman. 'Did you decide to follow us, Sergeant?' he asked, just as they reached the pavilion. He was still breathing heavily, evidence that at least he had tried until the end.

'Nah! I just got curious, that's all. I haven't been to a club game since I chucked playing myself, so I thought I'd come along to see what you boys were like.'

Lander gave a short breathless laugh; as he folded his umbrella McGurk glanced at him and noticed that blood was seeping from a slight cut beside his right eye, mingling with the mud. 'And what's the verdict?'

'The truth?'

'Plain and unvarnished.'

'You asked for it. You cover a fair bit of ground, but you never seem to put your hands on the ball. As for your big pal Symonds, your fucking trout can jump higher than him. You'd be better off at home looking after them.

'Sorry,' he added.

Lander shook his head. 'Don't be. Our coach is going to say a bloody sight worse when he gets us in that dressing room. I take your point about the fish, really; we should be back at Howdengate trying to sort out re-stocking. But if Art and I had stayed at home at such short notice, the team would have been light. The club could have landed in hot water with the RFU.'

'Unlike your two and a half ton of trout, which by now will be in very cold water . . . frozen in fact.'

McGurk shook the young landowner's hand, then climbed the stairs to the pavilion. Only the smaller of the two bars was open, and the lounge area was crowded. He stood his brolly with the rest, edged up to the bar, secured a pint of lager and turned away, to find Andy and Karen Martin smiling at him.

'The game's much better watched from up here, Jack,' said the DCS. 'I didn't know you were a member.'

'Guest,' the sergeant replied.

'Whose?'

He looked around. 'Yours, probably.'

'That's all right, then. This club needs all the income it can get. This social or professional? I saw you speaking to one of the Jed lads.'

'Social really. Mr Pringle and I saw him this morning; him and that big useless second-rower of theirs. He owns a trout farm, and the big lad's his manager. You'll never guess what happened to them last night.'

Martin's vivid green eyes narrowed. 'You're joking.'

'I wish I was, sir. But when it comes to security, these boys just won't take a telling.'

'Maybe not,' said Martin quietly. 'But you tell Dan Pringle from me that I want an action plan from him at Monday morning's divisional heads meeting. Three strikes, and someone's out.'

He sipped his orange juice, then shot the other man a curious look. 'Funny, Jack, when I saw you there I wondered if you were considering a comeback.'

At that moment the sergeant knew that he knew. 'I won't if you won't, sir,' he answered.

'My days are long gone,' he chuckled. 'Do you reckon I did you a favour, then?'

McGurk switched his pint to his left hand, put two fingers into his mouth and withdrew a dental plate, with four upper molars. 'I didn't think so at the time, sir,' he said, 'but I've still got a few of my own teeth left, so with hindsight I reckon you did.'

Thirty-seven

Bandit Mackenzie slid a plate of four chocolate doughnuts across his desk. 'Get outside a couple of these,' he said.

'One maybe. My diet's working.' Dell picked one up and dunked it in her coffee. 'You're splashing out, aren't you?'

'I thought I should in the circs.'

'What circs?'

He looked at her awkwardly, even a little guiltily. 'Well, it's like this,' he began. 'If we'd got a result this afternoon out of our wee bit of private enterprise, I'd have been able to square your overtime with the DCI, no problem. But I doubt if I'll be able to persuade him that an empty cassette box counts as a result . . . not unless it turns out to have Bible John's DNA on it.'

She laughed, ironically. 'How does your wife put up with you, Dave? You're the slipperiest bastard I know. One of your saving graces is that you're also the most transparent. I never had any illusions about being on double time this afternoon.'

She grabbed a second doughnut and popped it into a brown paper bag which lay on the desk. 'So I'll have this for later.'

He grinned. 'Still beats the St Enoch Centre on a Saturday though, doesn't it?'

'I wouldn't know,' she answered. 'I'm a reasonably affluent single woman. I prefer Princes Square.'

Mackenzie laughed. 'It's just as well I don't fancy you. You're way too pricey for me.'

She wrinkled her nose and flashed her eyes at him. 'Of course you fancy me. But your other saving grace is that you love your wife.'

'You're too fucking sharp by half, girl. You could wind up on point duty somewhere if you're not careful.'

He reached into a side pocket of his jacket for the cassette box. 'Here, stick a label on this, and get it to a technician on Monday.' But the container he laid on the desk held a tape, the recording of his interrogation of Ruth McConnell earlier in the week.

'Shit, wrong pocket.' He reached down to the other side, found the box which they had taken from John McConnell's kitchen, and laid it on the desk beside the other.

'Here, wait a minute . . .' He sat upright, eyes narrowing. 'They're different sizes.'

The sergeant leaned forward, peering at the desk. She took the tape from its box and tried to fit it into the other; it was too wide by a few millimetres.

'Then what the hell is it?' she asked.

'I'll tell you,' Mackenzie said, quietly. 'It's a video eight cassette box. And old John McConnell didn't have a camcorder.

'Gwennie; that big awkward bag your witness saw the woman carry into the house. A pound to a pinch of shit, there was a video camera in it. The bitch was filming him.'

She looked at him in disbelief. 'But why in heaven's name would she want to do that?'

'Heaven's got nothing to do with this.'

He leaned back in his chair once more. 'Yes Sergeant, your overtime is safe with me. The DCI will okay it for sure, when I report this to him. Who knows, he might even okay some for me.'

He smiled. 'I'll report it somewhere else too. I'm looking forward to hearing what Bob Skinner makes of this.'

Thirty-eight

'I suppose I should thank you, McGurk,' Dan Pringle growled into the telephone, 'although it might have occurred to you that it was down to me to break the bad news to the Head of CID that my division's on the way to becoming a laughing stock. I tried to call him this afternoon; I was going to give it another shot tonight.'

'I'm sorry, gaffer, honest. I couldn't have known that DCS Martin would be there, far less that he'd see me talking to Lander from the clubhouse bar. But when he did, I had no bloody choice but to tell him.'

Pringle sighed. 'Aye, I know son. I'm just a bit pissed off, that's all, and you're in line. "Three strikes and someone's out", indeed. Our Andy is not known for his sense of humour either; not when it comes to the job at any rate.

'So we'd better take him at his word and have an action plan in place for Monday.'

The sergeant's heart sagged at the use of the plural. He knew what was coming next.

'Did you have plans for tomorrow?'

'Well, yes, sir.'

'Aye, well so had I. We're both stuffed then. You said there are two other substantial fish farms on our patch, didn't you?'

'That's right. In Berwickshire, just north of Coldstream, and down near Langholm.'

'In that case, I want you to arrange for the owners of them both to meet the two of us on site tomorrow, whether they like it or not. If our weekend's buggered, so's theirs.'

Thirty-nine

When Sammy Pye answered the phone once more in Ruth McConnell's flat, Bob Skinner needed no further confirmation that his secretary's private life had taken a new turn. He smiled; he wondered what the young sergeant would make of her over the long-term.

He was still grinning when she came on the line; then he remembered why he was calling her.

'Ruthie,' he began, 'your pal Mackenzie's out to impress all of a sudden. He's been back to your uncle's house for another look around.'

'I hope he didn't turn it upside down,' she snorted. 'It took me long enough to tidy the place up when he left me there the other day.'

'I'm sure he didn't. He and his sergeant may have found something, though. There's just something he needs to check with you first, and I said I'd do it for him. It's about your Uncle John and his missing possessions.

'Can you tell me whether or not he ever owned a video camcorder, specifically a non-digital model, the sort that takes eight-millimetre cassettes.'

He waited, but only for a few seconds. 'No sir,' she said vehemently. 'I'm quite sure that he didn't. Apart from his music stuff, Uncle John wasn't a man for toys like that. Why, he didn't even have a video recorder, far less a camera.'

'You're absolutely sure of that, are you? Couldn't he maybe have bought a camera in the last few months of his life, one that you didn't know about?'

'Absolutely not, sir. He wouldn't have done that, and there was a good reason why not. I offered to buy him one for Christmas, a few years back. He told me not to. He said that one of the great regrets of his life was that he didn't have any cine film, or video, of Aunt Cecily, not a scrap.

'She had wanted him to buy a camcorder, but he had always refused. He said he thought the things were intrusive; they annoyed him whenever he saw them in holiday resorts and there was no way he wanted to be taken for a German.

'Then my aunt died and he realised what he had denied himself. But after refusing her one, he just couldn't contemplate buying one for himself, or letting me, either.

'No sir. No way.'

'Okay,' he said. 'Possibility discounted. That gives Inspector Mackenzie something to go on. Thanks.' He was about to hang up, but added. 'By the way, whose turn is it for the dishes tonight?'

He left her laughing, then called Bandit Mackenzie on his mobile number. 'Your box means something, Inspector,' he told him. 'Ruthie's dead certain that her uncle never owned a camera.'

'What does it mean though, sir?'

'I hate to think. I saw a home movie earlier this year and I never wanted to see its like again. I only hope . . .'

'Any advice?'

There was a silence. 'Think for yourself, Bandit,' Skinner said, finally.

'Why would she do it? We'll need to find her to learn that, I suppose.'

'Maybe.'

'Has she done it before?'

'Now you're cooking. So?'

'So I'll run a check through the central criminal intelligence unit for other suspicious deaths involving single old people with drug problems.'

'Why just old people?'

'That makes it difficult.'

'Who said it was going to be easy? You do that, I'll have a look in my hat; see if I can find another rabbit.'

Forty

The big, dark-haired solicitor looked merely nonplussed when the very recognisable figure of the Deputy Chief Constable stepped into the living room of the house just off Craiglockhart Avenue. When Louise Bankier followed him a few moments later, his expression turned to one of pure bewilderment.

He looked at Neil McIlhenney. 'I'm sorry, Mr Stanley,' said the big detective, answering his unspoken accusation. 'I had to be a wee bit circumspect when you showed me round yesterday.' He glanced at Skinner. 'All I told Mr Stanley was that we were looking for discreet accommodation for a VIP visitor to Edinburgh. I kept Miss Bankier's name out of it, just in case nothing came of it.'

'Naturally,' the DCC continued, picking up the explanation. 'If you read the *Evening News* yesterday, and a few other papers today, you may have seen a reference to Ms Bankier being in town. These stories are, to say the least, unwelcome.'

Keith Stanley had recovered his composure. 'I can imagine,' he exclaimed.

Skinner thought he caught an assumption behind his remark. 'I'll tell you, Keith, what I told the media. Ms Bankier

and I are old friends. She's also a public figure who is going
to be working in Edinburgh for a while and wishes to maintain
a semblance of a private life, rather than be incarcerated in
an hotel. She's asked me as a friend if I would help her find
somewhere suitable.

'You might think that this house, comfortable as it is,
seems a little modest for one of the world's leading film actors.
If you did, you'd be right; that's exactly why we're here. There's
an estate for rent out beside Dalmahoy. Louise could move
in there but it would be like running up a flag; it would be
just the sort of place where the press would expect to find
her.

'This, on the other hand, is an ordinary house in an
ordinary suburb . . . just like Ms Bankier's family home near
Glasgow, in fact . . . where people mind their own business
and do not observe their neighbours' coming and going. I
can't think of anywhere in Edinburgh where someone would
be less likely to pick up the phone and tip off the tabloids that
she was here.

'To back that up, of course, if you rent this house to Ms
Bankier, we will expect your client and your firm to be bound
by the normal rules of confidentiality.'

'Of course,' the solicitor exclaimed, 'but even at that, Ms
Bankier's a very famous lady and, as we all know, this is a
surprisingly small town.'

'Sure,' agreed Skinner, 'but if, through no one's fault, it
does leak and the paparazzi turn up here, they'll stand out
like a sore thumb, and they'll be moved on, like any other
loiterers.

'Now, would you like to show Louise around?'

Keith Stanley nodded. 'Of course.' He looked at the woman. 'Well,' he began, with a smile, 'this is the living room . . .'

Skinner and McIlhenney remained behind as agent and potential tenant left the room. 'There you are,' the DCC muttered. 'The word "stalker" was never mentioned.'

'You don't think we should tell him?'

'Big Keith's a professional; if he asks, I'll tell him. If not, that's his judgement.

'This was a good spot though, Neil. Nice house, and like you said, a piece of piss to protect. The film production company will pay a premium rent and a good security deposit. If Lou likes it, once we've gone, you talk to Keith about the things we need to do for security. Don't go into too much detail, but you can tell him that we want to install automatic openers to the driveway gate and garage door.

'The garage is attached to the house, with a steel connecting door, so that way you can drive straight in and Lou can go in without ever being in the open air. Tell Keith that we'll leave the auto openers for his clients when the lease expires, as an added sweetener . . . not that he'll need it; I saw the glint of money in his eye.

'Let's get everything done as quickly as we can; I want Lou in here by Tuesday.'

Forty-one

Looking across the table, Maggie Rose thought that Dan Pringle looked a little flustered. That struck her as unusual; she had seen Pringle happy, sad, angry and hung-over, but never flustered. She wondered whether, after all, the country air was proving too fresh for her veteran colleague, and whether sooner rather than later Andy Martin might suggest moving her to the Borders and him back to Edinburgh.

Then it came Pringle's turn to report and she understood. 'Another fish hijacking, Dan?' Willie Michaels exclaimed, only to have the smile wiped from his lips by a single glower.

'You can bloody laugh,' came the growl. 'I've seen the figures on pilferage of electrical goods from the factories in your area.'

'So have I,' said the Head of CID from the head of the table. 'Don't worry; that's next on the agenda. Carry on, Dan.'

Pringle shot another arrow-like glance at his West Lothian colleague. 'Very good, sir,' he said. 'Like I said last week, the danger has existed for a while. There's a cavalier attitude among some of these fish farmers; they think that insuring against theft is the only precaution worth taking.

'The first thing I want to do, sir . . . and here I'd welcome your involvement . . . is to speak to the major insurers and draw their attention to what's happened. I want them all to review their cover for these farms, at once, wherever they are, and to put the wind up the operators with big premium increases for those who don't follow police security advice.'

'I'll do that, Dan,' Martin agreed, 'and going by past experience, they'll agree to that suggestion. The only problem is that it'll take them upwards of a week to agree and longer than that to implement.'

'We've had two thefts in a week. What can we do in the short term to prevent another?'

Pringle's heavy eyebrows came together as he tugged at a corner of his moustache. 'The best we can, sir, given our manpower resources.'

'Given the cost of this scale of operation, I reckon that there are two other Borders trout farms that are worth doing.'

'What are the costs, Dan?' asked Maggie Rose.

'Two vehicles, four guys, somewhere to kill it quick and freeze it quicker.'

'And the take?'

'That's the thing, Mags. The estimate is that a total of seven tons has been stolen; that's about sixteen thousand pounds of trout. I'm told that if you sell it fresh to the big stores, depending on the market you might get one fifty a pound for it. Frozen you'll get less.

'If you process it, either smoke it or turn it into pâté, you'll get more, but these boys are unlikely to have done that. So even if they've managed to find a gullible market that would take it all fresh, their top take will have been twenty-four grand.

'Knock off expenses and split it four ways, and it's no' a hell of a lot to risk the jail for. So I'm expecting another theft, somewhere; maybe not on my patch, but somewhere.'

'Okay,' said Martin, 'we'll alert every farm in Britain, and we'll use the information to stir up the insurers as well. But what about the two other farms on your patch?'

'McGurk and I visited them yesterday,' replied Pringle. 'There's Langholm Rainbow Farm, and Country Fresh Trout, near Coldstream. Langholm's the biggest of the lot, but anyone that does it is asking for it; the owner, a man called Stephenson, has high-definition video cameras on high poles, and he floodlights the place at night. Plus the site's surrounded by an alarmed fence.

'He smokes or processes most of his fish on site, so he's at the top end of profitability. He assured us that he's never compromised with security.

'The other one, Country Fresh, is run by a woman. Her name's Mercy Alvarez; she and her husband started the place, then she divorced him and got it as part of her settlement.'

'Did you say Mercy?' Greg Jay looked down the table.

'Short for Mercedes,' Maggie Rose explained. 'It's a popular Spanish girl's name.'

'I could imagine this one being popular,' said Pringle. 'She's a real looker; just like you'd imagine a señora. Dark eyes, long dark hair.'

'Fine, Dan,' Martin interrupted, 'but what's her security like?'

'Crap. Same as Mellerkirk and Howdengate; an on-site

manager and no perimeter alarms. No alarms at all, in fact. She did say that she'd install video surveillance, though.'

'Did you believe her?'

'To be frank, no I didn't; she struck me as apathetic about the whole business. She was a bit aggressive, in fact. Still, McGurk left her details of insurance-approved installers.'

'Tell him to go back in a couple of days and see if she's done anything about it. I might just give her some encouragement myself.'

'Okay, but I had another thought.'

'What's that?'

'Why don't we install our own?'

'Why should we? Let her pay for it, and if she won't, let her insurance company shove her premium sky-high.'

'I didn't mean install it for her. I meant install our own set-up on the Q.T. There's a wee woodland overlooking the farm. We could stick a night-vision video camera in there with a timer and a long-life battery.'

Martin rubbed the back of his hand against his chin, as he considered the superintendent's suggestion. 'Would the tapes last long enough?'

'Set up two cameras, with two timers. We'll change the tapes and batteries first light every morning.'

'Costly, mind; we'd need high quality kit.'

'Divert it from the crime prevention budget,' Pringle suggested. 'It'll be money spent better than on telly commercials.'

The Head of CID laughed. 'The Boss would agree with you there. Okay, Dan; go ahead. You'll tell the owner, of course.'

'Ach, why should I? She'd never install her own if I did that. No, but as soon as this meeting's over I'll talk to the telecommunications people.'

'Fine,' Martin turned to Detective Superintendent Michaels. 'Right, Willie, about this pilferage epidemic of yours . . .'

Forty-two

Glenys Algodon looked around the living room, not even moderately impressed. 'It's all right,' the secretary said, in a slightly trans-Atlantic accent, 'but not when you compare it to the house the studio rented for you in Sri Lanka on the last gig, or even your own place in Beverly Hills.

'I mean, look how close the neighbours are.'

Neil McIlhenney felt his hackles rise; the woman had treated him like a taxi-driver when he had collected her from her shuttle flight at Edinburgh Airport, now here she was criticising the accommodation that he had picked out.

Louise Bankier defused the bomb inside him with a simple laugh. 'Compared to your flat in London, or mine for that matter, we're luxuriating in space here,' she said. 'What about the South African movie last year, when they wouldn't let us leave the hotel?

'Or that place off Malaysia where we did the location shots for that awful sci-fi epic? You and I, and the make-up girl, had to share a room; and the toilets . . .' She turned, grinning, to the big detective, moving across towards him. 'French style, they were, and the shower head was directly above you. Plus, there was no hot water on the island and the cold was in short supply, so you had to . . .'

She stopped herself short, blushing slightly, and laid the flat of her hand on his chest, still laughing. 'Believe me, Neil, this house is lovely, just lovely. Plus, as Bob said yesterday, it's just like my mum and dad's place in Bearsden.'

His anger was completely forgotten, dissolved by the music of her laughter and the warmth of her touch. He looked from her to Glenys Algodon. She was smiling too at the Malaysian memory, but he noticed that she did not blush. She was almost as tall as her employer, with copper-coloured hair that at first he had assumed was dyed, until he saw that her skin tone was a very light brown, indicating a mix of ethnic origin, a West Indian grandparent, perhaps or a Mauritian.

'I suppose so,' she conceded. 'But do you really want Clarence here at weekends?'

'I don't mind at all,' said Louise, 'if you don't, and if Neil's happy.'

Glenys's frown returned. 'Neil's in charge of my security,' the actress explained. 'He's a policeman, like his colleague.' She nodded towards a second man in the room, standing quietly beside the window.

'Excuse me, boss lady,' the secretary exclaimed, 'but what's this about? When we talked about this project at first, you said that you might stay in Glasgow with your father and your sister. Now here you are, holed up in a bungalow in the sticks of Edinburgh, surrounded by coppers.'

Louise looked up at the big inspector. 'Neil,' she asked, quietly. 'Do you want to explain?'

'Sure. Let's all sit down, though.'

'No, you go ahead. I'll make us all some coffee; I noticed

that someone's done some shopping for us.'

As she spoke the doorbell rang; McIlhenney went to the front door and opened it. A woman stood in the small porch; she could have been Louise Bankier in her twenties. 'Hi,' she said, with a smile. 'You must be Inspector Neil. I'm Lucy, Lou's sister.'

'Come on in.' The detective swung the door wide. 'She told me you were coming through to see her.'

He led the younger Bankier into the living room, taking her coat from her on the way, and hanging it on a hook in the hall. The reunited sisters embraced. 'Good to see you, Luce!' Louise exclaimed. 'You pitched up at just the right moment, as usual. I'm just about to make coffee. Come with me; there's stuff I've got to tell you.'

The two women headed for the kitchen, leaving the policemen alone with the secretary. 'Okay,' said Glenys sharply, as soon as the door had closed. 'What is this?'

'I didn't introduce myself properly at the airport,' he began. 'My name is Detective Inspector Neil McIlhenney. I'm the executive assistant to Detective Chief Constable Bob Skinner. We have reason to believe . . .'

'No bullshit!' the woman snapped. 'Plain talk, please.'

'Okay,' said McIlhenney. 'Lou's got a stalker. Someone set off a smoke bomb in her hotel room early Saturday morning; put her in hospital for a few hours. A week before that, she was in Regent Street with my boss, who's an old friend of hers; some bastard in a car, white male, dark Ford Mondeo, fired a shotgun at them. It was a blank, but DCC Skinner didn't know that at the time. He's made a few enemies, so he assumed at first that it was the real thing and that he was the target. Now we're assuming that Ms Bankier was.

'As long as she's working in Edinburgh, she's under our protection. Effectively, I'll be her bodyguard.'

'You mean living with us?'

'No, but I'll be very close. My house is a few hundred yards away, and we've installed an alarm system that's linked to there and to the nearest police station. We've got some toys in the garden as well, that'll pick up anything heavier than a cat as soon as he steps over the fence.'

She looked at him. 'Your wife's gonna love that.'

'My wife is dead,' he answered, coldly.

She flicked an apologetic glance at him then looked down. 'Hey, I'm sorry.'

'So am I.' McIlhenney nodded across to the other, younger, man. 'This is Detective Sergeant Stevie Steele; he's been detached from other duties to the investigative side of this thing, and he'll report directly to DCS Martin, our Head of CID and through him to DCC Skinner.

'First off, he's going to need to talk to you.'

'Sure,' said Glenys. All her earlier suspicion and aggression had vanished, leaving only concern. 'Inspector,' she asked, 'you said that your boss is an old friend of Louise. How old?'

'They were students together.'

'Ah. I wonder . . . Maybe it's him.' She smiled at McIlhenney. 'Louise has had a few male involvements in her life,' she explained. 'Warren Judd was the most serious, but that's over a while now. Yet I've known for almost as long as I've worked for her, that there was someone way back, someone who left a mark on her that ain't never worn off. I don't want to get too corny, but I've always thought of him as the love of her life.

'Friday before last, she told me that she was meeting someone for dinner. She didn't say who, but from the way she said it, and the way she looked . . . real nervous, unlike I've ever seen her . . . I knew that it was him.

'I got to get a look at this guy.'

McIlhenney turned to Steele. 'Stevie,' he murmured. 'You'd do well to forget you ever heard any of that.

'And you too, Ms Algodon. That's a part of Louise's life that you'd better keep very confidential.

'Now,' he snapped, suddenly. 'Sergeant.'

'Sure. Ms Algodon . . .'

'Glenys.'

'Glenys then. I know already from the Metropolitan Police that you've reported a couple of people to them as, shall I say, unwelcome correspondents. They were both interviewed immediately, and they were both found to be innocent; just fans who had taken adulation a bit too far.

'Very quietly, we've confirmed already that neither of these men was in Edinburgh on Friday night. One of them is dead, and the other is a recluse who conducts almost his entire life over the Internet.

'Can you recall what alarmed you about them?'

She shrugged. 'They were persistent, that's all; I thought they were possibly obsessive personalities, so I took no chances.'

'You're qualified to judge, of course,' said Steele, casually, 'having a degree in psychology.'

'How did you know that?' she shot back.

'Same way we know that your boyfriend, Clarence Sparrow, is a solicitor and a West Ham season ticket holder. We take our job seriously, Glenys; I'm sure you do too. I appreciate your ability to make sound judgements about Ms Bankier's correspondents. Can you tell me how you base these?

'First of all, what volume of mail does she receive?'

'Probably less than you'd think,' the secretary told him. 'Louise has a mature following, and the older you get, the less likely you are to write fan mail. These days more and more of it comes over the Internet. Louise has a website, and there's an e-mail address attached.

'There is an official fan club, and we receive mail through that. Also there are people who just write to "Louise Bankier, London" or "Great Britain" even, and these are passed on by the Post Office.'

'Do you get much crank stuff?'

'Very little. Most people just write to thank Louise for a particular movie, or for being like a friend to them. They ain't even looking for a reply usually, but they always get one, sometimes with a photograph, and it's always signed personally, and with a little PS message. She even insists on signing off her own e-mail, even if I draft it. I have her signature programmed in, and we can add it.

'When I get nasty ones, as I do very occasionally, I never show them to her. I send them a stern reply, signed by me, warning them off if necessary. I don't burn them or shred them, though; I keep them for at least two years, in case there's a repeat from the same source.

'Almost invariably they're signed too, with return addresses.

212

When they come in the mail, I always check them out and the addresses are always genuine. When they come in the e-mail, I pass them back to the provider, for them to deal with.'

'Have you had any nasty ones, lately?'

'Only one or two in the last six months; we don't get all that many. And as I said, they were all signed and addressed. They're in a file at the agency in London where I'm usually based.'

'Fine,' Steele nodded. 'I can have them checked out. What about your Internet correspondence?'

'Some, but not much. Net-heads are too scared of being blocked out.' She paused. 'There was one message, though, a couple of months back, that I didn't show to Lou. It came on Hotmail; it was unsigned and odd enough for me to check it out with Microsoft.

'All they could tell me was that the holder of that mailbox was someone called John Steed, and that he had logged on and registered through a cyber-café in Newcastle. Give me two minutes to boot up my laptop and I'll show you it.'

She picked up a bag which she had laid on a chair, unzipped it and produced a portable computer; clipped into the lid, beneath a transparent screen was a photograph of a smiling black man. The detectives waited as she switched it on and opened her e-mail folders.

She had just clicked on a file, and handed the computer to Steele, when the Bankier sisters came back into the room. Lucy wore a worried look; Louise followed behind her, carrying four china cups and saucers on a tray. She laid one beside the sergeant, on a small table, as he looked at the message, with McIlhenney peering over his shoulder.

'Hi Louise,' they read silently.

This is a message to thank you for the major contribution you have made to world cinema during your outstanding career. However, every bitch has its day, as they say, and it's in the nature of things that yours has to be over quite soon.

When that time comes, I hope that you will have a moment to contemplate the effect that you have had on the lives of the millions to whom you have provided an idle distraction, and that you will be able to judge at that time whether the sacrifices you have made along the way have been worth it after all.

John Steed.'

'What is it?' Louise asked.

'An e-mail I didn't show you,' Glenys confessed.

'Ah, one of them.'

'You know?' the secretary exclaimed.

'Of course I do,' Louise laughed. 'Not even an actress is vain enough to assume that she only gets nice mail.' She held out a hand to Steele. 'Let's see it.'

The sergeant glanced at McIlhenney, who nodded, grim-faced. She took the laptop from him and read. 'You see what I mean?' the secretary said when she was finished. 'It's odd, but you couldn't call it threatening.'

Neil McIlhenney and Louise Bankier exchanged meaningful glances. 'Until you see the signature,' said the detective. He looked at the others.

'You three are probably too young to remember the TV

series, and no bugger went to the movie they made a few years back.

'The name. John Steed; that was the name of the lead character. The series was called *The Avengers*.'

scenes and the bigger went to the movie they made a few
were back.
The name John Steed, that was the name of the lead
character? He

Forty-three

Bob Skinner was rarely surprised; but even he was taken
aback when Ruth buzzed through to his office to say that
Detective Inspector David Mackenzie was at the front desk,
asking if he might see him.

'The Bandit?' the DCC exclaimed. 'I wonder what the
hell he wants. Aye, sure I'll see him. Have someone show him
the way up.'

When Ruth showed the Lanarkshire detective into the big
wood-panelled office, she recalled his mockery of her boss at
their first, unfortunate meeting. '*Somewhere along the line*,'
she mused, as she saw the expression on his face, '*he has
learned respect.*'

'Well David,' said Skinner, as she left. 'Does your mother
know you're out?' He grinned at the younger man's momentary
confusion. 'I mean does your divisional commander know
that you're through here?'

'I've told Detective Superintendent Lillie that I had to
come through to Edinburgh to pursue my enquiries, sir.' He
frowned. 'How did you know she's a woman?'

'You'd be amazed by what I know. For example, you're an
Albion Rovers supporter . . .' The inspector's mouth fell open.

'Don't be embarrassed about it, son,' Skinner laughed. 'It's the main reason why I like you.

'Tell me though, did you tell the lady whom you were coming to see?'

Mackenzie gave a slight, awkward grin. 'Not exactly. She'd have gutted me like a fish if I'd told her that; I said I had to re-interview a witness.'

'But what if I hadn't been in? Didn't you think to call first?'

'I suppose I should have, but the thing is, it isn't really you I've come to see. I want another chat with Ruth.'

'Not under caution this time, I hope.'

'No, of course not; she isn't back on the list. So far, I've drawn a blank with my check on drugs-related deaths. The fatalities are nearly all on smack, and most of them found in derelict buildings, not drowned in their baths. No, I need Ruth's help again, that's all.'

'Let's see if she can, then.' Skinner leaned forward, picked up one of his telephones and buzzed twice. Less than half a minute later, the door opened. 'Christ, Ruthie,' he murmured, 'were you waiting outside?'

'More or less, sir. Mr Chase was in my office with about a day's worth of dictation; I just excused myself and ran.'

Skinner scowled. 'I must tell ACC Chase that anything he dictates over the weekend will have to be typed up by Jack Good. You've got your work cut out as it is, looking after the two of us five days a week.'

'It's part of his game plan, sir. He wants a secretary of his own.'

'He can have one,' Skinner retorted. 'But Good goes back

to traffic. That's the deal and I'll tell him, too.' He turned to Mackenzie. 'Sorry, David. We're washing linen here. Now, how can Ruth help you?'

'I want to take this investigation off on another tack, sir. I sat down yesterday and I reviewed everything we know about this death. There are questions all over the place; the drugs in the old man's system, the missing syringe that was used to inject him, the identity of the woman, the video camera, what happened to all his possessions and his money . . .

'Then it came to me that there's another gap in our knowledge – one that we can fill. We know very little about the victim himself. We know that his only two living relatives were Ruth's mother, his sister-in-law, and Ruth herself. We know that he was a member of Dullatur Golf Club for about sixty years, till he stopped playing. We know that he was a British Rail manager in Glasgow, until his retirement.

'But that's it; and it's all completely impersonal. It gives me no clue to what this man was like . . . and I should know that. So, Ruth.' He looked at her, directly for the first time. 'I'd be grateful if you would tell me about your uncle. What sort of man was he?'

She stared back at him, as if she was slightly puzzled by his question. 'What was he like?'

'Yes. For example, was he your favourite uncle?'

'Inspector, he was my only uncle: my late father had one brother and no sisters, and my mother is an only child.'

'I see. I knew you were his only niece, but I didn't realise that. It doesn't really answer the spirit of my question, though.'

Ruth caught his shrewd look. 'Would he have been my

favourite uncle if he had competition, you mean? No, probably not.'

'Why not?'

She sucked in her breath. 'I find it hard to say. I went to see him out of family duty as much as anything else; the fact that I hadn't seen him for months before his death should tell you something. I may have felt guilty if I hadn't phoned him for a while, but I didn't do anything about it.

'He could be a very remote man. Not cold, just remote. For example, I don't recall my father ever telling any funny stories about him. My dad had a great sense of humour; he loved people. Yet he never had anything to say about Uncle John, even about their childhood, and there was less than two years between them in age . . . Dad was the older. He and Aunt Cecily didn't visit us very often, and we rarely visited them. When we did meet, it was always very formal; I never remember much chat.

'Later, when I got a bit older, I used to duck out of even those occasional visits.' Suddenly she frowned. 'For a while I didn't feel comfortable with Uncle John.'

'Why?' asked Mackenzie, quietly.

'There was this one time,' she murmured. 'I'd be about thirteen, and my mum and dad had a party for my dad's sixty-fifth birthday, and his retirement. He was head teacher in a big secondary in Kilmarnock. Uncle John and Aunt Cecily were invited; I remember my mum being surprised when they came.

'Well, as I said, I was about thirteen. I was, shall we say, a big girl for my age, but I was still short of any sexual awakening. I didn't have a clue about any of that stuff; nothing to go on save tweeny chit-chat. Nevertheless, I was wearing a very short skirt and a stick-up bra, because I thought they were fashionable and my good old mum had indulged me. She's about twenty years younger than my dad. He was mid-forties when they met; he was married before,' she added in explanation, 'but his first wife left him for a bloke in Glasgow.

'Anyway, there was music at the party. I had a dance with my dad, and then my Uncle John asked me to dance with him. It wasn't the same as dancing with my dad, I can tell you. Thinking about it now, I remember it quite clearly.'

'Are you saying he touched you?' asked Mackenzie.

'No,' she said quickly. 'Nowhere he shouldn't, not in the way I think you mean, anyway. No, there was a slow tune playing, and he danced fairly close; he was leaning over me, then he gave me a hug, and I felt this enormous hard thing pressed against my abdomen. It was just for a second or two, until the record stopped; I wasn't scared . . . I suppose I was taken aback, more than anything else.

'I suppose that even then I must have known something about male equipment, but it took a conversation with a school pal to tell me that dear Uncle John had had a monster erection for his little niece. Looking back now, I have no doubt that he was letting me know it, deliberately.'

'What did you do?'

'Nothing. But I knew that I didn't want to dance with him again. Even after I found out for sure that he hadn't had a stick of rock shoved down his trousers. I didn't say anything to my mum or dad. The terrible thing is that a young girl in that position is afraid that if she does tell tales, she'll be accused of making them up. But I was very wary of Uncle John for a while after that; in fact, for about five years, until I was . . . how do I say . . . not sexually experienced, but sexually confident, I probably made a point, subconsciously, of never being alone with him.'

As she looked at the inspector, her eyes seemed to harden. 'There you are, Bandit,' she said, 'there's an insight into my uncle the victim. He was an old lecher.'

At first Mackenzie gazed back at her as if he could think of nothing to say. 'I wish that was the first time I'd heard a story like that,' he murmured at last. 'But I saw the same thing actually happen to a kid once, at a family party, just like you. She screamed though, and I nailed the guy who did it there and then. I charged him with indecent assault.

'That was the time I told you about; the time I nicked my own brother.'

For the second time that afternoon, Bob Skinner's eyebrows rose in surprise. 'Have you spoken to Ruth's mother yet?' he asked quickly.

'No sir,' the Strathclyde detective answered.

'You should,' said Ruth. 'Maybe he tried it on with her as well.'

Forty-four

Neil McIlhenney looked at the three beautiful women who sat in a circle facing him. Stevie Steele had gone, taking with him a printout of John Steed's enigmatic message.

'It's easier for me to give this advice than it will be for you to take it,' he said. 'But I don't want you to get this thing out of proportion. This bloke has made two extravagant gestures so far; unpleasant stunts they were, but stupid too because they were both very risky. For example, Central London is patrolled by armed response teams; if one of them had been in the area when he fired that shotgun, it could have back-fired on him. Fatally.

'We've also found a security tape in the Balmoral which may show a man flipping a room key behind the reception counter. The suspect's back is to the camera but it was still a reckless thing to do.

'If there is a next time . . .' the inspector muttered grimly, 'he's cooked.

'That said,' he added quickly, 'he's not going to do it here. No one will break into this house; I promise you that. You believe me?'

Glenys Algodon's eyes dropped to her lap; even Louise

222

looked hesitant for a moment. 'Of course,' she said, not quite quickly enough.

'Listen, Lou,' said Neil. 'If it makes you feel safer I will have an armed woman officer stationed permanently with you.'

'Thanks, but no, really. I have faith in you; I'm still just a bit shaken by what happened the other night, that's all.'

He smiled at her. 'I don't blame you; but it's going to be all right. Honest.'

'Inspector? Can I ask you something?' Lucy Bankier's question interrupted their exchange.

'Fire away,' he said.

'What about our house in Bearsden? I mean, is it conceivable that this man could try something there? Dad's quite frail these days, and I wouldn't want to worry him with any of this, but if there's a chance . . .'

'Lucy,' he told her, 'right now, your house in Bearsden is being watched by Special Branch officers.

'As my boss said earlier, this sort of incident is being regarded as a form of terrorism these days, and handled appropriately. I'm not SB, but I've been given this role for a variety of reasons, the best being that this is how Mr Skinner wants it. Otherwise, my colleague Mario McGuire or one of his team would be here.'

He chuckled. 'I'm better looking than McGuire, anyway.

'Be sure, Lucy, it would be just as dangerous for anyone to attack your house in Glasgow as it would be to try anything here.'

'That's good to know,' sighed the younger Bankier sister, sincerely.

'One thing though. Where did you leave your car? I assume that you drove through.'

'Yes. It's in the street.'

'That's fine for today. But in future, when you're through here, park it in the driveway of the house.'

McIlhenney rose from his chair. 'Okay, Louise,' he said. 'I'm off; hopefully you can get on with learning that script with no interruptions.'

She stood with him and walked him to the door. 'Oh, yes,' he added. 'There may be one. The Big Man will probably look in on you before he goes home.'

'My other jailer,' she murmured, with a smile.

'I'm sorry if it feels like that . . .'

'. . . but it's for my own good. Yes, sir, I know, but still, I am this man's prisoner, effectively.'

'No you're not,' he assured her. 'You can go where you like, when you like, with me.'

'Okay,' she shot back, still smiling, 'take me to a movie tomorrow night . . . any damned movie.'

He hesitated. 'In the dark? Among people who'd recognise you?'

'Hey,' she protested. 'I'm not hiding from the world at large, just from one man. And he's not going to try anything in a crowd, with you around. The worst that'll happen is that you'll have to watch me sign a few autographs.' She broke off, picked up what looked like a piece of card from the hall table, and handed it to him. 'That reminds me; I promised you this.'

He turned it over; it was a photograph, signed, 'For Neil, Lauren and Spencer, with love, Lou.'

'Hey, thanks!' he exclaimed, almost bashfully. 'Okay, tell you what.' He glanced at her enquiringly, 'How's your schedule tomorrow?'

'I read in the morning, then I have a production meeting here in the afternoon with Warren Judd and Elliott Silver. I'm executive producer on this project as well; it's part of the deal.'

'Well,' he said, suddenly tentative, 'once that's done, would you like to have supper with the kids and me; after that, you and I can go on to a movie . . . somewhere discreet, you understand.'

She smiled; it seemed to light up the narrow hall. 'Hey, I'd love it. I enjoy nothing more than just behaving like an ordinary human being; until you've lived in a goldfish bowl like mine, you can't know how precious that is.'

'Sure I can,' he murmured. She looked at him, but came nowhere close to reading his thoughts. 'Sure I can.'

Forty-five

Dan Pringle's description had been spot on, Andy Martin acknowledged as he stepped out of his sports car, after a bumpy journey up the sort of country track for which it had decidedly not been designed.

Despite his discomfort, he was glad that he had come; he was intrigued by the superintendent's investigation but had felt remote from it. As was the case with Bob Skinner, the ties of his supervisory role chafed him from time to time, and occasionally he felt compelled to loosen them . . . albeit less frequently than his friend and commander.

As he started to walk towards the woman, she turned in his direction. Mercedes Alvarez would have stood out in any crowd; she was, he guessed, in her mid-thirties, and looked as stereotypically Spanish as anyone he had ever seen, with jet-black hair and sparkling brown eyes which seemed to burn like coals as she glared at her unexpected visitor.

'Yes?' she demanded aggressively as they approached each other. 'You can't read the sign maybe; the one on the gate which says that this place is not open to the public?'

'Yes, I read it, Ms Alvarez,' the detective chief super-intendent replied, 'but I don't qualify as the public. I'm a policeman.' He introduced himself, but she was unmollified.

'Another policeman!' she protested. 'Two of you came to see me yesterday; they even asked me to meet them here. Wasn't that enough?'

'Apparently not. They reported to me that you seemed less than interested in what they had to say.'

'No. That's not so. Of course I am interested in my fish; of course I am sorry for what happened to those two other farmers, whoever they are.'

'I'm glad to hear it. In that case I assume that you'll follow their advice and install the security equipment that they recommended.'

He sensed her move on to the defensive for the first time. 'I'll look into it,' she said, dismissively. 'I'll have to see what it costs; maybe I can't afford it.'

Martin glanced around the big site, listening to the noise of the pumps, and the music of the running water which flowed constantly through the big tanks. 'You can't afford not to, Ms Alvarez. If you want to be able to insure your stock in the future, you're going to have to invest in alarms and a proper video system.'

'Who says?'

'I say. We say. The police, who are expending considerable time and money investigating the consequences of other farmers too short-sighted to invest in proper protection against theft. We say you'll have to, and you can be dead certain that the insurance companies will back us up.'

The woman flared up again, her Latin eyes flashing. 'You can't threaten me like that.'

Martin grinned at her, amused by her reaction. 'Sure I

can,' he told her. 'I can back it up too. Don't make me have to; install that equipment.'

She seemed to capitulate; finally she smiled at him. 'Okay, okay,' she exclaimed, raising her hands in token of defeat. 'I'll need to speak to Mr John, my bank manager, maybe . . . it's really him who runs this place . . . but I'll do it.'

'Is that Andrew John?' the detective asked.

'Yes. His office is in Edinburgh, but he comes to see me down here.'

'I know Andrew; I'll speak to him, tell him what the situation is. I shouldn't think there will be a problem.'

The smile left her face in an instant. 'No!' she snapped. 'You no' do that. That's my business; I'll deal with it.'

'Okay then, but you make sure you do. I'm going to send Detective Sergeant McGurk back here on Friday; I'll expect you to show him a functioning video set-up.'

'If you say so,' she grumbled. 'But I have an alarm; I have a video system. Kath,' she called to another, younger, woman, who was loading feed into a dispenser. She stopped, laid down the big paper sack, and walked towards them, a big strong-looking girl in the inevitable black rubber boots.

'This is Kath Adey,' said the Spanish farmer. 'She's my manager, and she lives here.' She pointed to a cottage on the far side of the tank complex. 'She sees everything, and she has a loud voice to shout "Help", if she needs to. Don't you, Kath?'

'Sure do, Mercy. You want to hear?' she asked the policeman.

'I'll take your word for it. Have you got plenty of groceries in that cottage?'

The manager frowned. 'I need milk, but otherwise I'm okay. Why?'

'Because if you're the only alarm system this place has for now, you cannot leave it until proper equipment is installed and running. Whatever happens, suppose you have an emergency call telling you that your granny's house is on fire and she's stuck on the roof, you do not leave that stock unguarded. Clear?'

The woman frowned at him, and nodded. 'Clear.'

'Do you have the number of the police station in Coldstream?'

'It's in the book, isn't it?'

'Look it up. Keep it handy. Just in case. I'm not saying that anything will happen, but still . . . It'd be nice if you and Ms Alvarez could get these fish to market rather than have someone else do it.'

He looked back at the Spanish owner. 'Friday, remember.'

She sighed. 'Okay, Friday. You send your man back on Friday.'

He gave her a friendly smile and made to turn back towards his car. 'He'll be here,' he said. 'Count on it.'

He drove carefully back down the rough track, turning at last on to a road which led to and through the border town of Coldstream. As soon as he was in open country, he eased his speed and dialled the central number of the Bank of Scotland.

He had to speak to two successive switchboard operators,

human screens between bank managers and an admiring public, before finally he was put through to Andrew John's office.

'I'm sorry, Mr Martin,' the banker's secretary told him, 'but Mr John's out of the office until Thursday. He has a series of meetings in England.'

'Too bad. I need to talk to him about one of his clients. Make me an appointment first thing on Thursday. I'll come to him.'

Forty-six

Age for age, Naomi McConnell was as attractive as her daughter; from Ruth's disclosure of the age difference between her parents David Mackenzie knew that she was in her early sixties, but she could have passed for ten years younger. He found it hard to believe that she had been retired from teaching for two years.

'This is very distressing,' she said, as she ushered the policeman into the sitting room of her neat bungalow on the outskirts of the seaside town of Ayr. In common with most Glaswegians, he had been taken there by his parents as a boy; in common with many, he had not been back since.

'For all that he was eighty, I was really shocked when I heard that he was dead. With all that golf he played, he always struck me as such a fit man that I thought he'd go on for ever. Now, to learn that there was something suspicious about it . . .'

'Ruth told me that someone drowned him in his bath!' she exclaimed.

'We don't know that for sure, Mrs McConnell,' the policeman cautioned. 'It's a possibility, but it'll probably never be any more than that. There were no signs of force on the body when we found it; we do believe that he was drugged though.'

'Drugged?' She looked and sounded astonished.

'We suspect that he may have been taking tranquillisers, or possibly having these administered to him.'

'My God. What sort of a world is this? Or what sort of a world was he living in?'

'That's exactly what we have to find out. That's why I'm here; to ask you what you knew of your brother-in-law.'

Ruth's mother drew herself up in her chair. 'As much as I wanted to, and that wasn't much. I hope I'm not incriminating myself here, but I never liked John McConnell. The last time I saw him was at Max's funeral . . . my husband's funeral . . . five years ago. Since then we've exchanged Christmas cards, but that's been it.'

'Why did you dislike him?' Mackenzie asked.

'I don't know for sure, but it was instant, I can tell you that. There was something creepy about him; I remember the way he looked at me this first time we met, and a few times after when I caught him off guard. I felt as if he was sizing me up.'

'I'm sorry to be blunt, but do you mean sexually?'

'That's exactly what I mean. I felt as if the man was undressing me with his eyes.'

'What about his wife?' he asked. 'What was she like?'

'Cecily?' Naomi McConnell threw back her head in a gesture which David Mackenzie had seen in her daughter. 'I never knew whether to feel sorry for him, or for her. In the end, I suppose I felt sorry for them both. They endured a sad, barren marriage for almost forty years, and they always seemed bored in each other's company. Max and I visited them as a duty rather than a pleasure, and entertained them on the same basis.'

The detective looked at her. 'Did Mr McConnell's attentions to you ever go beyond glances?' he asked, cautiously.

She drew in her breath. 'Well, I learned early on never to dance with him,' she snorted, with remembered indignation. 'In fact, I remember once, oh, nearly twenty years ago, at a party we had here when Max retired, I saw him dancing with Ruth. She was barely in her teens then, but she was a well developed girl. I probably let her over-dress a bit that night; she was gorgeous and didn't even know it.

'Anyway, as I said, I saw John dancing with her, and I just wasn't having it, so I walked over to the record player and stopped the music. He looked at me afterwards, and it was the only guilty look I ever had from him. I thought about asking Ruth if anything . . . anything untoward had happened, but she didn't seem flustered so I let it lie.'

'Your suspicions were spot on though.' Mackenzie blurted the words out in spite of himself.

'You mean . . .'

He nodded. 'Ruth told me exactly the same story yesterday. In the circumstances, and given her age, she seems to have handled it pretty well.

'Tell me,' he continued quickly, 'how did your husband feel about his brother?'

'Max tolerated John, but they were never close, by any stretch of the imagination. No, there was something between them. He never said so outright, and I never asked him, but I think that he either suspected or knew that John had had an affair with Lorna, his first wife. Mind you, to listen to Max talk about her you'd think she'd had everything in trousers. He was very hurt when she left him, and he stayed bitter about her for the rest of his life.

'She went off with a man John worked beside, in fact. Max held a bit of a grudge over that too.' She paused. 'Now he did feel sorry for Cecily; he thought it was sad that such an obviously a-sexual woman like her should be married to a man like him.

'I asked him once why they'd married in the first place, all he said was "Respectability". He believed that his brother was promiscuous; he even said to me that he thought he probably cruised the red light district of Glasgow in that big car of his.'

'So all in all, Mrs McConnell, you did not regard your brother-in-law as a very nice man,' the detective summed up.

'Not a bit,' she agreed. 'He was mean too. "As tight as a fish's . . ." Max used to say.' She laughed.

'And yet, in the last few months of his life, he gave away all his money and virtually all of his possessions of value . . . even his car.'

Naomi gasped. 'Ruth didn't tell me that. If that's the case, I can only suppose that the old fool compromised himself with a woman in some way, and that she blackmailed him.'

'Maybe,' Bandit Mackenzie murmured. 'But if she was blackmailing him, why did she take a video camera into his house, on the day he died? That's the biggest mystery of all.'

They looked at each other across the room.

'You said that your husband's first wife went off with a workmate of his brother.'

'Colleague,' Mrs McConnell laughed. 'John was management and never slow to let you know it. He didn't have workmates. But yes, Lorna went off with a colleague. I never knew his name though, and Max never mentioned it.'

'Perhaps John kept in touch with her.'

'Quite possibly, but she can't tell you anything now. She died about fifteen years ago. I remember John phoning to tell Max about it, to see if he wanted to go to her funeral. As far as I know, he didn't even send flowers.'

'Damn,' said the policeman, his frustration showing. 'Another closed door. I tell you Mrs McConnell; your brother-in-law couldn't have covered his tracks better if he'd tried.'

Forty-seven

Way back, when the world was young and James Proud was merely an Assistant Chief Constable, he met a young CID officer whose vision, commitment, and intensity were such that he made a bigger impression on him than any man had ever done before. He had marked that young man as one who, some day, would command the force, and from that time on had taken a personal interest in his career development.

Bob Skinner had known nothing of this at the time; he had been totally focused on his twin ambitions of cracking every crime he confronted and, possibly even more difficult, raising, as a lone parent, his young daughter to womanhood. He had been given time in each CID posting to gather experience and establish his track record, but once he had come within sight of the top of the ladder the rest of his climb had been rapid.

As Sir James Proud looked at him across the coffee table in his spacious office, he knew that only one act remained to bring about the final fulfilment of his vision; his own retirement and the installation of his protégé as Chief Constable.

Yet it was something which the two men had discussed

only tentatively in the past, and never once in those conversations had the deputy allowed himself to anticipate the time when he would sit permanently in the Chief's chair.

Even after an extended period in charge, during his boss's enforced absence on sick leave, Skinner had subtly avoided any detailed discussion of the future, or at least of the post-Proud era; so much so that the veteran wondered whether he might have developed an agenda of his own.

If he had, Proud mused, it was unlikely that Assistant Chief Constable Theodore Chase featured in it prominently, if at all. Bob Skinner was almost invariably tolerant of the views of others; he demeaned his own skills as a man manager, yet he had gathered around him the most gifted team of detectives on any British force, and in spite of his own inclination to keep hands on, had given them the leeway they needed to achieve results.

Ted Chase, though, was the exception; rule-defying, rather than rule-proving. From the moment that he had settled himself into Jim Elder's old chair, the newcomer to the Fettes Command Corridor had set out an agenda which seemed to have been designed to challenge Skinner's position and authority.

His peremptory appointment of Jack Good had started the rot; technically, the Chief could have vetoed it, but Chase during his excellent interview had subtly established that, in the event of his appointment, he would have some say in the choice of his personal staff.

Then there was his paper; his damnably well-crafted paper on the command structure of the force, and of the benefits of the Deputy being a mirror image of the Chief Constable, rather than someone whose different attributes and skills . . . however admirable they might be, as the document had made a point of acknowledging . . . had in the past caused crises in the relationship between the police command and the elected board which supervised its operations.

Proud Jimmy had hoped that Chase would have backed off, if not in the face of Skinner's clear hostility, then of his own mildly discouraging signals. But he had not; the man's ambition was built of strong materials. The old Chief had bought time by the simple ruse of saying that he wished to give Chase a chance to find his feet in Edinburgh, while he considered his thoughts at length.

He knew that this was merely postponing the crisis point, the moment when he would either have to tell Chase to fall into line, or put his paper up for discussion by the Board. Had no other considerations applied, he would, of course, have told the ACC what to do with his paper on Day One. However, he had more than a suspicion that, if he did that, Jack Good might carelessly allow a copy to fall into the hands of Councillor Agnes Maley, Bob Skinner's arch enemy. Although Sir James had tried to have Maley removed from the Police Board, he had failed and she was still around and capable of making mischief.

Still, he had been enjoying his period of peace, until that damned Civic Reception, at which the ACC's wife had made her debut and had behaved in front of Sarah Skinner, and even Chrissie, by God, as if she was Lady Chase already.

Fervently, the Chief Constable wished that he could discontinue his informal Tuesday management sessions with

Skinner and Chase; that he could see them separately, but not together. However, he knew that that would only have widened the rift.

Now, as he looked at Chase sipping his coffee as if he wanted to get it, and the last chocolate digestive biscuit, out of the way, he could sense a new storm well over the horizon, some heavy rain about to fall on his life.

'Okay, Ted,' he sighed. 'I can read the signs by now. Stop bristling; out with it.'

The ACC looked at him as if he had been caught sneaking a biscuit out of turn. 'I'm sorry, sir, if I appeared on edge. It's just that there are a couple of points I have to raise this afternoon, and I have a feeling that they may provoke a reaction.'

'Oh yes,' said Skinner, not helping the situation by smiling. 'And what are they, Ted?'

Chase continued to look at Sir James, ignoring his colleague's grin. 'I'm finding it increasingly difficult to share a secretary with the deputy, sir. I don't know how much work my predecessor generated, but I really am finding it difficult to secure enough of Miss McConnell's time for my needs.

'This week, for example, McIlhenney seems to be out of the office for long periods, and McConnell is having to cover for his absence. Why I was in her office yesterday, giving her dictation tapes, when the DCC buzzed. She simply jumped up, excused herself and left the room.

'It's just not good enough, sir. I insist either that she is replaced or that I am allocated a secretary of my own.'

Skinner's smile vanished; Proud sighed inwardly as the

first figurative raindrops began to fall. 'Don't you ever . . .' The words fell not far short of a snarl. '. . . suggest again, mister, that Ruth should be moved out.'

The DCC paused, waiting for Chase to return his gaze, but the ACC continued to look firmly at Sir James.

'Okay,' he exclaimed, eventually, 'I'll support your request for a secretary of your own.' Chase's head seemed to turn on a swivel. 'But Jack Good has to go.'

For a second or two, the Cumbrian's mouth worked like a goldfish tipped on to a kitchen counter. 'But, but . . .

'Absolutely no way,' he protested, turning back to Proud Jimmy for support.

'Sir, do I or do I not have the right to appoint my own personal staff?'

The Chief Constable studied his desk. 'As I recall Ted, you have a say in it; that much is certainly true. Of course,' he added, freezing the ACC's smirk, 'there are cost considerations. How would it be if we gave you your own secretary, and replaced Inspector Good with a promising young sergeant?'

'I couldn't accept that. I chose Good; I have great regard for his abilities.'

'Well, no other bastard does!' Skinner boomed. 'The man's your sneak. Do you think I don't know that? Do you think I don't know that you've had him going round out-stations, and even some principal divisional offices, making snap inspections and reporting back to you?

'The bugger's even been checking on CID. He wandered into Dan Pringle's office last week in his well-pressed uniform; all that was missing, apparently, was a swagger stick.

Dan advised him to fuck off, but I'll bet he didn't tell you that.'

'Well?' Chase exclaimed, raising his voice. 'I am responsible for operations; why shouldn't my exec. act on my behalf in visiting stations and asking whether they have any operational problems which we can help them solve?'

'In principle, because you shouldn't have an inspector even appearing to be checking up on a chief super. In practice because this one's a twat!'

'Chief!' the ACC shouted. 'I object to that language. What can the DCC have against Jack to mistreat a junior officer in that manner?'

Sir James sat quietly in his chair. Skinner, with an effort, hauled on the frayed reins of his temper. 'If you had consulted Jimmy, or me,' he said evenly, 'or anyone else before you were blinded by the shine of his shoes and the gleam of his badge, we'd have bloody told you.

'Jack Good's wife is an executive on the *Scotsman*; and she has him by the balls. We've had three serious leaks to that paper in the last few years, and Good is suspected of being the source, inadvertent or otherwise, in every instance. That's why he was stuck in the Operations Room for the duration, and only allowed out on special occasions as a bloody ornament.

'Then you swan in like a guardian angel and pluck him out of there.'

'You might have told me,' Chase complained.

'You didn't give us a chance. Once you'd appointed him, we couldn't simply say "no". We've got nothing we can pin on him; we had decided to keep him out of the heart of the action. There was nothing wrong with that, by the way; his record as an officer warranted his previous posting.'

The ACC sat back in his chair, silenced for the moment. Then a strange look came into his eyes; looking at him, Sir James Proud saw, for the first time, a sign of malevolence in him.

'Good has his uses,' he said quietly. 'For example, this morning he reported back to me on a visit he paid, on my instruction, to the telecommunications department.

'He told me that he had found a number of very odd installations made by that department over the last couple of days. Specifically, we have just installed a state-of-the-art alarm system in a house in the Craiglockhart area of Edinburgh. This is linked not only to the Torphichen Place Divisional Office, but also to a private address in the same area. On checking, Good discovered that it is the home of Detective Inspector McIlhenney.

'The installations were made on the personal instruction of the Deputy Chief Constable.

'Further investigation on Good's part revealed that the house in which the alarm system is fitted was leased yesterday to a film production company; the signatory of the lease was one Louise Bankier, an actress.'

Once more Chase focused his gaze on the Chief Constable, as he produced a single sheet of paper from a folder on his lap. 'Here, sir, is a cutting from Saturday's *Evening News*, which appears to link this woman with a senior police officer, who is unmistakably our colleague, Mr Skinner.

'Chief Constable, the inescapable conclusion is that the Deputy Chief has been using police resources to provide sequestered accommodation for his lady friend during her stay in Edinburgh.'

As Sir James Proud looked at Bob Skinner, he saw the colour drain from his face. He pushed himself to his feet with surprising speed and glared sternly at Chase. 'Thank you, Ted,' he said. 'Now leave the room . . . at once.'

The ACC stood, a smile of unconstrained triumph on his face, and slipped out of the side exit.

As the door closed, Proud Jimmy looked at the ceiling. 'Sorry about that, Bob,' he exclaimed. 'But at that moment, I thought you were going to kill him.'

Skinner was so enraged that he was breathing slightly heavily. 'At that moment, Jimmy, I might have. Even now, you may only have given him a stay of execution.'

The Chief dropped into the chair behind his desk. 'What the hell am I going to do about that man?' he said.

'Bring it to a head,' the DCC snapped. 'Put his paper to the Board, argue against it, and have it squashed. In the minutes, it'll read like a reprimand.'

'But what if they back it?'

'They won't. You still have enough on enough of them for them to be afraid to cross you. If I'm wrong about that . . . Well, I won't be taking any orders from that fucking blackshirt; I'll tell you that much.'

He sighed. 'But listen, that's trivial. My big problem is that Good knows about Lou, and that is dangerous given his suspected weakness for pillow talk. You know the whole story, because I told you straight away; I was hoping to avoid it, because I just don't trust the man, but now Chase has to be let in on it as well.

243

'You speak to him, if you will. I'll handle Jack Good; when it comes to putting the fear of God in people, you'll concede that I'm better at it than you.'

The Chief let out a sound that was half chuckle, half snort. 'You do that; then I'll send him back to the Ops Room tomorrow.'

'No,' said Skinner quietly. 'Keep him here until this is over; I want him close, where he can feel my hot breath on his neck, even though Chase won't dare send him out of this office again. Meantime, give the ACC a typist, just to keep him happy.'

Forty-eight

In a strange, private way Neil McIlhenney was in awe of his daughter, of her calmness, her maturity, and her remarkable common sense for her years. Since Olive's death, she had replaced her mother as the rock upon which his life was founded.

Therefore it was quite remarkable to see her in awe of someone else.

Louise Bankier had not just come for dinner; she had provided it. King-size specials from Pizza Hut had been delivered ten minutes after Neil had brought her round from her secluded address, and she had insisted on giving Spencer the money to pay for them.

They had eaten them, cut into wedges round the dining table, father and children, Marie the temporarily living-in nanny, and their guest.

Lauren had said very little during the meal; for once Spencer had gone unchecked as he had made the running with a series of quick-fire questions which ran the gamut of the movie industry, from Tom and Jerry to Tom Hanks. As Neil had watched her he realised that she in turn was studying Louise, a vivacious, vibrant female presence restored unexpectedly to her young life. He could not begin to read, far less understand all the thoughts which were swirling around in her pre-adolescent mind. However, he was reminded of something that his own grief, and their bravery, made him overlook too easily; the extent to which they too must miss their mother.

As they prepared to leave, Lauren and Spencer stood politely, ready to wish their guest goodbye. In keeping with the rest of the evening, the youngest McIlhenney had the last word. 'Dad's taking us skating in Princes Street Gardens on Saturday,' he said. 'Would you like to come too?'

'Hey Spence,' said his father with a grin. 'Don't push your luck.'

'How did you know I like skating?' Louise responded. 'Of course I'll come . . . if your dad lets me. I have to do what he says, you know.'

The children seemed to look up at him with a new kind of respect. 'Okay,' he said. 'As long as you continue to remember one thing; that Ms Bankier being here is not to be talked about at school, or to anyone outside this room. Understood?'

Spencer nodded. Lauren simply said, 'Father!', throwing him an old-young reproving look that he had seen so often before, and which never failed to tug at his heart.

Louise laughed. 'It's a date then. Hot dogs on your dad!'

He whistled as they stepped out into the moonless sodium-lit night. 'Add two more names to the fan-club,' he said.

'Two?'

'I always was a fan,' he murmured.

'That's good to know,' she answered, as he opened the car door for her.

'Where are we going, then?' she asked, as he slid into his seat beside her. 'Somewhere discreet, you said.'

'Yes; and somewhere I'll feel comfortable in the dark.'

'Where are you going to find an empty cinema in this town?'

'I'm not, but wait and see the next best thing.'

They had been driving for less than ten minutes, when Neil turned off Morningside Road, and parked close to a small, but well-lit cinema, one of the old-fashioned kind, rather than a modern multiplex. 'This is where I take the kids: the Dominion. We're going to Cinema Three; it's about the size of your average living room.

'You really don't mind going to *American Beauty*? I mean, you must have seen it.'

'No, honestly, I haven't,' she said. 'You may find this odd, but I don't go to the movies much.'

He led her quickly past two short queues of cinema-goers and past the box office. 'I picked up the tickets earlier,' he explained, 'and I had a quiet word with the manager. The only things I asked was that we go in first, so that I can eyeball the rest of the audience. There only are a couple of dozen seats, though.'

She said nothing, but looked sideways at him with a quiet smile.

Two and a half hours later, they stepped back out into the foyer. This time there was no slipping unnoticed past the crowd. Word had spread and scores of people were waiting, holding diaries, leaflets, future attraction fliers, scraps of paper, anything that would accommodate an autograph.

Neil stood back as she signed, studying every person as

they stepped up, noting the time she spent with every one, and the interest she seemed to take in them all.

Finally it was over. As they stepped outside, he asked her, 'Is it like that every time?'

'Pretty much,' she said, linking her arm through his as they headed for the car. She chuckled, enigmatically. 'But at least, tonight it isn't raining.'

Forty-nine

Stevie Steele didn't mind Newcastle, but he did have a strong aversion to wild geese. As he stood in the street outside the St James Internet Café, he fancied that he heard a fluttering of wings.

He had spent a good part of the previous day in front of a screen, studying the jerky images provided by the Balmoral Hotel's video security system, trying to put a face to Louise Bankier's stalker. Trying in vain.

Yes, there had been that one image; a slim man of medium height wearing a loose raincoat and a black hat. He had stopped at the reception desk, and stood there for a while, his back to the camera throughout, appearing, to Steele at any rate, to peruse some of the information leaflets on display there. Then the receptionist had turned to pick up a telephone; there had been a movement. Very little, no more than a flick of a wrist, and the appearance of something small flying through the air and falling behind the counter; only the appearance, that was all. Unless you added the fact that a few seconds afterwards, as the receptionist ended her call, the man had walked off, without turning, towards the hotel's side exit.

The only certainty that Stevie Steele had at the end of the

day was that there was nothing else on those security tapes. They were patchy in their quality and, worse, they switched from camera to camera. He had walked around the hotel and confirmed what he suspected, that each one had a red 'live' light and that anyone with half a brain would be aware when he was being filmed and when he was not.

The only other slim clue to the identity of the actress's persecutor was that one, cryptic e-mail message from the threateningly named John Steed. It was the only potential lead he had left, and he was even beginning to doubt that. Sure, its use of the word 'bitch' was offensive, but it was still possible that it was nothing more than a letter from a fan with an odd turn of phrase.

The only chance of finding out lay in the Newcastle café from which it had been sent. He opened the door and stepped inside.

Stevie Steele was something of a Net-head himself; he had a home computer and an e-mail address, through which he had built up a small network of friends around the world. He knew what a cyber-café was, a drop-off point at which those without their own Internet connection, or more likely, people travelling away from home, could buy on-line time, and coffee while they used it.

He could see their value in big tourist centre cities, and in airports, but he was slightly surprised that there was sufficient custom on Tyneside to drive such a business. As soon as he stepped inside he could see that his scepticism was justified.

The café side of the business seemed lively enough, but the three computer terminals which sat on desks against the far wall were all idle. A screen-saver was displayed on one, but the others were switched off.

As he looked at it, a middle-aged woman approached him; she wore a designer suit, and a pleasant smile. 'Can I help you?' she asked, in a tone which suggested that that was genuinely what she wanted to do.

'Mrs Egremont?'

'Yes.'

'I'm DS Steele; I called you this morning.'

'Ah yes.' The smile stayed in place, but behind it was something that he had seen many times before, the natural uncertainty sparked by a visit from a policeman.

He tried to put her at her ease at once. 'I'm grateful you could see me so quickly,' he said. 'It's nothing to do with you, really; I'm trying to trace a customer of yours.' He reached into his jacket and took out the printout of the Steed e-mail.

'This was sent on November the ninth through Hotmail, from this location. The User-id is "John Steed", but that mailbox hasn't been used since. I'm hoping that you can recall something about him that will help us trace him.'

Paula Egremont frowned. 'Is this nuisance mail?' she asked.

'You could say that.'

'Let me look at my diary.' She walked over to the till counter and took out a book from a ledge underneath. 'November nine, you said?'

'That's right; a Thursday.'

She opened the desk diary and turned over page after page until she found that date. Her lips moved unconsciously as she read. 'Yes!' she said, at last, with evident satisfaction. 'I do remember him. I had a visit from a coffee rep. that day; he had supplied me with some poor quality stuff and we had a row about it.

'While we were having it, the only other person in the place was my only Internet customer of the day. A young man, in his twenties; clean-shaven, wearing jeans, Timberland boots, or something of that ilk, and a heavy donkey type jacket.'

'You know him?'

She shook her head. 'Never seen him before or since. But the truth is I don't have all that many Net customers, so I tend to remember them fairly easily.'

'Can you tell me anything else about him?'

'He had a pale complexion, and he wore rimless glasses; could have been Gucci. We didn't say much to each other though. He came in, asked for a coffee, pointed at the machine and I switched it on. I'd just given him his coffee, when that damn rep. came in. By the time I'd finished complaining to him, he was signing off.

'He finished his coffee, paid and left.' She smiled, apologetically. 'That's all I can tell you, I'm afraid . . . apart, oh yes, I nearly forgot, apart from the hat. He was wearing a black hat.'

Fifty

Detective Sergeant Jack McGurk grumbled quietly to himself as he drove down the country road. Dan Pringle was a good guy to work for most of the time, but when he felt under pressure he tended to share it around.

When he started to indulge in creative thinking, anything could happen; his bright idea of keeping Mercy Alvarez' Country Fresh Trout under secret video surveillance was a prime example.

It was fine in theory, cost-effective policing that did a job without tying up teams of detectives round the clock, but in practice some poor bugger still had to go and change the tape every so often; first thing in the morning too, to lessen the chances of his being spotted. Of course, secrecy being the watchword, and Dan being too new in the division to know whom he could trust completely, that poor bugger just had to be Jack McGurk.

The sergeant had mixed feelings about his transfer to the Borders; it would mean a move south, away from the city. Even now he was living through the week in a furnished police flat in Newtown St Boswells. On the other hand Dan Pringle had more or less promised him that if he did the job for three years he would swing him a quick promotion to inspector.

That was a distant prospect, though, as he stopped beside the fence which bounded the woods in which the video cameras were hidden in a camouflaged box. He could approach through the trees without any danger of being seen from the farm, and the road was so isolated that he could leave without attracting any other attention.

The downside was that at daybreak the forest was still dark, and the trees were dripping wet. He took his rubber boots from the well of the passenger seat and pulled them on, then slipped into his Barbour, slapping the deep pockets to make sure that he was carrying the fresh tapes and fully charged batteries.

He made his way through the woods; it was Thursday morning and he was making the trip for the third time, so even in the gloom he knew the way fairly well. It had taken him half an hour to find the box on his first morning, and he had only just managed to avoid being spotted by the manager as she made her first round of the tanks.

The box opened from the back; he slipped the cameras out, one by one, exchanged the tapes, then replaced the depleted batteries. Finally, his job done, he risked a look across the clearing.

McGurk would have crept away had he not noticed the door; Kath Adey's cottage lay open to the morning chill, yet there was no sign of her. Quickly he glanced around the compound. The Suzuki jeep which he had seen on his first visit, and which he had assumed was hers was still there, parked beside one of the sheds. He listened; there was no sound but the beat of the pumps, and the steady splashing of the circulating water.

And then he looked at the tanks. Maybe the fish were asleep, for there were no signs of trout breaking the surface, no signs of fish snapping at the food, insect or artificial, which he had noticed there before. Yet there was something, something much bigger than any trout, something in the tank nearest the cottage, something floating face down.

'Oh shit,' Detective Sergeant Jack McGurk muttered as he forgot all about secrecy, breaking his cover to rush across the clearing, rubber boots flapping awkwardly as he ran.

Fifty-one

For many years, Andrew John had worn a beard. Although it had disappeared shortly after the arrival of its first grey hairs, Andy Martin imagined it in place still, as he took a seat in the banker's small office in a depressing concrete building in the Grassmarket. John was a good friend and occasional golf partner of Bob Skinner and had proved invaluable to him over the years, as a sounding board in the business sector.

'Sorry to drag you in here so early, Andy,' he began. 'But I'm only paying flying visits to my office this week. That's one of the bad things about the commercial side of our business.' He gave a quick, bright laugh, and glanced around the small dull room. 'Or maybe it's one of the good things.

'I spend more time in my customers' offices than I do in my own.'

'I used to be able to say the same,' said the Head of CID. 'Now I'm scratching around for excuses to get out of the office. I found one the other day, though,' he continued. 'That's what brought me here.

'I had occasion to pay a visit to a trout farm near Coldstream . . .'

'Oh,' exclaimed Andrew John, rolling his eyes at the

detective and leaning back in his chair. 'Country Fresh? The Welly-boot Contessa?'

'Apart from the fact that Contessas are Italian, not Spanish, that's the very lady.'

'What's she been up to?'

Martin held up his hands, palms outwards. 'Nothing. Nothing at all, honest. I went to see her because we've had a couple of major thefts from fish farms in that area. They both lost all their stock; had it hoovered up into container trucks through big suction hoses.

'In both cases their security was crap. My guys visited her after the second theft and saw that hers is too. She was a bit off-hand when they told her she should improve it, so I went down to give her a slightly heavier message.

'She told me she'd have to speak to you before she did anything, so I thought I'd have a quiet word with you too. We're about to recommend to the insurers that they get very tough with farmers who use their policies as alternatives to crime prevention provisions; I thought you should be aware of that when she asks you for spending approval, or an increased facility or whatever.'

'Thanks Andy,' said the banker. 'I appreciate that. Within these four walls, it won't make my decision any easier, though. I'm as exposed to that lady already as I want to be; to that whole sector in fact.'

Martin looked at him in surprise. 'Why's that?'

'Ach, most of these places are penny operations. There's so much farmed salmon on the market now, either raised here or dumped by the Norwegians, that it's depressing the price of trout. I used to have half a dozen trout farmers as clients; most of them estate owners who saw it as a way of making some extra money.

'Now I've got only two; Mercy Alvarez and one other. The other one's all right for now, because he's worked out that the only way to profitability is to add value to the stuff before you let it out the farm gate, by processing on site. Mercy, though, she just raises it quick and sells it quick, so she's dancing around the break-even line all the time. That's no use to me; I want to lend to businesses that are going to expand and become more substantial bank customers in the future.

'In that respect, fish farms are second last on my wish list.'

'What's last?' asked the detective, amused.

'Football clubs. They soak up tons of borrowing but how do you foreclose on them?'

'You don't; you sponsor them.'

'Ah, in an ideal world you only sponsor them, never lend. Let some other bugger do that!'

'So . . . has Mercy been in touch with you since Monday?'

'No. But I've been away from the office, remember.' He leaned across his desk and flicked through a pile of yellow message slips. 'Yes, there's a note here asking me to call her this morning.'

'When you do get in touch with her, what'll you say?'

'Ach, I don't know. What's the damage likely to be?'

'I can't say for sure, but I can tell you it won't be any more than next year's insurance premium, if she doesn't install . . .'

He broke off as his mobile rang. He took it from his pocket, excusing himself as he answered.

Across the desk, Andrew John saw the chief superintendent's face darken. 'Fuck!' he swore quietly. 'I'm coming down, Dan. Is Dorward on his way? Good?' He ended the call and put the phone away.

'The horse has bolted, Andrew,' he said. 'The fish have swum; use any analogy you fucking like. Your customer's farm has been done; only this time they've left a casualty behind, and it isn't a bloody trout.'

'What?' John gave him a look of pure incredulity.

'Kath Adey, the manager. Someone hit her over the head, then dumped her in a fish tank. She's dead.'

Fifty-two

Andy Martin made a point of learning by experience. On his second visit to Country Fresh Trout, he left his MGF in the care of a uniformed constable stationed at the head of the farm track and called for a police Land Rover to take him along the rough last leg of the journey.

Dan Pringle was standing at the door of the manager's cottage as his driver pulled up and he jumped out. A black panel van, with a spinning ventilator on its roof, was parked outside, its rear doors open. As the Head of CID approached his colleague he passed it, and glanced inside. A plastic coffin lay on the floor, its lid alongside it; he caught a glimpse of a white face, blue-tinged.

'Tell me about it,' he asked quietly.

'Jack found her,' said the superintendent, the only person on the scene, apart from Martin himself, who was not wearing a white tunic. 'He came to change the tapes in the video, and he saw the girl, floating in the tank.'

'What did the doctor say?'

'Just what I told you on the phone. He put the time of death at shortly after midnight, and said that the cause was probably cerebral injury rather than drowning. She was

260

battered about the head with something solid, then chucked in the tank.

'We found this, just beside where the body was floating. We've been all over the place looking for a murder weapon; everywhere save the tanks. They're not all that deep, but given the cold we'll need to use divers in dry suits if we're going to search them properly.

'The sub-aqua team's on the way down from Edinburgh right now. Effing and blinding all the way, I'll betcha.'

'Why the hell did the bastards have to kill her?' Martin muttered grimly.

'We'll maybe have an answer to that when we have a look at the tapes.'

'Maybe we'll have an answer to everything. Do we know if she received any phone calls, or tried to make any?'

Pringle frowned. 'Not with the cable cut, she didn't.'

The chief superintendent looked sharply at him. 'Where's the Alvarez woman?' he asked.

'I don't know. She lives in Coldstream, but she's not there.'

'Well you find her, Dan. Wherever she is; something stinks about this, and I don't mean the fish. I gave her till Friday to have her security installed, and this happens two days before.'

He shook his head, and slammed his left fist painfully into his right palm in sudden remorseful anger. 'That girl in the van. I told her not to leave the farm unattended; I read her the bloody Riot Act and told her that, whatever happened, she shouldn't leave the fish.

'I'm going to have these guys, mate,' he said, evenly, 'and

if Ms Alvarez does have anything to do with it, then God help her. Send McGurk and however many people it takes out to find her. Meanwhile, you and I are going up to Edinburgh to see the technical people and get as much as we can out of those tapes.'

Fifty-three

The head of Human Resources stared at Mackenzie as if he had just asked her to undertake a free climb, in winter, up the north face of the Eiger. 'You cannot seriously expect me to tell you that, off the top of my head,' Margaret Mair exclaimed.

The inspector looked at the top of her head, on which her hair was drawn into a tight grey bun. She reminded him of his first primary teacher, a warrior quite literally of the old school. For all his urbanity, for all his authority, he felt a memory of infant intimidation run through him.

He braved her glare. 'Of course I don't, Miss Mair,' he assured her. 'But I would like you to find out for me.'

'It's easy to say that, young man, but not nearly as easy to do it. You're talking about the old days of British Railways. This man McConnell retired fifteen years ago. Things have changed since then. We're privatised now, and many of the old personnel records simply don't exist any more.

'Those that do might have been transferred to Railtrack, or to ScotRail or to another of the operating companies. It would all depend on what Mr McConnell did.'

'Someone would be paying his pension, surely.'

'That's a different thing altogether. And besides, there are thousands upon thousands of pensioners.'

Mackenzie decided to change tack. 'But Miss Mair, I'm not necessarily talking about personnel records alone.'

'Human Resources now,' she nit-picked.

'Not even them. I simply want to speak to anyone who might have known this man, and with whom he might have had continuing contact over the years. Okay, he's been gone for fifteen years, but there must be some people still around in the organisation who remember him, and remember who his friends were.'

Her lips pursed. 'Mr McConnell didn't necessarily have any friends,' she said, unexpectedly.

'You remember him?'

'Yes, Mr Mackenzie, as a matter of fact I do. I didn't know him, you understand . . . He was a senior manager then, and I was only a junior executive . . . and I don't recall what section he worked in. However . . . assuming that it's the same man, and I suppose it must be . . . I do recall that he was not regarded as a very nice man.' She gave a brief, but severe nod of her head. 'Particularly by the female members of staff.'

The policeman saw her embarrassment, and took secret delight in it. 'Why was that, Miss Mair?' he asked ingenuously.

She sniffed. 'He had a bit of a reputation, among the younger girls at any rate. They used to call him . . .' She paused, and for that second he thought he saw her blush. '. . . they used to call him "Feely John". He had the name of being a bit of a toucher. Always accidental, of course, and given his rank, no one ever complained, but most of the girls didn't like to get too close to him.'

'What about the others? Were there any who didn't mind?'

'There were a couple of girls,' she said. 'There were rumours, shall we say. They were both flighty types, and neither of them worked here long. There was gossip once about someone walking into a room at an office party, but the detail of it never came to my ears.'

'*I'll bet it did,*' thought Mackenzie, '*but it'll never pass your tight old lips now.*'

'What about male colleagues? Do you recall anyone with whom he was particularly friendly? For example, I'm told that his former sister-in-law married a colleague of his. Her name would have been McConnell too; she died about twenty years ago. Does any of that ring bells?'

'No, it does not. As I told you, I did not associate with the man, nor did I even know his section.'

'In that case, do you know anyone who might have?'

'Mr Mackenzie,' she exclaimed, indignant once more. 'I am not a mine of information nor a hoarder of old office gossip.'

'I never suggested that you were,' he said at once, in his best mollifying tone. 'All I was hoping to do was to draw on your experience.'

The woman's stiff spine seemed to unbend just a fraction. 'Very well,' she conceded. 'If you leave the matter with me, I will search my memory further and consult other senior colleagues. Former sister-in-law, you said?' She pursed her lips again, as if she did not approve of sisters-in-law in the 'former' category.

'It may take some time, and I can make no promises. However, if you leave me your telephone number, I shall see what I can do.'

Fifty-four

'Y ou realise, gentlemen, that you are not going to be seeing a seventy-mil movie here?' Tony Davidson pointed out. The force's Director of Telecommunications had a reputation for plain speaking. 'This is not Hollywood; we cannot trace fleeing criminals by satellite in the dark. We may be able to tell where a specific dustcart is at any moment during its round, but that's about it.

'What we're playing with here is way short of being even as advanced as that.'

'Let's have a whack at it anyway, Tony,' said Andy Martin. 'We won't blame you for failing to work miracles, but there's a dead girl demanding that we all do our best. Dan and I will have to take a press conference later on today and it would be nice to have something positive to say.'

Davidson nodded and turned off the light in the small viewing room. 'For best results . . .' He pressed the start switch of a big video player which sat on a table, cabled to a monitor screen on a tall stand.

'This is the first tape,' he said, as a green-tinted image appeared on the screen. 'It has a twelve-hour slow speed capacity, so what we're looking for should be towards the

267

middle. It has a time display, so . . . I'll wind it forward to midnight.'

They waited, watching as the tape wound on, little or nothing changing save for the blur of the white indicators in the bottom left corner of the picture as the hours, minutes and seconds flashed by. Finally the technical director pressed a button and the numbers steadied, showing the record time as four minutes past the midnight hour.

On screen the shape of the compound could be made out; they could see the tanks with odd sparkles of green light from the ever-flowing water, as it caught the light from a single window in the cottage beyond. They listened, and could hear its constant soft tinkle and the dull sound of the pumps.

Davidson ran the tape on, switching from slow motion to normal speed, sending the time indicator turning faster, but still legibly.

Suddenly, with 01:12 hours showing on screen, there was a different movement. Quickly he froze the picture, then returned it to its original running rate. Looking intently, they saw the green ghostly outline of a figure walking across the clearing towards the house, a tall long-striding man. He was dressed in boots, and a long hooded jacket, and he appeared to be carrying something light in his left hand.

'What's that?' asked Pringle, of no one in particular.

'Could be a sheet,' Davidson replied, 'or a sack, or a tarpaulin.'

The man in the video walked straight up to the cottage. Right-handed, he banged on the front door . . . the knock was loud enough for them to hear above the splashing . . . then stood back, round the corner, out of sight from anyone who might open it.

'Freeze it,' Martin ordered.

The detectives and the technician studied the still frame on screen. 'I'd say that he wants the girl to come out, so that he can throw that sheet or whatever over her head. So why didn't she? Run it on, please, Tony.'

The scene played itself out; the man stood waiting, tensed, the covering now held in both hands. At last, they saw another movement, another figure, a little smaller than him, but stocky, behind him, moving towards him slowly.

'It's the girl,' Pringle exclaimed. 'She's come out the back door.'

She was almost on him when he dropped the sheet and turned. They saw the blur of movement as she swung at him, his hand coming up to catch hers, the two green-ghost figures together in a silent struggle. Then, as they watched, his right hand wrenched clear, with something in it. His arm rose and fell; there was a scream, another blow, another, fainter shout, then blow after blow after blow.

'Oh my God,' Davidson hissed.

'That's it,' said Martin. 'The plan was to throw that sheet over her head and tie her up while the robbery went ahead. But the poor lass had a go. She saw his face, and he killed her.'

'Someone she knew?' Pringle mused.

'Maybe, maybe not; but someone she'd have been able to identify.'

And then as they watched the screen was filled with green light, and the roar of engines came from the speakers. Four wide beams swung across the picture, two of them lighting up a dark shape, like that of a petrol tanker. Then the first shafts of light swung round and shone directly into the camera, obliterating all other images, even the time read-out in the corner.

'Dammit!' shouted Pringle in frustration.

They watched the film for fifteen minutes seeing only green but hearing the sound of the farm's machinery, harshly throbbing diesel engines, and something else louder than the pumps, the whoosh of fish and water being sucked from the tanks. Occasionally an indistinct figure would be framed against the light, carrying what could have been a long flexible hose, then would move out of shot once again.

Finally it was over. The noise of the suction engines stopped. As the three listened, they heard a single loud splash, then another, softer, then the slamming of vehicle doors. It seemed to take the camera some seconds to adjust to the darkness once more. When it did, the clearing was empty, and the scene was as it had been at first, save for the fact that the front door of the cottage now stood open, and that on the tank nearest to it, something – no, someone – floated.

The Head of CID punched the 'Stop' button on the player, killing what was left of the sound.

'I'm sorry,' said Davidson, in the darkness, even before he switched on the light. 'As I said, there are limitations to this technology. Shining a bright light into the lens of a night vision camera will bugger it, for sure.'

'The man, Tony,' asked Martin. 'Is there anything you can do to isolate and enhance that image, to get a face out of it?'

'No. I'm afraid not. Even if he hadn't been wearing that

hooded jacket, I couldn't get you the sort of definition you need.'

'How about those guys who appeared in shot carrying the sucker hoses?'

'Without the headlamps, probably, but with all that light behind them? Not a prayer.'

'Ah, too bad,' the Head of CID sighed, then brightened up almost at once.

'Still, Dan,' he said. 'It's not a total loss. We can wave those tapes about at our press conference. The killer and his pals; they're not going to know they're useless, are they?'

Fifty-five

Neil McIlhenney reflected on his day as he drove up Colinton Road. There had been an air of unmistakable tension about the place, and clear signs that something had happened. The ACC's new secretary, for a start, drafted in without warning; not a hint dropped by Ruth in his direction that Chase had won his unsubtle battle to increase his personal staff.

Then there had been Jack Good; he never could stand the boiled-shirt bastard, and even less so since he had made inspector and had shown himself to be the sort who glared when a junior uniform failed to salute him, and who insisted on being 'sirred' all the time, even by his contemporaries, guys who had known him for years.

But all that day, the same Jack Good had been a bag of nerves. He had bumped into him three times in the corridor; twice he had been coming out of the toilet, but on the first occasion, he had been leaving the DCC's room. On every encounter, he had been jumpy, like a man trying to get out of the path of a speeding car.

Yes, something was up all right, and he deduced that it had to do with ACC Chase, and that peculiar grin which he had been carrying all day. Bob Skinner often told McIlhenney more than he needed to know, but he never talked about anything that went on inside the Chief's room, unless there was a clear reason for it.

He had never suggested that tension might possibly exist between Chase and himself. He had never needed to, of course; Neil knew his boss well enough to understand that coppers like Chase were anathema to him. He had never mentioned Chase's notorious paper either, any more than had Ruth, who had typed it. He might still not have known about it, but for a series of heavy-handed hints from Good, which had eventually provoked him to exclaim one day, in his own small office, 'Jack, exactly what the fuck are you talking about?'

It had to be that damned paper that lay behind Chase's smirk. Yet if it was, why was his aide so clearly shiteing himself?

'Ah, *what the hell*,' he thought as he turned into his driveway, '*the boss'll tell me when he's good and ready.*'

He drove his car into the garage, checked with Marie that Lauren and Spencer were fine, then walked the short distance round to Louise Bankier's safe house. As he opened the garden gate, he saw, almost hidden behind a tall hedge, a silver-grey Renault Mégane hatchback. He glanced at the registration: Glasgow. Of course, Lucy's. Lou had mentioned that her sister was bringing her father through to see her.

He rang the bell; its echo had barely died before Louise swung it open. 'Hey,' he said, trying to look severe. 'I thought I told you not to do that; take a look through the peep-hole first.'

273

'I saw you coming up the path; and eyeballing poor wee Lucy's car too.' He smiled as he noticed that she sounded more Glaswegian than ever. 'Come and meet the guys,' she said.

Warren Judd and Elliott Silver had been gone by the time he had arrived the evening before to pick her up. He studied them both carefully, but politely, as she introduced them. Judd was a short, stocky man, about his own age, he guessed; he flashed him a smile and was taken aback by the hostility in the look which he shot back. Silver was ten years younger, in his late twenties, of medium height and light build, with soft features and, unlike his colleague, possessed of a ready, endearing smile.

Behind them at the window, another man stood. He was big; at least six two, bulky shoulders in a denim shirt, black hair cut close. McIlhenney's eyebrows began to rise, unconsciously, until Lucy walked over to him and took his arm. 'This is Darren Mason, my boyfriend,' she said. 'He's never met my famous sister before.'

Louise smiled at them, then exclaimed, with more pride in her voice than he had heard before, 'And last, but the opposite of least, the most important man in my life; Malcolm Bankier, my dad.

'Dad, this is Neil McIlhenney, who's sort of looking after me while I'm here.'

The old man in the armchair made to push himself up on a thick brown cane. 'You stay there, Mr Bankier, please,' said the detective, laying his left hand gently on his shoulder and offering him his right. He settled back then shook it, with a gnarled, twisted, arthritic claw, looking not at Louise, but at his younger daughter, who was perched on the broad arm of the chair.

'Who is he?' he exclaimed. 'She got another man?'

'Shh, Dad,' whispered Lucy. 'No, that's not it.'

The old man's face seemed to brighten up. 'Ah, he's yours then,' he cackled. 'Lucy's got a fella.' The young woman flushed.

'No, Mr Bankier,' said Neil. 'I'm not so privileged. I work for Louise. I'm responsible for her accommodation while she's in Edinburgh. I just looked in to check on her schedule for tomorrow.'

'Work for her, you say?' His voice, though wavering, still kept its cultured middle-class Glaswegian tones. He waved his stick at Judd and Silver. 'Like these two?' Suddenly, his eyes narrowed, and he beckoned the policeman towards him. As McIlhenney leaned over, Malcolm Bankier nodded towards Warren Judd. 'That wee chap there,' he hissed, loudly enough for everyone in the room to hear, 'watch him. Seen him before somewhere. Don't like him.'

Neil could think of nothing to say to fill the embarrassing silence, but the old man did it for him. 'Thought I'd seen you before too,' he said. 'With Louise; long time ago, when she was a lass and my wee Lucy was a baby. Not you though; someone else. Sorry.'

Lucy Bankier glanced up at her sister, who nodded. 'Come on, Daddy,' she said. 'Lou says tea will be ready; let's go to the dining room.'

'She never said a bloody word,' Mr Bankier grumbled, but he allowed her to help him to his feet, and out of the room.

When they were gone Louise looked apologetically at

Judd. 'I'm sorry about that, Warren,' she said. 'His memory's all over the place these days. He hasn't a clue what he's saying.'

'Don't worry about it.' The producer laughed, but, it seemed to McIlhenney, without real humour.

'I do though. For example, I worry for my sister, left in Bearsden to look after him. I give her nursing help, of course, but he goes through them at a rate of knots; I've had to move agencies twice. The Alzheimer's has changed his personality completely; for one thing it's made him a dirty old man . . . and I'm not just talking about his toilet habits.

'It makes me so sad; he's only seventy-five you know, and he wears a bloody nappy, yet there are men in their eighties who're as fit as fiddles. This started off as one of his better days, too.'

'Well,' exclaimed Judd, brusquely. 'We'd best leave you with him, then. As we agreed, don't you worry about tomorrow. Boy Wonder and I will take care of that. See you on Monday, to start the New Town shooting.' He turned on his heel and left the room, Silver in his wake.

'Your dad's not as wandered as all that, is he?' McIlhenney murmured. 'He's right about friend Judd for a start.'

'He never did like Warren,' she snapped. He felt rebuffed; she saw it and apologised at once. 'I'm sorry, Neil; I'm just a bit touchy on that subject.'

'So's he, I reckon.'

'Don't take it personally.' Then she smiled. 'No,' she said. 'Take it personally if you like.'

She paused, and looked at him. 'You know who he mistook you for, don't you?' she asked.

'I can make a pretty good guess.'

'How much has Bob told you?'

'Very little; only that you two were close a long time ago. But last Friday night when we drove back from Gullane, I knew who you were talking about. He was the one, eh? The big hurt, twenty-five years ago.'

'Yup,' she admitted. 'And isn't it strange now, that Dad should mistake you for him, you two being such good friends and colleagues and everything.'

She sighed. 'Daddy was furious, you know; furious with Bob, when we broke up. I never talked about him afterwards, you know, but once when I was visiting home, when Lucy would be about fourteen, he said something, in front of her, about having seen him on television.

'I had to tell her the whole story. Until that moment I hadn't realised just how angry he had been.'

She laughed. 'And then, on Monday evening, when he called in, she was here, and they met. I wondered how she'd react, but you know, she just melted. She fell for him on the spot, just like me two and a half decades before her.

'I tell you, it's just as well he loves his wife, or Bob Skinner could do untold damage in my family still!'

He chuckled. 'Speaking of families, I must get back to mine. I gather that you've called off your meeting tomorrow.'

'Yes. Glenys and I are having another day with the script;

the guys can finish the location recces. There's only one I want to do myself.'

'Where's that?' he asked.

'You'll find out,' she told him, mysteriously. 'On Saturday.'

Fifty-six

'Where did you find her, Dan?' asked Andy Martin.

'She turned up at her house in Coldstream, just after five o'clock. Two uniforms spotted her and detained her until McGurk picked her up and brought her up here to Galashiels. We're just about to question her.

'So far she's brassing it out, though: she claims she has no idea why we want to talk to her. McGurk was smart enough not to play along with her though. He's said nothing at all to her, other than that she's wanted for questioning. We've let her stew in it so far, but we're ready to talk to her now.'

'Have you seen her at all?'

'Not yet.'

'Has she seen a lawyer?'

'She was allowed to phone her lawyer in Coldstream. He's a real old country lawyer with more sense than to go anywhere near a criminal matter, so he's sent up the young lad in his office who does what little Sheriff Court work he has.

'He's just arrived, but he can see her at the same time as I do. Jack sneaked a quick look at him. He says he looks still wet behind the ears, but full of himself, puffed up like a rooster.'

'Nah,' said Martin dryly. 'There's a difference between a rooster and a lawyer.'

'What's that?'

'A rooster clucks defiance: a lawyer fucks de clients.'

The Head of CID cut across Pringle's laugh. 'What does McGurk think about the woman?'

'He reckons she's lying in her fucking teeth.' The superintendent glanced across his office at the sergeant. 'Mind you, Jack's still a bit upset, after finding that poor lass. He's desperate to nail someone for it. I'll make up my own mind about her.'

'Go and do it, then,' said Martin. 'Just remember, though; McGurk doesn't know as we do that it couldn't have been her hitting the girl on the tape.'

'No, but you don't know that wasn't her we saw framed in the lights of that lorry.'

'True,' admitted the Head of CID. 'Go do it then.'

Pringle hung up and nodded to McGurk. 'Come on.' He led the way out of the room downstairs and into the waiting area. He spotted the lawyer at once from his sergeant's description; no more than twenty-five years old, smooth-cheeked, looking precociously pompous in a pin-striped suit.

'Mr Mark Taggart?' the policeman asked.

'Yes!' the young man exclaimed. 'Inspector, I insist on seeing my client at once, or must I speak to your superiors?'

'That's "Superintendent" to you,' Pringle barked. 'Dan Pringle, divisional CID commander, and don't fucking threaten me, son. Now you come on wi' us and you'll see your client.'

'But I want to see her alone,' the young man protested.

'So does DS McGurk here, but we're all going to see her together, and you're going to keep your mouth shut and let us get on with our interview. This is a murder investigation, as I'm sure you know by this time . . .' The young lawyer gulped, almost comically, leaving Pringle to guess that any briefing he had been given before he left Coldstream might have been less than complete.

'Your client hasn't actually killed anyone, son, but she still has a few questions to answer about her possible knowledge of the crime. I'm not going to caution her at this stage; if I decide to in the light of anything she says, I'll stop the interview and advise you at once.

'Until then, you're in there because of my generosity of spirit, and that's all.'

Mercy Alvarez was waiting for them in a small, windowless room at the rear of the ground floor of the divisional headquarters building. The air was thick with cigarette smoke as the two detectives entered; Pringle felt an old familiar pang. The woman glared at them through the blue haze, but said nothing.

The female constable who sat silently with her rose and made to leave, until Pringle shook his head, signalling her to stay. He placed twin tapes in the recorder on the table, then switched it on, identifying everyone in the room for the record.

'We've got a problem with you, Ms Alvarez,' the superintendent blurted out, as soon as he had completed the formalities.

'What you mean?' she snapped.

'Well, there were only a handful of us who knew that as of Friday, you'd have video security installed on your farm. There was you, there was Jack and me, and there was our boss, Mr Martin.' He paused. 'Oh aye, and there was Kath Adey.

'All of which makes it very iffy that last night someone should have broken into your site and emptied out your tanks. In view of the short time that's gone by since the last robbery, it makes me wonder whether someone tipped off these guys that they only had a couple of days . . .'

'What?' Mercy Alvarez interrupted, her dark eyes widening. 'Country Fresh? Is been robbed?'

'Good,' said Pringle. 'I'm impressed by that reaction; maybe I was meant to be. But I'm not convinced. Someone told that gang that they had to do your place before Friday. Now it wasn't DCS Martin, and it wasn't DS McGurk, and it wasn't me. So that just leaves you.'

'Superintendent!' Mark Taggart exclaimed.

'Shut up, you! Did you set up your own farm to be robbed, Ms Alvarez?'

The woman's face twisted in anger. 'No I did not!' she spat. 'Anyhow, you miss someone out? What about Kath?'

Jack McGurk shook his head. 'We don't think it was her, Ms Alvarez.'

'Why not?' she shouted. 'Why you accuse me, not her?'

The burly superintendent leaned across the table. 'Because no one's bashed your head in, and chucked you in a fish tank,' he said, quietly. 'Because you're not lying in the fucking mortuary up in Edinburgh, with your brain beside you in a stainless steel dish.'

Dan Pringle was long past the stage in his police career when he believed that he could be surprised by anyone or anything. But right there, right then, Mercy Alvarez surprised him; she fell off her chair, in a dead faint.

An hour went by before a doctor certified that she had recovered sufficiently for the interview to proceed. She was so shaken that Pringle was convinced there and then that she had known nothing of her manager's murder.

His tone was gentler when he resumed his questioning. 'Let's start again, Ms Alvarez,' he said. 'When was the last time you saw Miss Adey alive?'

'At four o'clock yesterday afternoon, when I left the farm, to go home.'

'Okay, now I repeat my earlier question. Did you have any knowledge that your farm was going to be robbed?'

'No, I did not. I swear it.'

'Did you mention to anyone that the police were insisting that you install security equipment?'

'No. Why should I?'

'Do I have to spell that out?'

'If you do, Superintendent,' said the young solicitor, a little braver now, 'I shall have to insist that the rest of this interview takes place under caution.'

'Okay,' Pringle conceded. 'If she did set the place up to be robbed she's no' going to admit it, caution or not.

'I'll rephrase it then. Did you mention to anyone, however innocently, that you were considering installing a system?'

'I told my bank manager's secretary that that was what I wanted to see him about.'

'Do you know if Miss Adey spoke with anyone, after Mr Martin's visit on Monday?'

'She might have, but only by telephone; she never leave the farm after that. I guess she spoke to the video man.'

'What video man?'

'A salesman who came see us a few months ago. He left us information then, and a card. I told Kate to phone him.'

'Was his name Anders?' asked McGurk.

'Yes, I think that was it.'

Pringle looked at the sergeant, enquiring. 'I found a leaflet and a card by the phone in the cottage,' he explained. 'There was an entry in Miss Adey's diary, too; she had an appointment with Raymond Anders, of Eildon Security, at four this afternoon on the farm.'

The superintendent drew McGurk into a corner. 'Let's find out whether he kept it,' he whispered. 'Let's find out too, but very quietly, whether he paid any unsuccessful sales visits to the other two farms.' The tall detective nodded and left the room.

'Just one other thing, Ms Alvarez,' Pringle continued, 'for now at any rate. Where were you all day today, when we were trying to contact you?'

'I was with my boyfriend,' she said, hesitantly. 'His name is Glenn Lander. He had a dinner party last night; I stayed over and all day. Four of us: his cousin from England was there, with her husband. He's a policeman; an important policeman, I think. His name is Ted . . . Ted Chase.'

Fifty-seven

'There's nowhere else to go, sir,' said Stevie Steele, his frustration written all over his face. 'This bloke exists, all right, this man calling himself John Steed, but I'm no closer to him now than I was at the start.

'I took the best still print from the Balmoral video that the techies could provide for me and showed it to the woman in Newcastle, but she said that she couldn't have identified her own son from the view it showed.

'She said that the guy's hat in the print looked similar to the one her customer wore, but let's face it . . . a black hat's a black hat.'

'Aye. I've got one myself.' Andy Martin sighed. 'That's the second time in quick succession that I've been let down by a video tape. Give a copy of the print to McIlhenney; maybe Louise Bankier or her secretary will spot something in it.

'Apart from that, there's only one other thing you can do, and that's pursue the possibility that this lad really is called John Steed, and that his message was badly worded but otherwise innocent.'

'I'm doing that already, sir,' Steele replied. 'The police on Tyneside have reported back to me already; they've turned up three John Steeds; one's in jail, another's in his eighties and the third is a hemiplegic.

'I even asked them to check on people named John Stead, just in case the man might have mis-typed his own surname when he sent the message. No joy there either. I'm waiting for other forces to report back; I've asked for traces as far south as Middlesbrough, and also in London and in our own area, where the two incidents have occurred.'

'Fair enough,' said Bob Skinner, turning away from the window of the Head of CID's office. 'It all has to be done, but you'll get nothing from it. Big Neil's first instinct was right; the name's a phoney, part of the message itself. We'll trace Mr Steed when he has another go at Louise, and not before.'

'And he'll find that difficult while she's under surveillance,' Martin suggested.

'Agreed, but next week, Lou starts location work on her movie; that's when she'll be vulnerable. We can protect her, and we will, by blocking off the streets where they're filming; she'll have a dressing room trailer too, but she'll still be an open target to an extent.'

'What about the crew, sir?' asked Steele. 'Are they being checked out?'

'Of course they are, sergeant,' said the DCC, testily. 'DI McIlhenney's getting a list this morning from Judd, the producer; everyone on the team from Elliott Silver, the director, right up to the tea-boy. He'll run a PNC check straight away . . .' He sighed. '. . . and come up with fuck all too, apart from a couple of pot-smokers.'

'What about Judd himself?'

Skinner frowned at Martin's question. 'He was the first one Neil checked. He and Louise lived together for a while a few years back; they talked about getting married, but she decided that she'd had enough of that game. Judd didn't like it, they had a major argument, and they split up, but not before he thumped her.

'She almost turned this movie down because of Mr Judd, but she liked the part, her agent pressed her and finally, he apologised. So she agreed.

'Do not worry, Andy. His was the first name out of the hat when this all blew up. He was even in the hotel on the day that smoke bomb was planted in Lou's room. But he is not the man in the hotel video and he was not John Steed in Newcastle. The physical descriptions just don't match up; the guy in the black hat is slim, and Judd's a wee bull of a fellow.

'On top of that, from the moment that he arrived at the Balmoral, all the way through their tour of Edinburgh, during their meeting afterwards, and right up to the moment he left, Lou swears that he was never out of her sight, and that Silver was with them the whole time too.'

The big DCC scowled. 'I'd love it to be Judd. It'd give me a chance to teach him not to knock women around. But it isn't.' He looked at Steele. 'So that's where we are, young Stevie; waiting for the stalker to pull another stunt. I hope he does too; I don't want him just to fade away. I want him caught.

'Now, will you excuse us, please. I have to talk to Mr Martin about something unconnected with this.'

'Of course, sir, I'll find DI McIlhenney and give him that print.'

As the door closed behind him, Martin looked at Skinner. 'Well?' he asked.

'Yes.' A grin spread across his face. 'I've spoken to him, interviewed him even, with the Chief Constable present. Mr Chase and his lovely wife Estelle were indeed entertained by Mrs Chase's cousin on Wednesday night. They dined on fish soup prepared by Ms Alvarez, braised venison prepared by Mr Lander, and praline ice cream prepared by Häagen-Dazs.

'The Assistant Chief Constable having consumed no alcohol all evening, he and his good lady began the drive back to Edinburgh at 12.45 a.m., leaving the young lovers slightly the worse for the third bottle of Paternina Banda Azul rioja tinto, and about to retire for the night.

'We left him pondering the possibility of being subjected to aggressive cross-examination by a hungry Advocate Depute.'

'That was nice of you,' laughed the Head of CID. 'It won't come to that, though. Dan phoned me a while back; Raymond Anders, of Eildon Security, who failed to turn up for his four o'clock appointment with Kath Adey yesterday, has also visited the Mellerkirk and Howdengate trout farms in unsuccessful attempts to sell them video surveillance and alarm systems.

'Every copper in the Borders is looking for him, but he's disappeared. Dan's about to issue a press statement with a description, and an appeal for public support in tracing him.

'Looks like he could be our man.'

Fifty-eight

'Just like Rockefeller Plaza.' Louise Bankier looked along the ice rink, thronged with circling figures on silver skates, some steady and assured, others much less so. 'They do this every Christmas time?'

'Yes,' Neil replied. 'Skating in Princes Street Gardens; it's a tradition already, even though they've only been doing it for a few years. Nice though, especially on a day like this.' He leaned forward on the green park bench, tightening the laces of his left boot. The morning was crisp and cold, the ice hard and inviting.

Spencer and Lauren leaned on the fence at the entrance to the rink, waiting, watching as their father checked the fastenings on the shiny new boots which Glenys Algodon had acquired for Louise the day before.

No one took any notice of them as they readied themselves to take to the ice. The actress wore tight black trousers and a heavy parka with a fur-trimmed hood so enveloping that it hid her face as effectively as a mask.

'Okay,' he said, as she leaned her weight on his outstretched left arm. 'Away you go, then.' She pushed herself away and set off, deliberately and carefully, after the children who were circling and pirouetting with fearless confidence. At the very first turn, her legs went from under her; she fell, with a bump. Lauren gasped, Spencer laughed, then Neil was beside her, helping her to her feet.

'Here,' he chuckled, 'I thought you said you could do this. I'm supposed to be looking after you; if you turn up for filming on crutches next week I'll be back on the beat.'

'I can skate,' she insisted, with mock indignation. 'I'm just out of practice, that's all.'

He steadied her, his strong hands on her waist. 'Get away with you, lady, it's like riding a bike. You never forget.'

'Okay, so let me go and I'll show you.' He released her and she set off once more, slowly, but more steadily this time. He skated easily alongside her, watching her closely until finally she gathered confidence and began to move more easily.

'You're quite good,' she told him, when she felt able to speak.

'For a flat-footed copper, you mean?'

Her laugh had a breathless edge. 'If you say so.'

'I played ice hockey when I was a kid,' he replied, evenly. 'After I chucked it, I didn't skate for a while, during my porker years, but then I started roller-blading with those two, and it seemed natural to take them on to the ice and show them the real thing.'

'They're really good.'

'Ah, but so am I.'

'Show me.'

'Nah. Too many people on the ice; plus, I don't want to draw attention to us.'

She saw him glancing around. 'You're always watching, aren't you?'

'Always.' At that moment, an unsteady skater, a young man, veered in their direction. Neil swung smoothly round, putting his body between the approaching figure and Louise, then catching him, steadying him and sending him gently on his way.

They skated on for around twenty minutes, Lauren and Spencer weaving patterns around them, until finally she called, 'Enough!'

They left the children to their ice ballet and skated off the rink, reclaiming their shoes from the kiosk and changing into them on their bench. That done, they leaned against the fence, watching the action on the ice, wincing as the occasional beginner came to grief.

'Hey,' she asked, glancing at him from the depths of her hood, 'what did you mean, earlier . . . your porker years?'

He smiled, with a touch of shyness. 'I used to be a far bigger boy than I am now. Olive used to go on at me about my weight. My father died of a heart attack at Spence's christening and she was always worried that the same might happen to me.

'I just laughed it off; I was big, sure, but I wasn't that unfit. I could still chase the bad guys. And, like everyone else, I had this notion that I was immortal, that the two of us were. Then Olive fell ill, and we knew that we weren't.

'I didn't entertain the idea that she would die; right up to the very last second in that wee side ward, I didn't believe that she would. But the mere thought that she could, that was enough.

'One of my nightmares is that anything might happen to me while those two are still kids, while they still need me. So

I do everything I can to make sure it doesn't. I'm thirty pounds lighter than I was back then. I go to the gym, run a bit, and play football with the boss's crowd once a week. I drink very little alcohol any more, and I'm careful about what I eat.

'Plus I have a job that takes me out of the line of fire.'

She looked at him, surprised. 'Then what are you doing with me?'

He scratched his chin. 'That's a good question. I asked it of myself and I asked it of Olive . . . I talk to her a lot, you know; all the time, in fact. The answer is that I'm doing what she would want me to do.' He gave her a confessional smile. 'She likes you, you know.'

'I'm honoured,' Louise whispered, sincerely.

'So?' he asked her, suddenly, ending that moment. 'Warren Judd?'

'My last big mistake,' she said. 'And he will be. I thought I knew everything there was to know about men; I thought I was always in control. I thought that he was safe, but he was anything but.

'I made it clear . . . or I thought I had . . . that I wasn't interested in marrying again. I believe I'm jinxed in that department. But Warren started on about it, and he wouldn't let go. I told him to forget it, but he kept bringing it up.

'Finally, we had a big argument and I told him to get out of my house and out of my life. He did . . .' Her voice dropped to a whisper, '. . . but before he did, he beat me up, and he raped me.'

When she was able to look at him again, she saw him as she had never seen him before. His face was dark with anger. 'The little bastard,' he growled.

She laid a hand on his arm. 'No, Neil, no. It's in the past; let it stay there. I've dealt with it, and with him. He crawled to get me to do this movie; I made him, believe me.

'God,' she said suddenly. 'I don't know why I told you that . . . not that last bit, at any rate. I have never told anyone about it before. Don't ever say anything to Bob, please. He doesn't know the whole story; it scares me to think what he might do.'

'Don't worry,' he assured her. 'I won't do that. But if Judd ever gives me half an excuse, I'll beat him bloody.'

She took his hand and squeezed it. 'Don't waste your anger. I've never had any luck with men. For the last ten years, I've attracted nothing but maggots.' She gave a short bitter laugh. 'When that effete little twerp Elliott Silver made a pass at me last year, that was it; that was when I decided to give up the species, for good!'

Fifty-nine

'Is this what it's going to be like from now on, Jack?' Mary McGurk complained, looking at her husband as he adjusted the knot of his tie and slipped the narrow end inside the retaining loop. 'Is it?'

'It's my job, love.'

'It's your job to have every weekend ruined?' she said, scornfully. 'It's your job to drop everything and go tearing off south even though we've had this party on the kitchen calendar for the last two months? It's your job to jump every time that man Pringle phones?'

He nodded, feeling his patience run out. 'Yes. It won't always be, but for now it is.'

She grabbed her jacket from the bed and began to put it on. 'Well sod that! I'll beat you to it; I'm going out. You'll just have to stay in with the baby.'

'Fine,' he shouted at her. 'You do that. You just do that, you selfish wee bitch! Go on out and leave me with the kid. You know what I'll do? I'll have a uniformed woman constable here inside ten minutes and I'll be on my way. So yeah, go on, make your fucking gesture, and slam the door on the way out so the bloody neighbours know too.'

She stripped the jacket off again and threw it at him; one

of the steel buttons caught him just above the eye. He felt sharp pain, and then a warm trace as a thin line of blood began to run down the side of his face.

'Thanks,' he said, coldly, ripping a tissue from the box on the dressing table and pressing it to the small wound.

'Sorry,' his wife whispered. She sat on the bed, her eyes glassy with tears. 'Jack,' she murmured, 'it's just not fair.'

He sat beside her. 'No love,' he agreed. 'It's not; but don't blame Mr Pringle, and don't blame me. If you want to, take it out on this man Raymond Anders. He's the guy who's in the frame for bashing that girl's head in on Thursday.

'Now he's been arrested at his sister's house in Leeds, and Pringle and I have to go and get him, then bring him up to Gala for questioning.'

'But couldn't someone else go?'

He shook his head, his mouth set tight. 'No. This is a murder investigation; it's down to us to pick this boy up. If you want to understand why, I'll bring home the photographs, and let you see them.'

'No thanks,' she retorted. 'I don't want any of that coming into this house.'

'But Mary, I'm part of that. It's what I do.'

'You don't have to do that. You could ask for a transfer back to uniform, somewhere in Edinburgh, not down in the sticks.'

Jack McGurk sighed. 'Are we back to that again? Love, we can't stay in Edinburgh. This is a case in point. Once we're living down there, things like this won't be nearly as big a hassle.'

'Of course they will,' she snapped. 'It'll be worse, I don't know anyone down there. I'll have nothing to do down there. I'll be like one of your prisoners. Can you get this through your big thick head? I don't want to go to the Borders, however nice and twee and country bloody casual you try and paint it.

'I want to stay here, Jack. I'm an Edinburgh girl, first and foremost.'

He stood up from the bed, checking quickly in the mirrored wardrobe door that the cut above his eye had stopped bleeding. Then he picked up the blazer which, earlier, he had hung over the back of a chair, and slipped it on.

'Funny,' he said, as he reached for the door handle. 'I thought we were a couple, first and foremost.'

Sixty

'I should be immersing myself in my part, you know,' she told him, with mock severity, as they headed down the A68. 'I should be in the process of turning myself into an Edinburgh criminal lawyer, as my craft demands.

'I should be spending the day talking to Bob's daughter, picking up hints and tips from her, rather than heading off for a day out in the country with a flatfoot like you.'

'Is that so?' he drawled. 'Point one, it was your idea to head out of Craiglockhart so that Glenys and Clarence could indulge in whatever it is young couples like them are supposed to indulge in on Sundays. Personally,' he offered in an aside, 'I usually watch football on telly with my son.

'Point two, brilliant and full of promise as Ms Alexis Skinner may be, she's a corporate lawyer. If you want to splash around or whatever in the realities of the Scottish crime scene, you're much better off with a career polisman like me.'

Cold Saturday had continued through the night; there was snow all around as they climbed Sutra Hill, but the road was well gritted and wet, rather than icy.

'So? Tell me about it.'

'Tell me about your lady lawyer,' Neil countered.

'She's a QC for a start. She's approached by a friend, whose husband has been arrested and charged with murder and she agrees to take the case.'

McIlhenney took a hand from the wheel. 'Hold on a minute. Who wrote the script?'

'Elliott did; in collaboration with a Scottish crime novelist.'

'They've dropped a clanger then . . . unless your lady lawyer's bent. Is she?'

Louise shook her head. 'No. She's a heroine, a straight arrow.'

'She's broken the rules nevertheless. She's not allowed to accept a brief directly from a client; she'd have to be instructed by a solicitor.'

'Is that true?'

'Of course it's bloody true. If you want me to be your technical adviser, you've got to trust me.'

She turned in her seat and looked at him, eagerly. 'Would you be? Our technical adviser, I mean, like for real?'

He whistled. 'Not a chance; not officially. But from the sound of things you need one. Alex might not do criminal work herself, but she knows plenty of advocates. Give her a call and she'll introduce you to someone.'

'But I don't know Alex. She doesn't know me.'

The big policeman laughed. 'One of the things I like about you, Louise, is that most of the time you forget who and what you are. If it makes you feel more comfortable, ask the boss to ask her.' He pointed to his mobile, which was clipped into a car adapter. 'Call him now, if you like.'

'No,' she said. 'You do it for me. I don't like to call Bob at home. Sarah was very good when we had dinner the week before last, but woman to woman, she won't want to hear too much of me.'

'You're too sensitive, but if you like, I'll call Alex myself and ask her for a couple of introductions. They'll be on the payroll, yes?'

'Sure. Elliott and the writer can pay for her, since they've screwed up.'

'Hard woman, you.'

'You better believe it,' she chuckled. 'Whatever crap we talk at Oscar time, our business is money-driven. I'm working with Warren because I know that, together, we'll bring the project in on time and within budget.'

'So what happens to the lady lawyer?'

'It's a complicated script; she's intrigued by her client; she falls for him in fact. As she speaks to the witnesses she becomes more and more convinced that he's been set up. She decides to do some freelance investigation of her own . . .'

'Stop!' he cried out. 'Don't tell me any more. You really need that technical adviser. I suppose that all the coppers are bastards too.'

'Absolutely.'

'Ah well,' he laughed, 'that's accurate enough.'

He took the Kelso turn-off at Carfraemill, driving more slowly since the road had been used less heavily than the main trunk route and, consequently, the surface was less certain. Eventually, he took another turning, and headed up a twisting hillside track; a few miles on it seemed to peter out.

He drew up in a deserted parking area. 'Okay,' he said. 'Let's see how good those walking boots are.'

They changed into their heavy country footwear, and into thick windproof jackets and gloves. 'What is this place?' Louise asked, looking at a finger-post on the edge of the parking area.

'Part of the Southern Upland Way. It's a walkers' route that links the east and west coasts. Normally it would be busier than this, but the snow overnight must have kept folk away.'

'That's good,' she murmured.

He led her up the track, heading east, with the sun shining over their shoulders. Patches of gnarled grass and brown, twisted heather showed through the covering of snow, and the walkers' pathway was still well defined. They reached the crest of the first hill after a few minutes and looked around the moorland.

'No trees,' Louise commented, surprised.

'No. This is the western edge of the Lammermuirs. If we walked far enough this road would take us to Longformacus, then to the coast.'

She looked around the rolling land. 'What's that over there?' she called to him, pointing to her right into the distance.

Neil followed the direction of her finger. 'I've never noticed it before, but it looks like a trout farm.'

'Won't the water freeze in weather like this?'

'Nah, they keep it circulating.' He took a small pair of binoculars from his pocket. 'It's beside a small river, a tributary of the Tweed, I'd guess. They'll pump water out of that and through the tanks. That looks like quite a big operation.'

He paused and squinted through his field-glasses again. 'The boys down here have had a lot of trouble with these places just lately,' he said as he spoke. 'Thefts, but the most recent one turned very nasty.

'That place looks pretty secure, though. Floodlights, high-mounted video cameras; all they need's a guard on a tower with a machine gun. Who knows,' he joked, 'they might have one of them inside that Portakabin.'

He put the glasses away and they set off again, up the next hill. As they stood together at the top, Louise took his arm.

'Can I ask you something, Neil?' she said. 'How do you manage to stay as . . . what's the word . . . controlled, I suppose? Don't you ever feel bitter? Don't you ever feel angry about what's happened to you and the kids?'

She was standing slightly above him on the slope; on his eye-level as he looked at her.

'I tried, at first,' he answered. 'Somehow, I felt I should. I thought about joining a mass action against the tobacco companies, until I realised how silly and vindictive that would have been. Olive smoked when she was a kid because everyone else did, including her mother. Okay, the bloody things were advertised, but so's beer, so's chocolate, so are saturated fats, so's sex. So what would I have got into there, suing companies whose shares are probably helping to grow my life insurance policies, my ISAs, and my pension fund, because my wife exercised her right to choose?

'Don't misread me, Lou. I told you yesterday about my

301

nightmare; the one about me pegging out while the kids are still young. I have others, though; dark dreams, dreams with no conclusion.

'But it's the daymares; they're the hardest to cope with. There isn't a day in my life goes by without me being back in that consulting room, listening to a man who was trying to keep the grief out of his voice as he gave my wife what he knew was a death sentence. There isn't a day when I'm not back in that wee room in the Western, at the end, listening to the click of the diamorphine pump.

'I overcome them by focusing on the positive side of her illness. On her determination, her cheerfulness, the way she never let fear get to the kids, not ever, on the things we did together, on the laughs we had together, in the early weeks and months of it at least. On her sheer courage, Lou; her sheer unbeatable courage.'

She saw the tears that he was unable to keep from his eyes.

'Afterwards,' he continued, not caring about them, 'at first it's indescribable; what it feels like, the numbness where a part of you's been ripped out.

'You wait for the pain to stop; eventually, the immediacy of it does lessen, but you come to terms with the fact that it will always be there, as long as you live. You come to understand other things too, very clearly; most of all, that two souls became one at the instant you and she met, and that although now they may be disjointed, that is only a temporary condition, only for a while.

'All of us, all of the bereft, we find our own truth in the midst of our tragedies. That's mine; I know that one day, our two souls will be one again, as they were when we were both alive. I have nightmares, yes, but I have a constant vision too, one in which Olive and I cruise the cosmos, together.'

'Do you believe in God, then?'

'I believe that we are all God, or at least that we are all part of something which for want of a better word we've come to call God, or Allah, or Jehovah, or that big shiny thing in the sky, or whatever . . .'

'And until that day comes, until you're reunited? How do you live your life?'

'As best I can, as happily as I can, enjoying my own body while I'm living in it, enjoying my kids as they become adults, enjoying their kids . . . however it pans out.

'I'm not afraid of another relationship. I get as horny as the next single man; but anyone who becomes involved with me has to understand that one thing is not negotiable. She is also going to have to be someone Olive would like, because she's going to be very close to her.'

Abruptly, a violent shiver seemed to pass through him. 'Hey, come on,' he exclaimed. 'Let's get moving or we'll freeze to the ground.'

He steered her forward down the track. 'One more hill,' he said, 'then we'll turn back.'

They trudged on together, down then up another crest, the steepest of the three they had tackled. Louise was breathing hard by the time they reached the top. Neil took a hip-flask from another of his pockets and handed it to her.

'What's this?' she gasped. 'Whisky?'

'IrnBru,' he grinned. 'I don't drink, remember . . . especially not when I'm driving.'

He watched her as she drank, deeply from the flask, not daintily from its cup.

'So what about you?' he asked, as she handed it back to him. 'Do you have a soulmate?'

She shot him a quick, almost furtive glance. 'I think so, but his is taken.'

Neil was silent for a moment. 'You might be surprised. He has a special soul; dark and mysterious, I suspect, but there's a lot of it to go around. There's more than one of him: that's as well as I can put it.'

He drew a great breath. 'Did you mean all that stuff yesterday, about giving up men for good?'

'Sure I did. I've been married twice and both times were disasters; my other relationships were no better, culminating in the episode with Warren. I've known other women with similar track records, and for a while, I thought like most of them that all those guys were to blame for not loving us enough.

'Then after the last one, I tried to put myself in the shoes of all those partners, and for the first time, it occurred to me that in most cases, the bulk of the fault had been mine. Since I was a young girl I have been obsessed with acting, not out of ego . . . at least I don't think so . . . but because I was addicted to it as strongly as an addict is to crack cocaine.

'I have been impossible to live with for any length of time. Short-term, that was fine. People tell me that I'm good-looking, successful, rich, and some have even added that I'm very good in bed, any man's dream. But as every relationship developed, I became more and more remote, as my partners, quite justifiably I see now, wanted more of me than I was prepared, or able, to give.

'So . . . and when young Mr Silver, who's as sexually interchangeable as anyone I've ever met, came on to me, it really was the last straw . . . I decided to withdraw from that world.'

She gave her deep throaty laugh. 'That I would have no more of men,' she murmured, 'that I would live the rest of my days as a Garboesque figure, alone, independent and unto myself. That was my clear vision of my declining years.'

'Was?'

She nodded.

'Until when?'

This time Louise was standing slightly below him on the hill. She looked up at him; at his dark hair, flecked with grey, at his soft blue eyes, and the web of lines around them, at his once-broken nose, at his expression which to some suggested stolidity, but which in fact he had fashioned over the years to mask a developing intellect.

She took hold of the front of his jacket, drew his face down to hers, and kissed him, lightly, on the lips.

'Until very recently,' she whispered.

Sixty-one

Pringle and McGurk had said nothing at all to Raymond Anders, from the time they had collected him from his holding cell in the West Yorkshire police headquarters building in Leeds until they had installed him in similar accommodation in Galashiels.

They had watched him squirm anxiously, seated beside the sergeant in the back of the car; they had listened to his occasional pleading question about where they were going and how long the journey would take. Yet deliberately, they had said nothing; not one single word.

Now, on Sunday afternoon, refreshed, and having gone over the assembled evidence, they were ready to begin. Anders had been formally cautioned by Chief Superintendent Charlie Harrison, the uniformed divisional commander, and advised that he was being held on suspicion of murder; he had been advised to call a solicitor and had chosen Geoff Lesser, a formidable High Court practitioner from Glasgow.

Suspect and solicitor were together when the two policemen walked into the interview room.

'Are you two ready to talk to me now?' asked Anders plaintively as they sat down opposite him and loaded the tape recorder. Pringle made the formal identifications for the record.

'Thanks for confirming, Mr Anders,' he continued, with a glance at Lesser, 'that we've had no informal discussions with you prior to this interview of the matters under investigation. Would you just repeat that for the tape; that we've said nothing to you until now.'

'Not a fucking word,' exclaimed Raymond Anders. He was a tall man but he sat hunched at the table, fair hair dull and needing shampoo, dandruff on the shoulders of his dark jacket, stubble on his long sharp chin.

'Thanks, that's sufficient,' said Pringle, pleasantly. 'Do you know why you're here?'

'They told me in Leeds; something to do with the murder of a girl on a trout farm.'

'Who said anything to you about a trout farm? I thought our colleagues in Leeds simply detained you in connection with a murder investigation.' The superintendent caught the quick glance from client to solicitor. 'No point looking at Mr Lesser,' he said. 'We haven't discussed the case with him either, and he's not going to lie to the tape for you.'

'So. How did you know about the trout farm?'

'I guessed. I heard it on the car radio; that was it.'

'Which station?' asked McGurk.

'Radio Borders.'

'Hold on a minute. Does that mean that your sister was lying to the police when she said that you arrived at her place at just after five on Thursday night?'

'No! I did. She was telling the truth.'

'In that case,' said the sergeant, 'prepare to lose your

driving licence. The news of Miss Adey's murder wasn't broadcast on Radio Borders until four thirty. It's a very local FM station, so to hear it you couldn't have been further south than Alnwick.

'You must have been doing around two hundred miles an hour to get to your sister's when you did, yet still hear that broadcast.'

'Maybe it was Radio Scotland, then.'

'They didn't broadcast the news until just after five, and you can't pick them up in Leeds.'

'Congratulations,' said Pringle. 'That's maybe no' the fastest opening lie I've ever heard in a formal interview, but it's up there with the best. Would you not agree, Mr Lesser?' The lawyer scowled at him.

'Okay,' the superintendent continued. 'Let's cut away the fat and get to the meat of this. I'm going to accept that you got to your sister's when you both say you did. Where did you leave from?'

'Hawick; that's where my office is.'

'Right, that's a two-and-a-half-hour drive to Leeds, minimum, in good traffic conditions; so you must have been on the road by quarter to three. Correct?' Anders nodded vigorously, starting a small white dandruff storm falling towards the table.

'But you had an appointment with Miss Adey, in her diary, in her handwriting, timed for four o'clock on Thursday afternoon. More than that, you'd a date with your girlfriend on Thursday night. Actually, son,' he whispered, confidentially, 'I think she's your ex-girlfriend now.

'As far as I gather from the boys in Leeds your sister and

her kids looked in perfect health. So, what made you up stakes, just like that, and bomb off south? Could it be that after the robbery at Country Fresh Trout went horribly wrong, after instead of being blindfolded and tied up in the dark Miss Adey wound up with her skull smashed in? Could it be that you panicked and ran for it?'

'I don't know anything about her getting killed,' Anders protested. 'I don't know anything about the robberies.'

'Robberies?' Pringle exclaimed. 'Since when have we been talking about more than one robbery? No, son, I'm interviewing you, no' the other way around. I'll get to the others later, and then you can get to telling me how you connected them.'

'In the meantime,' Jack McGurk broke in, opening the briefcase which he had brought into the room, 'we want you to tell us about this.' He took out a clear plastic bag and laid it on the table. It contained a thick wooden baton, around fifteen inches long, with a large lead weight set in one end. It was blackened and scorched, but still clearly identifiable.

'This was found by detective officers, when they searched your house in Hawick under warrant on Friday morning. They found it in an old oil drum in your garden shed.' The sergeant fixed the suspect with an icy look. 'It had been in a fire, but forensic examination identified hair, blood, tissue and bone fragments which were sticking to it, as coming from the murder victim.'

'McGurk's an angler,' the superintendent offered. 'He reckons the thing was probably used to kill fish. We found the bones of a small trout in a plate in Miss Adey's kitchen.

The lassie probably helped herself every so often, for her supper.'

'Her Last Supper,' said McGurk, grimly.

'Don't be dramatic, Jack,' Pringle chided. He looked at the solicitor. 'In the drum,' he told him, quietly, 'we found the remnants of a large hooded waxed cotton jacket which had been soaked in petrol and set on fire. This club, which was the murder weapon for sure, had been wrapped in it.

'We've got a video tape which we can show you. It was taken at night and you can't identify the people in it, but we know that one was a tall man in a jacket very like the one which was burned, and that the other was Miss Adey, because it shows her murder. She tried to defend her employer's property with that thing. It was taken from her and her skull was bashed in with it.

'That's bad enough in itself for your client. Now I'll get to the other robberies. This was the third inside two weeks from a trout farm in the area; the total value of the stock stolen being around thirty-five thousand pounds, give or take a few.

'We know that all three thefts were committed by the same gang. There are two other linking factors; all three farms had very poor security, and all three had been visited by your client in failed attempts to sell them video surveillance systems.

'There's one other odd wee fact too. The second robbery happened after the resident manager . . . the very large resident manager . . . had been lured away by a bogus call telling him that his father, who's recognised as one of Hawick's top bevvy merchants, had been severely injured on his way home from the pub. Our man here just happens to drink in the same boozer as Mr Symonds senior; but the licensee told us that he wasn't there that night. His girlfriend was, but he wasn't.

'I don't think you're going to argue with me if I suggest that the Fiscal will support charges of murder and theft against Mr Anders, on the basis of what I've shown and told you.'

'No,' Geoff Lesser agreed, with a heavy sigh. 'I'm not. In fact, I propose that you do just that, to put Mr Anders' detention on a proper legal footing, and to enable me to consult with him properly and at length about his defence.'

Ten minutes later, the two detectives were back in Pringle's office; Anders had been charged formally, and left alone with the lawyer.

'That was easier than I'd thought,' McGurk mused, aloud. 'I didn't expect that Lesser would just roll over like that, and let us charge him.'

'Me neither,' said the superintendent, 'but I know why he did. Suppose he'd pulled out all the stops, and we'd bailed Anders, *pro tem*. The rest of the gang must be feeling pretty insecure right now. The boy's probably safer in the jail; that's what his lawyer's thinking.'

'Maybe,' McGurk agreed. He was staring at the window, absently.

'What's up?' asked Pringle. He reached into a compartment of his desk and produced a bottle of whisky and two glasses. 'Come on. Let's have a nip to celebrate.' He poured two small measures, and handed one to the sergeant.

'You still worrying about your wife?' he asked.

'Yes. But that wasn't what I was thinking about.'

'Oh aye?'

'Yeah. I didn't mention this before the interview, not just because it would have muddied the water, but because I wanted to be certain. Now I am.

'That boy Anders . . . I've seen him before.'

312

Sixty-two

'He's dead sure of that?' the Head of CID asked.

'He says he's "Under oath" sure, and big Jack's not a fanciful lad. He says that on the afternoon after the Howdengate robbery he went to Raeburn Place on a whim, to watch Lander and Symonds play for Jed Seconds . . .'

'Yes, I know; Karen and I met him in the bar afterwards.'

'Well,' Dan Pringle continued, 'when he was walking across to the pavilion after the game, he saw someone go up to Lander and speak to him. Lander answered him, then he saw Jack, broke off his conversation with the other guy straight away and came across to talk to him.

'That other bloke was Raymond Anders.'

'Hmm,' Andy Martin murmured. 'That's interesting, I'll grant you. I'm not sure what it tells us, if anything, but it's interesting. Why should Anders show up at Raeburn Place? Guys from Hawick are not likely to go up to Edinburgh to watch Jedforest seconds. That's like a parish priest having a season ticket at Ibrox.'

'Whatever the reason is, it wants checking into.'

'What was Lander doing on the night of the robbery?'

'His girlfriend. He mentioned that he was in bed with her when big Symonds phoned him from Gala.'

'And Symonds? We know, do we, that he actually did go to the hospital?'

'Aye. Two nurses in the A and E remembered him. They said he was in a right state; he took some persuading that his father wasn't there after all.'

'I wonder if Lander has more than one girlfriend, or if Mercy Alvarez gave him an alibi, just as she and ACC Chase gave him one for the night when her farm was done.'

Pringle gave a soft hum. 'Aye, now there's interesting right enough.'

'Especially,' said Martin, 'since I seem to recall the lady saying to me that she didn't know the other farms that had been robbed. Dan, maybe Anders is bang in the frame for this girl's murder, but we know for sure he didn't act alone. There's the footprints, and more. There were two tanker trucks so that means at least two people.

'No,' he said sharply. 'At least three. On the tape, after the girl was killed, both trucks drove up at once.

'Dan, don't get too pleased with yourselves, you and McGurk, for nailing Anders.

'I understand why you let Geoff Lesser talk you into charging him at that point, and leaving him with him. I'm not as patient as you, though; not on this. I don't just want this guy; I want them all.

'The two of you, get back in there with your prisoner, take the gloves off and lean on him; I want names out of him.

'You tell him from me that the Crown Office will press for every day he holds out on us to become another year added on to the judge's recommendation on the minimum sentence he serves before parole. If he wants to be out of jail before he's fifty, he'd better talk to you.'

'All right, sir,' murmured Pringle, with a sigh. 'Can it really not wait till tomorrow, though? The boy's locked up, and Jack's just about to go on up the road. He's having problems at home,' he added. 'Mary's no' happy about the move.'

'Tonight, Dan. I sympathise with McGurk, but unless you can find someone else experienced to sit in with you, it's down to him. If he likes, I'll ask Karen to talk to his wife, and you and I can see what we can do.

'But I want Anders leaned on, and I want it done now.'

The Head of CID paused. 'Oh, and just in case you think I'm copping out, I'm about to delight Mrs Martin by spending the rest of my Sunday night digging up insurance company managers. I intend to find out the total insurance loss on all three farms.'

Sixty-three

'What's wrong?' she asked. 'Have I been too pushy? Or have I just made a total fool of myself?' She looked at his profile in the faint green light of the car's instrument panel; smiling as he gave a small involuntary shudder, as if he had just switched off his auto pilot.

'I'm sorry, Lou,' he said. 'I was miles away there.'

'I asked you whether I had upset you, back there on the moor. Will I find myself with a new minder tomorrow?'

'Christ, no,' he exclaimed. 'You've stunned me, that's all. You took my breath away. I mean, what brought it on?'

'I don't know for sure,' she answered, laughing softly to herself. 'But thinking back, I remember wondering whether, maybe, for all my adult life, the man I've been looking for is the sort who puts Irn Bru in a hip flask.'

'Shh for a minute,' he said. 'Let's pull in somewhere for a bite, and damn the punters. We can't talk about this in the car.'

After they had climbed down from the moor their circular route had taken them through Kelso, Duns and on to the A1 at Grantshouse. Neil looked at the road signs and saw that East Linton was only half a mile ahead. He turned off the single carriageway trunk road, into the half-hidden village, drove across the Tyne bridge and pulled up close to the Drovers' Inn.

Happily, the roadhouse was quiet and they were shown straight to a table for two in the dining room upstairs. They ordered a glass of white wine for Louise, a bottle of sparkling mineral water and two seafood platters with side salad, then sat silently as the wine was poured and the bottle opened.

She smiled at him, mischievously, as he took his first sip. 'Like I said,' he began, 'I'm stunned. Gob-smacked. I don't know what to think, and I sure don't know what to say . . .

'Other than this. I find you very attractive; but I'm not talking about the publicity photo or the face up on the big screen. You're beautiful on the inside, Lou, and that's where it counts.

'But what I don't understand is what the hell you can see in a big dumb polisman like me, given the world you live in, with all these bloody superstars and everything.'

She ran the tip of her right index finger round the rim of her glass, which lay untouched on the table. 'Much the same thing. I haven't felt the faintest flicker of attraction for a man in the last three years, although . . .' she smiled again, '. . . my line of work being what it is, I have had a few propositions put to me.

'You're not like anyone I've met, not in a while; not for as long as I want to remember. You're a warm, open-hearted, caring man, and you are not in the slightest affected by who I am . . . or by the person I'm supposed to be. Nor by any other of those bloody superstars, if it comes to it.

'You see through all that; when you look at me, I can tell

you're just looking at Louise Bankier from Bearsden, and that's all I am.'

He shook his head. 'Not all. It's who you are, and it's enough. Maybe I'm afraid to look at the face up on the big screen. Maybe she would overwhelm me.'

'No. You look through her to get to me; you just strip her away.'

'So what are you saying? What are you asking? Are you asking anything?'

'I don't know. I'm afraid to say any more than I have. And I don't know what to ask of you. I do know this, though; I mustn't trifle with you. You don't deserve any more hurt in your life, and I certainly won't be the one to inflict it.'

'You couldn't,' he told her. 'Not you; it's not in you to hurt me or anyone else. Anyway, I'm beyond hurt now, beyond any hurt I can imagine, at least. I've found my truth, my certainty, and that's my shield.'

'But what about the loneliness? Does your shield protect against that?'

He looked at her for a while, without replying, spinning his glass in his fingers, watching the bubbles in the water, as if he was considering something. Finally, he laid it down. 'Let me tell you a story; a true story, true as I'm sitting here.

'In the days and weeks after Olive died, I experienced certain physical things, signs you'd call them, of her presence around me, on another plane. The very day after, in fact, I lay down on the sofa, alone, and closed my eyes for the first time in over twenty-four hours. As I lay there, I felt a line of pressure above my eyes, firm yet not painful, not like a headache.

'I knew that it was her; I knew instinctively that part of her essential being . . . we use the word soul, and it's as good as any other . . . was merging with mine, binding us together.

'A few weeks after that, I had a dream. I was drawn towards, and eventually came to a bridge. I could see her on the other side, but I couldn't cross; she knew I was there. She wasn't smiling, but she was content that I could see. I knew then that she had brought me there.

'The bridge was grey, and so was everything around, but I knew also that, when I can cross, I'll see colours the like of which I've never imagined.'

She made as if to speak, but he held up a hand to stop her. 'No,' he said softly. 'That's not the story.

'A few months later, the Big Man insisted that I take the kids and go off to his place in Spain for a couple of weeks. So we went out there, and lay beside the pool, and went to the beach, and all the time, I felt this great space around me, empty, yet not empty.

'Then, one night I was lying in bed in Bob and Sarah's guest room, asleep, and dreaming about Olive. All of a sudden, I woke up.' He snapped his fingers suddenly, making her jump. 'Abruptly; just like that.

'There was someone there, lying beside me. It was her; she was there, in my arms. We couldn't speak, either of us. We just hugged, and we cried. Then after I'm not sure how long . . . more than a couple of seconds, anyway . . . she just faded, melted away, leaving me alone, but with a huge feeling of relief.

'I lay there for a while, until eventually, I went back to sleep, back into the dream from which I'd awakened. But next morning, it was all still there, as clear as it had been at the time.

'Now I know, Lou, that inevitably, you're sitting there thinking, "The poor man," or some such, and that it was all part of the same dream. Yet what I've told you is as pure a truth as I can give you. Just like you, I've had many dreams; bad ones, good ones, dark ones, bright ones . . . aye, even wet ones when I was a teenager.

'But I've never, ever, had a dream that I could touch. I've never, before or since, had a dream that cried on my shoulder . . . and neither, I'll bet, have you.'

She looked at him, unaware of the tears in the corners of her eyes and shook her head.

'Olive told me many things in that wordless encounter,' he continued. 'Most of all, though, she told me to be patient, that it would take as long as it took, but that it would be all right. Until then, she was letting me go to get on with my life.'

He frowned. 'Why did I tell you this? Yes; the loneliness. There is none, not any more; it left me that night. I find the patience part of it difficult from time to time, but when I do the kids are there to get me back on track.

'So don't you worry about hurting me, love. It's the other way round; given what you've been through, it's me who has to worry about hurting you.'

'As you said earlier,' she told him. 'You couldn't if you tried. It's not in you.'

His eyebrows rose as he topped up his water glass. 'Are you so sure? I know enough about your career to remember that a while back, you won an award for *Wuthering Heights*. Back there on the moor, don't you think you might have been replaying the role?' He grinned. 'Imagine me as Heathcliff!'

She laughed, a suppressed giggle at first, until it escaped into a long peal of beautiful sound. 'Not for a minute,' she exclaimed, more Glaswegian than he had ever heard her, and loud enough for two other diners to turn and look towards their table. 'Heathcliff didn't even carry a hip-flask, far less fill it with ginger.'

Sixty-four

Geoff Lesser was not a happy man. He glared at Pringle as the two came face-to-face in the divisional HQ's reception area. 'I was halfway back to Glasgow,' he complained. 'What the hell's this about?'

'Let's just say we've had a change of heart,' the superintendent growled. 'We've decided to offer your boy a deal, but it'll be take it or leave it, and it'll be now. I'm sorry to mess you about, but the Legal Aid'll pay for it, as always.'

'Yes,' said Lesser, with a hint of a grin, 'but slowly as always.

'But what do you mean a deal? My client denies all charges, strenuously.'

'He can get as strenuous as he fucking likes. Strenuousness does not impress juries, and you know it; they expect strenuousness. They're impressed by evidence, and on the basis of that, Anders is on the Peterhead bus already.'

'Ah, but he will say that someone could have burned that coat and that baton in his shed, someone who wanted to frame him for the robberies. As you rightly said, he had visited all three farms, in the course of his everyday visits, and in attempting to sell them his systems had himself pointed out to the managers their vulnerability to the type of theft which was subsequently committed.

'What appears to be evidence for the Crown, is in fact evidence for the defence.'

Pringle nodded, amiably. 'Time will tell, sir.

'Let me guess,' he continued. 'I suppose he did a runner after he received an anonymous telephone call warning him that the police would be after him for the girl's murder.'

'Very good, Superintendent. You've worked out what happened.'

'Oh, that I have, Mr Lesser, that I have. Come on and let's see what the poor victim of miscarried justice has to say about it.'

The detective led the way back to the interview room, where Jack McGurk and a uniformed constable were sitting, silently, with Raymond Anders. The room was blue with cigarette smoke.

'Right,' Pringle barked at the prisoner. 'You can put that out right now. It took me long enough to give up; I'll be buggered if I'll indulge your habit.' He snatched the cigarette from the man's hand and ground it out in the ashtray which lay on the table.

He switched on the tape. 'This is a resumed interview with Raymond Anders, by Detective Superintendent Pringle and Detective Sergeant McGurk, Mr Geoff Lesser, solicitor, also being present. Prisoner remains under caution.' He looked at the constable and jerked a thumb towards the door. 'You can go, son.

'Right, Anders,' he began, setting himself down on a chair. 'This afternoon was the ritual dancin'. This is the serious stuff now. You're cooked for this and no messing; since we saw you this afternoon, the technicians have found blood remnants on a scrap of the coat you burned.'

'I didn't burn it!' the prisoner protested. 'Someone else must have.'

'This is after you had the anonymous call that caused you to do a runner?'

Anders' eyes narrowed slightly. 'Yes. It must have been. It would have been the same bloke, likely.'

'Ah,' said McGurk, speaking for the first time. 'A bloke with a set of keys to your house?'

'No, of course not.'

'Son,' Pringle sighed. 'The jacket and the club were burned in an oil drum inside your garden shed. That was a daft thing to do, but I suppose you didn't want the neighbours to see you. However,' he looked at Lesser and let out a great bellowing laugh, 'it wasn't nearly as fucking daft as locking the shed door after you'd done it.'

The solicitor stared up at the ceiling.

'Don't piss us about any longer, Raymond. We didn't press you on this this afternoon because we hoped that Mr Lesser might have persuaded you that the smart thing to do would have been to name your accomplices. I'm sure he suggested it to you, but you've taken the stupid option.

'I'll give you one chance here. Tell me who else was in on the robberies. I can't promise this, but I might be able to persuade the Crown Office to accept a plea of guilty to the robberies alone, if you name your accomplices in Court. As things stand you and you alone are going away for life.'

Anders was as white as his solicitor's shirt, but he shook his head.

'The prisoner declines to answer,' said McGurk to the tape.

'Look son,' said Pringle. 'Be sure of what you're facing here. This is a brutal murder committed in the furtherance of theft. There's no chance of this being talked down to culpable homicide. This will be a life sentence. The Crown won't leave it at that though; they will ask the judge to throw the book at you, with a minimum sentence recommendation that will make you an old, old man by the time you come out.

'Mind you, you might not want to come out by then. You might fancy settling down with a nice bloke for the next twenty-five years.'

'I never killed her!' Anders screamed.

'Raymond!' his solicitor warned, but in vain.

'I never touched the woman, I swear it. I was waiting in one of the trucks when she was done.'

'What about the coat and the bludgeon?' McGurk asked, harshly.

'I was given them to burn.'

'By whom?' Pringle barked.

'Superintendent,' Lesser interjected. 'I must advise my client to say no more.'

'That's the last thing you should advise him, Geoff, and you know it. Now answer the question. Who gave you the coat and club to burn?'

'I can't tell you. I never knew his name.'

'Bollocks. Who was it?'

'Can't tell you.'

McGurk grabbed his shoulder and turned him to face him. 'Was it Glenn Lander?'

'Who's he?' Anders bleated.

'You know him. You met him the day after his farm was robbed. I think you arranged to see him at Raeburn Place, to tell him that the robbery had gone fine.' Anders looked at him in astonishment, and the sergeant knew that he had hit the mark.

The prisoner turned, desperately, to his solicitor. 'I want to go back to my cell, sir,' he pleaded.

'Raymond,' said Lesser, solemnly, 'at this stage, it may be in your interests to co-operate.'

'I want to go back to my cell!'

The lawyer shook his head. 'Very well.' He looked across at Pringle. 'This interview is over, gentlemen.'

'I might as well tell you, Geoff,' the superintendent said, as he switched off the tape, 'that the boy really did a bad job of burning that stuff. He says he didn't kill the girl, but he did manage to leave part of the baton untouched by the fire, and we've got his palm-print off it.

'He'll be in court for remand tomorrow morning, as per the usual routine. You've got till then to persuade him to change his mind.'

Sixty-five

The alarm buzzed once; its red signal light flashed once, but Neil McIlhenney was not asleep. His right hand flashed out and hit the 'cancel' button inside a second. In the same movement he swung out of bed, snatched up his jeans, sweater and shoes from the floor, slipping silently into the trousers, not bothering about underwear or socks as he slipped out into the hall.

There he unlocked his desk with a key on his chain, took out a Glock automatic pistol, and slipped it into a pocket of his heavy outdoor jacket as he pulled it on over his sweater. He left the house within a minute of the alarm's warning, having made barely a sound.

He ran down Colinton Road as quickly as he could safely manage in moccasins on the slippery pavement, and turned into Craiglockhart Avenue, skidding to a halt as a red glow behind the houses close by told him the reason for the emergency signal. As he broke into a run once more, he heard a car; crashing gears, screeching tyres then the roar of an engine as it sped away into the night.

Twenty yards down the Avenue he slipped and fell, thanking his lucky stars that the Glock was on safe as he landed on it. He ignored the sharp pain, pushed himself to his feet, and ran on, until he reached the cul-de-sac where Louise's rented home stood.

He had made it in less than three minutes, yet the house was an inferno. The front door was consumed, and through it he could see that the wildfire had spread almost instantly along the acrylic hall carpet and up the varnished wooden staircase which led to the two attic bedrooms.

Whatever had happened, it had been so sudden, so cataclysmic, that none of the neighbours had yet been awakened . . . nor, as far as he could see or hear, had anyone in the house. He took out his mobile and keyed in the direct number of the Torphichen Place office where the back-up alarm was situated.

It was answered quickly. 'This is McIlhenney,' he snapped. 'There's a fire at the house; major outbreak. All available appliances, at once, ambulances, the whole fucking shooting match.'

As he ended the call, he saw, to his horror, a figure appear in one of the bedroom windows. It was Glenys Algodon; she was naked, silhouetted by the flames behind her, as she struggled with the handle of the double-glazed window unit. He held his breath as he watched her, knowing that there was nothing he could do, no one else he could call who would help.

At last, the window swung open on its central hinge; as it did so, he heard her screams for the first time and saw the blaze behind her, fuelled by the inrush of air, reaching out as if to feed on her.

'Get out!' he bellowed. 'On to the roof, then jump!' He vaulted the steel driveway gate, into the garden and ran for the bungalow. 'Now, Glenys, I'll catch you.'

She did as he said, and slithered, still screaming, out of the half-opened window, then rolled, over tongues of flame which were already licking through the tiles, down and off the roof.

He reached her, but only in time to break her fall; her weight sent him sprawling beside her on the lawn. She rolled around still screaming, with her hair on fire. He beat it out with his bare hands, then dragged her as far away from the house as he could, noticing as he did so that her back and buttocks had been turned into one large blister by the heat.

He held her, firmly, face down, talking to her, soothing her, until her screams turned to whimpers, and stopped, finally, as she slipped into a daze. He took off his heavy jacket, slipping the gun into the waistband of his jeans and his mobile into a pocket, and covered her, gently.

As he did so he heard an indignant, scared voice behind him. 'What are you doing?' it demanded.

McIlhenney turned, to see a middle-aged man in dressing-gown and pyjamas, peering down at him, over the garden wall. 'I'm having a fucking barbecue,' he roared. 'What did you think?'

The man recoiled. 'Are you a neighbour?' the policeman snapped.

Nod. 'Yes. Next door.'

'Well, get back in there, bring me a blanket or something like it, then make a strong cup of tea.'

'For the young lady?'

'No. For you. The young lady will be going off in an

ambulance in a minute. When she does, I'm going to want to talk to you.'

As he spoke, the first fire appliance swung round the corner into the cul-de-sac, siren silent but blue lights flashing. 'Go on,' the detective shouted, more kindly, to the neighbour. 'Get me that blanket, now.'

The firemen did not see him at first as he crouched by Glenys; instead they cleared the locked driveway gate as he had done, hoses connected to the nearest hydrants, playing water on the roof and shooting it at the front door. Behind them, another appliance arrived, then, as the neighbour appeared with a travelling rug, an ambulance.

McIlhenney wrapped Glenys carefully in the blanket, then stood and waved to the paramedics. As they ran across, a white-helmeted figure jumped from the second fire engine, spotting the policeman as he did.

'Neil?' DO Matt Grogan called out. 'What the hell are you doing here?'

'I live round the corner. I'll speak to you later; I'll want to know how and where this started.' As the veteran firefighter strode towards the blaze, the detective helped the ambulance crew as they lifted the casualty and placed her, still face downwards, on a stretcher. She was still dazed, but as they lifted her over the low wall, she looked at him sideways, and he could see that she was numb with horror. 'Clarence, Louise . . .' she whispered, and then her eyes glazed over once more.

'Oh Jesus,' McIlhenney murmured, feeling himself shivering, but not from the cold of the night.

He took his handphone from his pocket and dialled a

familiar number; as always, the man on the other end was wide awake, although the call was answered on only the second ring.

'Yes Neil,' Skinner said, quietly and evenly. His bedside phone had a readout which identified incoming numbers, and sometimes, callers. 'What is it?' He knew that at 1 a.m. the call would not be trivial.

'I'm at Louise's place, boss. There's a fire; it's still burning, but the place is gutted. My alarm went off, and I got here double quick, but it was well alight by then. Matt Grogan's here; hopefully he'll give us an idea of how it happened.'

'And . . .' Skinner did not have to say more.

'Glenys got out, Boss. A bit scorched, but she'll be okay. I'm afraid for Clarence Sparrow, her boyfriend; I thought he was catching the last shuttle home to London, but . . .'

'Louise, man, Louise. Did she get out?'

McIlhenney took a deep breath. 'Lou was never in the house, Boss. She was with me.'

'With you?' Skinner's exec. heard the astonishment in his voice. 'Did you have her up for dinner again?' he asked. It was the first time in McIlhenney's life he had ever heard him ask anything remotely like a stupid question.

'No, Boss. She was asleep when I left her.'

There was a long silence, yet during it the two men seemed to say things to each other, things which were for life. 'Then you'd better go and tell her what's happened,' the DCC said at last.

'I've got to have a word with the neighbours, Boss; and with Grogan.'

'They can wait until I get there. No, off you go and see
Louise; you don't want her to be waking up and wandering
down there looking for you.'

Sixty-six

'So Clarence was still there,' said Lou. She was sitting on Neil's sofa, her hands wrapped around a mug of coffee. Her eyes were red and blotchy, she wore no makeup, her hair was tangled, and she was dressed in a tee-shirt and Neil's black towelling dressing-gown, but she was still beautiful.

'Yes, love,' he said, quietly. 'Since the last time we saw them, he must have decided to stay the extra night. And clearly, from what she said to me, Glenys assumed that you'd come back in after they'd gone to bed.'

She leaned against him, her head on his shoulder. 'As she would,' she murmured. She slipped a hand, warm from the mug, into his and squeezed it. 'You were right, love. There's someone watching over us.'

He pressed his face against her, kissing her hair. 'Never doubt it,' he whispered in her ear.

It was as if for that moment there was no one else in the room; a fact that was not lost on Bob Skinner and Andy Martin as they stood in front of the fireplace. Eventually, McIlhenney remembered their presence.

'Sorry Boss. This situation's become a bit . . . well, unprofessional, I suppose.'

'Who gives a damn?' said Skinner, with a quick look that

put his assistant at his ease. 'Because it did, Lou wasn't in that house, and thank God for it.'

'But poor Clarence was,' she reminded him.

He winced. 'Yes. Poor Clarence. Matt Grogan said that they found him in the bedroom doorway. He's seen similar before; the victim's in bed, hears these funny noises outside; he's half-asleep and opens the door to investigate.

'Whoosh! The fireball's sucked in and he's right in the middle of it. Ms Algodon was lucky she got out.'

'Does Matt have any theory about how it started?' asked Martin.

'Yes,' the DCC answered, 'and a pretty good one at that. The perpetrator climbed over the driveway gate, walked up the concrete path to the front door . . . knowingly or otherwise avoiding triggering the geophones we put in the garden . . . and put three cans of petrol up against it. Then he put detonators in each one.'

He glanced at his two colleagues. 'Know what Matt thinks he used? Big firework rockets, one in each can. He linked the three fuses together with a single petrol-soaked cord, lit the blue touch-paper and withdrew, effing sharpish.

'The explosion would have been soft, probably not enough to wake the neighbours, unless they were sleeping with the windows open . . . unlikely in December. However, it would have blown the front door in . . . triggering your alarm, Neil . . . and torching the place in seconds.'

'You took how long to get there?' he asked McIlhenney.

'Under three minutes.'

'Nevertheless, that would have been enough for the blaze

to have been impenetrable, even without the second explosion.'

'What second explosion, boss? I never heard anything.'

'No, it would have happened seconds after the first. There was a box of highly inflammable aerosols in the hall; they gave the fire a sort of turbo-charged effect, according to Grogan.'

He looked at Louise. 'Any idea what they might have been?'

She nodded back at him. 'Yes. They were hair spray; we're due to start filming this morning, and since we're shooting in street locations, I had arranged for the make-up person to call at the house first thing and fix me up there.'

'Who dropped them off?' asked Andy Martin, quietly. 'Who knew they were there?'

Louise looked up at him, for a few seconds. 'They've been lying there since Thursday. Elliott Silver brought them with him when he arrived for our meeting. I remember telling him just to leave them in the hallway.'

'This is the same guy,' McIlhenney exclaimed, 'who tried his hand with Lou a while back and got sent down the road.'

'But Neil . . .' she protested, twisting round to look at him.

'But what, love? Tell me something; does he have a car here, or does he travel by taxi?'

'He has a hire car. Why?'

'Because when I was running down Craiglockhart Avenue, I heard a motor, taking off sharpish.'

Skinner looked at Martin. 'Talk to him, Andy. Have a serious talk with him. Where's he living, Lou?'

'He's renting a flat in the New Town. On India Street, in fact, where we're due to begin filming this morning. You'll find his address in my Filo, in the hall.'

'You better postpone that. Your director could be busy for a bit.'

'I'll call Warren; he's in the George Hotel.'

'Don't worry about that,' Skinner assured her. 'I'll call in on him myself.'

'Meantime,' he continued, 'what are we going to do with you? Maybe we should move you into a hotel suite?'

'No,' McIlhenney retorted. 'Lou stays here.'

'But Neil,' she said. 'What about the kids?'

'They'll be fine.' He looked at the DCC. 'Anyway, we may wind up locking up Mr Silver before the day's out . . .' He frowned. 'But even if we don't. We're finished pissing about now, Boss, aren't we?'

'Too right,' said Skinner. 'If Lou is going to stay with you, then we make this a fortress. Armed officers front and back from now on, round the clock. Spence and Lauren get taken to school and brought back by car.' He paused. 'Better still. They can come to ours; it's near the end of the school term, so a couple of weeks or so at Gullane Primary with Mark won't harm them at all.'

'Deal,' said Neil, looking at Lou. 'You okay with that, love?'

She hesitated. 'I'm okay with it except for one thing. I don't want to put you in danger.'

He laughed. 'Try and keep me out of it. Okay, Boss,' he said to Skinner, pushing himself up from the sofa. 'I'll keep the kids off school this morning. They'll think it's Christmas come early.'

'Fine. I'll pick them up this afternoon . . . unless Silver confesses everything.'

'Which you don't think he will?' asked McIlhenney, quietly.

Skinner drew in his breath in a familiar hiss. 'No, I don't,' he admitted. 'If it was him, then delivering those aerosols personally was a stupid thing to do. And this boy hasn't done a single stupid thing so far.'

'Apart from persecuting Lou in the first place,' McIlhenney growled. 'That will turn out to have been very stupid.'

'Indeed,' the DCC agreed, moving towards the door with Martin. 'And taking a shot at me, even if it was a blank. That too.'

'Right, Andy,' he said, as McIlhenney saw them into the small hall. 'You'll brace Silver right away.'

The Head of CID nodded. 'Yup. I'll have to postpone my divisional heads' meeting this morning anyway. Dan Pringle's in court with the guy we nailed for the fish farm jobs.'

'Mmm,' said McIlhenney idly. 'We saw one of them yesterday, on the edge of the moors just off the Carfraemill to Kelso road. A big one it was, too . . . with a video security system, you'll be glad to hear.'

Martin stared at him. 'Is that so?' he murmured. 'Dan Pringle showed me a list of all the trout farms on his patch, and I'm dead certain there wasn't one there.'

Sixty-seven

Policemen are used to being wakened from their slumber in the middle of the night to be told of catastrophe, disaster and death. Film producers, on the whole, are not. Warren Judd looked a bundle of nerves as he perched on a chair in his George Hotel suite, sipping black coffee from a jug provided by room service. He was shivering, not from the cold, for the room was warm, but from nerves.

'Do you know how the fire started?' he asked, his voice shaky.

'We're still in the realms of theory,' said Skinner, truthfully. 'I won't speculate.'

'But you do know that that man, Glenys's partner, is dead?'

'His name was Clarence Sparrow, and if he isn't dead, he's a bloody phoenix.' It was the policeman's turn to shudder as he recalled what Matt Grogan had shown him under that tarpaulin. 'Glenys Algodon got out by the skin of her teeth, and of her back. She'll be in a lot of pain and discomfort for the next few days, and she'll have a new hair-do for a while, but she will be all right.'

'And Ms Bankier definitely wasn't there? You're sure about that? I mean if the fire was that bad . . .'

338

'Mr Judd,' the DCC said, slowly. 'I have spoken to Louise. She is shocked, but in good health.'

'Why wasn't she there? Where was she? We start shooting tomorrow; it isn't like her to have late nights while she's working.'

'She had a dinner-date; she hadn't got back when the fire started.'

'Dinner date? With whom?'

Skinner frowned as he looked at the producer, sensing old passions, old jealousy within him. But he sensed nothing else.

'With Neil, her bodyguard,' he told him, abruptly. 'They went out for the day, they had supper and then they went back to his place.' Judd's cup slipped in his fingers, spilling coffee on to the George's expensive carpet.

'She . . .' he whispered.

The DCC stared at him hard. 'Neil's a fine man,' he murmured evenly. 'One of the very best of people; as is Louise, as Louise has always been, as she was when I knew her first, when you were not as much as a black cloud on the far horizon. She deserves someone like him, and if you ever grudge her that, mister, or reproach her, or wish her anything but the very best of luck, then in Neil McIlhenney and me, you will have made two of the worst enemies that a man could possibly have.'

'But who is he?' Judd croaked.

'He's a policeman. He's my executive assistant. Lou's been under our discreet protection since she's been in Edinburgh. She has a stalker, a persecutor. Before tonight there have been two incidents, one in London and one in Edinburgh.

Neither was a lethal attack; tonight's was.

'We're looking for a slim-built man in his late twenties, who signs himself John Steed in e-mails, but whose name that, quite certainly, is not.'

'What about my movie?' the producer exclaimed. 'Are you shutting me down?'

Skinner grinned. 'Whether I would or wouldn't do that is academic. Your co-producer won't have it, and that's that. You're going to lose today, while we make revised security arrangements for Louise, but you should be able to start shooting tomorrow.

'However, from now on, no one is going to know where Louise is staying; neither you, nor your director, nor the co-stars . . . not even Glenys, when she recovers. That knowledge stays within my team.

'I'll also be putting a man on set, so that no one can booby-trap any of your props. You'll be responsible for checking everybody on set. You see one unfamiliar face, you shout bloody murder.'

Judd nodded his head. 'Whatever you say, boss. I'll call the unit manager right now and tell him to stand everyone down for twenty-four hours. We can reschedule and make up the loss over the next couple of weeks.

'The only days I can't change are the Hogmanay street party stuff . . . but that's wild footage, doesn't involve the cast . . . and next Saturday and Sunday; we've got the okay to shoot the big closing scene in Parliament Hall. We set up overnight Friday so we can film both days if necessary.'

'That's fine. No worries there. There's only one other thing you're going to have to do. Telly have been to the fire scene already and the press will be all over it very soon, so my media manager is going to have to issue a statement confirming that there's been a fatality.

'Sparrow's parents will be advised of his death first thing in the morning. Once that's done, I want you to issue a statement expressing regret and explaining that the house was occupied by members of your production team, including Louise Bankier's assistant.

'You should add that Lou is shocked by Clarence's death and by Glenys's injury in this tragic accident. You can lie in your statement. I can't.'

He left the producer in his suite, to come to terms with everything that had happened, and to begin revising his schedule.

Sixty-eight

Elliott Silver's address had been easy to find. Louise Bankier was one of those traditionalists who still carried a Filofax, rather than an electronic notebook. And like all Filo-freaks, she updated hers daily and took it with her, everywhere she went.

Neil McIlhenney found it without difficulty, scribbled it on a clean page in the 'notes' section and handed it to Andy Martin, as he was leaving.

Martin enjoyed driving through the empty streets of the city at night, listening to the frying sound of the tarmac beneath the wide tyres of his MGF, driving fast through lights which normally were blocked with daytime traffic. He zipped through Holy Corner and Bruntsfield, on into Lothian Road and past the new office blocks which had changed Edinburgh's skyline in recent years, finally taking the unnecessarily complicated route which led him to India Street.

Elliott Silver had made his temporary home on the basement level of a tall grey tenement building. He parked in the street outside, looked around the other vehicles until he found a Mercedes A-class, with the rental company tag still hanging from the rear-view mirror. He laid a hand on the hood, but it told him nothing; it was cold.

The Head of CID trotted down the steps, checking his watch as he went: 4 a.m. 'The man should be well asleep,' he murmured to himself, as he rang the doorbell. There was no answer; not until the third ring. Eventually the blue-painted door swung open, framing a leggy blonde woman, wrapped in a silk dressing-gown, back-lit and made transparent by the hall.

'Yes!' she snapped. 'What the hell is it? Where's the fire?'

'Craiglockhart,' he said, 'but it's out now.' He flashed his warrant card. 'DCS Martin, Edinburgh CID. I want to see Mr Silver. Is he in?'

'What's up, Gracie?' a sleepy man's voice sounded from the depths of the hall. 'Is it some drunk? 'Cos if it is . . .'

'It's the police, Mr Silver,' Martin called out. Then the man stepped into view and he recognised him, even unshaven, in boxer shorts; a face from a hundred screens, and many more magazine covers. That of Ralph Annand, Louise's co-star.

Unbidden, Martin stepped into the hall. 'Elliott Silver,' he repeated, 'I'm told he's living here. Is that true, and if so, is he here?'

'Yes!' The third voice came from the bedroom door; a man, fair hair tousled, leaning naked against its jamb. 'I'm Elliott. Now what the fuck do you want?'

'As little as I can get away with,' Martin replied, his legendary patience wearing thin. 'Where were you between midnight and two o'clock?'

'Here, in bed.'

'Okay.' He turned to the woman, thumb jerked towards Annand. 'Him I know. Who are you?'

'Gracie Annand,' she replied. 'Ralph's wife.'

'Right.' His green gaze flashed back to the director. 'So who's to say you didn't slip out. Were you in bed alone?'

Elliott Silver gave a long bored sigh and shook his head.

'So who else is here?'

'No one, Mr Policeman.'

'But you weren't in bed alone.'

'No.'

It was Andy Martin's turn to sigh. 'Okay,' he asked, 'which one?'

Silver flashed him a wicked, triumphant smile. 'Both of them, Mr Policeman. Shocked?'

'To the core, sunshine,' said the detective, 'to the very core.

'Now go and get some kit on . . . all of you . . . and get your sore and sorry arses back in here. Because it's my turn to shock you.'

Sixty-nine

Skinner's car stood outside the George, no obstruction to traffic, since it was only just after five. He thought about driving home but saw no point in wakening Sarah, or the baby, earlier than necessary. And so, instead, he drove down towards Fettes, stopping only to pick up a couple of filled rolls in an all-night café in Stockbridge. The night security staff came to something approaching attention as he parked in his reserved space, opening the door for him before he reached it.

Tiredness was beginning to catch up with him as he unlocked his office; he debated whether to grab a couple of hours' sleep on the couch, or to attack the rolls instead. His mind made up, he switched on the coffee filter which stood, ever ready, in the corner. The bread was fresh from the baker's oven, not too well fired, buttered and filled with egg mayonnaise. He ate them with pleasure, and chased them with strong coffee, then looked around.

'How many mornings like this, Bob?' he asked himself aloud. 'Caught in limbo in the nothing hours; nothing happening, nothing to do but think. Too many, especially in the time between Myra and Sarah . . . Christ, in the time between Sarah and Sarah.

345

'I was worried about big Neil, too, facing the same thing. Then he goes and surprises the shit out of me; him and Lou. Fucking big dark horse that he is! Let's hope, eh?'

He looked around, feeling suddenly self-conscious, as if there was a chance that someone might catch the DCC talking to himself in the night. Suddenly a thought caught him, and he laughed quietly. 'Not so daft a notion with Chase around.' He opened the deep drawer of his desk. 'Better just check to see if he's hiding in here.'

And then he noticed the small table beside his desk; the bank of telephones on top, and on the second shelf beneath, the fax. His private, secure fax, with a plastic tray suspended from it, a tray that was no longer empty.

Intrigued, glad to have something to do, he took the message from its holder and scanned it. There was a cover sheet headed, 'Private, Eyes Only,' above an impressive crest, bald eagle surrounded by the legend, 'National Security Council of the United States of America', which was followed in its turn by a second line, 'From the Office of the Deputy Chair.'

Skinner grinned as he pictured his old friend Joe Doherty, whom he had known since his days as FBI resident in London, before a college buddy had become President and set him on the road to greatness; he saw his thin, lined, sallow face, the slimness of his build which made him seem smaller than his five feet nine.

As he began to read, he heard his mid-western drawl.

When he had finished the three-page message he put it down with a faint tinge of excitement. He reached out for his outside line, then stopped, considering. Finally he exclaimed, aloud once more, to the ghosts in the room, 'Ah bugger it! Why should I be awake, and him asleep? The boy's got to learn.'

He took a card from his wallet, where he had tucked it away, picked up the phone and dialled David Mackenzie's mobile number.

As he had expected, the Strathclyde DI was too good a copper, too keen, too inquisitive, too scared to miss out on anything, to switch off his hand-phone while he slept, or to divert calls to the night shift. After a few rings, a sleepy voice came on the line, mumbling a 'Hello'.

'Bandit? It's DCC Skinner. Glad you're awake.'

'Sir, it's . . .' the voice slurred.

'That's right, it's quarter to six. Say sorry to your wife for me, then go downstairs, get a great big notepad, and call me back on the number I gave you.' He hung up the telephone and waited, looking at the second hand on his watch.

One minute and twelve seconds later, the phone rang. He grabbed it, grinning. 'Good man,' he exclaimed. 'It's going to be worth it, I promise.

'How are you getting on with old man McConnell?'

'Slowly. Someone in the ScotRail office is looking into his record for me, but she's doing it grudgingly and bloody slowly. I doubt if she'll come up with anything.'

'Fuck her.'

'Is that an order, sir, because if it's all the same to you . . .'

Skinner chuckled. 'Okay, just forget her for a while. I've got a new tack for you, one that will awake your basest instincts. Remember I said a few days back that I'd do some brainstorming of my own? Well, listen to me and I'll tell you what I've been up to.' He raced on.

'What do we know about the late John McConnell?

'One, he was a keen golfer. Irrelevant to your investigation.

'Two, he was a dirty old man. Possibly relevant to your investigation.

'Three, he was apparently into jellies. Highly relevant to your investigation.

'Four, someone ripped him off for most of his liquid assets. Again, highly relevant to your investigation.

'Five, he's dead. The reason for your investigation.

'Agreed?'

'Yes sir,' said Mackenzie, wide awake now.

'Good. So let's join the dots. Forget the golf; that's nothing. What we have is a young woman who by some means or another, gets this old geezer hooked on drugs.

'The means? Well, he's an old lecher with a penchant for the young stuff, so join those dots up too.

'She feeds his addiction, but at a cost. Over a period of a few months, he gives her all his money, she withdraws it, posing as his niece. Also she sells his prize possessions and does a runner with that money too. We're talking a total rip-off in excess of one hundred thousand.

'Finally she's got the lot. So one day she turns up, feeds him a final shot, and while he's orbiting around Venus, immerses him in a scalding bath and drowns him. Are you in any doubt, Inspector, that that's how it happened?'

'No, sir, none at all.'

'Which leaves us with that video camera. Why the hell did she take that video camera with her on that last visit? One reason only: to make a movie. And why the hell,' Skinner asked, 'would she do that?'

'Because she's a fruitcake!' Mackenzie exclaimed.

'Maybe she is, maybe she isn't. I've met a lot of fruitcakes in my career, son, and all but a very few of them had a purpose behind the things they did. So, I continue to ask, why did she film the old boy?'

'We'll need to find her to find that out, won't we?'

'Ah, but Bandit, maybe by finding out we'll find her. That brainstorming I've been doing has focused on that. Listen,' he said, urgently. 'Young girl, old man . . . dirty old man . . . home movies. It's porn; beyond a doubt. It's a porno movie.

'But add in the drugs element and you take it up a notch. Not just sex but sado-masochism. Finally add in the fact that the old man winds up dead. Is your blood running cold yet, Bandit? Because it should.

'I have a friend in the States, who has access to just about everything, including FBI investigations into the pornography industry. We're way behind the column in Britain in that area. Sure, we're good at catching the sort of dirty bastards who collect kiddie pics, but there's all sorts of stuff going on that we don't have a clue about.

'The Americans do; the FBI wage a real war on it, but there are places where even they can't go. The CIA have been involved as well; and even they can't cap it. Pornography has moved on from the corner shop . . . way, way on. It's a major Internet industry now, and it shows just what a dangerous thing the Net can be.

'There are all sorts of sites that can be accessed easily; some of them offer membership, some of them just one-off sales, but they all involve money, collected through credit cards. You imagine it and you can find it, and with the right kit and enough credit in your account, you can download it. Guys like us might lock you up if you're caught, but you won't be.

'The softer of these sites are tolerated; the hardest might not be but they can't be stopped either, because they operate outside regulation, outside the US, outside Europe, in South America, in the Far East, in Asia . . . in bandit country. Sometimes they move their administration around from place to place; that includes the accounts, always hard to spot, through which they collect their dough.

'Potentially the money in it is better than drugs, and easier.'

Skinner paused. 'Still with me?'

'All the way', said Mackenzie breathlessly.

'Okay; this is it. At the very end of the pornography industry there exists something so awful we don't even like to think about it . . . the snuff movie. A film which is the ultimate in sexo-sadism, a film in which the torture and death on screen are not simulated. They are real.

'They've been around for a while, of course, since back before the video days, made mostly in South America. But with today's technology . . .' He paused, letting the suggestion strike home.

'So, Bandit, what if, just what if mind, the lady with the video camera was making a snuff movie, with old John McConnell as the star?'

'Why, sir? Why?' the inspector exclaimed.

'Maybe you said it yourself. Fruitcake? But remember, on

the Internet you can upload to a site as well as download from it.'

He took a sup from his cold coffee. 'I can't answer any more whys but here's another what if. What if this woman didn't make any mistakes? She couldn't have known that the old dear across the road would eyeball her taking the camera into the house. So what if by taking the syringe with her, and leaving the cassette box, she was leaving us a message?'

'Jesus,' Bandit Mackenzie whispered. 'What sort of a mind do you have?'

'I ask myself that sometimes. I suspect it's much like your own; it's been around longer, that's all, so it's more experienced in contemplating evil.'

He went on quickly. 'So back to my friend in the States. He's come up with a list of potential websites; the sort of Net location where one finds extreme pornography. What I suggest you do, Inspector . . . suggest, mind, I've got sod all to do with this investigation . . . is get yourself a computer with a modem and get looking.

'But be sure you use a mainstream connection. If you try to log on through the Strathclyde Police computer address, you might just find yourself blocked out.'

The DCC chuckled again. 'You got that pen handy?'

'Yes, sir.'

'Good. Here you are then. I hope you have plenty of paper . . . it's a long list.'

Seventy

'So he's not talking?'

'Not a cheep, Andy. Not a dicky-bird. I talked to him right up to the moment he went up before the Sheriff, and Geoff Lesser went as far as he could to persuade the lad to turn Crown Evidence, but he was having none of it. So he went into court, the charges, murder and theft, were read out, he made no plea and he was remanded in custody.'

'He'll be in Saughton by now.'

'Honour among fish rustlers, d'you think?'

'Maybe, but more likely terror. I think that he's just plain scared of someone, another member of the gang.'

Andy Martin heaved a sigh. 'Maybe after he's been locked away from them for a week or two he'll start to feel braver. Tell Lesser that there's a deal on the table; we'll drop the murder charge in exchange for names in the witness box. We'll also ensure that he never spends a single day in the same prison as another gang member.

'That will be open to him until we catch the rest of the gang ourselves, with indictable evidence against them.'

'I'll tell him,' said Dan Pringle. He looked at the Head of CID. 'Christ, Andy man, you look knackered.'

'I feel it,' the DCS confessed. 'I've been up most of the bloody night.'

'Karen no' sleeping, is she?'

'That was the night before last. No, we've got an operation going up in Edinburgh, and it took a bad turn on us. I wound up rousting three unsavoury citizens out of their bed . . . and I mean bed . . . at about half four.'

'Have you not been home since?'

Martin grinned. 'Sure, but by that time Karen was awake, and being sick.'

'She no' over that yet?'

'I'd hoped so, but not quite. I'm told we go on to cravings next; spam and mango pizzas at two in the morning, that sort of thing.'

'Not necessarily. With my wife it was just baked beans; but they can bring problems of their own . . . especially in the winter, when ye canna' sleep with the windows open.'

'Anyway,' said the Head of CID, steering the discussion back on to professional lines. 'With one thing and another, I decided to scrub the Monday briefing altogether and come down to Gala to see you instead.

'Give me a state-of-play report on the fish farm investigations.'

Pringle nodded. 'Sure, but let me get McGurk in.' He stepped out of his office for a few seconds, and returned with the bean-pole sergeant following behind.

'Right sir,' he began. 'The story so far.

'We have Raymond Anders in custody and charged. He denies killing the girl, but admits to driving one of the trucks at the Alvarez place.

'We have Mercy Alvarez spending the night on which her farm was raided in bed with Glenn Lander, after having dinner with Assistant Chief Constable Chase and Mrs Chase, who stayed long enough to clear them of any possible involvement in the robbery.

'We have Glenn Lander spending the night on which his farm was raided in bed with Mercy Alvarez, having entertained another cousin until just after midnight.

'We have Raymond Anders making contact with Glenn Lander at Raeburn Place on the afternoon after his farm was done, we believe to tell him that the stock had been moved successfully.

'We have the robbery taking place the day before Anders was due to meet Kath Adey to sell her a security system.

'We have the gang going along to Country Fresh prepared to restrain and blindfold the girl, only for her to be killed when she fights back.'

Martin nodded. 'Yes to all those; we've got Anders and through Jack's sighting at the Accies match, a strong link to Glenn Lander.

'Now, why was no apparent attempt made to lure Adey away from the farm? I suggest that it was because they knew she wouldn't go, because I had given her and Mercy Alvarez a very clear warning that she should not. So they didn't even try; they cut her telephone line instead, so she couldn't raise the alarm.'

'What if she had a mobile?' asked McGurk.

'They don't work in that gully. Someone knew that too. I have no doubt that it was the same person who knew that it was pointless trying to get her to leave. Strong link number two: Mercy Alvarez, who told me that she didn't know the other fish farms that had been robbed.'

'Two out of three,' said Pringle.

'Yes. Now what of the third? What about Mellerkirk? How does that connect?'

'It doesn't, sir.' Martin looked at McGurk as he spoke. 'There's no connection between Lander or Alvarez, and Sir Adrian Watson, not one that I've been able to make, at any rate.'

'Oh there is a connection, Jack. A very clear one. We've all been thinking in terms of maybe ten or twelve grand apiece as the proceeds of these robberies. In other words, okay, but maybe not worth killing over. However, the insured losses in each of the three farms are, Mellerkirk, thirty thousand, Howdengate, forty thousand, and Country Fresh, forty thousand. Total, one hundred and ten thousand pounds, spread over three different insurers so it doesn't show up too fast.

'What do you have? Three businesses operating on the edge of profitability; anyone who steals their fish is actually doing them a favour, for they can restock with the insurance lift and still have a tidy sum left to reinvest, or reduce debt, or whatever. Of course if they're stealing their own fish themselves, they're doing even better, aren't they?'

'They are indeed,' Pringle agreed. 'We're pretty close to nailing Lander and Alvarez. Now all we need to do is tie in that bastard Watson.'

'If it is him,' Martin countered. 'Adrian Watson's worth about seven million quid cash. On top of that he owns the estate, and he has two fucking Botticellis hanging on his walls. What the hell's he doing involved in a thirty-grand insurance scam, especially one with murder involved?'

'His fish are worth stealing, though. Especially . . .' He stopped in mid-sentence and a big grin spread across his face, wiping away all his earlier weariness.

Pringle stared at the Head of CID; the grin was infectious, it spread to him. 'What is it?' he demanded. 'What the hell have you been hiding up your sleeve?'

'It's funny,' said Andy Martin slowly, 'that a good copper's a good copper all the time. Neil McIlhenney was out for a drive yesterday with a friend. He took her down to the western end of the Lammermuirs, to the far end of the track that takes the walkers to Longformacus. While he was up there, he spotted a fish farm.'

'But there's no fish farm there, sir,' McGurk protested. 'I've listed them all and I've visited them all. There just isn't one there.'

'You're right, Jack. There isn't, according to the local environmental health department, or to the Scottish Executive Department of Agriculture, or to the Trout Farmers' Association. Sammy Pye checked with all of them this morning, and called me while I was driving down here.

'It doesn't exist, but it's there nonetheless, because big Neil says it is, and so does the lady who was with him. I have a feeling that if you look at Raymond Anders' business records you might find some unexplained equipment purchases that can be explained right there.'

Martin leaned back in his chair. The grin was far from extinguished. 'Sammy checked something else for me too . . .

bright lad, Sammy. The land in that area is owned by a family trust; there's not much you can do with it other than graze sheep, shoot and fish the river that runs through it.

'The trust was established by a rubber planter who bought the land when he came back from the Far East sixty years ago. He must have seen the war signs in the air and got out in the nick of time. It's administered by a small firm of surveyors to the landed gentry, based in Edinburgh.

'There are only two trustees now; the planter's daughter and her son. His name is Gates: Bill Gates.'

'The . . .' exclaimed Dan Pringle, then ran out of adjectives '. . . bastards.'

'Aren't they just. They steal their own fish, take the insurance money, or nearly all of it, and restock at a profit, having transferred the originals to another site for sale in the normal way at top market prices.

'Total take, probably fifty grand each, after they'd paid off Anders and the third man in the team.'

'So what do we do now,' Pringle mused. 'Lift them?'

Martin shook his head. 'Too soon, too soon. You'd get Gates, but if he kept quiet, the Crown Office wouldn't act against Lander or Alvarez on the basis of the evidence we have at the moment.

'We have to catch them together. I don't envy you the job, Dan, but it's got to be done. We have to stake out that farm, until they all show up.'

Seventy-one

Karen sat in her car and took a deep breath and looked up the narrow path which led to the terraced house. 'Well, Sergeant Neville,' she whispered to herself, 'if you had known that this came with the territory, would you have taken it on?'

She saw a curtain move in a ground-floor window. 'Of course you would,' she answered herself. 'Doesn't make it easy though.' Steeling herself, she stepped out of the car.

The front door opened before she reached it; the woman who awaited her was in the second half of her twenties, only a few years younger than she was herself. She was casually dressed in a Hard Rock teeshirt and designer jeans, but she wore them well. Her dark hair was wavy – permed, Karen guessed.

'Mrs Martin?' the woman in the doorway asked, unnecessarily, for she had been expecting the visit. 'I'm Mary McGurk; come on in.'

She showed the visitor into her small living room; a toddler sat in the middle of the floor, playing intently with a plastic hammer and bricks. 'This is Regan,' said her mother. 'We called her after the guy in *The Sweeney*. Jack's idea, but it suits her.

'Look at her. She's about as good at the DIY as her father.' She glanced at her visitor again. 'Here, have we met?'

Karen grinned, pleased to be recognised. 'Yes; at a CID dance a couple of years ago. You were with Jack, and I was with Sammy Pye. I was DS Neville then, in the Head of CID's office. I still am in a way . . . I married him a few months back.'

'Yes; I remember now, you were the girl in *that* dress. Fast track to the top, eh?' said Mary McGurk, with a light laugh. 'You're off your mark in another way too, I see. When are you due?'

'The early summer, actually. God, is it that obvious already?'

'Well, you're quite well endowed naturally . . . who could forget that dress, come to think of it . . . so . . .'

'Hah,' laughed Karen, 'tell me about it. I expect that I'll have boobs like mountains for a few months, but that after that they'll be off to the deep south.'

'No,' the other woman smiled, 'that's not necessarily how it goes. Good luck to you anyway. There'll be times when you're grateful for the company, if nothing else. Now, would you like a cup of tea? It's made.'

'That'd be nice, thanks.' As she waited, in an armchair, Regan put down her hammer, crawled over and climbed up on to her lap. 'Aunty,' she said in a clear voice.

'Get you down off there!' the mother scolded as she returned.

'Ah, leave her alone, she's fine.'

'Fine, but a bit erratic still, though. Put her down if she starts to feel warm; these new nappies are good, but they don't work miracles.

'So, Mrs Martin,' she said, as she put a cup of tea and a two-finger KitKat on a small table beside her chair, 'what brings you here?'

'For a start, I haven't come to act the grand lady. It's Karen, okay?'

Mary McGurk nodded.

'Andy, my husband, said I should come, but not before Superintendent Pringle spoke to Jack and he agreed.

'I've had a bee in my bonnet for a while, Mary, about the police service and the way it handles its officers. Now, although I've left the force, I'm actually in a position to do something about it.

'When a police officer has a problem on the job, if he . . . or she . . . has a close call, or he sees something that's really hard to take, then there's very good established machinery these days to deal with the consequences. The force . . . our force at least . . . is as interested in a person's emotional well-being as in his physical fitness, and that stretches from the rawest police cadet to the Chief Constable.

'For example, Andy even had counselling himself earlier on this year . . . but keep that to yourself.

'There's a flaw in it. We . . . listen to me, talking as if I'm still part of it . . . give support for on-the-job developments, but we tend to forget that there can be trauma down the line as well, especially if the officer's partner isn't part of the force. When coppers marry coppers, like Andy and me, or like

Maggie Rose and Mario McGuire, there's a built-in under-standing in the relationship, just the same as when teachers marry teachers, doctors marry doctors, social workers set up home with social workers, and so on.'

'But when a copper marries an art teacher, you mean . . .' Mary interrupted.

'No, I didn't. I'm still speaking generally here. In my own case, when Andy goes out of that door every day, for all his rank I know that there are risks because of the way he does his job; you do not always get to deal with nice people. Ironically, his predecessor rarely set foot outside his office, yet he was killed in a plane crash coming back from a meeting in London.

'I can live with these risks, because I've been exposed to them myself and I can keep them in perspective. But it has to be more difficult for you to watch Jack go out on an investigation where someone's been murdered and where the person who did it is still at large.

'Now the fact is, the risks are minimal, but they're always going to be there, in your mind. When the niggling stress they cause is compounded by something else . . . like in your case a career move to another division . . . then too damn right it's going to affect you.

'And because of that it's inevitable that it's going to affect Jack.'

Karen held up a hand. 'I promise you this. Jack has not been running around the Borders moaning about his bloody wife or anything like that. But he and Dan Pringle work very closely together; Dan likes him and he cares about him, so even if Jack tried he couldn't hide his worries from him.

'What I'm getting round to saying here, Mary, is that I believe that there should be a proper support group for officers' partners as well as for the men and women themselves, and I'm bloody well going to see that it is set up.'

Mary McGurk opened her mouth to speak, but in the end only a sigh came out. 'You're right in what you're saying,' she murmured at last. 'I do feel remote sometimes, but . . .'

'Can I ask you a straight question?' Karen interposed. 'Suppose Jack wasn't a detective, and this move wasn't happening. Would you two still have a problem?'

'No. Not through me, anyway. I love him.'

'Okay, I want you to tell me what we can do to help, but first, I have to make a point. This is a disciplined service and Jack was in it when you two married. In this set-up, in the lower ranks, you don't always get to apply for your job. Very often an officer is offered a posting with his long-term career development in mind. In a force like ours, with a big geographical area, that can sometimes mean moving house.

'That's what's happened with Jack. He wasn't posted down to the Borders because Detective Superintendent Pringle likes the way he makes coffee, or thinks he's fun to have around. Dan took him down there because he believes that he's a damn good officer, who could fill his own shoes one day; divisional commander and above.

'At the moment he's living Monday to Friday in a reasonably comfortable police squat down in the division. That's not ideal for him, and it's bloody awful for you, with the baby, and even worse since the job can have erratic hours.

They don't have many major investigations down in the Borders; just your luck that he should pitch up there at the start of one.'

'Maybe,' said Mary, 'but what if I move down there and it's just the same, with him never being home? It's such a big thing, moving house; and at least in Edinburgh I've got my family, my friends.'

'Look, we can't solve all your problems. If you put enough pressure on Jack, he can ask for a move back up town, and he'll get it. It'll be CID too, not back into uniform, unless that's what he wants. But it will slow down his career development and it could prevent him going as far as he might.

'So what can we do to make this move as positive for you as possible? You're an art teacher. Would you like to go back to work, part-time or full-time? We'll get you a job. Would it be easier for you to move south without the big commitment of buying a house? Fine; keep this one, put a tenant in it, a young copper maybe, who'll look after the place or else. We'll find you a nice place in a nice community that you can rent until it's time for Jack's next move, which will probably be to a divisional detective inspector job. Do you want to get to know people down there? As a first step you can join the police partners' support group that I'm setting up. I've only sent out one mailshot, and I've got two hundred members already, one third of them in the Borders.'

'You can do all that?' asked Mary. 'Even a job?'

'I called round the education departments before I came here this morning. I'm a trained teacher too; I know the ropes. There's a job going in a secondary in Galashiels that you could start after Christmas. Full time or mornings only; up to you.'

'Can I talk to Jack about it?'

Karen looked down at Regan, who was sleeping on her lap. 'I think that would be a pretty good idea, don't you?'

Seventy-two

'Take it away, Jackie,' said Dan Pringle. 'You're looking a happier boy this morning, even in this freezing bloody pit.'

'You're looking a bit smug yourself, sir, if I may say so.'

'You and Mary got things sorted out then?'

'For the foreseeable at least,' said the sergeant. 'She's going to give it a shot. She's going for an interview with the Council head of education on Monday, then once this thing cracks we're going to look at places to rent in and around Gala.

'She's also going to help Karen Martin set up this support group of hers. The way things are going she'll have no bloody time for Regan and me when she gets down here.'

'Aye, well, we'll no' be sending the DCS's wife out to counsel you,' Pringle rumbled.

'You boys still okay in here?' he enquired, conversationally rather than solicitously.

'Fine, sir. DC Donovan and I have never been more comfortable. Have we, Jason?'

'No, Sergeant,' the young detective constable agreed, not bothering to hide the irony in his voice. 'But so far, it hasna' rained.'

The three were seated on folding chairs in a deep camouflaged hide which had been dug out, under cover of darkness, on the crest of a hillock just over a quarter of a mile from the supposedly non-existent fish farm. Its walls were lined with black plastic to contain the damp; a small butane gas heater burned in a corner of the ten-foot square trench, and a camping stove stood beside it with a kettle coming to the boil. The sloping roof, which used the line of the hillside, was planking with heather laid over the top, and it was ventilated by the slit window through which its occupants were able to keep watch on the floodlit enclosure.

'The man still there?' the superintendent asked.

'Yes,' McGurk replied. 'Still the same story; no one's come or gone since we set up here overnight on Monday. The bloke's living in the Portakabin near the entrance. He comes out every so often to load the automatic feeders and check the stock then he goes back in again. Always he wears this big parka thing with a hood, so we can't get a good look at him.

'One thing, though; he's got a rifle in there. We don't get all that many gulls this far inland, but he's shot a couple that have come close.'

'Has he now,' said Pringle. 'That makes this a siege in that case. When we take this place down, we'll have armed officers in the team.'

'Sir,' Donovan called out suddenly, peering through the observation hatch. 'There's something going on here. There's a tanker arriving.'

McGurk grabbed his non-reflective field glasses and turned to look out of the viewing slot. 'Right enough, boss,' he said, although Pringle was peering over his shoulder. 'A big vehicle, not unlike a petrol tanker, or the sort of machine they use to pump out septic tanks; one man in the cab. The guy's out of the Portakabin and he's opening the gate.'

As they watched, the driver of the tanker eased it carefully through the gates and took up position, within reach for its long flexible hose of two of the eight large tanks. Satisfied, he left the engine running and jumped from the cab.

'Fucking hell, it's Gates,' McGurk called out in a stifled shout.

As the three policemen watched, the Mellerkirk manager and the hooded man unfastened the suction pipe from the side of the tanker and positioned it in the tank on the left. Then Gates stepped up to a control panel mounted beside the door and pressed a button. A new sound overrode that of the engine, the higher-pitched noise of a pump at work.

'Jack,' said Pringle, 'I want him followed when he leaves here. I'll stay here and keep an eye on what's happening. You two get down the hill and into your Land Rover and be in position to follow when he moves off. No radio, just in case. We keep in touch through our mobiles.'

The sergeant nodded and led Donovan out of the hide, taking care to disturb the sloping roof as little as possible as they left.

The pumping operation continued for twenty minutes, until both tanks had been emptied. As Gates and his companion stowed the hose once more, Pringle took out his mobile and called McGurk's number. 'Ready Jack?'

'Yes sir.'

'Magic this, isn't it?' said the superintendent. 'It's just like being a real polisman again. Okay, he's on the move. Call me when you get where you're going.'

He ended the call and watched as the tanker turned awkwardly within the compound, then drove back out of the gate. The hooded man closed it behind him, then went back inside his Portakabin.

Pringle sat back and waited. He made himself a mug of tea from the kettle on the small gas stove; eventually, he made another. At last, his mobile played its little tune. 'Yes?' he answered eagerly.

'You're not going to believe this, sir,' came Jack McGurk's drawl. 'Gates has just driven up the track to Mellerkirk.'

In his hide, the superintendent laughed quietly. 'The audacious wee so-and-so,' he said. 'The insurance money's come through, and Gates is selling Sir Adrian Watson's own fucking fish back to him, at top dollar, you can bet.

'I wish I could find it in my heart to feel sorry for the arrogant bastard, but when this comes out in evidence in the High Court, it'll be the talk of the New Club!

'Job well done, Jack. Let's keep the other two under close observation. Then all we'll have to do is wait until they show up, take identifiable photographs of them on site and they should be ours.'

'Save for one thing, boss. Same old problem, how do we identify the fish?'

'Fuck that; we're past that now. We'll just charge them all with murder and theft, and stand back, so we're not trampled in the rush to be the lucky one who's allowed to shop the others and become a Crown witness.'

Seventy-three

'Are you sure it's safe to leave Louise on her own?' asked Bob Skinner.

'Yes,' replied McIlhenney emphatically, 'there's no problem. I thought I'd take the chance to come into the office, since they're shooting a scene in the Laigh Hall this afternoon; you know where that is, just about directly below the Great Hall itself. It's a part of the building that we can control quite easily. No one's getting in without identifying themselves to a uniformed officer.

'Everyone involved on the shoot has to carry a laminated photo-pass, signed by Warren Judd, no less.'

'They'll become collector's items,' the DCC grunted sourly.

'I doubt it. There's too many of the bloody things; there are a hell of a lot of people in a full-scale film production crew you know, especially the sort of big-budget jobs that Lou works on.'

'Listen to the expert. How's the filming been going anyway, Mr de Mille?'

'Remarkably smoothly, considering that they lost Monday. Silver split the crew into two, so they could film simultaneously

369

on different locations; Lou's not in every scene herself so it was simply a matter of dividing up the extras.'

'They're all checked out too, I hope.'

'To be sure. They all have photo-passes as well, even Lucy, Lou's sister; she's got a walk-on part.'

'She's a thesp too?' said Skinner, surprised. 'I didn't know that.'

'Well,' the inspector sounded hesitant, 'it isn't as simple as that. She'd like to be, but she's got a couple of big obstacles . . . no joke intended. She looks too much like her sister for a start; she'd have difficulty establishing her own identity. On top of that, she's not a very good actress.'

'Ah, that's unfortunate.'

'Lou's got her a couple of jobs, on the back of which she has an Equity card, but she didn't exactly shine in either of them. Still, when she asked for a part in the new movie, Lou got soft and told Silver to write her in.'

'What does she play?'

'Lou's character's sister, what else? She's only got a couple of lines, though. One in the Laigh Hall today, and the other in the big climax scene; they're shooting that in the Great Hall over the weekend.'

'It's not finished already is it?'

'No,' said McIlhenney quickly. 'They've got another week of location shooting after this, then they break for Christmas, and come back to do the Hogmanay stuff.'

'And during the break?' Skinner asked. 'I mean, there's no reason to suppose we're going to have caught this bloke by then. Have you given any thought to that? No, I suppose I mean has Lou given any thought to it?

'If she's still under protection . . .' he went on. 'You have to spend Christmas with your kids . . . Christ, I should have thought this through, before I allowed you to move her in with you, whatever your personal relationship.'

'In spite of your personal relationship!' he shouted. 'I have messed this up. I should have moved her in with Mario and Maggie, not you.'

'Sure,' his assistant said quietly. 'If you'd done that at the start. Aye, and if Alex hadn't been working that Friday night, Lou and I might never have met. But she was, and we did, and there and then things started to happen between us without either of us being aware of it, until the truth dawned.

'Don't worry, I'm a big boy; well-fired in life's furnace you might say. I'm not disregarding the possibility that Lou's feelings might change once this clown's caught and the strain is off her. It was just about the first thing I asked her, in fact. She said no; that she's sure. In any event, I know how I feel about her, and that's got sod all to do with being her knight in shining armour. It's man and woman, pure and simple.

'So let me ask you this, Boss.' He stopped. 'No, let me ask you, Bob, man to man. If Sarah was under this sort of threat, would you delegate the job of protecting her, or would you allow the Chief to delegate it?'

Sitting on the edge of his desk, the DCC smiled at his friend. 'No, I would not,' he answered, truthfully. 'As you know damn well.

'Doesn't alter my question, though. What are we going to do during that Christmas break to get you and the kids together, yet protect Lou?'

371

—————— Quintin Jardine ——————

'She's thought about that too. We haven't discussed Life After John Steed, as you might put it, but the Christmas question has come up.'

'Lou has four homes,' said Neil. 'One in London, one on the Côte d'Azur, one in Ireland, where she's officially resident, and one in Beverly Hills. It's on an estate with its own security, and she wants us all to go there for Christmas.'

'If we did, d'you think your pal in the States could fix it for me to carry a firearm?'

'I know he could.' Skinner grinned. 'Don't shoot anyone unless you have to, though. It could get messy.'

'I promise, boss. In that case . . .'

He was interrupted by the ringing of the DCC's private line. Skinner frowned in momentary exasperation, then picked it up. 'Yes,' he snapped.

'It's Dave Mackenzie, Mr Skinner. I'm going to need your help.' The Strathclyde DI sounded anxious.

'Sure, if I can. What do you want me to do?'

'Can you have a word with my superintendent?' asked Mackenzie plaintively. 'I've spent all week logging on to porno websites. In the process, I've run up this bloody enormous bill on my credit card for material I've downloaded. If I'd known what I was getting into I'd have cleared the spend before I started; I didn't, though. When I went to the DCI, he crapped himself and referred it up the line.

'The Super went ape-shit, and demanded to know exactly what the fuck I've been up to. I had to show her the list you gave me; now she's demanded to know exactly where the fuck it came from!

'I tried to tell her that I had a source to protect. She told me that in that case I could protect him even more by paying my own credit card bill. I'm in it deep, sir. Can you help me?'

Skinner laughed. 'I reckon I can,' he said. 'Is this your divisional commander you're talking about?'

'That's right.'

'You're in luck, Bandit. She and I went to the same primary school in Motherwell; not only will I fix it, I won't even need to tell her that I got involved in your investigation after you threatened to lock up my secretary.'

Mackenzie sighed with relief. 'Thanks sir,' he exclaimed, 'I've been trying to imagine having to explain to my wife that I've wiped out our Christmas spending power by downloading porno videos.'

'That's okay. I'll pull another string and have you set up with an untraceable AMEX account for the rest of it.'

'Ah,' said the inspector, 'I don't think I'm going to need much of it. This is where I get to the good news; I think I've got a result.'

Skinner, in his swivel chair, sat bolt upright. 'You've what? Son, I thought I'd probably sent you on the dirtiest wild goose chase of all time and you're telling me you've got something?'

'Yes sir.' The DCC could almost hear the young man beam. 'I found it on a website on your list called www dot mortestrellas dot ec.'

'Death Stars,' Skinner translated. 'What's the dot ec bit?'

'Ecuador, I think. The site narrative's in Spanish and English. It's desperate stuff, sir. A series of short videos of girls made up to look like pop stars being abused and then stabbed or strangled. There's an on-site disclaimer that says that all scenes of violence are simulated,' Mackenzie's voice grew grim. 'But they're not, sir, be sure they're not.

'Among these I found a series of videos offered for download, under the title, Blue Star Falling, numbers one to six.

'So far, I've downloaded the first two. They're different, sir. The . . .' he paused for a second, '. . . performers, are an old man and a young woman, both naked, and in action . . . her more than him, though. She's wearing a mask, but he isn't. The downloaded quality isn't all that great, and I've only seen old John McConnell once, on a mortuary slab after he'd been dead in his bath for a fortnight, but . . .'

'Good for you, Dave,' said Skinner. 'What are you going to do with it?'

'First off, sir, I want to show it to you. At some point I'm going to have to show it to Ruth to get an identification, and I'd like you to look at it first.'

'Charming. But I started you off on this, so I suppose that's only fair. I'll tell you what to do; download the rest, then link it all together. If you can transfer it to VCR then do it. If not, store it on Zip discs or whatever it takes and bring it through here. We can look at it with my technicians; I'll have them isolate an image of the old man and enhance it as far as they can. We'll show that to Ruthie; nothing else.

'I'll get you a shot of the woman too. Mask or not, it might help.

'Come through here tomorrow morning, ten o'clock. We'll be ready; bugger jurisdiction now, Bandit. This investigation doesn't have any borders any more.'

He hung up. 'Would you credit that?' he said. 'The boy's got a result; he thinks he's found Ruthie's uncle starring in a South American porno movie.'

'You rate that boy, don't you?' said McIlhenney.

Skinner nodded. 'More highly with every encounter. He reminds me of a young bloke I knew once. He's got the gift.'

'What's that?'

'Luck, and he pushes it.' He looked at his assistant. 'Lou's on a secure set tomorrow, yes?' McIlhenney nodded.

'Come and meet him, once you've dropped her off. I don't relish watching what I think he's going to show us, so I wouldn't mind some company. Besides, another set of eyes might see something Mackenzie's and mine don't.'

Seventy-four

David Mackenzie leaned back in his chair and looked at Gwendoline Dell as she entered his office. 'Off the hook with the Super?' she asked.

He wiped his hand across his forehead in a mock gesture. 'Thank God,' he said. 'Or thank Bob, at least.'

'Good for you. Now are you going to tell me what landed you in it in the first place, and what you've been doing all week while I've been running myself ragged trying to find John McConnell's grandfather clock, not to mention his girlfriend?'

'No,' the inspector replied, seriously. 'I won't expose you to it until I have to, and even then I'll think twice about it.'

'Sexist pig!' she exclaimed. 'Don't you go treating me differently to a male officer.'

'Don't worry; I'm not. I wouldn't let anyone see this stuff unless it was absolutely necessary.' He swung his chair round to face the computer which sat on a table beside his desk. 'Now bugger off, Gwennie, and don't come in unless I call you.'

The sergeant turned and left, with a frown and a disdainful sniff. Mackenzie pressed the start-up button of the PC. He was waiting for it to boot up, when his phone rang. He picked it up. 'I thought I said no calls,' he told the switchboard operator.

'This is one you said you would take, sir,' the man replied. 'Miss Mair.'

The inspector's eyebrows rose; he smiled. 'Put her through.'

'Miss Mair,' he said, heartily as the call was put through. 'Margaret. What can I do for you?'

'Don't be familiar with me, young man. You can do nothing for me, I assure you. I, on the other hand . . .'

Seventy-five

'What time do you have to be on set tomorrow?' Neil asked too casually.

'Why?' she smiled. 'Do you want rid of me, already?'

'Not for one second. But the boss has got someone coming to see him and he's asked me if I can sit in on the meeting.'

'In that case, my dear, you can drop me off any time you like.' Louise paused, as if she was considering something, touching her lips in one of the trademark gestures which were familiar to millions of movie fans around the world.

She caught him looking at her, and clenched her fist quickly. 'I can't stop doing that,' she said, 'not even on camera. Catherine the Great, one LA hooker, a lady brain surgeon, several stressed-out housewives and now a Scots criminal lawyer have all had that same mannerism.'

'I'll bet it suited them all too.'

'It looked pretty daft on Catherine the Great, I have to say. In this case, though, it was masking a brilliant idea. Do you think that the kids would like to come on set tomorrow? We're shooting the big surprise ending, but if we put them on Scouts' honour, or Guide's honour or whatever it is these days, I'm sure they'll keep the secret till the movie comes out.'

'Hey, could they do that? I've got this complicated arrangement for Spence, with the boss bringing him up town, and Mario . . . That's my pal Mario McGuire. You haven't met him yet; he's head of Special Branch and his wife's a detective super . . . picking him up from Fettes and taking him to his mini-rugby at Murrayfield. But I'm sure that Lauren and Mark would love it. Wait a minute while I make a phone call.'

He went into the hall, returning a few minutes later. 'Sorted. Sarah will take them to Parliament House for ten o'clock, then she'll leave the two younger ones with Alex and go shopping. You are one popular lady right now, I'll tell you. Never mind the kids; the greatest gift you can give a mother with five youngsters on her hands is an afternoon of freedom in Jenner's and John Lewis.'

As he looked at her, he saw a peculiar expression cross her face. 'What?' he asked.

'Oh nothing. You just walked over my grave, that's all.' She tapped her chest. 'Once upon a time,' she said, 'one of my most secret dreams was to be able to take pleasure myself from a gift like that; to leave the kids with someone, indulge myself, then go home in the knowledge that they, and their dad, would be waiting for me.

'Long gone, that dream.'

He took her in his arms and held her close, rubbing his face in her hair. There was much that he could have said to her, but not at that moment.

Eventually she looked up at him. 'What about Christmas?' she asked quietly.

'Yes. Come what may, suppose we catch this man

tomorrow, the kids and I will come with you to Los Angeles. I'll book the flights tomorrow.'

'No,' she said firmly. 'I'll book them.'

'Hey,' he protested. 'That isn't part of the deal.'

'Yes it is. It's my Christmas present to you. It's more than that, in fact; it's a very inadequate thank you for all you've done for me, for all you're doing, for all you're giving me. So please me by saying not another word about the subject.' She stopped his reply with a kiss.

'There's only one other thing I wish I could do for Christmas,' she murmured.

'What's that?'

'Give my dad his mind back. But all the money in the world won't do that. He's all alone now, there in his head. In every respect in fact. He has no friends any more. Most of them drifted away years ago; there was one old guy from his working days, but even he seems to have stopped coming around now.'

She sat on the sofa, pulling him down beside her. 'My life's going to change in a lot of ways, love. One of them will be the amount of time I give to my father. Being back here for this movie, seeing him the other day as he was, made me realise how selfish I've been, and not only towards him.

'I thought I could discharge my obligations with money by paying for nursing care and such like. But in reality, I've just abandoned him, dumped him on my kid sister, made him her problem while I've gone on pinning gold stars on my CV. You know what's going to happen to me at New Year? They're going to make me a bloody CBE!

'When they offered it to me, months ago now, I accepted because I thought it would be nice for my father. Nice for him? They could be turning me into a giant carrot and he wouldn't notice the difference. Lucy was delighted for me, of course, but that didn't make me feel any better.

'Things are going to be different. Dad's always resisted the idea of going into a nursing home. But he's a kind man and if he could still think straight he would accept that it's inevitable. So I'm going to make it happen. He'll be looked after in the best place I can find, and I'll be there to see him every week.'

'And where will this place be?' Neil asked.

'Close, love,' she whispered. 'As close by as I can find.'

Seventy-six

'There's nothing positive yet, sir,' said Jack McGurk. 'I'm on observation here at the moors site, and co-ordinating. Mr Pringle is watching Lander's place, and Donovan, my DC on this job, is parked at the Alvarez woman's house.

'Half an hour ago she left Coldstream, heading north, then ten minutes ago, Lander left his house. Superintendent Pringle said I should call you to keep you advised.'

'Good for Dan,' Andy Martin retorted. 'But what about Gates? Who's watching him?'

'Gates is ours, sir, any time we want him. He owns the secret site, and he used the fish there to restock Sir Adrian Watson's farm. Even if we can't do him for theft and murder, there will be about twenty other things that the Crown Office can throw at him.'

'Not good enough. At the very least, I'm going to charge every person at the scene with that girl's murder. We know where Lander and Alvarez were, but Gates is unaccounted for. I'm betting that he was there. I want him, Jack; I want to see him go down with a life sentence.'

'I hear you, sir. I'll keep you in touch as things develop.'

'No. Tell me once you have a resolution. Meantime, I'll call your divisional headquarters like Dan asked me to and have an armed response team put at your disposal. If you do have to go in there, there will be no chances taken with that rifle.

'Are any of you three carrying?'

'I am, sir. Donovan's not qualified, and Mr Pringle won't, not any more.'

'In that case, should you have to go in there, you will lead. You know the procedure; clear warning given, then fire in response to a perceived threat. Take no risks with officers' lives. You know that there is an armed man on that site; I am ordering you to make the assumption that everyone there is carrying. I'm timing that order at eight twenty-seven Saturday morning, December the sixteenth. I'll back your judgement, all the way.'

'Very good, sir.' McGurk understood what he was being told. As he signed off the call, a cold chill of fear ran through him.

He went back to the observation slit of the dugout on the moor, and watched the site for ten minutes more before the muted tone of his mobile rang out again. 'Jackie?' Dan Pringle. 'Yes sir.'

'We've trailed them both to Sir Adrian Watson's estate; not to the fish farm, but up an access road to somewhere else. We're out of sight in a lay-by near the road end. We can't go any further; all we can do is wait here and hope like hell that there isn't another way out.'

'Can you take them down there, sir?' the sergeant asked, hopefully. 'They're bound to be meeting up with Gates.'

'Not good enough, son. They could say they're all getting ready for a Ramblers' Association hike. We have to get them together on that site, or identify them there individually. Only then can we . . . Haud on a minute!' The superintendent broke off.

'Jack!' he resumed breathlessly, after a few seconds. 'Two tankers have just come out of that access road; Alvarez is driving one, and Lander the other. It's a pound to a pinch they're heading in your direction. We'll follow them, but well out of sight. I'm not going to blow this by having them spot us.

'Is your armed team set up?'

'They'll be on their way by now, sir.'

'Right. Call divisional HQ and have them given precise instructions to proceed to your hide flat-out. But Jackie, it's touch and go who'll be there first. Whatever else happens, once those two trucks go into that compound, they do not come out. Understood?'

'Sir.' This time the chill of fear turned into a shiver which it took McGurk some time to control. He had never felt so alone. His heart was pounding as he peered through the slit, watching the site, waiting, listening for the sound of a police vehicle at the foot of the hill behind him, until, after God knew how long, two long white tanker vehicles appeared up the rough track, the first one blowing its horn as it approached, rousing the caretaker from his cabin, bringing him out to open the gate.

He watched as the two vehicles drove into the compound, taking up position between the rows of tanks, among the six which were still full. And still, he was alone.

'Where are you Dan?' he whispered, but it brought him no nearer. 'Oh shit.'

He slipped backwards out of the hide and began to run, crouched, moving crab-wise round the side of the hill, trying to stay invisible to Lander, Alvarez and their warden. He could hear the tankers pumping as he moved, and hoped that they had no super-fast setting.

At last he came to a small clump near the gate, and hid behind it, gathering his breath and his nerve.

'This is it, Jack,' he said, drawing his pistol, the Walther with which he had always felt most comfortable on the firing range, the gun which he had never before drawn, far less used, for real. Switching off the safety, he launched himself from his hiding place and ran to the gate.

'Armed police officer!' he shouted at the top of his voice, but too late to stop the site-watcher, who had seen him as soon as he broke cover, from reaching his Portakabin and diving inside.

The others still had their backs to him, watching their tankers as they sucked up the fish. 'Lander! Alvarez!' he shouted again. 'Armed police. Stop what you're doing and turn around with your hands raised.'

Although she was further away, she heard him first; she turned as she was told, and he, seeing her, followed suit. His hands were still at his side as he walked towards the detective, with the woman behind him, as if she was trying to use him as a shield. 'I only see one of you, sergeant,' he called out. 'Don't you, Harry?'

As he spoke, the minder stepped out of his shelter, rifle in his hands. 'And Harry's got a bigger gun than you.'

McGurk levelled the Walther. 'Drop it or I'll . . .' he shouted, but as he did, the man snapped his weapon to his shoulder and sighted it at him. He dropped to a crouch; and pulled the trigger. Not one, but three shots rang out.

Even after the post-mortem and the official enquiry, Jack McGurk never knew, because he was never told and never asked, whether the man had died by his bullet, or that fired by the marksman from the armed response team, standing on the crest of the hill. But he did know how close he had come himself. For the rest of his life, a tiny crescent-shaped nick out of his left ear would always be there to remind him.

The three of them – McGurk, Lander, Mercy Alvarez – stood, or crouched, frozen by the echoes of the gunfire, until a shout shattered the silence. 'You two! On the ground, now! Face down, hands on head.'

The two fish farmer lovers did as they were told, instantly, lying there as Dan Pringle and DC Donovan marched past the sergeant, to frisk them roughly and cuff their hands behind their back with plastic ties. Finally they were hauled to their feet.

As the armed team swarmed into the compound, McGurk walked over to the dead man. 'Who was he?' he wondered.

Dan Pringle came to stand beside him. 'I can tell you that. He used to work at Mellerkirk, until he got laid off after the first robbery. No wonder; Gates had another job for him.'

'His name was Harry Conroy,' said Glenn Lander. 'He was Ray Anders' father. Ray's mother did a runner when he was a kid, and he and his sister were adopted by a family in Yorkshire. Ray traced his old man eventually, and came back up here to set up his business.'

The estate owner looked at Pringle. 'I'll tell you everything,' he said. 'It was all Gates' idea; Ray tried to sell him a system and when Watson wouldn't buy, he told him that his place could be knocked over easy, just like ours. He'd tried to sell to Mercy and me before that.

'Gates thought this was a great idea. So he approached us; he told us that if we kept clear of our farms on certain nights and asked no questions, we'd both make a buck. We didn't know he was going to balls it up, and that Harry would kill the girl.'

Jack McGurk hit him; a huge right-handed punch on the side of the head, far harder than any he had ever thrown on the rugby field. 'No, you bastard,' he snarled at the unconscious figure on the ground, fingering his bleeding ear, 'but you'd have let Harry there make my Mary a widow.'

Pringle patted him on the shoulder, and turned to Mercy Alvarez. 'I've got a vacancy for a Crown witness,' he said. 'Gates planned the whole thing, Anders is going down because he was there when the girl was killed, Harry's dead, and that other one on the ground there, he's having the fucking book thrown at him, whether or not the ACC's married to his cousin.

'You tell us the whole story he just started, and you'll be charged with defrauding your insurance company, you'll plead guilty, and you'll get a couple of years, max. If you get a really good lawyer, the judge might even suspend it. What do you say?'

She looked up at the burly policeman, a gleam in her dark eyes, as her lover began to stir on the ground at her feet. 'Where do I sign?' she asked.

Seventy-seven

'What's the big surprise ending, by the way?' Neil asked as he and Louise stood at the entrance to Parliament House which had been allocated to the film crew.

'I'm not telling you that!' she said with a smile. 'You'd find out if you were here to see it, but as it is, only the kids get to know.'

As he spoke, Sarah's Freelander was waved by a security guard into the area between St Giles' Cathedral and Parliament House. She drove towards them, past the parked cars, and the equestrian statue. As soon as she stopped, the nearside doors opened and Lauren and Mark jumped out.

Sarah leaned over in the driving seat and she looked at the couple. There was still something behind Neil's eyes, something that would always be there, but for the first time since his wife's death, the big policeman looked content, as if a kind of peace had come into his life, as of course it had, against all hope and to his complete surprise.

'You two are looking pleased with yourselves,' she said.

'Are we?' Louise replied. 'I don't know why he is. He's going to work.'

He squeezed her shoulder. 'What are you talking about? So are you.'

She laughed. 'You know, even after all these years, I forget that sometimes. When it's a scene I really fancy, it's like going out to play.'

'Have a good game, then,' said Sarah. 'And thanks for helping free up my Saturday.'

Neil leaned over and closed the passenger door. As she drove off, Louise took each of the children by the hand, and turned towards the hall. She raised herself slightly on her toes and kissed him. 'Have a nice day,' she whispered, as Lauren's eyes widened.

He saw them into the building, into the safe-keeping of the uniformed police at the entrance, then walked the short distance to his car.

The Fettes headquarters were on Saturday mode, and so he found a parking space at the front of the building, beside a red Ford Ka which seemed to look slightly self-conscious beside Bob Skinner's BMW.

'The DCC said to tell you he's in the technical unit, Mr McIlhenney,' the door officer advised him. Neil nodded and set off along the twisty route to Tony Davidson's kingdom. He rapped on the technical director's door, opened it, and stepped inside. Davidson himself was absent, but at his meeting table sat Bob Skinner and another man. McIlhenney sized him up: early thirties, leather jacket type, a bit flash maybe, confident, but clearly in awe of the boss.

'Neil,' said Skinner, 'this is the Bandit. DI Dave Mackenzie. David, Neil McIlhenney, my exec.'

As they shook hands, Neil completed his appraisal with a look in the eye. Yes, he liked the bloke, even if he had given Ruthie a hard time.

'Tony's off working his magic on the downloads that Dave brought with him,' the DCC explained. 'They're videos, and we think they may show Ruthie's uncle.' Quickly he filled McIlhenney in on the background to Mackenzie's Internet trawl.

He had barely finished before Tony Davidson returned, to summon them to his neon-lit viewing room. 'I've cleaned up Mr Mackenzie's files as best I could,' he said, 'and edited them together into a single video. For ease of viewing, I've done a fast transfer to a Betacam tape, linked to a twenty-eight-inch monitor.' He handed Skinner a black device.

'Bob, there's the remote. I've seen what's on there, and frankly I don't want to see it again.' He turned and left the room, switching off the lights as he went.

Skinner felt himself tense as he pressed the 'play' button on the device. The monitor screen flashed grey for a second, then black, then the title appeared. 'Estrella Azul Caída,' he read. 'Blue Star Fallen.'

It vanished and a caption appeared, also in Spanish. He translated it for the others. 'Dark star at play. The dark side of a famous lady? It is for you . . .

'What the hell does that mean?' he murmured, as figures appeared, their movements slightly jerky from the download, but clear enough. An old man, silver haired; a woman, wearing a white carnival mask, much younger, long-limbed, dark hair well cut, above shoulder-length. Both naked, her flesh firm, his sagging, but still showing solid musculature. Left side on to the camera as she teased him, coaxed him, stirred him, first into life, then into prodigious size.

'Jesus!' McIlhenney murmured, looking away in disgust as she straddled him. When he looked back, he could tell by the lighting and the position of the camera that the scene had changed. Something else too; the old man seemed diminished, weaker, slighter in his build, if not in his genitalia, as the woman bent over him, her right side to the camera.

'Jesus!' This time it was Skinner who blasphemed, but his was an exclamation of horror. He froze the image on the scene. 'David,' he snapped. 'Leave us alone for a minute.'

The Strathclyde detective looked at him, puzzled, but obeyed without question. As the door closed behind him, the DCC stared at his assistant. 'Look!' he said, his hand pointing towards the screen. 'That birthmark on the woman's right hip; in the shape of a blue star. Louise has one, exactly like it. A few years back, she did a movie with a nude scene. It showed that birthmark; I remembered it straight away.'

McIlhenney looked at the image, then back at his friend. He read shock in his face; saw that he was shaking. 'No, Boss,' he said quietly. 'Lou used to have a birthmark like that one. But not any more. She had another nude scene in her last movie but one; a long one. She didn't fancy the idea of showing it again, and so she had it removed, surgically, and new skin grafted on where it had been. As it happened, the director shot the scene mostly in darkness, so it didn't show.

'The graft wasn't perfect. There's still a faint mark there. I asked her about it, and she told me all about it.

'That isn't Lou, but it's some sick cow who wants us to

think that it is; someone who knew about the birthmark, but doesn't know that it ain't there any more.'

The sound of relief which burst from Bob Skinner was more of an explosion than a sigh. 'Bandit!' he shouted towards the door. 'You can come back in now.'

As the young inspector re-entered the room, he pressed the 'play' button once more. They watched the home movie to the end, to the last awful scene. The woman, still naked, still marked, injecting the poor, sad, old man, needle into a vein in his erection, making him jump with pain, holding him until the drugs took him to the edge of a stupor. Then the bath, hot, steam obscuring the lens but not enough to hide his feeble struggle, first as he felt the scalding heat, then as she held him beneath the surface, her hands and forearms protected by long rubber gloves.

And then it was over. The three policemen sat, breathless, staring at the screen, silent until Mackenzie spoke. 'Do you think it was McConnell?' he asked.

'I'm sure it was,' Skinner answered. 'Ruth showed me a photo once.'

'And the woman, sir? The way you reacted back there. Do you know her?'

'We were meant to think that it was Louise Bankier, the film actress,' said McIlhenney quietly. 'It wasn't, though.'

'Bankier?' the younger inspector exclaimed. 'One of John McConnell's old workmates was a bloke called Malcolm Bankier. I was tipped off by a contact in ScotRail. He lives out in Bearsden. I went to see him last night, but he's fucking ga-ga. There was no point even trying to question him; poor old bugger doesn't know whether it's breakfast time or Easter.'

McIlhenney's eyes narrowed. 'Who else was there when you saw him?' he asked.

'There was a nurse, and his daughter. Lucy, her name was. Here, was that Louise Bankier's old man?'

Skinner ignored the question and picked up the telephone on the table. 'Get me Detective Sergeant Steele,' he ordered the switchboard operator. 'Wherever he is. I'm in Mr Davidson's viewing room.' He replaced the phone and sat waiting, he and McIlhenney staring at each other, eyes locked together, oblivious of the third man in the room.

Skinner answered the return call halfway through the first ring. 'Stevie? DCC here. I want to ask you something. From the Balmoral video you saw, from the description the woman in Newcastle gave you, could John Steed be a woman?

'Think hard, man, before you answer.' He waited. 'You sure?' Another pause. 'Thanks.' The phone slammed down.

'Stevie says yes. He says it could have been. And so could the person in that car in London.' Skinner's gaze flashed back to Mackenzie. 'Bandit! The woman the neighbour saw. Long hair, yes?'

'Sir.'

'A wig. Long, like Ruthie's hair; photos around the house, I'll bet. And in the bag, more than a camera and a stand; a wig cut like Lou's hair, and a mask. It's Lucy, Neil. She made that movie. She killed the old man. She's Louise's stalker.'

McIlhenney stared back at him, struck dumb for that moment.

'Where is she now?' Skinner asked.

'At the Great Hall, in Parliament House, where Lou's

393

shooting her big scene. And with Mackenzie's visit last night, she'll know we're . . .'

Before the door of the viewing room had swung closed behind him, Neil McIlhenney was at the end of the corridor.

Seventy-eight

The blue-suited guard looked up, startled, as the big figure burst through the narrow swing doors. 'Yes sir?' he began, but McIlhenney ignored him and walked straight up to the uniformed constable guarding the entrance to the Great Hall.

'Anything happening?' he asked.

'All quiet, sir.'

He opened the brass-bound door and stepped inside. The finest public room in Scotland was perfectly quiet, yet it was full of people. Together they formed a tableau, each in position beneath the mighty hammer-beam roof, lit bluish by the great movie lights, some splashed with colour from the enormous, illuminated, stained glass window which dominated the south end of the hall.

There was not a sound, until Elliott Silver broke the perfect silence. 'All right, people,' he cried out in his high, airy voice. 'We all know what's happening here, so let's . . .' He broke off. 'No, no, no!' he screamed. 'That light's all wrong. There's too much on Louise. Makes her look as if she's got a halo and she isn't even fucking dead yet.'

Neil heard a quiet 'Tut!' to his right and looked sideways

to see his daughter, standing beside Mark, both of them in the care of the tiny make-up lady.

As the lighting cameraman made adjustments to the set-up, he edged over towards them, still looking around. Then a figure moved, beside the great statue of Lord Stair; it was Lucy. Their eyes met and from that moment there was no more doubt, only understanding, no more questions, only truths.

In her gaze he read success, triumph, exultation. He looked for pity, but saw a hatred that seemed as old as time. He looked for madness, but saw only vicious satisfaction as if she knew she had won. And he did not know why. He did not know how.

He looked back across the hall, to centre stage. For the first time he saw Lou, her back to him, wearing an advocate's wig and a dark trouser suit. Facing her he saw Ralph Annand, a hard expression set on his face. His left arm was loosely around the throat of a third actor, a young girl, and there was something, something the policeman could not see, in his right hand, as it hung by his side.

He felt a tug at his sleeve, and looked down. Mark McGrath, Bob Skinner's adopted son, looked up at him with his wise young eyes. 'Is that a real gun, Uncle Neil?' he whispered.

He looked again, until he saw what Mark could see from his viewpoint, through the ruck of bodies. Ralph Annand was holding a sawn-off shotgun. He gasped, and then as if from nowhere Warren Judd was standing before him.

'What happens in this scene?' McIlhenney demanded. The producer looked at him as if he was insane. He took a fistful of his jacket and lifted him on to the points of his toes. 'Tell me!' he hissed.

Judd's eyes started out of his head as the policeman's grip tore out a forest of chest hairs. 'Lou's client, that's Annand, is guilty after all. Someone smuggles him in a shotgun. He takes a hostage, she tries to block his way, and he shoots her.'

As Neil's mind raced, Silver's voice slashed through his shots. 'Okay everybody, take one and . . . action!'

He dropped Judd and looked over the heads of the crouching production crew, as Annand tightened his grip on his mock hostage and raised what was indeed a very real gun. He could see that the actor was locked in concentration, and in any case he was afraid to shout. Instead he ran straight forward, bulldozing his way through everything in his path over the ten yards between him and the gun, flattening Silver as the outraged director tried to block him, reaching Annand's awareness and his body at the same time, grabbing his right arm and swinging it upward as his finger tightened on the trigger . . .

Even under such a high roof, the explosion sounded huge as the actor fired both barrels of the sawn-off, upwards, harmlessly away from Lou. Annand's face twisted as he swung at McIlhenney with his free arm. The policeman head-butted him between the eyes, then dropped him like a stone, under a shower of coloured glass fragments from the stained glass window, which had just disintegrated above their heads.

He grabbed Lou, and held her to him, protecting her from the particles. All around him, he was aware of people diving for cover.

'Was it him?' she whispered. 'Ralph?'

'No, love. Not him. I'm sorry, it was Lucy. Somehow, she switched blanks for real cartridges. It's been Lucy all along.'

'No!' She twisted in his arms. 'Don't say that!'

'It's true, honey. I'm so sorry, but it's true. Do you know a man called John McConnell?' He felt her nod.

'An old friend of my dad's,' she murmured. 'Strange man. He used to visit. Lucy called him Uncle John.'

'Well, Lucy killed old Uncle John, and filmed herself doing it. She tried to make herself look like you. She tried to make people think that you had done it.'

She began to sob; he felt tears soak his shirt. 'She was out to ruin your career; to ruin your life if she could.'

Elliott Silver's woman-like scream from the back of the Great Hall seemed to tear them apart. Neil relaxed his hold on Louise and followed its direction. The make-up woman lay on the ground, stunned. Above her stood Lucy, holding Lauren, his daughter, just as Ralph Annand had held his screen hostage, but with a cuticle knife pressed to her throat.

'Okay Daddy,' she shouted, hoarsely. 'Bring your car keys over here. Your little girl and I are going for a ride.'

He looked at Lauren, signalling to her with his eyes that she should keep calm, that he would make it all right. He walked towards her, reaching down as if for the car keys, but in reality for the Glock which was tucked into the waistband of his denims, finding time to wonder how it could ever be the same between Lou and him once he had blown her sister's brains all over Parliament House. He was aware of Bob Skinner, and of Mackenzie, watching from the doorway.

Bob knew what he was going to do all right and stood there motionless, as if signalling him to get it over with.

'You know why,' Lucy shouted as he walked towards her. 'There's my life, and there's hers; her with her fucking Oscars and me with only simple bloody Darren to give me relief from the pain of watching our father shit in his nappy every bloody day in his life.

'You know that, don't you?'

'Sure,' he said, evenly. 'But those days are over, kid. All over.'

He was almost on top of her, his hand on the butt of the pistol, ready for a point-blank shot, when a small voice rang out from behind her. 'Drop it, and put your hands up.'

Lucy's eyes widened as she turned her head and her grip on the knife slackened. It was enough; he let go of his gun, snatched the weapon with his flashing left hand, then punched her with his right, once, on the temple, pulling the blow slightly but still knocking her senseless.

He grabbed her round the waist as she fell, and as he did, he saw Mark, frightened, but brave, still holding Ralph Annand's abandoned shotgun, which he had retrieved from the floor in the panic, creeping round behind Lucy as she focused her gaze on Neil, to ram both barrels into the middle of her back.

Lauren looked up at him with her mother's eyes. 'Sometimes, Dad,' she said, 'I'm even more proud of you than I am normally.

'Now what,' she asked, 'is this with you and Louise?'

He gazed at her in astonishment then exploded into laughter, grabbing his daughter and embarrassing her by throwing her into the air, then hugging her to him, as Lou arrived to hug them both.

When the hubbub, the confusion, the panic was over, when the unit doctor had sedated Lucy, before her transfer to hospital under police guard, when he had treated Elliott Silver for hysteria and straightened Ralph Annand's nose, when Bob Skinner, long since, had taken the children off to join Jazz and Seonaid, he took Lou away, out of the Hall, up the stairway and into the deserted Signet Library.

'I'm so sorry, Neil.' She exploded into tears once again as he sat her down beneath the great tiers of books which held much of the story of Scotland's law.

'What should you be sorry for?' he asked her gently, stroking her hair.

'For what my sister's done, for what I made her do. For what she did to your daughter.'

'Shh, love. Lauren's seen worse than that in her short life. For one thing, she's seen her mother die. You have nothing to reproach yourself for, and don't ever let me hear you do it again.'

She looked up at him, tear-stained. 'I love you. D'you know that?'

He hugged her. 'I was hoping . . .'

'What's going to happen to her, Neil? What if I don't press charges?'

'Those are the least of them, honey,' he said, sadly but truthfully. 'Even if you don't, Lucy still has to answer to Ruth for the awful things she did to John McConnell. She still has to answer to Glenys for Clarence Sparrow.'

'But she's crazy. She must be.'

'There's crazy and there's crazy. The law has its own definition.' He paused, looking for and finding a handkerchief to dry her tears.

'Listen,' he murmured thoughtfully. 'Maybe I shouldn't tell you this but the boss would do the same if he was here.

'There's a guy called Kevin O'Malley; he's a psychiatrist. Call him tonight and put him on a retainer; it will be better for Lucy if he's on her team.

'He's the best, and if he says that she is unfit to plead, or was suffering from diminished responsibility at the time the crimes were committed, the Crown is not likely to argue with him. If he wasn't working for you, he'd probably be on their team, telling them the same thing, but best to be sure.

'Whatever happens, Lucy's going away, love. It's a matter of where and for how long, that's all.'

He heard a diplomatic cough from the doorway, and swivelled round to see Bob Skinner, returned, standing behind them.

'I heard that advice, Inspector,' he said. 'You were dead right. So right in fact that I've already phoned O'Malley.

'Tell me something, Lou,' he asked. 'Have you got any of your own money in this production?'

'Not likely,' she retorted. 'I'm Scottish, remember. Anyway, if they've got me, they don't need my money. Why d'you ask?'

'Because the project's going to be on hold for a long time. It'll take them about three years to mend that broken window next door.'

Seventy-nine

Bob Skinner was late for work on the following Monday morning. It was one of those rare days on which he felt slightly fragile, after the short-notice dinner party which he and Sarah had thrown the night before for Neil and Louise, and Andy and Karen Martin.

He had just settled in behind his desk when his internal telephone rang. 'Come in and see me for a minute,' the Chief Constable asked. '*Unusual*,' he thought as he crossed the hall. '*Why the summons?*'

Proud Jimmy looked at him quizzically as he entered his office. 'Coffee?' he invited.

'No thanks. I've got one across the hall.'

'Ah fine. Have you managed to mollify your pal the Lord President of the Court of Session?'

'Just about,' Bob replied. 'I spoke to him on Saturday night. He's a bit upset about the mess in his Great Hall, but he's pleased that everyone walked away from it afterwards. The guy who's really pissed off though is Warren Judd, the producer. He's having a hell of a time persuading his insurance company to cough up for the reinstatement of the window. They seem to think that he should have been able to prevent anyone bringing live rounds on to his set.

'He's asked me to put in a word for him.'

'And will you?'

'Not for him, the little shit. I will for the window, though. It's a national treasure and it must be restored.'

'What news of the girl?'

'O'Malley needs more time with her, but provisionally reckons that the Crown will accept that she had diminished responsibility at the time of the offences. They'll take pleas on two charges of culpable homicide, and she'll go to hospital for however long it takes . . . which as you and I both know, could be for ever.

'That'll not be the case with Dan Pringle's job, though. Three of them are going down for life for that girl's murder, and one for the attempted murder of McGurk as well, even though he didn't fire the shot.'

'How is the sergeant?'

'He's got a sore ear, but a change of underpants and the rest of the month off with his wife and kid should see him all right.'

Skinner frowned. 'What did you want me for anyway?' he asked. 'Or was that it?'

'No,' said Proud Jimmy. 'I thought you'd like to see this.' He handed him a sheet of paper. 'The Scottish Executive Information Directorate are releasing it at midday. Take it away with you and read it over your coffee.'

Skinner nodded and left the Chief's room, walking back to his own. Settled behind his desk he picked up his mug and read the note.

When he had finished, he began to laugh . . . and laugh . . . and laugh. He laughed so loudly that eventually his door opened, as Neil McIlhenney and Ruth McConnell came unbidden to investigate.

'Read that,' he said, choking as he passed the paper to the inspector.

McIlhenney frowned, then did as he was told.

'*Press release,*' he began.

'*HM Chief Inspector of Constabulary announced today that Assistant Chief Constable Theodore Chase, of Edinburgh, has been appointed an Assistant Inspector in his office, with immediate effect.*

'*Announcing the appointment, HMCIC Sir Ross Montgomerie said, "Although he has been in Scotland for only a short time, Mr Chase has impressed me greatly with his dedication to his duties and with his appreciation of the traditional values of police work. He is a fine addition to my team."*

'Is this for real?'

Skinner nodded, still almost speechless. 'What an operator!' he said at last.

'Who?' asked McIlhenney. 'Chase?'

'No, you daft bugger! The Chief! How I would love to know what the hell he's got on Montgomerie to have managed to pull this one off.' He shook his head. 'What an operator!

'Oh, Neil,' he called out, his composure restored as his two assistants left. 'Ask Inspector Good to look in on me, will you, please.'

Eighty

The great bell rang midnight, amplified by loudspeakers all along Princes Street. 'Happy New Millennium,' said Neil. 'Last year was only a rehearsal, you appreciate.' He kissed her, long and sweet, then kissed his daughter, and shook hands formally with his son. Above their heads fireworks exploded and cascaded from the Castle Rock.

'Thanks for Christmas in Los Angeles,' he murmured in her ear.

'No,' said Lou. 'Thanks for this; it's much better.'

'Ah,' he muttered. 'This is all sweetness and light now, but wait for a few hours. Last year they had three armed events in Leith alone, in the first twelve hours of the year.'

'God, you coppers have a cynical view of mankind. How am I going to fit into your life, I wonder?'

'I don't know,' he said seriously. 'How are you?'

'Like a glove. At the very least, I'm taking a long sabbatical from the film business. You've got me for keeps, if you want.' She pressed her hands to his chest. 'Don't worry,' she told him. 'I won't try to supplant Olive in here. I know I can't.'

'No. So just be yourself; you've got your own place in here.' He nodded at the children as they gazed up at the pyrotechnics in the sky. 'And in theirs too. You don't need to be their mother; being you will be enough.'

He grinned, big and infectious. 'Hey, remember what you said a few weeks back about me walking over your grave? Premonitions don't have to be ominous, you know. Maybe what I was really doing was kick-starting your future.'

She leaned against him. 'In that case . . .

'Neil, I'm only forty-two, and these days, lots of women my age . . .

'How would you feel about that?'

He looked down at her, smiling, and drew her to him. 'We can but try,' he answered in her ear, as the rockets soared and the crowds roared. 'My love, we can but try . . .'

Skinner's Trail

Quintin Jardine

Elated after the birth of his son, Assistant Chief Constable Bob Skinner is quickly brought back down to earth by the grim reality of a murder in one of Edinburgh's prosperous suburbs.

Found knifed to death in his luxury villa, Anthony Manson was known to the city's CID. The victim had run a chain of laundrettes, saunas and pubs throughout the city, but for some time the police suspected these to be a front for a drug distribution network. But whoever killed Manson was particularly cunning in covering their tracks, leaving no clues or leads to pursue.

But then another seemingly minor crime, involving property fraud, takes Skinner from Scotland to northern Spain, following a complex and blood-soaked trail that leads back to Edinburgh and Manson, involving vice, corruption and the merchants of death . . .

Praise for Quintin Jardine's novels:

'Well constructed, fast-paced, Jardine's narrative has many an ingenious twist and turn' *Observer*

'A triumph. I am first in the queue for the next one' *Scotland on Sunday*

'Perfect plotting and convincing characterisation' *The Times*

978 0 7553 5772 7

headline

LB 01|14